WARRIOR ETERNAL

PRIMEVAL

Sam Hain

Copyright © 2024 Sam Hain
All rights reserved
First Edition

Fulton Books
Meadville, PA

Published by Fulton Books 2024

ISBN 979-8-89427-421-8 (paperback)
ISBN 979-8-89427-422-5 (digital)

Printed in the United States of America

Prologue

It is said that while legends are born, they can never truly die, but they live on and grow far beyond their origins. And while the legends may become lost over time, they are never truly forgotten.

These were the words that were spoken to Primus, who was one of many in a group of fresh recruits standing before the commanding general of the army of the city of Meftif in the land of Crizia.

The city was near Alabel River and, in comparison to its neighbors, was not the largest or most opulent city but was more heavily fortified than the rest because of constant attacks by pirates that sailed up and down the river, looting many ships of their goods and burning the fields of many of the farms that fed the city. It was because of this that Primus had enlisted as soon as he was able.

The armies of the city had established a rule long ago. No man could join before his eighteenth year. The reason the ruler of the city had given was simple—if you survived until your eighteenth year, you were more likely to have already married and started a family.

This gave the soldiers a reason to fight harder and also meant that there was a better chance of fathering a child, so that if the man were to fall in battle, his line would carry on. Meftif's population would not fall, and the city would always be defended.

Primus's father had fallen in a battle with a rival city, north and across the river, when he was in his thirteenth year, and his mother and younger sisters had fallen to pirates when he was in his sixteenth year.

The only reason Primus was still alive was that he had been courting a childhood friend that day, hoping to woo her and, by extension, her family and win their approval to wed. He had had trouble convincing them up until that point as he had been but a farmer.

Once smoke was seen rising from the direction of his home, Primus had rushed back to his farm in a state of panic, only to witness the destruction of all he had known. Primus held his mother as she died in his arms, burnt and bloodied, and he swore on all the gods that he would put an end to the pirates, no matter the price.

With the loss of his farm, Primus had known that he also lost the chance to convince his beloved's family to allow them to wed, as they would never allow their daughter to wed someone who could not provide even the most meager of existences to their only daughter.

Primus had begged and pleaded with them to give him a chance, and eventually, they relented. He could marry their daughter only if he proved himself successful in battle and earned a station as an officer. To that end, Primus began to train.

He went to the house of his longtime friend Niran, with whom he had spent much of his childhood. The two were at once the best of friends and the worst of enemies.

Their rivalry had long been known on the outskirts of Meftif, one constantly trying to outdo the other. Primus had lost most of their fights and challenges until then. Being of a slight build, it was easier for Niran to overpower him.

But after Primus's farm and family had been slaughtered, the tide of the fights began to turn, and Primus's daily training had eventually molded his body. The soft body of his youth gave way to a hardened, lean form, so much so that others on the outskirts began to compare him to a wild cat or a jackal. In just three seasons, Primus had begun to resemble what he had hoped to become—a predator, a hunter, the taker of life.

As he entered his seventeenth year, Primus now bore a body knotted with thick bands of corded muscle, barely contained under his golden-brown skin, his arms thick, chest deep, and legs that looked powerful enough to crush a boulder.

Yet despite his much-increased size, he had lost none of his speed and in fact seemed to only have gotten faster, whipping around the other men with the swiftness of the wind, bending as a reed yet striking with all the strength and power of a lion.

But perhaps, most impressively, what had grown the most was Primus's savagery. Once he had begun to fight, only victory would stop him, as time and again, he picked fights with older, more experienced men, ordinary traders and farmers, and even the occasional trained soldier.

Time and again, Primus had found himself lying on the hot sand, bruised and bloodied, only to stand once more and face those with whom he had been fighting. No matter the beating Primus took, he never yielded, and he began to fight once more. Eventually, when his opponents would begin to tire, Primus would strike with a fury not seen until that moment, raining blows down on them without mercy.

As time went on, Primus became a more skilled fighter, eventually able to win brawls against several men without ever being touched himself, bobbing around them like a heron and striking with the precision of a cobra.

This sort of behavior eventually landed Primus in front of a law setter who had wanted to imprison him for a number of years after he beat seven men nearly to death with nothing more than his bare hands.

Primus then argued in his own defense, telling the law setter and everyone else present in the room that he did not wish to fight and that it was not his desire. The crowd laughed for a long time after this, but once they had quieted down, Primus began to describe things, not, as people might have thought, with his childhood.

Weaving the happy tale of his youth, the telling became bitter before long as the death of his family and the destruction of his home were talked about in great detail, along with his pledge that he would wipe out the pirates for what they had done.

And it was to that end that he fought now and had fought so much so as to hone his skill in combat, that when he would join the armies of Meftif, he would slaughter all who stood before him to ensure that others would not face the same loss. By the time Primus was finished telling his story, the day had nearly given way to night, and there were several onlookers who were sobbing.

"So this is why you stand before me. It is not because of an urge to fight and kill for your own sake. It is to fight for the sake of your fallen family and the families of others. And since you are still a season away from joining the army, you are unable to put the skill you have developed to proper use yet. This all sounds correct to my ears. However, I cannot help but ponder something you said much earlier in the day.

"Primus, you told me that you do not like to fight, yet you yourself have told me you've spent much of the last year or more fighting. Why, then, do you lie to me and to these people when you clearly have a love of battle?" the law setter asked.

"Forgive me, my lord, for I had no intention to lie. If I had not made clear enough before now, let me set your mind and the minds of those gathered here at ease. I am not a violent man by nature. In point of fact, I would rather be left alone, that I may keep to my own and the few friends I have. I would not be out fighting with soldiers, guards, tradesmen, and the like if circumstances had been different.

"No, I fight now because I feel I must, and so that when I am allowed into the ranks of Meftif's armies, I will be the best prepared and most vicious warrior I can be, so I may prove myself in the eyes of my captains and the eyes of the family of my beloved. That I may earn a station of my own and raise my family. And that I may have my vengeance, if it is within my power. That is why I fight. It is not for personal glory or a love of battle. It is so that I may live through the battle, so that I may know peace after the wars are over," Primus said earnestly.

"Your words ring true and honest to my ears. Very well. You will avoid being sentenced to the dungeon as long as you cease to start these fights with anyone else. Stay out of trouble, and on the morning of your eighteenth year, you may enlist in the army. As long as I do not see you before me again, no one will stop you from doing so.

"And to make it so that this does not happen again, you will be permitted to go to the army and watch them train so that you may practice their fighting styles on wooden pillars using wooden swords. They will allow you access to the training fields once they have completed their daily instructions," the law setter stated, holding aloft a small red square cut stone for a moment before bringing it down on a larger black stone that sat on the carved bench to his right with a resounding crack. People began to stand and make for the streets outside the building.

Primus himself sat down to think on one of the stone benches that had been recently occupied. He decided that he would not just watch the soldiers train but would also begin to train with them whenever he could.

He would ask the captain of the guard, whom he had seen training the new recruits, if he may practice with them, and if the captain would not let him, Primus would watch from a distance and mimic the soldiers.

He would run, jump, and otherwise follow all their movements so he might reach the same level of physical proficiency that the soldiers displayed. And when the training field emptied for the day, he would begin to train with the wooden weapons he was allowed. He knew that this would be demanding, but he had been preparing himself for this for nearly two years.

Night had fallen by the time t Primus made his way back to the home of his friend Niran, with whom he had been living since his farm and family were burned. It was well past the time of the evening meal, and Primus had not eaten all day, nor did he expect to.

Primus reached for a mug resting on a shelf above the enclosed stone firepit, on which the family cooked their meals, and opened a barrel next to the cook fire that contained water from the river not far off. As Primus took a long, deep drink from the mug, he heard a slight sound behind him, the soft sound of a single pebble being turned over on the floor.

Primus spun around, his left hand raised to block an incoming attack, his right pulling the mug back, turning it so the rim would be the first point of contact so as to inflict the most amount of pain and end this fight before it began.

Primus locked eyes with Niran, and both of them tensed, stopped, and stayed perfectly still, as if they had chanced on a snake. Niran chuckled and sat down on one of the chairs that rested against a nearby wall. Primus slowly lowered his hands, breathing heavily.

"So the mighty warrior returns," Niran said playfully. "To what do we owe this great honor? Has the law setter seen fit to grant you lands and titles and riches beyond your imagination?"

"No, he gave me exactly what I had hoped for," Primus said wearily.

"What? He allowed you to go and train with the soldiers?" Niran asked.

"In a manner. I can begin training tomorrow after they have left the field using the wooden training weapons. I can try to do what they do, as they do it," Primus said.

"Primus, are you sure this is still what you want? This is really the only path you see forward?" Niran asked.

"It is. This is the only way I can be at peace with myself and the only way I could have Turia. Remember, the deal was that I could have her if I win a name and station for myself," Primus stated, resigned.

"I know that, but there are other ways, my friend. You might be a savage fighter, but you have to remember that this isn't a game or a fight with me or any of the other men around here. We may now fight on even footing, and while one of us might take on several men at one time and walk away either unharmed or with very few injuries, that won't be the case soon. These men are trained killers. That is their job. They are the takers of life, the bringers of death, the last thing many men will ever see," Niran said.

"Do you think I don't know this? Do you think I treat this like a game? I nearly killed someone yesterday, and while the thought made me feel sick, I know that there is a purpose to what I do. I know what these men do, and I wish to join their ranks. I've prepared for this now for a long time, and finally, my plan will come to fruition," Primus countered.

"Well, be that as it may, promise me that you'll be careful. I do not want to lose my friend. We have had many adventures in the past, and I would like to have many more in the future. I also wish for your betrothal to Turia to come as well so that I could be an uncle to your children, as you have been to mine." With those solemn words, Niran rose from his chair and departed to his bed to lay next to his wife for the night.

Primus continued to sit for a while, thinking about what Niran had said. Of course, he couldn't turn from this path now. He had worked for too long to get here, and it was now the only thing he knew. Even if he could forge another path for himself, there was not much else he was good at doing.

He could work the land, that he knew, and he had apprenticed to one of the smiths for a time shortly after the burning of his home. That was until he had challenged the smith's son to a fight. The fight ended with one of the larger rough grinding stones falling on the foot of the smith's son, breaking it. And shortly thereafter, he was thrown out of the forge and into the street, being warned never to come back.

Though he seemed to have a talent for it, that path seemed lost, as his former master had gone to seemingly every other smith nearby and told them all that Primus was a danger to their forge and of how he had damaged his son's foot. Even though it had been an accident, no smith would take him after that.

Outside those two things, fighting was the only other thing Primus knew and the only thing he had any skill with, although he hated it. The sound of blood rushing through his veins, his heart beating in his ears, the vibrations that ran through his arms with each blow, the smell and taste of blood. Primus hated every second of it.

Yet it was the only path that was now available to him. And Primus was determined to become the very greatest warrior in Meftif and possibly the greatest warrior to walk the land. With his skill and determination, he would forge for himself a new life. He would rise through the ranks of the army and carve out a place of honor and glory for himself. And when he was finished, he would drop his sword, his shield, and spear, and he would live the rest of his life in peace.

Chapter 1

Primus had done as the law setter had instructed, and he had reported to the training field the next day and had spoken with the instructor, Thak, who had instructed him to watch the soldiers and to follow along in their footsteps, albeit at a distance.

He ran, he jumped, he pushed his body up from the ground, he sparred with the air, he swung imaginary swords, and he shot imaginary bows. After the soldiers had departed the field, he took up their wooden swords and began to swing them at the wooden posts that represented enemy soldiers, beginning to move slowly at first, going back over the movements that he had watched throughout the first half of the day.

Once he was more familiar with the movements with the added weight in his hands, the wooden training swords weighing twice as much as a real sword, or so he was told.

After Primus had exhausted himself with the sword, he then walked over to the bows and arrows. Selecting a bow and grabbing a leather tube that was sealed at one end and full of arrows, Primus started toward the firing line before stopping and turning back, bringing a second tube with him.

There, he began to fire arrows toward the other end of the field, where there were large blocks of dried reeds, wrapped tightly on each end with a leather thong.

The first number of arrows Primus loosed at the reed target did not find their mark but instead went either left or right and fell short by one-quarter length of the field.

But soon his arrows began to hit the reeds. However, the grouping of the arrows was not consistent, and Primus realized that this would not be as easy as he had hoped it would be.

As the days had worn on, Primus had become more and more proficient with the weapons he was given. He had soon grown comfortable with the wooden sword's weight and even began to use two of them in one hand, doubling the weight while still practicing for hours to increase his endurance.

Within a month, every arrow that he fired at the reeds found their mark, and the pattern became tighter, until Primus had achieved such proficiency that he began to split some of the arrows that were already buried in the reeds, and the bow's drawstring, which had been a slight challenge to pull back, felt no heavier than a feather.

Primus also began to practice using his left hand as well as his body was beginning to become lopsided in his muscle distribution, and, he reasoned, if he was ever unable to use his right arm, he would still be able to fight effectively as well as confusing an enemy by changing his fighting style and his handedness, a tactic that he knew would unsettle even the most hardened of warriors.

At first, the prospect of following along with the soldiers had excited Primus, but as his eighteenth year drew near, he found that he was becoming bored with his training, as it was so limited. He knew that what he was doing was important to him. However, it was frustrating to be so close yet so far from his goal.

What was making things more frustrating, however, was something that was out of his control. Several times now, the soldiers and their instructors had left for days at a time, running out away from the river and into the desert.

They were not marching, as Primus had first thought, but running with a full pack of arrows, full armor, weapons swinging from their belts, or slung across their backs.

When they would return several days later, the same number would always return, albeit they looked exhausted, haggard, and covered in dust, stinking of sweat. Primus did not know where they were going, and he was, at present, unwilling to follow them. It wasn't because he was scared, but he did not want to risk leaving the regiment that was given to him by the law setter.

If it was to be reported by anyone that he was not training as he had been allowed, there was a chance, however slight, that he would be prevented from joining the army. If that were to happen, Primus felt that he would have been lost.

The day finally arrived. On the eve of his eighteenth year, Primus did something that he had not done since he had begun his self-imposed quest.

He took the day for himself, deciding that the best thing for him was to enter the city and spend the day wandering Meftif's streets. He had seen so little of the city in his life, spending most of his childhood outside the city walls, only occasionally making a trip into the city to help sell his crop once the harvest was over. Even the metal smith he had apprenticed to had lived and worked outside the city walls.

Meftif itself was a large sprawling city, although its central building, where the ruler of the city lived, towered over the rest of the city. At nearly a thousand feet in height, it was a dominating and imposing structure, high above the rest of the of the landscape, and was visible for miles around.

This had two effects, as it would mark the city from a distance, making it easy for all to find their way to the city, but it also provided visibility for the scouts who were stationed atop the tower, constantly on the lookout for enemy soldiers.

As Meftif was roughly in the center of Crizia, it was a shining beacon of man's accomplishment, a testament to the builders of the city nearly five hundred years before, and a sign of the strength of arms that belonged not to just the city but also to Crizia.

Never had the walls of the city been breached despite the frequent attacks against the city that had suffered in the past, occasionally from within their own borders, as well as attacks from outside their borders.

Meftif was also large enough that it could house the entire population of Crizia within its walls in times of crisis, capable of holding over one hundred thousand people.

With a city so vast, Primus knew that he could easily lose himself while exploring the city, wandering for hours without truly seeing anything. The soldiers' barracks were not within the city walls and were instead just outside each of the city's four main gates.

This was to ensure that no matter which direction an attack might come from, soldiers would always be nearby, ready to defend Meftif at a moment's notice, although a large-scale attack from outside forces had not happened in quite some time.

Most of the attacks in recent memories were from other cities in Crizia, their leaders hoping that they would be able to take control of Meftif for its strategic importance. However, even those had ended in recent years.

So Primus wandered the streets, turning first one way and then the other, with no clear direction in mind. He passed shops selling all manner of items, some imported from around the world, others made within the city walls.

He passed shops selling spices from the far east, where more nomadic people wandered with large herds of smaller than average horses, and leather products made from the hides of goats raised along the great grassy steppes closer to Meftif, though still thousands of miles away.

He passed other shops selling various pipes and bags loaded with tobacco which came from the far west, from across the great sea, and various fruits and nuts from the same regions.

He passed open markets selling birds of paradise from the lands to the south and the other lands that he knew were in the far southwest of the world, a land covered in dense ancient jungles, bordered by high mountains along most of its western coast.

He passed by stalls and stands selling trinkets and ornaments from the far north across the small sea and decorative carved masks from the far south on the other side of a vast desert.

All these items and more were brought here for sale and trade, and although most of the people of Meftif would never see these lands themselves, they would often tell stories of the lands and peoples who lived there. Some had swarthy skin tones, and others were so light as to be akin to linen. Others were short with oddly shaped eyes, and still others who were only slightly darker in skin shade than Primus, who dwelled deep within the jungles and atop the high mountains, in cities that were often blanketed by clouds.

Despite the oath that Primus had sworn and the promise he had made to Turia, there was a part of Primus that wondered what it would be like to visit these lands and meet the people who lived there. To visit these lands after gaining his commission and winning glory in battle.

These musings eventually turned into daydreams, and Primus allowed himself to be carried throughout the city, floating on the river of his curiosity and his imagination.

His daydreaming was cut short, however, when Primus noticed something, or rather *someone*, lurking behind a pillar, half hidden and watching him. How long this person had been following him, Primus did not know. He turned toward the pillar and prepared himself to fight as the figure slipped away, but this time, it was a fight only to defend himself.

Primus knew that if he had to fight, he would not be able to fight with everything he had every other time in the past, because if he did, he would be barred from joining the army. If he had to fight, he could only slow the person down, possibly throw them into a wall or just scare them away.

Primus had no shortage of enemies, and he rapidly thought of a list of those who were in the city who would hold a grudge and would try to get their revenge. Primus rolled his shoulders and broadened his stance, walking now with his feet spaced shoulder width and balled fists as he rounded the pillar, ready to meet his enemy. Standing in front of him was Turia.

Primus let his guard down and felt a knot of tension ease in his back, which he did not realize he had been carrying up until that point. Turia stood half in the shadow cast by the large pillar next to her, her hazel eyes sparkling slightly in the half-light, her waist-length hair pulled behind her into a neat braid.

Her white tunic seemed almost to shine in the light and almost to glow in the shadow, and her teardrop-shaped face wore a mask of equal parts worry and relief. She looked at Primus for a long moment, with her hands clasped behind her back, biting her lower lip softly as she nervously shifted her slight weight from one leg to the other.

She crossed the few feet between them in an instant, and before Primus quite knew what was going on, she had wrapped him in a warm, tight embrace, her lips pressed tightly to his as she kissed him deeply. Primus hesitated only for a moment before embracing her as well, pulling her closer. After a long moment, Primus broke off the kiss.

"Turia, why are, uh, I mean, what are you doing? And what are you doing here?" Primus asked somewhat sheepishly, his cheeks feeling slightly warm.

"I came to see you. I haven't seen or talked to you in a long time now, and I miss you. I've been coming here every day for a week now, hoping to find you here," Turia said.

"But that still doesn't explain why you've been following me or why you decided to start coming here," Primus said.

"Because you join the army tomorrow, and I know that I won't be able to see you much after that. I haven't seen you in months now, and I won't see you until you're done with your training. You've been watching and training with the soldiers since the law setter told you that you could do this. You've been training and trying too hard to get where you want to be, where you feel you *need* to be, and you've put everything else behind you and ignored it all," Turia said, her tone shifting from pleading to accusatory.

"I know I haven't seen you in a long time. I haven't come to visit. I haven't taken a day off training until today. I've been trying to hone my body, build my endurance. I've been trying to do all of this for you. You know the promise I made and the only way we can be together properly," Primus said softly, his face falling slightly and his eyes becoming glassy.

Turia reached out and gently caressed Primus's face, holding it in her slight hand as if it was a hollow glass orb that would shatter at the slightest touch. She looked deep into his eyes, and after a moment, he slowly brought his face close to hers until their foreheads touched.

They stayed like this for a long silent moment, simply enjoying their closeness and the timelessness of this moment. Eventually, Primus gently pulled himself away and broke the touch.

"So now that you're here, what do you want to do? I do have all day, after all," Primus said with a smile slowly spreading across his face, an action that erased years from his face.

"Well, what do you want to do? I followed you for a little while now, but I still can't quite tell what you're in the city for. You've wandered right past a lot of things that normally you're interested in. You didn't stop at any of the shops or stalls. You just walked past and glanced at everything.

"You used to love the things from across the lands and the seas, and you haven't, thank the gods, looked at any of the brothels, but you also haven't stopped for anything to eat. Should we go get some food?" Turia asked.

"Well, I wasn't really hungry earlier, and I really just wanted to come into the city and wander for a while. I didn't really have anywhere in mind to actually go. I don't have any money since I don't have any kind of way to make money," Primus said, looking away from Turia and back toward the city.

"Wait, you haven't had a proper way to make money? How have you been getting food to eat? And where have you been living? The last time I talked with Niran, he said you weren't living with him and his family anymore."

"Well, I've been sleeping in an unused storehouse next to the barracks. Thak had a bed moved into it, and the soldiers have also been feeding me. I can have all the food and water I care to eat or drink. I just have to eat once the rest of the soldiers are done. The only thing I'm not allowed is any of their beer.

"I could just take some of the mugs and fill them out of the large barrels there. They aren't watched, but I don't want to take it. I don't know if anyone is checking the barrels, but I do know that if I do, I'll be disobeying my orders. I have to practice this now because if I disobey my orders in a battle, I'll be put to death," Primus explained.

"Well, have you had anything to eat today? Could I steal you away from the soldiers and your training for a bit longer? I did find something the other day that I think you might enjoy a lot. Come on," Turia said with a sly smile and a wink then turned and walked away slowly.

Primus stood where he was for a moment, thinking over her proposal. Then with a slight shrug, he started to follow her. He knew that she must have something else planned later in the day, as Turia had done things like this in the past, although what it was this time, Primus could not have guessed.

The next several hours seemed to pass both with surprising speed and with shocking slowness because of their meandering path through the city, generally heading toward the northwestern portion of the city, and the leisurely pace of their stroll.

Their conversation meandered from one subject to another in much the same manner as their walk, and they spoke of many things, including Turia's studies, which included learning how to run her father's trading company. They did not have a large company, just three barges which were floated up and down the river, mostly moving wheat and barley to the granaries and back.

Though their fleet was small, they made more than enough to support themselves because of a few changes that Turia's father made to their barges, changes that enabled them to float in shallower waters while carrying a few dozen extra bags of grain. While the family trade would usually be given over to the eldest son, Turia had insisted that she wanted to learn as well in case something were to ever happen to her siblings.

In these and many more discussions about less important matters, such as the crane that Primus had seen hunting along the riverbank two days ago, the hours passed, yet no time seemed to have passed at all.

They were content in each other's company, and just being near made a knot of tension in Primus's stomach vanish, a knot that had been there since the last time he had seen Turia, which was so many months ago that he had lost count.

After a time, they came closer to the center of the northwestern quadrant. The section of Meftif was mostly warehouses. During the harvest, when thousands of tons of goods were brought in from the surrounding areas, they would be stored overnight or sometimes for two before being loaded back onto barges or wagons to be shipped to towns and villages farther away from the city to process or portioned out to be sold to various shops within Meftif.

Everything from raw ore to polished helms, raw wool, and intricate rugs so large and detailed they would fill a grand hall, raw grains and sacks of flour, canes and beats to large bags of crystalized and refined sugar. Though nearly every type of product came to be stored at the warehouses, many of these same warehouses went unused for large portions of the year.

This was due in part to so many of the goods being bound to other destinations. The raw wool would be sent away to several villages to be spun into the fine threads, which would then be sent farther away to be woven into the large and sumptuous rugs, which would then find their way back to Meftif the next year, either for sale within the city or to be loaded onto ships, which would then set sail, whether to the far north, the far south, the far east, or the far west.

As it was, Primus was puzzled why Turia would bring him here. There were some shops selling ground meats and cheeses wrapped in thin flour shells nearer the city wall. However, this particular area was nothing but empty warehouses.

Just as Primus was finally about to mention this to Turia, she stopped suddenly and looked to the left. A doorway to one of the warehouses stood open just a fingerbreadth. She took Primus by the hand and rushed inside, closing the door quietly behind her, peeking through the small window set within the door as she did.

"Turia, what is going on? Did you see someone out there? Are we about to be attacked?" Primus asked in rapid succession, fists tightening, widening his stance for balance, his heart already drumming in his chest.

Turia did not look at him. She only continued to stare out of the small window, which sat around halfway between the door and its frame. Primus took a moment to survey the immediate area.

Turia had led them inside a medium-sized warehouse, although it was still nearly sixty feet tall, five times as wide and six times as long. It was almost entirely empty, save a few low walls made of cloth sacks full of flour. Not a single other person was in sight, and all was deathly quiet.

After a little more than a minute, Turia lowered herself fully to the floor. Despite being tall enough to see outside the window normally, she had still been standing on the tips of her toes.

She turned toward Primus then with an impish grin that he found both intriguing, somewhat amusing, her amusement being infectious enough to put a smile on nearly anyone's face.

"And just what is so funny?" Primus asked, the corners of his mouth rising slightly.

"That we're both here, all alone. In this big empty warehouse. You sure got yourself all worked up over nothing. I just wanted to make sure we weren't seen coming in here, is all," Turia said as she slowly made her way toward him, swinging her hips from side to side.

"So this is what you were planning then?" Primus asked, his eyes leaving her face as he watched her sway toward him.

"Mm. And there's one more surprise for you too. Remember, I've got you all to myself today. No one knows where we are, and no one is expecting us for quite a while," Turia said, her voice becoming low and breathy, and she slowed as she drew closer to him, her eyes burning.

She gently took Primus's face in her hands and stood on the tips of her toes again, and she embraced him again, first gently and then with force. Primus returned the gesture as they began to move as one toward the sacks of flour. The silk bags that contained the fine powder felt incredibly soft under their bodies as they lost their balance and toppled over.

* * * * *

It was late afternoon by the time they had exited the warehouse and later still by the time they made it back to the southern edge of

Meftif. Once they were close to the gate, Turia bought them both two long and thin skewers covered in chicken and pork cubes and interspaced with large chunks of peppers, onions, and other vegetables.

They ate more than they normally would as they were both ravenous. They also drank their fill from a nearby public water fountain as they were absolutely parched, all the while smiling and laughing with each other. Sometimes over a quip, sometimes over nothing at all, simply happy for each other and giddy from their earlier exertions.

After they had eaten their share and drank their fill, they made their way outside the city walls. They knew that they both had to go back to their respective homes before dark, Turia for fear of her father's wrath and Primus for a good night's sleep, as his induction was the very next morning.

They started to say goodbye to each other as the light of sunset bathed everything in sight with its soft golden hues. Primus was once again struck, as he so often was, by the Turia's beauty.

The angle of the golden rays lit her from all sides, and she seemed to glow with an inner light all her own. Her almond-shaped hazel eyes, the gentle curve of her jaw, her small nose, her high cheekbones, the curve of her waist, and the wideness of her hips.

It ensnared every thought in Primus's mind, and for a moment, he felt his thoughts muddy and was unable to form a coherent thought. Instead, he flashed a warm and very gentle smile at his love. And she seemed to lose all thought as well, for her only response was to bow her head a little, blushing slightly before returning the smile with a wink.

Though they were supposed to be saying goodbye to each other and making their way home, they reached for and held each other for a long, silent while, swaying back and forth slightly, as if to a tune that only they could hear.

When they eventually pulled away from each other slightly, they began to speak again, though nothing of any significance passed between them, and before either of them quite realized what was happening, the sun had set below the horizon, and darkness was once again beginning to creep over the land, as if the night were a sentient thing, intent on devouring every shred of light and land it could reach.

"Well, I guess we should probably go our separate ways now. You're going to be in plenty of trouble once you get home, I wager," Primus said with a half smile.

"What about you? Aren't you breaking curfew right now?" Turia said, turning her head ever so slightly so as to look sidelong at him.

"Maybe a little, although I doubt anyone will notice me come or go, especially at this time of night. That might prove beneficial to us though, especially if you want to…" Primus trailed off, raising his eyebrows quickly and breaking out into a full smile.

"Oh, I thought I would have worn you out after this afternoon. I think I'm glad to be mistaken," Turia said playfully, adding another wink. "The only trouble is that if I don't leave now, I fear I never will. Besides, you said it yourself. Father will be furious with me for being out after dark."

"Well, I know that there isn't anything I could do to convince him differently," Primus said.

"But you will. I know that you will. You've been training so hard and so long for this, and even though I do not wish to be parted from you for so long, I will wait for you as long as is needed," Turia said.

"Thank you," Primus said, his voice suddenly thick, the lump in his throat making it difficult to breathe.

"Of course. Promise me you'll be careful from tomorrow onward? I couldn't bear it if something were to happen to you," Turia said, her eyes looking suspiciously wet.

"Nothing will happen. I promise. You have my word. I'll be as careful as I can," Primus said, choking the words out.

"Thank you. I love you, Primus."

"I love you, Turia."

They embraced once more, holding tightly, almost afraid to let go, as if they believed they would never see each other again.

Then after a moment more, they released their grip, quickly turning their backs on each other so that they would be forced to part ways. It was with a heavy heart and heavy footsteps that they parted ways.

Once Primus made it back to the storehouse that had served as his bunk, he undressed and climbed into his cot, covering himself with the thin blanket that had been provided to him. He strove to calm his thoughts and sleep.

For whatever tomorrow would bring, it would be the beginning of a new chapter and his chance to make a better life. Eventually, Primus drifted off into a deep slumber, watching as the stars wheeled behind his eyes. Fantastic visions awaited him at every turn.

Chapter 2

Primus awoke in the gray light of predawn. He was looking out of the small window set within the door to the storeroom. The landscape and city had both a peculiar angularity and flatness to it, as if everything in the world had been painted on an enormous canvas and hung on a wall as large as the horizon itself.

Gray though it was, the very first rays of golden sunlight soon began to stretch their long fingers into the sky, and as it began to brighten, the world was once again bathed in color.

Once the sun began to show itself, slowly cresting the horizon to begin its long arc above the world, Primus got up from his cot, stopping only briefly to tear off a small chunk of bread.

It was a meager breakfast. However, he had not slept well, and even the thought of a large meal made him feel nauseous. Though he did not suffer from nervous fits like so many others did, Primus could not help but feel a certain sense of apprehension regarding what was to come.

He made his way to the training field, noticing several men who were trickling on to the same field. They were all lining up before a large pulpit that must have been moved to the center of the field sometime during the night.

There was very little talk from the other men who were slowly gathering on the field. Although whether their silence was due to fear or excitement, Primus could not be certain. Whatever their true feelings were, they seemed to be hiding them well, and Primus strove to do the same.

The sun hung a fingerbreadth above the sky before the last of the men seemed to have made it to the field, standing without arrangement or order. The occasional whispered conversation could be heard. However, they were always stilted and somewhat awkward and would end very quickly after they began.

Around a quarter of an hour had passed when, from the other side of the field, the commanding general of the soldiers strode onto the field. His entrance was simple and without fanfare or announcement. As the general made his way to the pulpit, what few whispers there were to be heard died out completely.

Not a single person moved, only watching with rapt attention until the general stood on the pulpit before them. The general looked them over closely, inspecting the men before him with the same gaze that one might give to a herd of cattle or other livestock, somewhat interested, albeit in a rather detached way.

However, when the general looked at where Primus was standing, they locked eyes for a moment, both staring intently at each other. The general broke the stare then addressed the crowd.

"It is said that while legends are born, they can never truly die, but that they live on and grow far beyond their origins. And while the legends may become lost over time, they are never truly forgotten. There is much that you will learn and do here. Here you will grow. While you are all considered men, many of you are all still more boy than man.

"Here we will shape you, make you into fine warriors and fine men. Though we have been in a time of relative peace, we must constantly be vigilant, always prepared for the day that we will be called on to act. To do that which others only dream of. To perform deeds that would cause weaker men to give in and give up. To take the easier path. This you will do and much more. Yesterday marks the last day of your old life. Today marks the beginning of your new life.

"I will not drag this speech on longer than necessary, however. I have said all that I needed and all that I wished to say. Raise your arms now in salute. You may put them down once I have left my position. And know that once you put them down, you are no longer ordinary men. You are soldiers of Meftif." The general finished his speech as all the men lifted their arms in salute.

He turned to make his way off the pulpit when he paused. The general turned his head slightly to look Primus directly in the eyes again, once more holding that long and unblinking stare, as if he was staring into Primus's soul. After a much shorter moment than before the speech, the general turned and walked away.

Primus thought little of this, however. His mind turned again and again to the one incontrovertible fact that had consumed most of his dreams and what had kept him in such a shallow sleep for a large part of the previous night, pulling him from his dreams at regular intervals. This was finally the day.

The culmination of everything he had worked for since the day he had lost his family and his home. His chance to build a life, and for his most secret hope, a desire that he had never told anyone, not even Turia.

While there had been no large-scale wars between the various cities in two hundred years, that did not necessarily mean that all the cities had friendly relationships with one another. There was always talk of when the next war between cities would be, but beyond speculating when old hurts and grudges might finally spill over into open conflict, there was not much else to do but wait.

However, there would be no further waiting, as the other soldiers who had walked with the commander onto the training field were now marshaling the newly minted soldiers away from the field and over to a table that was positioned near the main hall.

There, the men's names would be taken down, along with their days of their birth and any other needed information, such as if any were fathers, and if so, how many children they had fathered.

Once this information was taken, the men were directed off toward one of three lines, each of which stood near one of the large buildings at the southern end of the training field. When it was

Primus's turn, he was surprised when the man sitting at the table did not ask for his name and tried to wave him on.

"You're waving me through, but you haven't taken my name, age, anything," Primus said slowly, his confusion evident.

"Everyone knows who you are, Primus, and we found out what we needed to and already have it written. Follow the lines down the center column there," the man behind the table said with a slight smile as he pointed in the direction of the center column.

Primus smiled as well, nodding to the man, and started toward the center column. That he had already been recognized for his tenacity and his efforts to train where and how he could and that his name was already becoming known, to some extent at least, among the soldiers left Primus with a strange feeling.

He had never sought attention of the type he had just received, although the feeling was not unpleasant, and Primus allowed himself to bask in the feeling for a brief moment before letting the slightly glowing warmth fade from within his chest.

The rest of the day passed with surprising speed. Once he was at his designated line, there was a little more time for Primus to wait, as there were many others behind them who needed to have a record made of them.

After that, the door to the building opened, and after all the men had made their way inside, several armorers came forward and began to outfit the men with their weapons and equipment.

Every man was given a fairly large round shield and dagger, as well as a new tunic and sandals made of more durable material so that it would survive the training to come.

Some were given swords. Some were given four-flanged metal maces, which were made by using immense pressure to fit the flanges to the metal rod. A few more were given pikes, and roughly half of the men were given bows and quivers full of feathered arrows.

Most men, however, were given simple spears. Each stood roughly the same height as Primus himself, with a haft made of flame-hardened wood. The short but broad blades were attached to a cone of metal that was pinned in place on either side of the haft.

Altogether, they were slight in weight and felt very easy to handle, and the image of so many spears in the hands of so many men brought to mind the thorny branches of sawtooth nettles that grew in abundance far away from the city, along the riverbanks, sharp and impassible.

Primus thought it strange that so many men had been given that particular weapon and decided to speak up, asking the armorer while he was being fitted.

"Spears are easy to make, easy to replace. You don't need too much wood if you have to fix a broken one. There isn't much metal either, so the smiths can make new ones quickly and easily. They've even been designed the way they have to both easily pierce enemy armor and be easily sharpened when they dull," the armorer explained while trying to find a chain mail shirt that would fit over Primus's shoulders.

"The way that you're going to be training, you'll know how to use every weapon efficiently. That way, no matter what you march into battle with, you won't be in as much danger if your weapon breaks or is lost. You might train as a swordsman, but you'll be a spearman if you need to be. Does all that make sense to you?" the armorer asked, looking sideways at Primus, one eyebrow raised. Primus nodded in return.

"Good. Now then, you've got your armor. You've got your new clothes. You just need your weapon and a shield. The man after me is the last one you'll see, and then you'll be shown to your barracks. I know you've been sleeping in that storeroom, so you're probably ready for a night's sleep in a proper bed. Tonight, you'll get one, provided you're not too sore to sleep, of course," the armorer said, a small smile turning up the corners of his mouth.

Primus made his way to the last armorer and received his shield and was given a sword. Two of the men in front of him received a spear, and the man behind him was given a mace. After this, they were all quickly waved through a nearby door, which was done so that no one was delayed overmuch inside the armory.

Once outside, Primus and his group were led down to the barracks. From there, they were divided into groups of thirty, and then each group was led to their sleeping quarters.

The insides of the barracks were larger and more spacious than what Primus would have believed. There were several feet between each bed and a small stone cupboard next to each bed, above which there was set a small window, and there was a long gap between the foot of each bed.

This created a sort of hallway between the beds, large enough for three men to walk shoulder to shoulder. Each of the small windows had a curtain that could be raised or lowered, but the cord for doing so was actually at entrance, next to each window.

There were no names on the beds, and there were no tablets with letters carved into them to indicate which bed belonged to anyone. And in any case, Primus could not read. He made his way to a bed like everyone around him was doing, selecting the third from the entrance on the left. He began to look through the cupboard, which was entirely empty.

Before anything else could happen, the man who led them to the barracks uttered a wordless shout. Everyone stopped where they were and turned to stare, unsure of what was about to happen. He continued to look over the room with an unblinking gaze for over a minute. Of all the men, Primus was the only one to match his stare.

"Welcome to your new home. The rules are as follows, and pay attention. You will be awoken at dawn every day. You will dress and report to the kitchens. After you eat, you will begin by drilling with your weapons until you have moved past understanding and proficiency and into the realm of art. You will become masters of not just your assigned weapon but also with every weapon here, and you will know every single inch, every notch, every imperfection you will remember, and you will be able to draw me a picture of it with your eyes closed.

"Once you're done with your weapon training for the day, you will move on to archery practice and combat practice. You will become as skilled with a bow as you are with your weapons, and you will learn how to fight both with weapons and without. Afterward, you will be moved indoors. If you do not know how to read, you will be taught how, and you will also be taught to think critically. You will learn battle strategy, how to create and read sand tables, how to write in and break coded language. You will learn to identify weather and wind patterns. In other words, you will be taught how to think like a soldier. Between combat practice and archery, you will be given your midday meal, and after your studies, you will be given your evening meal.

"Drilling with your weapons will take place every day. However, nearly everything else will be done as seen fit by my superiors. Should they decide that you will lift logs and break rocks for a day, you will lift logs and break rocks. If they decide you are to study all day, you are to study all day. And should you show promise in any particular area or if you impress my superiors enough that they begin to take a special interest in you, you will be rewarded accordingly. Now as this is the first day for almost everyone here, your training will begin tomorrow. Today, you will be guided around the training grounds and be shown what you will be expected to do." The soldier finished his speech, and as he turned to leave, he looked back briefly.

"We'll be back soon. Everyone, take a moment to settle in and put away any items you may have brought with you into the cupboards next to the beds." And with that final note, he left the building, leaving Primus and the other recruits alone.

The silence that followed was brief, as most of others began to talk with one another about this and that. Primus, however, was not paying attention.

He simply opened the cupboard door and began to put some of the clothing he had received inside. His armor and weapons he put in the stone chest that he found under the bed, which seemed to have been made for the express purpose of storing those items.

His sword and dagger each fit neatly into a carved-out space. His shield sat under his armor, along with his helm. Closing the box and sliding it back under his bed, Primus looked over the rest of the men with him.

Most of them were still putting their belongings away, and some of them had finished. Those who were finished were starting to change out of whatever they had worn to the ceremony that morning, and Primus followed suit, stripping down and donning his new attire, which smelled as if it had been freshly washed.

No one really tried to start a conversation with him, although a few asked his name, so Primus sat in silence for a while on his bed.

After some time had passed and everyone had put all their weapons, armor, and clothing away, the same man returned and bade them all to follow him. Once everyone had left the barracks, the soldier made his way to the front of their little group and began walking. Everyone followed behind, like chicks behind a mother hen.

The soldier led them around the training grounds, showing them where everything was located, from the privy to the archery range; the combat field, which was set slightly apart from the rest of the training grounds; the kitchens; the library; and the laundry area, where any torn or severely soiled clothing could be brought to be mended and cleaned.

The men were also informed that the set of clothing they had received earlier in the day were one of several, which would be washed after being worn. Several extra sets of clothing would be provided if needed or if given leave from the barracks.

The tour of the training grounds ended near the barracks, and the men were informed that even though it was now midafternoon, they were free to roam the training grounds for the rest of the day, that they may revisit any of the areas that they had been shown whenever they pleased, or that they could go back to the barracks for the rest of the day.

Primus had no interest in going back to the training fields for the day. He had seen them from a distance already for quite a while. Nor did the library hold any interest for him since he could not read yet.

Instead, he made his way back to his barracks alone, content to sit and review the things he had been shown and create a plan for himself and review the things he believed he needed to work on come tomorrow morning. His introspection was short-lived, however, as when he opened the door, the general was sitting on the end of his bed, flanked by two soldiers acting as guards.

Primus froze when he saw them, as if he had chanced on a viper, and they likewise when they saw him. They stood there for a moment, staring into each other's eyes, and Primus imagined that they were likely trying to find the most effective way to kill him should he move in any kind of threatening manner. But after a brief pause, the general raised his hand.

"Ah, I see. You are called Primus, are you not?" the general asked. Primus nodded. "So you're the man who I've heard so much about. You've trained next to the soldiers for months now. You've joined their ranks, and yet standing here, it almost looks to me as if you would rather not be here. So tell me, why have you joined us?" the general asked.

"I joined today because the law setter told me that I could join as long as I stayed out of any more fights and stayed out of trouble," Primus answered simply.

"No, I mean what led you to believe that joining us was the best choice? Why do you believe you are on the correct course right now?" the general asked, his intense eyes boring into Primus the same as they had done earlier.

The intensity reminded Primus of the looks he had exchanged earlier in the day. However, they seemed more intense now, as if they were searching for something deep within him.

"I joined because I don't feel like I have any other options available to me. I don't have a good relationship with many merchants or smiths in the city. I can't read, and I have no money to buy any land to farm, which was the profession I grew up with and which was going to be my life," Primus said flatly.

"Good. Will you come with me to my quarters? There are a few things I wish to discuss with you before you begin tomorrow."

Primus nodded again, and without further delay, the general stood and exited the barracks, his guards following swiftly behind him. Once they were all outside, the guards flanked Primus, standing close to his sides. Their meaning could not be clearer. If he were to try to attack the general or anyone else assumedly, they would strike him down where he stood.

The general led them through the maze of buildings and into Meftif, and after turning just two streets, they arrived at a rather large estate with a sprawling garden. Ivy strangled the front and side of the estate, which, being so close to the wall, was covered in shade for a majority of the day.

Low walls surrounded the estate, broken by a gate made of twisting metal, intricately carved with patterns that meant nothing to Primus but that he knew were not meaningless. The gate was not locked, and they entered the garden and walked the short path to the main entrance.

During the short walk, Primus noticed many flowers that he had never seen before. Some were white with a deep bulb, on which sat a single stalk and a sweet smell. Others were such a dark shade of purple that they appeared almost black when in the shade. Still, others were a vibrant red with thorns growing along their stems, and around all the flowers hung a soft and pleasant aroma.

Through the entrance, the doors of which were a deep brown and finely carved so that on each door at roughly head height, Primus beheld a snarling visage of a lion ready to pounce, so lifelike that he was sure they were about to leap from the door and tear his flesh from his bones.

On the other side of the imposing edifice was a large hall from which branched various hallways and rooms, and several servants were walking from one room to another, some carrying trays of fruit, some carrying clean linens, and some carrying scrolls and folded sheets of parchment.

From there, Primus was led to the second floor of the estate, up a large staircase made of the same richly colored wood as the doors and which wrapped around the upper floor, and down a short hallway and to a large study. The shelves were lined with books and scrolls stretched from floor to ceiling while several highly padded chairs were spaced apart near the bookshelves, placed near lamps that would provide light for reading no matter the hour, day, or night.

A large desk made of a wood so dark that it appeared black sat at the end of the study, although whether the wood was naturally that color or was stained black with age, Primus could not tell.

The general strode across the woven rug that covered a large portion of the spacious room. That was covered with a series of colored lines woven throughout it that formed a pattern of such dizzying complexity that Primus felt as if he could stare at it for days and still not find where one line started and one ended.

The rug held his attention until the general sat down behind the desk and waved his hand. As he did this, his two guards departed the room and closed the door, although Primus did not hear their footsteps as he would have expected to if they had left the room unguarded. The general motioned for Primus to sit in either of the chairs in front of the desk and continued to gaze at him with the intensity that Primus had already come to expect from the older man.

Primus took his seat and matched the general's stare. Neither of them spoke, and they continued to gaze at each other until Primus noticed the meager shadows coming through the window were growing longer and longer, and he guessed that by now, it must be late afternoon or evening, although he never looked away from the older man in front of him.

"So despite everything I've heard about you, you seem to have learned the value of patience," the general finally said, leaning back in his chair, resting his elbow on the chair and his head on his fist.

"You can't succeed in either the immediate future or the distant future unless you can sit and think things through," Primus replied, his voice hoarse from disuse.

"This is true. And it is the future that I wanted to speak with you about," the general said.

"The future?" Primus asked.

"Your future, to be precise. I've heard some of your story, but I would like to hear a full account of yourself, your experiences that led you here, and what you plan to do now that you are here. As I said, I have heard some of it already, mostly as rumors that spread through the soldiers' ranks. But I want a true and honest account of everything that led you here, starting with what you were doing the day you lost your home," the general said as he pulled a cord behind him, and a hidden door opened to reveal two pitchers.

The general stood then and poured a chalice from each pitcher and gave two of them to Primus. One chalice was filled with water, and the other was filled with wine. He was silent for a moment. Then he took a large drink from his water and a sip from his wine and was silent for another few moments.

Primus then started with how that fateful day had begun, leaving early in the morning for Turia and his attempts to convince her father that they should wed, how someone had come in a few hours later and pointed to the pillar of smoke rising in the distance and his mad dash home, hoping that somehow, there was something, *anything*, that he could do to help his family and his misery when he could not.

He then spoke of his attempts to reason with Turia's father afterward and of his difficulty maintaining a job and ultimately of his promise, that if he could win his fame and fortune on the battlefield, he would be allowed Turia's hand.

Thereafter, at the general's request, Primus detailed the training he had imposed on himself to prepare himself to join the soldiers and his trial by the law setter. After that, Primus spoke of the training he had done since, following the movements and behaviors of the soldiers from afar, and how he had progressed as well as what skills he did and did not have at the present moment, including not being able to read or write. By the time he had finished his account, night was almost upon them. The general was silent for a short while, digesting the flow of information.

"You expect much of yourself. Well, in any event, you have proven that you have the determination and tenacity to choose a path and follow it. But beware, Primus, the path you have chosen is a hard one. There are many opportunities within the army, and you absolutely may earn the glory and honor you are chasing. But beware, Primus, for there is a cost that must be paid. Whether it is time, blood, or missing limbs.

"You most likely have heard the rumors that there is another war on the horizon. These are not merely rumors anymore. Several other cities are currently building their armies up, and we have received reports that they intend to launch an attack on Meftif. We aren't sure when they will attack, but this is the largest buildup of soldiers in living memory.

"There is much room for a man to grow here, and if you truly wish to earn your commission as an officer, you will soon have the opportunity to do so. But you must know that you could be injured or killed during the coming battles. The cost could be quite high. So I will ask you this only once. What price are you willing to pay for this life you envision for yourself?" the general asked, and Primus answered immediately.

"Whatever I must. I've come too far to fail now or to back out of this, and no one else would take me anywhere. I will pay anything I must to have this," Primus answered, stone-faced, his voice hard.

"Well, luck be with you, Primus. I don't know why, but I have a feeling you're going to need it. Now then, you missed your midday meal, and the hour is quite late. I'm sure you're hungry. Will you eat with me tonight?" the general asked.

"It would be my honor, sir," Primus replied, a smile tugging at the corner of his mouth.

They left the study and made their way to a large dining hall. However, the only ones seated at the table were the general and Primus, who thought better of asking if the general's wife or children would be dining with them. They spoke of many different topics, although none as serious as what had been discussed earlier, and soon it was time for Primus to go back to the barracks to sleep for the night. At the door, the general stopped him.

"Once you learn to read, I will personally instruct you in some of the finer arts of warfare. There is much that I can teach you and much for you to learn if you're willing," the general said.

"I would like that very much, sir. Thank you for your offer," Primus said, taken aback by such a proposition.

"It is no trouble whatsoever. I look forward to our lessons, and I will be watching your career with great interest," the general said, smiling for the first time.

With that, Primus bade him good night and was escorted out of Meftif by the two guards who had accompanied him earlier that day. Once back at the barracks, Primus was surprised to see that all the other men were asleep, which Primus was grateful for, as it meant that he would not have to answer questions regarding where he had been.

As Primus lay down, he returned to his conversation with the general, wondering what he could have meant with his warning and going over and over what price he might have to pay. But he knew that whatever the price, he was willing to pay it if it meant that he would achieve his goal and realize the dream that he had worked toward for so long. He was slowly slipping into sleep, visions of what could be his began to dance behind his eyes, and as sleep overtook him, his last thought was of Turia.

Chapter 3

Primus awoke out of a shallow and troubled sleep. While his dreams initially started off pleasant, a mix between real memories of Turia and fabricated days with her, they had eventually taken a darker, more twisted path. Strange shapes and patterns began to appear around the edges of his vision before giving way to ruined landscapes. Strange creatures, hulking monoliths that he had no desire to meet, shuffled around the edges of the tortured lands, sometimes sliding into the wavering half-light that resembled the way that light patterns shifted on the bed of a river.

Then his dreams shifted again, and he beheld a warped version of the training field that he had spent so long observing. On it, though, were not men but what appeared to be shadows which twisted and writhed as if they were made of flame.

The individual shadows fought with one another, sometimes merging and sometimes retreating far away, but always, they continued to fight. Primus watched these silent apparitions fight for a time, unable to look away. Then his dreams shifted once more.

The scene before him was one of such chaos, devastation, and confusion that Primus was taken aback as he looked about. In the distance, to his left, was Meftif and some of the army, mostly archers, while everything else around him, whether he looked forward, backward, or to his right, was swarming with not only soldiers of Meftif but also soldiers whose tunics were dark from the vibrant red of his own.

My own? Primus thought, and he belatedly realized that he was dressed for battle as well, blood dripping from his sword. He looked at his shield, which was notched, dented, and missing the top six inches, sheered away by some powerful attack he must have stopped. His helm was missing too. As for his body, more viscera stripped his arms and trickled down his legs. The normally light red tunic he wore was now dark, stained as it was with blood. Though he was covered in blood, he was not sure if any of it was his.

He looked at his feet and noticed with a shock that a left arm was lying on the ground in front of him, shield still attached to the forearm, while a man lay directly in front of him, clutching the mangled stump near his shoulder, more blood gushing from the wound. His cries were barely audible over the sound of the battle, which raged around him with the fury of a thousand storms. He was spinning quickly, trying to gather more information. It looked as if the soldiers of Meftif were winning, as there seemed to be fewer troops from whatever force opposed them.

Primus looked up then and saw the general near the line of archers. He was pointing and gesticulating wildly, standing atop a large box, bellowing orders at his soldiers, trying to rally them to his position and form a more effective front line against the tide of oncoming soldiers. It appeared to be working as a large knot of men had already formed around him, pushing the scrum of battle back from their leader.

Then from somewhere off to his right and slightly behind him, a spear sailed through the air. Everything slowed down, and every detail stood in sharp relief. Primus could see every scratch on the sword the man in front of him was holding, count every imperfection in his armor, every tear and frayed thread on his tunic.

The spear moved through the air slowly, as if it had been set in a slow-moving stream and not thrown through the air. Primus found himself running forward without realizing it, moving at a speed that would have shamed a diving eagle, the very air itself seemed to hold him back.

Primus opened his mouth to call out to the general to warn him to do something. But as loud as his shout was, the battle was louder still. The general did seem to hear him and looked in his direction then toward the spear, but it was too close. There was no time to duck behind his shield, no time to move.

The spear struck the general midchest, sliding through the chain mail as if it were made of the flimsiest paper. The general took half a step back as the force of the impact struck him fully and the spear slid to a stop, the tip emerging from his back and tugging slightly at his armor. He was still for a moment then collapsed onto his side, his body as limp as an empty sack of flour.

Primus sat bolt upright in bed, panting hard, covered in sweat. It was still dark out, and everything was quiet. The other men slept in their beds, some snoring loudly, some quietly, while others simply breathed, lost in whatever fantasies their minds conjured for them.

None of them were awake, which meant that Primus had not shouted or cried out in his sleep, and he must not have cried out when he woke up. He cast his gaze around the room once more then rested his head in his hands.

He could not explain why, but that dream had been different from all others he had ever had. It was too realistic. Any other dream he could ever remember. There was always something slightly off-kilter about the world, whether it was the way another person or Primus himself looked or sounded or how they acted or behaved. There was always something pulling at the seams of the world, always something to let him know that he was dreaming.

None of that was present this time. The sand had been hot on his feet. The sun felt as it should. The shouts and battle cries were sharp. The sound of metal striking metal sounded like a bell ringing. The feeling of being covered in drying blood was as sticky as he remembered it from butchering hogs. Even the pounding of his own heart now matched what he felt in his dream.

That didn't feel like a dream. That felt like it was really happening. Or maybe it's going to happen. There's no battle going on right now that the general is a part of, and even though he said that other cities are building up their own troops, it didn't sound like they actually amassed enough men to launch a full-scale war. Maybe that is something coming in my future. I'll tell the general about it the next time I see him. I'll pull him aside and go over everything, Primus thought, trying to calm his racing heart.

He shivered slightly and lay back down, drawing the blanket in close as he turned over and slowly drifted back to sleep.

* * * * *

When dawn arrived, a drum sounded from somewhere just outside the barracks, its deep notes reverberating through the buildings. Everyone got out of their beds and got dressed in their new clothes, and they donned their weapons before leaving for the training field. After just a few minutes, and when everyone was gathered, Thak marched onto the field, followed by four other soldiers.

The other soldiers broke off on their own, and from the front of the group, they began to work their way to the back, laying about many of the men with swagger sticks, marshaling them into five blocks, shouting to form neat lines as they went. Though there was some grumbling from the men as they were initially hit, the entire process only took two or three minutes.

Once the blocks of men were formed, the four soldiers returned to Thak and stood rigidly in place with their arms at their sides and legs close together.

"You men are supposed to be standing at attention!" Thak bellowed. "You will stand in formation here every morning unless ordered otherwise. You will be at attention, and you will not move or speak unless ordered otherwise. You will wait for me or one of my lieutenants here, and you will follow their orders the same as if you were following mine.

"We will instruct you in the arts of warfare. You will hate us now, and you will love us when you are finished. Your body will be pushed to its limits. You will learn discipline, and when the time comes, you will defend Meftif with honor. We will tolerate no dissent. Do you all understand?"

"Yes, sir!" the men bellowed back.

"Good. Today we will teach you the proper way to use the weapons you have been given, and we will see where each of you stands in unarmed combat as well as armed combat. Do not think, though, that we will allow you to hack yourselves to pieces. You will use wooden weapons when you fight each other. Do you all understand?" Thak asked.

"Yes, sir!" the men bellowed.

"Well then, let's begin!" Thak said, smiling.

* * * * *

When everyone reached the training field reserved for weapons instruction, Primus and the men stood with several feet of space between them and proceeded to go through the motions. Although Primus knew these well enough and he could most likely perform them in his sleep, he followed the direction since he had never been allowed too closely to the training field.

Drilling with the weapons was different from simply mimicking the movements as he had done so many times before. The biggest difference that Primus noticed was the extra weight from his weapons and shield.

Their heft caused him to stand a little wider than usual and stand more on the balls of his feet than the more flat-footed stance he had used until now. Thak and the lieutenants directed Primus and the others to go through the various forms and poses, not focusing on speed but precision, flowing from one pose to another with slow and deliberate movements.

After nearly two hours of practicing with all their various weaponry, the group then marched in formation to the archery range. Once there, Primus and the men were allowed to rest briefly and quench their thirst under some shaded stables at the back of the range where the practice arrows were stored. After around a quarter of an hour, when everyone had rested and drank their fill, everyone took up a bow and two quivers of arrows.

Thak instructed them first on how to string a bow, which involved hooking their heels behind the lower end of the bow and bending it over their legs so the bow would have enough curvature to attach the string to the top. Primus had an easier time with this as his larger stature allowed him to bear down on the bow with greater strength.

After the bows had been strung, the instruction on how to accurately fire started, with Thak once again demonstrating the technique, his arrow sprouting from the red-painted center dot of the straw target two dozen yards away.

However, what Thak had made appear so easy and natural was far from it, and Primus struggled to make his arrows find their mark with the same accuracy. Despite his prior training, his arrows were not consistently placed. Primus was far from the only man to struggle with this, however.

Most of the men around him were as inconsistent as he was, if not more so, although Primus did find a small bit more success as he neared the bottom of his second quiver. This came from slightly turning his left hand so the bow sat at a slight angle, and the arrow rested partly against the bow and his hand instead of resting solely on his hand and partly extended forefinger.

After they had all retrieved their arrows and refilled their quivers, Thak instructed all the men to return to their positions, this time not firing at their own pace as they had before but on command. Thak also had them hold their drawn bows for a time as well, not firing immediately, as well as firing as rapidly. Several men were unable to hold their shot as long as Thak instructed and released their arrows by accident.

When this happened, the men who were unable to hold their arrows in place were ordered to step back from the line and to repeatedly run around the stables until instructed otherwise.

After emptying both of their quivers and retrieving their arrows for a second time, Primus and the other men were allowed to break for their midday meal. After they had eaten, they were marshaled into a large theater adjacent to the kitchens, where they were given instruction of what various battle lines and troop formations looked like and a description of the best ways to defend against such positions.

After they had all digested their meals so it would not slow them, and after they had their fill of battle tactics, which Primus had found to be incredibly interesting and made a concerted effort to remember everything he had learned, the men were led back outside. Once at the combat arena, the men were paired off with each other by Thak and the lieutenants. Curiously, the combat arena was covered in soft and springy hay.

Primus and the other men were then instructed on the soldiers' style of fighting, which did not just involve punching and kicking but also grappling. They soon progressed beyond maxims and began to apply what they had learned with one another. They took turns throwing their partners onto the ground, and the purpose of the hay became clear. It softened the impact of being slammed repeatedly onto the ground.

Once everyone was sore and dusty, they began to fight each other in the same pairs that they had already been practicing in, but with their fists covered with soft fabrics to better absorb some of the impact of the blows and prevent anyone from getting too hurt, as well as being told that in no uncertain terms, they were not to injure themselves too badly. Finally, they were given their wooden weapons, as well as some lightweight padded leather armor.

At both of these exercises, Primus excelled, barely being touched by the fighting. Although these blows did unsettle him, Primus knew that he could improve to the point that he was nearly untouchable. This he knew he would need to do if he were to survive any encounters on the battlefield, and from his dream the previous night, he knew that that time may be rapidly approaching.

By the time Thak instructed them to break off their training for the day, Primus and everyone else with him were tired and sore and covered in dust as the sun hung just slightly above the horizon. The day was not over, however, as the men were given one final task.

They were led to a long wooden trough that was suspended around seven feet off the ground. There, they were instructed to strip naked and step under the trough. After a moment, Thak pulled a rope at one end, and suddenly, water began to pour down from small holes that had been bored into the wood, and they were showered in water, allowing them to wash the dust and sweat from their bodies.

It took several minutes for the water to run down to a trickle, and once dressed again, the men were instructed to go to the kitchens for their evening meal and were relieved of duty for the rest of the day. Primus knew that this would be the only chance he would have for the rest of the day.

"Sir, could I have a moment to speak with you?" Primus asked as the rest of the men made their way to the kitchens.

"Of course, Primus. What can I do for you?" Thak said, a smile spreading across his face for the first time that day.

"I was hoping to speak to the general, sir. I have a matter I would like to discuss with him," Primus said, wary of revealing too much information.

"I'm sorry, Primus. He was given a missive early this morning. He left the city and won't return for a few days. I can have a missive made to send to him if it's urgent, though," Thak said, noticing how Primus's face fell slightly.

"No, it's not urgent, but please let him know that I'm looking for him when he comes back. It could be nothing, but it could be something," Primus explained, hoping that it would not sound suspicious.

"Of course. Now go on. You need a meal and a change of clothes. You can leave your current clothes in a stone tray that's in the barracks," Thak said, smiling and motioning toward the kitchens with his left hand.

Primus bowed his head and started toward the kitchens. Legs of roasted mutton and savory bread danced behind his eyes, and the taste of beer was on the tip of his tongue. Despite this, he went with a certain amount of trepidation, hoping the general would not be away for too long, as the dream could be more significant than either of them realized.

Chapter 4

The following week came and went without much change in Primus's daily routine. He had no more nightmares as vivid and realistic as the one before his first day of training, although he had been unable to speak with the general until very late in the week. During that time, Primus had excelled at all the exercises that he had been presented with due to his greater-than-average strength and speed.

His understanding of battle tactics rapidly developed, and he began to challenge the situations that were laid out by Thak and the other instructors, which included one scribe and two scholars, both of whom had extensively studies the battles of the past.

Primus was able to point out where the flaws in past strategies that had cost numerous troops or had resulted in severe losses and develop a plan of his own. These plans were nearly always better than those of the soldiers who had fought at the time.

What baffled Thak, the scribes, and the scholars was that they admitted to showing only what was known at the time, hiding the rest in what they termed a *fog of war*. This kept Primus and the others from knowing how many enemies they would actually face, as well as the disposition of the enemy and many other things besides, such as if reinforcements were on the way.

Each time a new battle scenario was presented, Primus would study the scenario in silence for a time, sometimes waiting until Thak asked for their thoughts, sometimes interjecting and speaking out of turn. The first time this happened, Primus was instructed to lie down on the ground and push his body up before lowering himself back down to repeat the process.

This did not stop him from doing it again at the soonest opportunity he noticed. The first time, the punishment was immediate, but Thak and the others debated if Primus was correct. The second time, Primus was not punished immediately and was asked how he came up with his plan.

Primus then explained his thought process, highlighting how the defending troops would have a better knowledge of the land surrounding them, how that could be used to set traps to be used against the enemy troops, and even how the defending troops could move out of their position to make it appear as though they left their defenses defenseless, baiting the enemy into a place they would not be able to escape from.

This seemed to impress the scholars, while the scribe simply stared blankly at Primus. Thak roused himself after several seconds of deep thought, congratulating Primus on finding a solution to this battle. He was later informed that this had been one of the worst losses that Meftif had suffered, and that if Primus had been in command, it would have been a near-certain victory instead of the bloodbath it had been in reality.

Over the next three days, Primus would interrupt the lessons with his own thoughts, which invariably proved helpful, and seemed to gain a great deal of respect from his fellow soldiers as a result. Though they had not yet been taught to read, they were informed that they would be starting those lessons in around a month, once their bodies had been conditioned, and once they had a better understanding of battle tactics.

On the evening of the fourth day, and near the end of combat training, several horses could be spotted riding toward the city. Though they had been at a great distance, as they began to draw closer, it became easier to make out the figures riding. Curiously, though, one of the riders appeared to be glowing. As they drew level with the training field and individual men could be picked out, Primus and the others realized that the glowing man was the general, resplendent in gold mail.

The level of wealth that the general displayed was staggering to Primus. Although the first thing he had seen was the gold mail, the general's helm was also encrusted in precious gemstones. The pommel of his sword contained a ruby the size of a hen's egg.

Primus started toward the horses, intending to hail the general and speak with him about the dream. However, he had not gone more than a few feet before one of the lieutenants, a man by the name of Caius, smacked him across his shoulder blades. Primus stayed where he was for a moment, staring after the general before returning to his partner.

Once combat training was over and the day was nearly done, Primus and the others washed their bodies as they had every day before, and then Primus sought out Thak as he had several days ago. Thak was already walking toward Meftif and was a considerable distance from the wash station.

Primus had to run to catch up with Thak. Primus shouted for him while still a little way behind him, and Thak turned toward the sound, stopping when he realized someone had called his name. Primus caught up with him soon after, stopping to catch his breath for a moment before speaking again.

"Thak, do you remember what I asked you a few days ago?" Primus asked.

"Yes, Primus, that you needed to speak to the general about something. I'm actually on my way to his estate now. Head on back to the barracks. I'll let him know you're looking to talk with him and send a runner for you once we've finished up," Thak said while turning to leave.

He's tense. Something is definitely wrong. I hope I find out what they're hiding sooner rather than later, Primus thought as he made his way back to the barracks. He had just changed out of his soiled training clothes and into a tunic and some comfortable leggings that had been cut off midthigh and made to lie down on his bed when there was a knock at the door.

No one knocks on that door, not Caius or Thak or any other solider. But that can't be the runner yet. Thak and the general would have barely begun. Unless there's something horribly wrong, Primus thought as he stood up and walked over to the door.

Standing on the other side was a soldier. Nothing denoting his rank was visible, and he was breathing was ever so slightly labored.

"Are you Primus?" the man asked.

"I am," Primus answered slowly.

"Your presence is requested at General Targrave's estate," the man said.

"General who?" Primus asked, confused.

"General Targrave. The man Thak said you were looking for earlier today, the man with whom you ate dinner with before he left the city," the man said bluntly. Primus realized, belatedly, that he had failed to ask the general's name at any point during that dinner and that he had never asked Thak either.

"Ah, I'm sorry. My mind wandered a little," Primus said as he stepped out of the barracks, lying to hide his lack of knowledge and awareness.

The soldier said not a word but simply turned on his heel and began to run at an unhurried pace. While Primus was able to keep pace at the beginning, he soon began to pant, while the soldier began to take deep, steady breaths. He appeared to be far more used to running than Primus was.

I have to build my endurance up. I might be able to fight for a while, but I can't even keep up with a simple run? I wonder if that's something Thak has planned at some point. He's been a soldier for a long time. He has to know that I don't have the stamina to do something like this for a long time, and probably the rest of the men too, Primus thought as he struggled slightly to keep up with the man in front of him.

Soon they came upon General Targrave's estate, the gardens still in full bloom. However, the outward appearance of the estate did not match the inner, where several servants were running to and fro.

Some of the captains seemed to be slightly panicked, while others looked to be dancing on the edge of insanity.

All were running about the estate as if they were chickens who had recently had their heads cut off. Primus stifled a chuckle at this, for despite his exhaustion from the run here and the evidently dire situation, he found the imagery associated with his silent observation to be quite humorous.

Making their way through the manor, they arrived at the study, which was guarded by the same two soldiers who had accompanied Primus and General Targrave at their first meeting. The guards waved them in without comment or question, apparently recognizing either one or both of them.

Inside was a scene of confusion. Several soldiers were walking through doors hidden within the walls, which would likely take them to other rooms within the manor, and, Primus suspected, out to the grounds beyond the house. From there, soldiers or messengers could leave the grounds to deliver their messages or to perform whatever task they had been assigned.

Several high-ranking officers and General Targrave were crowded around a table that had been moved into the room. The table was piled high with maps and books and scrolls of every shape and size, and all were urgently talking to each other or General Targrave, each trying to make themselves heard above the din. The soldier who was with Primus started toward the table, and Primus followed, weaving between men around them, as if everyone in the room was engaged an intricate dance.

"Ah, Primus, you're here. I'm sorry, but I didn't know that we were going to call you here so soon. Have you at least had a bite to eat yet?" Thak asked, a look of intense relief washing over his features as soon as he laid eyes on the younger man.

"No, I went back to the barracks first to change first. I thought that I would have a few minutes before heading over for some food," Primus said somewhat ruefully.

"I'm sorry to hear that. We'll be here for a while yet. I'll send a message for two of the cooks to stay late so you can at least have a hot meal," Thak said, signaling to the soldier who had brought Primus to the estate. The soldier nodded and left the room quickly to deliver his new message.

"So why am I here, sir?" Primus asked.

"Because Thak requested you to be here," General Targrave said flatly, the tension behind his voice clear. "Apparently, you have knack for finding winning strategies for battles of the past."

"I requested you here because we have a problem, Primus. A really big one," Thak said gravely.

"What problem?" Primus asked, careful not to appear enthusiastic despite the excitement within him rising at his first real chance to impress his superiors.

"General Targrave just returned from a meeting with the generals of three other cities, all of whom apparently united sometime last year. They kept their alliance a secret until now, but they've been pooling their resources, preparing and planning. Our spies told us as much, but we didn't know until recently what exactly they were planning. So several days ago, when General Tar—" Thak was cut off.

"Enough. I was there, and I don't need hear it again. War is nearly upon us. Three cities have united against us, and we have precious little time to prepare for it ourselves. Before I go any further, I want to tell you which cities they are. Sodom, Gomorrah, and Angra," General Targrave said.

His words struck Primus like hammer blows. Each one seemed to drive the very breath out of him more and more and pound him deeper and deeper into the floor. His earlier excitement vanished. He was stunned, and despite preparing himself for this for years now, Primus now felt very small upon hearing this news.

"When do they plan to attack us?" Primus asked, somehow managing to keep his voice from trembling despite feeling his heart rate triple.

"Did you honestly expect them to tell us, *boy?* In the game of war, the element of surprise is often the greatest weapon. They wanted to meet with me to try and offer a preemptive peace negotiation. I rejected their offer," General Targrave said, practically spitting the words past his teeth before continuing.

"Even though we had the chance, we didn't take it. I would rather crawl in the mud than roll over and give these *vermin* even an inch. While leaving, though, we did notice that the training grounds they had was larger, easily able to hold three times the usual number of troops, but they appeared to have been constructed in haste. Between all three, I would estimate that we would be facing around ten thousand men."

To Primus, it felt as if his heart stopped, and his stomach twisted so violently he could feel the muscles in his abdomen shift. A cold feeling began to permeate his being despite the sweat that had broken out across his body.

"If we're facing down that many men, we have to put out a call to arms. Everyone who was a soldier and left has to be called back. Without them, we have maybe, what? Two thousand or so men?" Primus asked while racking his brain for other options to increase the number of fighting men. Other than conscripting citizens, no other way seemed viable, or at the very least palpable.

"We have already thought of this, and we have already contacted the scribes so they can begin work on the orders," General Targrave said dismissively.

"We should also put out a call to anyone who was thinking of joining the soldiers. Post papers all over the city and outside of it to try and entice more people to join and to let them know what's going on," Primus said immediately.

"We won't even have time to fully train you, let alone anyone else who joins up to fight with us," General Targrave said, who was now sounding increasingly irritated.

"We'll have to speed up the current training as well, learn only what we need to now, and everything else can come later. If there *is* a later that is, or we'll have to learn more than one new thing at a time. Perhaps combat training as a unit while also going over tactical positioning. We also would have t—" Primus was cut off before he could finish.

"Enough!" General Targrave roared, and the room came to a standstill. "I have been in command of this military since before you were born. I have learned from the finest warriors of my grandfather's time and my father's time. I have no need for you, who are still more boy than man, to plan *my* wars for *me*. Begone now. Go back to the barracks and sleep," General Targrave finished with a wave of his hand and looked back down at the map.

Primus stood stunned for a moment as the clamor slowly resumed throughout the room. Thak, however, gave him a sympathetic look that was mixed with some other emotion that Primus could not quite identify, although it looked suspiciously like admiration. Thak continued to gaze at Primus for another few moments before turning his attention back to the table and the general.

"Sir, if it's all the same to you, I'll take Primus back to the barracks myself. The watchmen have all been alerted, and every gate is closed with orders not to open unless is one of us," Thak said.

General Targrave grunted in the affirmative and made a noncommittal waving motion with his hand. Thak turned around immediately and took Primus by the shoulder firmly, though not roughly, and marched him out of the manor. Once outside, they slowed down, and Thak surprised Primus by steering him not toward the gate but away from it instead, although still staying near the wall. After they were far enough away from the estate, Thak finally spoke.

"That was both genius of you and very brave Primus. And thank you, by the way. I've wanted to tell Targrave off for a while, but my station and discretion always got the better of me," Thak said while releasing Primus's shoulder and slowing to a leisurely walk.

"Wha…what do you mean?" Primus asked, shaking his head in confusion.

"Targrave likes to think he's such a great leader, that he's taken everything into account and that he can't make a single mistake, like he was blessed by the gods or some nonsense. The problem is that he's gotten worse over the years, and now basically everyone can see it if they look at his decisions for more than a few seconds," Thak said. "You really don't get it, do you?"

"Get what?" Primus asked as he slowly began to realize what had just occurred.

"Targrave didn't send any message to the scribes. He didn't think to call soldiers who left their swords and shields behind or even to shorten the training of the new group. He didn't do any of that. *That's* why he was so upset with you. You effectively called his bluff in front of most of the high-ranking officers," Thak explained.

"He offered to teach me the arts of warfare just last week," Primus said in disbelief.

"He probably saw something akin to promise in you. That perhaps you could be led to believe what he wanted you to believe. Namely that he's going to be able to handle any threat that comes his way. What you just showed tonight, in less than a minute, is that Targrave is not what he appears," Thak said

"I wasn't trying to insult him," Primus said defensively.

"Insult is putting it lightly. You *humiliated* him. No one has ever been able to so plainly show how poor of a job he really does. Before you came in, he was starting to discuss the possibility of using some buried stakes in the ground as a possible deterrent. He didn't even consider the possibility of trying to find more men to help us fight, like I told you earlier, but you also showed that there are serious gaps in his reasoning. Not that he skipped a step or two when trying to put together a plan, but that he never even looked at the steps needed," Thak said.

"That makes me dangerous to him," Primus said as the reality of the situation to sunk in.

"It makes you a rival. It makes you someone he has to look over his shoulder for. It endears you to the others in a simple way that he never could. In short, yes, it makes you incredibly dangerous to him. But there is one other important thing you're missing," Thak said softly.

"What's that?" Primus asked, afraid he already knew the answer.

"It means that even though you might have a better mind for all things war, he won't let you have any say in what's going to happen. That was actually why I had Targrave send for you earlier. It was because he was going to immediately move to build defenses for the city. I was going to have you look over the plans and suggest where to build defenses, set traps, and just try to make it more difficult for enemy soldiers to make it to our position," Thak said.

"And I destroyed any chance of being able to do that when I said what I said," Primus said softly, nodding.

"Oh, you burned your chance so severely that not even your chance's ashes are left. But don't look so down. When one door closes, a window opens," Thak said, smiling once again.

"What? What are you talking about? What window?" Primus asked.

"Oh, it's some phrase that's existed since forever ago. What that means is that when one opportunity dies, another is born. Your new opportunity was with the other men still up at the estate. They suspected that Targrave didn't have much in the way of plans, but your quick thinking gave them some hope that *someone* will be able to give them half a chance at victory." Thak said, pointing at Primus.

"Me? But what can I do? You heard Targrave back there, and you said it yourself. I don't have a chance now," Primus said, unsure if he was feeling angry or depressed.

The one thing I wanted, my officer's commission, just disappeared, and Thak still thinks there's a bright side to all of this? Primus thought.

"You do have a chance. Most all of those men will follow Targrave's orders if there is no other alternative. But you gave them an alternative," Thak said. On seeing Primus's confused expression, he continued, "*You.* You proved to them you can think on your feet, and Targrave sent you away before you could say anything about planning defenses. *I* talked to them earlier about how amazing you've been doing in your studies so far, and you proved your value.

"The way it looks now is that if you could stay calm and collected like that, not shout at Targrave in return, and combined with what they've heard about you prior to today, they're far more likely to listen to you now. That hope that you gave them means that whatever the plan Targrave dreams up, they'll follow it, yes, but only until they can say that they did as ordered and not face an insubordination charge.

"Beyond all of that, the ranking officers know that Targrave has always been inept when it comes to planning any defenses in the war games we sometimes play. He'll give them his plan, and like I said, they'll follow it. But they won't be happy about it, and they'll be looking to you to guide them. Tomorrow, I'll bring you a map of Meftif and the surrounding area, and I'll draw on it where the defenses are going to be placed, along with the most likely directions an attack will come from.

"You'll study it and change what needs to be changed, from troop placements to barricades to traps, and I'll pass the plans along. This way, the defenses that won't work can still be built to appease Targrave, but the actual defenses will be in place, and much stronger for it. We'll have to operate in secrecy, but at least then Targrave won't be able to stick his nose in our business and muck up your plans," Thak finished, looking quite pleased with himself.

"You're talking about going behind Targrave's back, committing insubordination, and possibly treason. What happens if Targrave notices? I find it a *little* hard to believe that he wouldn't know about a second set of defenses being built. And more than that, how am *I* supposed to direct men who are building these defenses and, from the sound of it, possibly direct them in battle? All of this when I just joined a week ago. You've been a soldier for how many years? How am I supposed to do this when I don't have the experience?" Primus finished, exasperated.

Though he sounded angry, all he felt was disbelief mixed with fear, as if fate was taunting him.

"You can do this because while you don't have the experience, you seem to have a gift for this. The men won't just be following you. They'll also be following me, if only just a little. They know me better than they know you, and I can ease any fears or doubts that they have," Thak said reassuringly.

"You make it sound so easy," Primus said dryly.

"You make it sound too hard. One thing you'll learn is that while I might be a bastard on the training field, I'll support every single man here if I believe that they have the potential. And you'll also learn that we're all much easier going than the rumors that we spread," Thak said with a sly smile while Primus stopped and gaped at the man.

"You didn't really think we would put someone to death for swiping a mug of beer or an extra loaf of bread, did you? We know what we're like and what we can get up to. To put it another way, we know what the limitations are. We actually have more freedom, not less. Now don't go and tell anyone else about it. If word gets around, we may lose some of the freedoms we enjoy. Now don't you have a sweet someone waiting for you?" Thak said with a knowing look. Primus could only nod, dumbstruck by the revelation.

"Well then, I'll make sure she gets a message tomorrow letting her know that you're free most evenings after training. All you really have to do is avoid the two sentries near the barracks. Or don't. They most likely won't stop you if you're with someone," Thak said with a shrug and a roguish half smile.

Primus opened his mouth several times, but no words came out, only a slight croak. Thak laughed deeply.

"Come on. It's getting late, and you still need a meal. Then it's off to bed. We've got a big day ahead of us tomorrow!" Thak said, wiping a tear of mirth from his eye as he draped an arm over Primus's shoulders and started to lead him toward the kitchens.

Primus chatted about nothing in particular with Thak until they reached their destination, whereupon he took his leave, explaining that Targrave would want his councilors present while he attempted to create something that would pass for a defensive formation.

Primus sat down and began to slowly eat his meal of roasted pork and assorted vegetables, his appetite gone for the moment as he mulled over everything Thak had told him. Soon, though, he began to eat in earnest, finding himself ravenous as the reality of his new situation settled in.

He was safe from death from his own soldiers, he would be planning and leading the upcoming battle, and he would have a chance to earn his commission and build the life he wanted. He would even be able to see Turia more often now, which brought a smile to his face as he consumed the last of his beer, wondering just how much trouble they would manage to avoid when they next met each other.

Chapter 5

It was during the midday meal when Targrave appeared to address the men. Primus had not spoken so much as a single word about the conference to anyone after he had been dismissed the night before, although he had been asked about it by a few of the men in his barracks. He told them only that they would find out soon.

All the men who had been training with Primus were completely silent while Targrave spoke, first telling of his summons, of his meeting with the military leaders of the other cities, and finally of the coming war. Several of the men looked pale, as if they might be sick. Two of them were, but no one broke the silence. Targrave attempted to extol the men for their training so far, hoping to rouse them from their stupor, but he was unsuccessful.

Targrave also informed them all that their training schedules would be quickened to prepare them all for the fight to come. He bade them farewell then, still trying to fire their imaginations and speaking of the glory and honor that they would win for themselves, that their names would be sung in every hall from the far western sea to the far eastern sea.

No one spoke for the rest of the meal, and not much more was eaten. When the time came for their afternoon tactics lesson, everyone shuffled quietly into the room and took their seats. Thak was not waiting for them as he usually was, so they simply waited in silence.

They did not have to wait long, however. After around five minutes, Thak entered the room, although instead of the large charts and maps that detailed battles and wars of the past, he now hung on the wall a set of letters and a large map of Meftif and the land surrounding it.

"Well, you all know that the situation has changed. You're not preparing to be soldiers in a time of peace. You're now training to be killers, warriors, defenders. Since we now don't have the time to teach you everything that we normally would, we're skipping right over most of the prior wars and battles. Today, we're going to work on two things in particular, and today we'll be going longer than usual. Today, we're going to discuss the best way, or ways, to defend Meftif, and we're going to start teaching you how to read and write," Thak said, and the lesson began.

The discussion ranged from barricade placements outside the city to the placement of archers on the walls and rooftops within the city. In case the walls or gates of the city were breached, where could defensible positions be constructed, both prior to any fighting and also after it had started.

After that, the discussion turned to traps that could be set, such as spike pits in the sand or holes dug in the sand and covered with wooden planks that would then have sand poured over top. The effect would be that one man or several could hide inside the hole. Then once the enemy soldiers had passed over them, the men inside the hole would lift the planks and attack from behind.

After what Thak had dubbed the *planning stage* was over, he began to teach the men their letters. To speed the process up, those who could already read and write were tasked with helping those who could not. The process would not end when the lesson was over, however, and those who knew how to read would continue to work with those who could not until every man knew his letters and would be able to both read them out and write them down.

"The reason this is so important is because most people can't read. That means that if you have to try to get a message to someone and you don't want it to be known what is in that message, it's best to do it in a form that most people can't understand. You can also send messages to each other or to me or any other soldier and know that they will understand whatever you're trying to say. But the most important thing of all is that this is where a lot of your orders will come from. They will be written down and handed off to you, sometimes as a unit, sometimes as a battalion, sometimes as just an individual message for you and you alone," Thak said after teaching them what each letter meant and how it was pronounced.

The rest of the lesson simply involved attempting to write out the letters in order and comparing them to the ones that hung next to the map. Nearly everyone on their first attempt produced nothing more than incoherent scribbles. Only three were able to produce anything that even resembled the writing next to the map.

On his second attempt, however, something in Primus's mind shifted, and like a key to a lock, something connected where before there was only an empty section of his mind.

His letters looked far clearer and much more like the letters next to the map, and Primus felt as if he better understood how they could be strung together to form words, sentences, and eventually whole books. However, while he understood more now than he did before, he was no faster at writing or reading, although he was sure that would come with time.

Primus was surprised at the feeling that learning to read and write had given him. It was a pleasant experience, one that was soothing to him. It helped ease the knot of tension that had formed earlier that day near the base of his skull. He had not expected that he might enjoy being a scribe, although the thought of tediously sitting in one place day after day, writing out the same lines over and over again, did not appeal to him.

I might enjoy something like this once we win this war. If we win this war, that is, Primus thought as he went over his letters a fourth time.

Once the rest of the men were able to create at least a passable reproduction of their letters, Thak had them move on to writing out their names, as well as some of their likes and dislikes. This, he told them, was to improve their understanding of how the letters would look as they formed different words and sentences. This would help them improve their spelling and grammar so that anyone else who knew how to read would not find a jumbled mess of misspellings or other errors that could cause the meaning of the message to be confused.

"In the right hands, a message you send could be read by someone who is about to do something incredible with the information you gave them. In the context of the coming war, you could be writing out a warning of approaching reinforcements. But if you can't spell correctly, instead of saying that there are many reinforcements, you might incorrectly say that there are *no* reinforcements coming. If your writing isn't clear, one message could be mistaken for the other, and that could prove disastrous," Thak explained before telling them to put down the hollowed reeds that they had been using to practice their writing.

It was now late in the afternoon, but they were not finished with the day yet as combat training had yet to be completed. This time was different, though, as instead of pairing off, Thak instructed half of them to take the left side of the combat field while the other half was to take the right side. He then spoke to each group separately.

"Before we do anything else, remove your tunics so you can identify each other. You're going to need to keep track of who's who. They're going to keep their shirts on in the other group. You're going to be the attacking group. Your job is to capture the enemy commander, which is going to be that man over there, the last on the right. Primus will be your leader, and you will protect him as best as you can. He is going to come up with a plan once I talk to that group and once they get into a formation suitable for defending against you. Once you capture the enemy commander, the fight is over. Try not to beat each other too much. None of you have on the proper armor, and we can't afford any of you to be in bed, injured. Not this time. Primus, start planning," Thak said as he turned and jogged to the other side of the field.

Several of the men with Primus began to ply him with questions as they removed their tunics and stood in just their short pants, but with a motion of his hand, he silenced them. He was being careful to watch where the man who had been labeled as the enemy commander moved to.

After some shuffling around, he watched as the man who had become his target was shuffled into the center of the group, which then formed a densely packed wedge shape. The shape looked as if it was made to break the charge and force Primus and his men around to the sides of the formation. The advantage of this was that it would spread Primus and his men apart, but the weaknesses numerous. After another moment of silence, Primus stepped in front of the men to address them.

"So I won't waste anyone's time. They're set up in a way that allows us to encircle them. They can use their shields to make a defensive line that could shove us back. But that's almost exactly what we're going to do too. We hit the point, and as soon as we do, we spread out on each side until we have them surrounded, and then *we* can set the pace of the fight. A few of us will also have to charge their line. Shield up, tuck it in close to your body, and when you run up, jump and spin. Use the spin and your speed to knock their shields away. That'll open them up, and we can start to break them up and get to their commander." Primus waited a moment to ensure that everyone understood his plan.

He turned on the spot and hefted his wooden sword and shield before shouting and charging forward. The men followed, and Primus could hear as they let out battle cries of their own, some shouting, others whooping. Primus arrived at the front of the wedge, and without waiting for his men to begin to spread out and encircle the defending group, he jumped and spun, breaking through the line of shields and ending his spin by throwing his shield arm out and striking several more men, knocking them over.

Inside the knot of men, Primus found that they were so densely packed that most of them could not move properly. They had no room to swing their weapons or bring their shields up to block any attack that Primus could unleash.

The defenders, now surrounding Primus, backpedaled, trying to find room to swing their weapons, but they were stopped by

Primus's men behind them before they got too far. Primus ducked a savage crosscut from the man in front of him that would have taken him in the head if it had landed. He jabbed the end of his sword into the man's belly, who fell back clutching his belly and gasping for air.

The next attack Primus let fall onto his shield before quickly retaliating with a cut of his own, aimed just above the man's left knee. The wooden sword bounced off the man's thigh, and he hopped back, howling in pain.

Primus charged forward again, but rather than spinning to push the men in front of him aside, he simply raised his shield and lowered his head as he plowed into three men who were standing too closely together, knocking them into the men behind them, tripping them and clearing a space in front of him. All of this happened slowly to Primus, and it seemed as if minutes had already gone by, but he knew that it really had only been seconds since he entered the formation.

Primus leaned back to avoid the next attack directed at him, which would have hit him in his sword arm just above the elbow, and he retaliated with an upward slash that struck the man on his forearm, causing him to drop his wooden sword. Primus struck again, bringing his now raised sword down toward the now defenseless man in a fast two-hit attack. At the last second, he changed the angle of his attack and struck the man next to him on the shoulder, causing him to also drop his shield.

Just then, two men of Primus's group were at his side, and together, they pushed farther into the defending formation. Not that there was much left of it now, Primus realized, as he stopped for a moment to refocus and take in how the mock battle was progressing.

His men had surrounded the defending formation entirely, pressing in on them and limiting their ability to swing their weapons. Primus could also see knots of his men dotted here and there, each small group not only pressing the rest of the defenders closer together and further limiting their ability to fight but also breaking up the defenders into smaller pockets and dividing the attention of the defenders.

Primus charged with the two men who had followed him into the breach he made, and together, all three of them charged forward two steps, using all of their combined strength to force the men in front of him even farther back. With a roar, Primus swept his shield arm aside, sending two defenders to the ground. He made a move toward one man who had his back turned while he was fighting with another of Primus's men in front of him.

Primus rapped him on the head, hard enough to hurt but not hard enough to injure him, while the man to his right dealt with the defender facing him and the man to his left pushing forward to join with the other attackers. Others of Primus's forces began to do the same thing, breaking the defending group up into ever smaller groups that could be easily overcome.

Primus was panting now, sweating, and covered in dust and stray stalks of hay, but he could see that he was winning. He spotted the enemy commander, and without pausing to consider whether it was a good idea, he charged forward, but rather than trying to knock the shields in front of him away by performing the same spinning jump as he had earlier or by simply ramming them as he had previously done, Primus stopped in front of what was left of the defending line and swept his shield across his body.

This backhanded strike was strong enough and came at an odd enough angle that the men in front of him could not hold on to their shields properly. One man dropped his while another man nearly dropped his. Primus jumped over the men as they crouched to try and recover, landing behind them and placing his wooden sword on the enemy commander's left shoulder, resting the flat of the mock blade on his shoulder while keeping the edge toward the neck.

The fighting around them came to a stop, and as Primus stood panting. The man who he had been instructed to beat stood completely still, looking around with wide eyes, confusion written plainly across his face, as if he were unsure what had just happened to him. He almost looked as if he expected to keep fighting.

Thak approached the now motionless clump of men slowly. His eyes roamed over the intermingled groups as he appeared to be taking in the sight around and before him. He finally stopped in front of Primus before looking slowly, first to his left and then to his right, before returning his gaze to Primus.

"H-how?" Thak stuttered.

"How what, sir?" Primus asked.

"How did you do that so quickly? You won this little battle in three minutes, maybe a little less," Thak said softly.

"I saw the formation, realized it would be better suited to an offensive charge than a defensive line, and I knew that we could fairly easily circle them. That would cut off any chance for them to change tactics or formations, and we could squeeze them together as well, making it harder for them to fight back," Primus explained, walking through the steps he had used in his reasoning.

"Ah. And that spinning jump?" Thak asked.

"I knew my speed would carry me into the line, possibly through it, but I would be surrounded by shields, pressed in on all sides, and unable to move. So the jump was more than a little risky, although it did seem to catch them off guard. The spin let me in past their shields, and I could use my own shield afterward by just extending my arm. Effectively, it let me push my way through, and since they were all pressed so close together, they couldn't fight back against me very effectively. Most of them couldn't even find room to swing their own weapons," Primus explained.

"But how did you know that you wouldn't be captured immediately?" Thak asked incredulously.

"Well, I didn't. But I knew that my men were behind me and that they would most likely be right behind me when I did what I did, since if I was captured, they would lose the game," Primus said with a slight shrug.

Thak continued to stare at Primus for almost a minute with what the younger man slowly came to realize was a slight sense of awe. Primus was unsure of what the source of the awe was, however. It could have been the speed with which he won. It could have been the speed with which he came up with his plan, as that had taken him less than thirty seconds. It could have been the ferocity that Primus attacked with, or perhaps it was everything, all coming together and allowing his plan to come to fruition perfectly. Or it could have been something else entirely.

"We're done for the day, men. Go on now. Clean up, eat your evening meal, go back to the barracks, and work on your letters until you need to sleep. Primus, once you get cleaned up, you will follow me to my quarters. I need to speak with you privately," Thak said as he bent down to help one of the men to his feet.

"Have I done something wrong, sir?" Primus asked as he did the same.

"No, but I have a pressing matter, and I want to speak with you about it," Thak said.

Primus said no more but continued to help men to their feet. Though no one was seriously injured, many men had large bruises already spreading across various parts of their bodies. Several of the men were limping due to being hit on their knees or legs, and large angry welts were visible across their thighs. Several men also had torn tunics, several bloody scrapes, and large discolored blotches were visible beneath the thin cloth.

Once they had all rinsed the filth from their bodies, Primus collected his things and walked over to Thak, who silently turned and began walking away from the barracks at an angle. Primus tried to get Thak's attention several times, but the older man stubbornly refused to answer, and after a moment, Primus withdrew and was taciturn as well.

Just inside the walls of the city, Thak turned down the first street on his right, stopping at the third house and producing a key from somewhere along his belt. Thak unlocked the door and stepped inside, and Primus followed. The home was smaller and less opulent than Targrave's manor, but it felt more inviting.

Several brightly colored drapes hung in front of the windows. A small pot with several flowers was the centerpiece of a round table that sat next to the oven. A large bookshelf sat next to several comfortable-looking chairs, and candles sat half burned in their sockets.

The house appeared deserted, as the only sounds Primus could hear were the sounds that he and Thak made. Thak moved around the kitchen and opened a cupboard, filling the air with a sweet and salty aroma. He pulled out a plate piled high with thick cut slices of ham, which appeared to have some kind of glaze drizzled over it.

A large pot of stew was also removed from the cupboard, as well as two loaves of bread. Thak lit a fire, and after he had built it up, he set out the ham and stew up to warm before sitting down opposite Primus.

They continued to sit in silence until the aroma of the food had filled the house. Thak retrieved the ham and stew, making a plate and bowl before placing one in front of Primus. Thak then returned to the cupboard and retrieved two cups and a jar that sounded as if it was only halfway filled with liquid.

Thak unstopped the jar and poured some of the liquid into each cup, giving one to Primus before sitting down with his own meal and cup and tearing a loaf of bread in half. Primus began to eat some of the ham, and after grabbing the other half of the loaf of bread, he began dunking it into his stew.

Thak had leaned back in his chair after he had sat down and proceeded to cross his legs and hold his cup, resembling for all the world a statue while ignoring his food. After perhaps five minutes more, he finally uncrossed his legs and leaned forward.

"That was some show you put on for me and my lieutenants earlier today," Thak said before taking a small sip from his cup.

"What do you mean? How was that a show for you?" Primus asked.

"I mean that was the new defensive formation that we worked on for a full season before you joined us, and you decimated it in seconds. If that had been a real battle, you probably would have been killed with that stunt you pulled. But that doesn't even matter much, because even if you died doing that, you would have broken that line, and every man in it would have died or been at the mercy of your men. You would have forced them to surrender. That's why it was a show, because you made a mockery of a new line," Thak said evenly.

"I'm sorry. I didn't know that that would cause you any trouble," Primus said, looking down at his plate, his appetite suddenly gone.

"Don't be sorry. Targrave came up with the initial formation. Decided it was time to test it out, I guess. He probably hoped that it would change things a bit. Well, he was right. It changes how we look at his plans," Thak said with a smile, sipping his drink again.

"Wait, then why did you seem upset earlier if what I did was actually a good thing?" Primus asked. The knot that had begun forming in his stomach eased although did not abate entirely.

"Because I at least had to put on a show for the benefit of the men in training. I told them the truth of who came up with it. Don't get me wrong either. I was genuinely surprised by how quickly you overpowered them," Thak said, his smile widening. "Drink up, by the way. That's my special stuff."

"So why did you tell them who created the formation? What is that going to do?" Primus asked as he picked up the cup, which he noticed was filled with a golden-brown liquid.

"Not so fast!" Thak said as Primus drank from the cup. He struggled not to spit it out as the liquid burned a tract down his throat and warmth blossomed in his belly. Primus gasped as he finished swallowing, coughing slightly as his eyes watered and his nose tingled.

"I probably should have warned you. It's really strong stuff. It's from across the sea, apparently made with secret techniques on plains as large as a country. I think the man I bought it from all those years ago called it amber whiskey. I only break out this for special occasions. My marriage, the birth of my children, and now this," Thak said wistfully.

"Wh-why? What's so special about this?" Primus asked, his voice unexpectedly hoarse.

"Because you just handed Targrave a defeat he can't ignore, or turn to his advantage somehow. I'm going to be completely honest with you Primus, I think Targrave is going to get us all killed in this war. But you have the potential to turn that around, because you have a talent for spotting an enemy weakness and exploiting it, or as was the case earlier, you can spot an enemy's strength and turn it against them. Without any prior training by any soldiers or any other means, that's very impressive." Thak said.

"So that's why you gave me some of this. It's a celebration," Primus said, lifting the cup and taking a sip. The whiskey still burned his tongue and throat, but not as badly as it had earlier.

"Exactly. I also wanted you to come here tonight because my wife went to visit her family, and she took the children with her. I also warned her that she should be ready to leave the moment I tell her to, because if I'm telling her to leave, it's because we're about to be attacked. She made up a few plates for us earlier as well," Thak said, finishing softly as he looked down at his cup. He continued to stare into its depths for a moment more before taking a large drink.

"I think that was the right thing to do. I don't know if I'll be able to fix all of Targrave's mistakes, but I'll try. Hopefully, you won't have to send them away at all, and it's just a false alarm," Primus said, his ears growing warm as he felt the whiskey taking effect.

He wasn't joking. A drink and a sip and I already feel it strongly, Primus thought.

"Hopefully, but I doubt it. The others sense weakness, and they'll take advantage of it if they can. But that's not what we need to focus on right now. I brought a map with the preliminary defenses on it here so you can look it over. Spot weaknesses and strengths. Targrave's plans aren't particularly good, although there does seem to have some semblance of actual planning that went into this," Thak said as he stood and retrieved the map from on top of his bookshelf.

Primus and Thak moved their plates out of the way but kept them close by as neither of them had finished their food. Thak unrolled the map and placed it in the center of the table. Another rolled map was placed to the side so that changes could be made without alerting anyone that any changes were being made.

Using some small stones to hold down the corners so that they did not raise by themselves, Thak settled into a chair next to Primus as they began to look over the plans that Targrave had created the night before.

Chapter 6

Several hours later, Primus and Thak stood up from the table, stretching their sore legs and trying to get their blood flowing again. It was tedious work to undo Targrave's many mistakes. The defensive map of the city had been worked on extensively, and although most of the placements had to be moved, there were a few that could serve a purpose, and as such they had been left alone, although the vast majority of the placements had to be altered.

Most of the defensive formations were placed south of Meftif, away from the city walls. However, the placements would leave the farms vulnerable to an attack. Primus, however, had not believed an attack would come from the south but rather from the east, along the Alabel River, which ran straight to the south but curved slightly toward the north, such that it turned and missed Meftif, turning gradually toward the northeast. The Alabel River flowed from north to south, and the cities that had allied themselves against Meftif all lay to the north.

Primus had reasoned that the most likely point of attack would come from the river due east rather than from the south, as that would put troops closest to the city. It would also have the benefit of not subjecting enemy troops to possible attacks by farmers and other tradesmen who lived south of Meftif along the river. This would slow their progress, and it meant that any troops coming through the area would have to either take prisoners or simply slaughter all the men, women, and children they encountered.

While Primus believed that this was not above the soldiers, he also had explained to Thak that any prisoners taken would mean that men would need to be left behind to guard them and shrink the size of the effective fighting force that could lay siege to the city. The most effective and efficient way, then, would be to try to launch an attack that would begin early in the morning and would target the eastern gate. If enemy forces could make it past the defending soldiers and inside Meftif and then make for the citadel in the center of the city, they would capture the heart of the city.

Once that was captured, any invading force could spread out and wipe out any defending force street by street until the whole of the city was brought under their control. It would then be a simple matter to convince the farmers and tradesmen outside the city not to stand against them once they realized that Meftif had fallen and that the city was no longer theirs.

Therefore, Primus had placed several traps that would help to thin out the enemy lines, as well as a warning system that could allow him and the men. He was trying to defend the precious moments needed to muster their forces and not be caught unawares. The traps consisted of several rows of spike pits that would be dug deep into the ground and covered with a sheet, which would be staked at several locations around the pit. The sheet would then be covered with a fine layer of sand, which would drag the sheet down slightly, and a mound would be built behind it, giving the entire structure the appearance of a small dune.

Spikes would also be buried in each hill as well, so any soldiers attempting to climb over would injure their arms or legs if they fell onto a spike, or if Primus was very lucky, the enemy troops would impale themselves if they tripped. This was something that gave Primus the idea to also tie a taut rope across two stakes and to bury it as well, although only under a small amount of sand, as the soldiers' feet would sink in slightly, and the rope would catch their toes and sandals, which would not trip everyone, although it would trip a few. Those few could mean the difference between victory and defeat.

The first two traps would be constructed identically to each other, while the third would have a small dune created and with spike traps on either side, while the fourth would have the trap behind. This would keep the soldiers guessing as to where the traps actually were, and it would both slow the advance of the soldiers and cause fear to begin to spread through their ranks. One might never know if they were about to step into a trap.

To push the soldiers into the correct path, Primus expected the enemy to make their approach at the river's closest point to Meftif, and a small trench was to be dug. It was to be a foot deep and with more sand brought to create dunes along the side of the path, effectively making a low wall. In addition to filling in the middle of the path with smaller dunes, as to appear natural and well-worn path. This would force the enemy down the only path that Primus wanted, although to accomplish this, the path would need to be very wide, and the spike traps would also have to be very wide north to south, but east to west could not be more than a few feet across to avoid forcing too many troops off of the path.

Primus also saw opportunity in another area that could cause mayhem among the soldiers by having several groups of archers bury themselves under blankets, much as the spike traps, lifting only a corner of the sheet for enough visibility to fire but not high enough to leave themselves exposed. They would use arrows tipped with scorpion venom and attempt to target officers, which would leave the men more disorganized and at a greater disadvantage compared to Primus.

Finally, several different defensive formations would be used, but they were to be spread out slightly until they resembled the shape of the crescent moon. They would close in on the attackers from the front and the sides, and if it seemed feasible, Primus and his men were to try to encircle the attackers and hem them in, making it harder for them to move, in addition to cutting off their retreat and thusly making surrender more likely.

The warning system that Primus designed was simple in its effectiveness. Several men or pairs of men would be stationed by the river in small huts that were to be built solely for the purpose of watching for enemy soldiers. The men stationed at each hut were to fish during the day and stay inside at night.

If the enemy were to come during the day, each man would have a square of polished glass that they would angle toward the next hut, flashing a blinding light at them several times to warn of approaching soldiers. If the soldiers arrived in the gray light of pre-dawn, a large campfire was to be lit, and the men inside were to start cooking. The firelight would alert the next hut and so on down the line until the fires were visible from Meftif.

If they arrived in the middle of the night, it would be more difficult to explain the fires away, and the men inside would likely be killed, and the soldiers would be more dangerous if they realized what was happening.

While discussing the exact placement of the fires, Primus had an idea that struck a chord within him. He explained to Thak his idea to take small clay pots and fill them with pitch and then to stuff the top of the small pot with a cloth, which could be lit from a torch and thrown onto the enemy force. This would cause confusion and panic among the soldiers, although few would actually be killed by the trick.

The weakening of the soldiers' morale and the hope that some would lose it entirely might cause the surrender of some of the enemy troops was the main purpose of this tactic, although both Primus and Thak disliked the idea. However, they knew it was necessary if they were to win the coming war.

While discussing the defenses and the planning had taken relatively little time and had gone over smoothly, Primus and Thak spent much more time discussing the more pressing problem—Targrave. He would block any attempt to reinforce the areas that Primus had indicated and could even have Primus thrown out for insubordination. While the insubordination claim itself would be valid, the reason behind it would not be, as Targrave had already proven inept on several fronts, such as the location and placement of the defenses, which included breaking the men up into small blocks of around thirty and then to space them out, with the archers in the middle of each group.

Against a smaller force, this might have been an option, as the smaller groups could move about more freely and go where they were needed most, and quickly as well. However, against such large numbers, this would not be effective, as the archers would be spaced too far apart to adequately fight the enemy force, leading to the possibility that they would be picked off or overwhelmed, as opposed to Primus's plan, which involved keeping the archers as far from the front line as possible and keeping them as large blocks, whose arrows could block out the sun and lay low many soldiers before they ever reached Primus.

After quite a while, though, Thak and Primus had devised a plan to build the defenses and not alert Targrave to their plan. The method for this would involve Primus and those with him running into the desert for days at a time, as Primus had seen the soldiers do before.

"So, Thak, I've been meaning to ask you. What do you and the others all do when you run out into the desert for, how long, three days at a time or so?" Primus asked.

"Oh, that. Well, we actually do pretty much exactly what it looks like we're doing. We go for a run, and we try to keep that pace up for as long as we can. No one really can keep up at first, but by the end of the normal training regiment, nearly every man with us can run at a fairly easy and loping pace," Thak explained.

"For three days?" Primus asked, awed by the endurance it would require.

"Mmm. Three days, and some can also go for three nights. No food, no rest for three days, until we get back. We're actually going to be starting that for you and your group here in the next few days. We normally don't start so early, but with war on the horizon, we can build your bodies enough to fight, but endurance is the thing that'll really land you in trouble," Thak said.

"How do you mean?" Primus asked.

"You're the perfect example, Primus. You fight like nothing I've ever seen before, but you're panting after just a few minutes into combat training. You might not be too tired to continue, but that's only here. On an actual battlefield, unless you can find a way to fall back from the front for a few minutes, you're going to be fighting for a long time. If you get too tired or your mind starts to cloud from exhaustion, you're more likely to make a mistake," Thak said.

"And my mistakes will get me killed, or the men killed, or both," Primus said, and Thak nodded.

Although the idea of running for so long did not sit well with Primus, he learned afterward that shorter rest periods would be given where the men would be allowed to walk, but gradually, these would get shorter and shorter. They were also to run along the Alabel River so that a fresh supply of water was always available to them so that no one would die of thirst.

This, however, would work to their advantage. Rather than slowing to a walk or stopping altogether, they could simply start building the defenses and the pathway from the river to Meftif when they arrived. Primus even suggested that rather than running only up and back down the river, they would run toward Meftif and away from the river before stopping and turning back.

This would start to wear the trail into the ground. That would hopefully become more like the pathway that Primus envisioned. However, the first such run would go up and down the river as planned so that the huts could be built, or at least they could be started now and completed on subsequent trips.

To actually build the traps presented a logistical problem, as bringing the necessary tools and materials with them would be difficult. The extra weight that each man would have to carry would slow them down, and it was possible that Targrave would notice the tools missing if he were to inspect the storerooms. Finding sheets of cloth large enough to cover the traps would also be difficult, as no bolts of cloth that size were easily available without a requisition order, and such an order would likely have to be signed by Targrave.

It had been decided that Thak would be the one to try and obtain the linens as he might be able to order them for training purposes. The wooden stakes would be another issue that Thak would have to deal with, although this would be significantly easier, as simply requisitioning more wood for Targrave's placements would need an explanation that was easily believable due to *mistakes* in cutting the lengths needed.

And so with a plan in place, Thak and Primus left the house and started back toward the barracks, discussing small details on the way, such as who would answer to whom and the timing of certain things, such as when the men were to leave on their runs. That detail, it was decided, would be best handled by leaving before the sun came up and returning after it had gone down, so as to make it harder to see what the men were carrying with them. If Targrave was watching, the darkness would hide the extra tools that had been brought along, or if it was late enough, Targrave might well retire to his quarters, and the men would be entirely unobserved.

Near the barracks, Thak left Primus, as he still had to write his report of the mock battle that Primus had participated in and address the weaknesses that Primus had found within the formation. Primus walked slowly in the general direction of his barracks. He could not help replaying the mock battle over in his mind as well as the numbers of troops he would soon be facing. He wondered if they would be able to accomplish what was needed in the time he had left. It was not until that moment that he wondered if any of the men with him would report to Targrave what they were doing, but after some thought, he discounted the idea.

Most of the men won't know the difference between this and what they would have been doing anyway. And if we have to, we'll tell them. I hope that today and in future mock battles, I will earn enough of their trust that they won't say anything. Some of them already trust me enough that they'll go along with it, but I don't know about everyone yet, Primus thought, trying to set his mind at ease of what should happen if he were found out and doing his best not to think of that outcome.

Near his barracks, he spotted another figure approaching. It was too dark to make out who it was, possibly one of the sentries on their nightly rounds, so Primus paid them no mind. However, when the figure reached his barracks and stopped, Primus looked closer.

It was too dark to make out who it was, and although it was unlikely that whoever this was meant him harm, Primus could not help but clench his fists. It was possible, however unlikely, that one of the other men in the camp meant him harm, possibly as retribution for earlier in the day, or because they were ambitious and saw Primus as a threat to their own goals, or even someone sent by Targrave to intimidate him.

His fears were unfounded, however, as the closer he got, the smaller the figure appeared to be, and closer still, the curve of hips and the swell of breasts became visible as well. After crossing the final twenty or so feet that separated them, Primus saw that it was Turia, standing at a slight angle to accentuate her form.

"Well, I see you still have to take a minute to realize it's me. I saw you coming a long way off," Turia said with a slight smile as she turned to face Primus.

"Hey now, it's dark out, and people have snuck up on me before," Primus said. A broad smile split his face, and his tone was playful.

"Oh, really now? And what exactly did you expect little old me to do?" Turia asked as she walked over to Primus, hips swaying as she went.

"Hmm, I'm not sure, but something like this." Primus leaned in and kissed her as he finished his sentence. Turia broke the kiss a moment later.

"Oh no, a soldier taking liberties, I see," Turia said as she leaned back, placing the back of her hand on her forehead in false shock.

"Oh, what ever shall you do now?" Primus said flatly deliberately, enunciating each word as he fought back a chuckle.

"So why is my man coming back so late? You weren't off getting yourself in trouble, were you?" Turia said as she swatted playfully at Primus.

"Come on, when have you ever known *me* to get in *trouble*?" Primus said, leaning forward slightly and putting his hands on his chest.

"Hmm, I can think of one or two times. Like a few weeks ago at the warehouse," Turia said with a wink. Primus smiled and winked back.

"Really, though, why are you back so late? I was told you would probably be back later because the captain of the guard wanted to speak with you. I waited until it was late before coming here, but it's so late now. What's wrong? You look sad now," Turia said, suddenly concerned.

"Well, I know we joke about getting in trouble, but we might all be in a lot of trouble soon," Primus said softly. "Let's take a little walk. I have a few things I need to tell you."

As they walked around the training grounds, making sure to keep well away from the entrance and any sentries, Primus told Turia of all the events of the last week. He told her how he was learning to read and write and the knack he seemed to have for it, of how he excelled at spotting flaws in battle strategy and how to correct for them, how he struggled little with combat training, and finally of Targrave's return with news of war.

"They're really going to attack us?" Turia asked in shock. Primus could only nod in response. "But why? We haven't attacked them. We haven't done anything to provoke them, and there's been peace for so long now. Why?"

"Thak and I think that it's because they can either see or sense that Targrave is weak. That our forces aren't what they were in the past, and that means that they have a chance to bring down the biggest and the strongest. They could set themselves up as the leaders of Meftif and, by extension, effectively Crizia as a whole," Primus said.

"How man...how many men would you be facing?" Turia asked.

"Ten thousand, if the reports are right," Primus said grimly.

Turia stopped suddenly, rooted in place. She pressed a hand to her temple and swayed in place. She looked as if she had been struck.

"No," Turia said softly.

"What?" Primus asked.

"No, I won't let you. I won't let you go into this. You can't fight in this war. You're going up against ten thousand men. You're going to get killed," Turia pleaded, tears already streaming down her face.

"Turia, please, don't cry. It's okay. It's all right. I promise it'll be okay," Primus said as he wrapped his arms around her shoulders, hugging her tightly.

"No, it's not all right. It's not. You're going to get hurt, and I can't. I can't do it. I can't sit there and watch you get hurt or die," Turia sobbed.

"It's okay. I promise. Please hear me out," Primus asked softly as he stroked her hair. After a short while, when her sobbing had slowed to sniffling and the occasional hiccup, she nodded slightly.

"You wondered why I was back so late, and you knew I was spending some time with Thak. We were drawing up plans to deal with this," Primus said.

Turia looked up at him, her face pale, and streaks of silver ran over her cheeks. Her eyes were still wet, and she looked like she could cry again at any moment.

Primus proceeded to explain everything that he and Thak had discussed and planned for earlier in the night, everything from the most likely landing place, to the traps, to the deception that he and Thak would have to implement to see this through, as well as his dressing down at Targrave's estate and the suggestions he had made there and how they were implemented. He then proceeded to tell her about the mock battle that had been staged earlier in the day and the implications it would have in the coming war.

With each revelation, Turia seemed to grow happier, if only slightly, as he outlined the methods that he would use to ensure victory. Finally, he told her of his dream, stressing the point of how real everything had seemed, how tired he had seemed at the time, as if the battle had been raging for some time, and finally of Targrave's death.

"With Targrave dead, it would likely fall to Thak and me to keep the men from running. I didn't tell Thak about the dream or Targrave, for that matter, although I initially wanted to. The problem is that with the way he leads, he's going to get us all killed. If he's dead, yes, it'll leave a hole for us, but one that I'll try to fill. By the time we get to that point, I'll hopefully have earned the trust of most of the men. Or at least enough of it that I'll be able to lead them, at least for a while," Primus finished. Turia was silent for a moment, contemplating everything she had just heard.

"You're taking on a lot of responsibility with all this, and you're risking a lot too. You're sure you won't get caught? And you're sure that you weren't hurt?" Turia asked, and Primus shook his head to both of her questions.

"I promise, everything is going to be okay. You'll see," Primus said softly as he cupped her chin with just his index finger and lifted her head slightly. She kissed him then, and afterward, they embraced, swaying softly. Then they began to walk the training grounds again for a while, talking about this and that, and nothing important passed between them. Eventually, the time came when they both realized they needed to leave each other so that they would be rested come morning.

Primus led her near the entrance then helped Turia out of the grounds, past the sentries. They kissed each other goodbye and good night. Primus watched her go, thinking of everything that was to happen in the next several weeks until the war began. Above all else, Primus hoped that Turia would be safe. Though he had refrained from doing so, Primus knew that he would ask Turia to leave the city for safety, just as he knew that she would never leave while he was still here.

Then Primus roused himself, shaking his head and shoulders, much like a cave bear ridding himself of flies. These thoughts, he knew, could wait until the next day.

Better get to bed. I've got a long day ahead of me tomorrow and an even longer week. I'm going to have a hard enough time sleeping tonight with everything I talked about with Thak. I just hope I'm right. Otherwise, I'll get myself and a whole lot of the men killed, Primus thought. He slipped back into the shadows, the darkness enveloping him completely, folding around him like a blanket.

Chapter 7

The following two months saw surprising progress, from the construction of the defensive traps and pathway, to the huts, to Primus's endurance, to his ability to lead. It had been a surprise when, on the morning after Primus and Thak created their own plan for the defenses of Meftif, Targrave appeared on the training field before any weapons training or target practice could take place. Targrave informed everyone present that he would be overseeing combat training from that day onward, and that any reports on how training was progressing were to be made on the spot.

Targrave's stated intention was to observe combat practice and see with his own eyes whether or not everyone was as proficient as they seemed to be in the reports. Primus, however, knew that there was more. Under the smooth veneer of watchful curiosity he wore, Targrave's eyes and the hard line of his jaw told a very different story. He looked as though he had barely slept. Dark circles and bags rested under his eyes, like overfull waterskins.

Thak must have written the report and delivered it to Targrave, and the knowledge that something he had worked on for months was dismantled in minutes by a man at least a third younger than himself must have weighed heavily on his mind. Primus caught Targrave several times throughout the rest of the morning staring at him with an emotion that he could not quite place. It seemed to be a mixture of envy, hatred, disdain, and…was it *fear?*

Shortly thereafter, Targrave decided to cut the training and target practice short, instead instructing everyone to move to the combat field. There, he had the men separate into four separate groups, each of about equal size. He then went to each group and spoke softly enough that no one in the other groups could hear. When Targrave made it to Primus's group, he instructed them that they were an attacking force and that they would be the only ones to attack. This put the group at a firm disadvantage. However, it was left up to them to decide how they wanted to attack.

Primus looked out to the other three groups, each one assuming a different defensive formation that he was unfamiliar with. Primus guessed that these were Targrave's inventions, that it was partly this he had spent time the previous night, although based on how long it was taking each group to position themselves even after Targrave had left them, Primus realized that these had been created in haste, as the war report took prominence. However, Targrave still had to find a way to recover from the blow that Primus had dealt to his pride, and the formation sizes and differences were meant to facilitate that recovery.

Primus had taken a moment to look over each formation then turned to the men with him and instructed them how to best deal with each formation. Afterward, Primus and his men broke off from one another and seemingly made to attack each formation simultaneously before they all turned toward the farthest defensive group and charged. With attacks coming from more than one angle, the men inside were quickly pushed back, although not beaten. Primus then shouted a signal that he had previously given to his men, and they suddenly turned and ran full tilt toward the rightmost group.

This sudden turn took both groups off guard, and Primus broke through the formation with ease, although again, while pushing the group back, did not beat them. After whooping, a third of his men went to engage the final defensive group, which until now had not seen any fighting. After only a handful of seconds, Primus ordered a retreat, and most of his men began to make their way into the center of the field, where they assumed a circular formation then covered themselves with their shields and crouched. The next men in line covered the top portion of the shields of the men below them, leaving just a tiny gap between which they could see out to the crush of bodies around them.

From between these gaps, several men with their wooden poles that functioned as spears began to jab outward into the crush of men. The attackers had become the defenders, and they tried to press their advantage. However, none of the formerly defending groups could make much headway, and more than one fell to the ground gasping for air after a pole knocked the wind from their lungs. Primus shouted one more time, this time calling the men who were not inside the protective layer of shields to him.

He, along with several others, had stayed outside and continued to fight on the fringes of the scuffle. From there, all but one of the men came to his side as he fell upon the others from the rear. Primus led the charge into the cluster in front of him, knocking several men over and rapping several others with his weapons, and the men with him did the same.

The distraction, coupled with the fact that the former defenders realized that Primus was not with the men behind a shield wall, caused the overeager defenders to turn around, leaving their backs exposed. And all three groups, which had all clumped together in an attempt to deal with where they believed the true threat lay, were swiftly beaten. Of the men that Primus had attacked, most turned to face him, and in their haste, they failed to realize that they were being beaten from the back.

As they began to realize that the threat behind them had not simply vanished, they began to turn around, tangling and tripping their fellow soldiers and causing further confusion. Some continued on, hoping they could still win this fight if they captured or incapacitated Primus, although they were now forced to defend themselves on two fronts, and this proved more difficult than they had originally anticipated.

Although it took a further four minutes, Primus and his group of men proved victorious once again. The ploy of Primus using himself as bait had gone over flawlessly, and he allowed himself a satisfied smile, happy to bask in the warm afterglow of victory. The same could not be said of Targrave. He stomped over the field and stopped directly in front of Primus, staring at him with the same intensity as their first private meeting. But underneath the somewhat blank look he received, Primus could see the cold fury just below Targrave's smooth exterior. Targrave worked his jaw back and forth for a brief moment before looking first left, then right, before returning his gaze to Primus.

"How did you do this? What thought process did you use to come up with whatever you would call this?" Targrave demanded.

"I looked at the size of my group and the size of the other groups. I knew that in terms of outright numbers, we couldn't win. We would be surrounded. So attack one group, then attack the other two at the same time to draw them in, in case they were waiting for the first group to fall. Once they're all fighting, climb over each other to strike back, retreat, and make a circular wall of shields to keep them out. Leave some gaps to see through and to poke a spear through.

"I stay back after ordering the retreat so I can use myself as bait, and when they turn around to try and capture me, they get attacked from behind because they are too eager, and they forget to look behind them," Primus explained easily, as it was simple and straightforward for him. It did not appear to be so simple for Targrave, who simply stared at him, blankly now, the fury having melted as he listened to Primus.

"And how did you know that they would come after you?" Targrave asked, perhaps a little too calmly.

"I wasn't completely sure they would, but if today had the same rules as yesterday, then their job was to capture me or slap me with a big wooden stick. So if I stayed back and made myself a bit of a target, then I could be a distraction. It was a risk for me to do, sure, but I was able to divide their attention enough that I was able to come out of this victorious," Primus said, gesturing to the men lying on the ground and to those who had fought with him, who now stood behind him.

"Ah, I see. Very well then," Targrave said as he seemed to shrink in on himself. Without another word, he turned and left the combat field. Nearly every man stood up and began to congratulate Primus for achieving victory when it appeared that defeat was the only possible outcome. Primus was not celebrating, however, as he watched Targrave leave the training grounds. His step was slow, and farther away from the crowd, he appeared to stagger slightly, as if he, too, had participated in the fighting and been struck hard in the head.

After that incident, Targrave had appeared at least once every week at the combat practice field, sometimes twice. Each time, there were new formations that were inherently flawed, and each time, Primus emerged victorious. It became obvious to everyone that the defenses were being hastily thrown together, and Targrave appeared a little more disheveled with each loss.

Although no one had spoken to the other men, Primus saw how they began to regard him with what he began to understand as admiration and loyalty. Even though he had beaten everyone black and blue countless times, his quick mind and his ability to win consistently had raised his standing among the men.

Also during this time, the preparations had begun. The mornings now only consisted of archery for around a half hour before Targrave put the men to work building his defenses toward the south of Meftif. The construction would last until shortly before the midday meal, which was served a little earlier than it had previously been. A large portion of the afternoons were spent learning to read and write.

Some long-past battles were still used to teach, although these now were only battles that would be close enough in scale to be comparable to Meftif's current circumstances. Targrave would rarely sit in with these lessons, and when he did, he was entirely silent, oftentimes choosing to enter after the room had been filled and doing so quietly that not even the faintest whisper of sound escaped him to alert anyone else to his presence.

Once a week, Thak would lead the men on their run away from Meftif and into the desert. Primus struggled here at first, as not only was he not used to running, but he was also unaccustomed to the overfull pack that he would carry. Inside the pack were digging instruments and several small mud bricks. Most of the men carried similar tools with them as well.

The construction of Primus's fortifications and traps seemed to make little headway at first. The huts were built first, and they were built with little effort. Running through the desert, on the other hand, to create the illusion of a safe pathway seemed to be compounding misery with madness.

The men did not seem to be able to wear in a path as fast as Primus would have liked, and they were only able to dig for so long before everyone made their way back to the Alabel River for water. To top off everything, to strengthen the men and to make them as tough as they could be, they were not allowed to bring any food with them, which made their exertions, mainly digging the trenches and sharpening the stakes, much worse.

While they were running, at least the pace could be maintained once the men were all at speed, but stopping every so often and starting again was tougher on their bodies, and shifting from running to digging was also difficult, as now there was not even the constant breeze to cool them. They made so little progress on this that Primus began to fear that his plan had doomed them all and that their time might have been better spent trying to build up Targrave's defenses more. Worse still, Primus feared that some of the men would either accidentally reveal the plan if Targrave was close by and listening into conversations on the training field, or they would deliberately go to him.

Either scenario would be disastrous for Primus and Thak as well, as they would both be responsible for the insubordination, and they both would face severe consequences. Despite this, Primus labored on with the others, desperately trying to project a calm and collected appearance. Thak helped with this somewhat on the first run. He had explained to the men that he and Primus had created a different plan than the one Targrave had, and the project would need to be completed in secrecy.

Primus's fears were unfounded. The ranks began to swell as more and more men were called back to fight and as more and more men joined of their own accord. As the ranks swelled, so, too, did the force that could construct the pathway and the traps, which became longer and wider than they were originally intended. Several more layers were added, and Targrave was none the wiser.

While this suddenly made it much easier and the plan began to come together with surprising speed, Primus was still unsure why no one had said anything about it to Targrave, even in passing or an overheard comment. One night, after returning from a run, Primus stopped Thak and pulled him aside. He then raised his questions to the older man.

"Well, Primus, they're not talking because of you," Thak said with a bemused look on his face.

"What do you mean because of me? What did I do? Do I scare them?" Primus asked, taken aback.

"No, you don't…well, actually. You probably do scare *some* of them. You're stronger than most of them. You're taller, and you're clearly smarter than a lot of them. You do have a bit of an intimidation factor, absolutely. But that just makes them not want to approach you at first. No, there's a completely different reason the men haven't breathed a word to Targrave," Thak said.

"And? What's the reason?" Primus asked, continuing when he saw Thak lower his head, struggling not to laugh. "Come on, you know something I don't, and this is important."

"It's because of *you*, Primus. You're the reason the men won't say anything," Thak said, a large grin splitting his face.

"M-me? B-but how am *I* the reason?" Primus asked, now thoroughly confused.

"Primus, the men are kind of…I don't know exactly how to put it. They're kind of enamored with you. You've proved you can fight and win. You can lead effectively in the mock battles. You've come up with a plan that they think is better than Targrave's. You keep finding solutions to the problems that I give during lectures. You…you do so much. You're able to do all of that and more.

"They admire you, Primus. They like you, and more importantly, they've become loyal to you. They believe you'll lead them into this war and lead you to victory. They have more faith in you than they do in Targrave. Because of that, they'll follow you to the ends of the earth, and they won't say a word," Thak said earnestly. Primus was silent for a moment.

"Okay, I can believe that the men who I started with believe all of that. But what about everyone else who either joined or was recalled? Why do they stay quiet?" Primus asked, speaking slowly.

"They stay quiet partly because the others stay quiet, but mostly because of you too. You're developing a bit of a reputation here, and it's a very good one. They all trust you enough not to sell you out to Targrave. Don't be worried about that or upset by it. Just be grateful we both get to keep our positions and our heads," Thak finished, placing his fist near Primus's shoulder and holding it there for a moment before bringing it down and gently pushing it into Primus's shoulder. Primus moved with it, although he said nothing about the friendly gesture.

Thak had left Primus alone after that. What he said troubled Primus, although he could not identify the reason for it. It could be that he was simply not used to the idea that he would be so well-liked due to the years he had spent living with Niran, spending all his days training or getting into fights.

I mean, it's not like it's a bad *thing that people are starting to like me now. I just don't know what to do. It's been years now, and all I've been known as until now is a menace, someone to be kept away from, not someone to be* admired. *Still, though, if it means I can have my commission, if it means that I'll be able to protect Turia, the most important thing I care about right now. If it means there'll be peace here, I'll take it*, Primus thought.

In addition to not knowing how he should feel about being liked, Primus was also unsure of how to take the news that he effectively was no longer alone. He had been mostly solitary for years, only spending any real amount of time with another person when Turia sneaked away to see him or the occasional day that he had spent with Niran and his family.

In the end, he had decided to simply accept the new information and to make as much use out of it as possible. He knew now that the men would follow him, and that was enough. Together with their admiration, these two things would greatly aid Primus if his dream was to become reality. If Targrave really were to die in the coming battle, Primus knew that the men would need to see him standing up and taking command. Otherwise, their resolve might still break, and the men would flee. If that happened, Primus knew that Turia would be in danger, and he knew that he would never allow any harm to come to her.

Another two weeks went by, and suddenly, preparations were nearly complete. The only things missing were several stakes, which would be easy enough to move during the next run under the cover of darkness, and even if those stakes were never brought to the traps, they were still formidable.

Pits had been dug in the sand, and bows and quivers full of arrows had been stashed away, waiting for the day that they would be used, alongside a small sealed jar of scorpion poison, which had been painstakingly collected from several dozen scorpions over the previous two months.

Primus had, quite by accident, discovered a way to make the scorpions produce their poison nearly on command. While handling one several weeks ago, the small pot still had had a cloth seal over its mouth which someone had failed to remove. While the scorpion's body was still being held, the stinger had accidentally been let go of, and the scorpion struck. Only the sheerest of luck had saved Primus then as the pot was being moved into place at the time. The tail pierced the cloth instead of Primus's arm.

When they pulled the pot and scorpion away seconds later, a small wet patch was visible on the cloth, and Primus realized that the scorpion had released its store of poison into the pot and cloth by mistake. After this revelation, the poison was able to be gathered much faster than it had been, as the scorpions did not need to be killed each time and could be held for several days to extract the most possible.

Thak had encouraged Primus to address the men at that point, and Primus had reluctantly agreed. He suddenly found himself standing before a sizeable portion of the army, wishing he were anywhere but there. He had no clue what he was going to say before he opened his mouth. But once he did, Primus found that he could not stop the flow of words, although he was never able to remember what he had said. For Primus, it only seemed to last for mere moments, a slight blur of sweat and the heat of the evening sun, which was nearly touching the horizon when he started his speech.

However, on finishing the speech to a thunderous cheering from the men, Primus walked away from the small hill he was standing on to deliver the speech, and he was surprised to see the sun had disappeared below the horizon. Thak congratulated him for giving such a riveting speech and said he believed he could single-handedly fight a hundred soldiers of Sodom without so much as a scratch on himself.

With the preparations done, the full scale of the runs were able to take place. While Primus had built his endurance up over the past two months, it was still not adequate for what he and the men with him experienced when running now for three days straight, no food or rest. Building the fortifications had been a time-consuming and tiring process, but the run was constant, while the work was slightly intermittent.

As a result, Primus and most of his men struggled somewhat to keep pace and not to stop to catch their breath. However, due to running with all the materials and supplies that were needed to build the defenses, as well as build and furnish the huts enough that they appeared to have actually been lived in for some time, their bodies were stronger, and they were able to quickly build the remainder of their endurance up. Thus, when they reached the Meftif again after three days, not one man among them was even breathing hard.

Primus saw more of Turia in this time than he had in the previous months. They spent most of their time wandering the training field at night, keeping away from the sentries and speaking of the general goings-on in the world. Although they often sneaked off to more secluded places on the field, and events would carry on much as they had before, Primus could see the worry beginning to wear on Turia.

She eventually confided in him that she could not seem to move past the image in her head of Primus lying dead in the sand. She told him how she had had a similar dream to his own, but the bloody sands that stretched on toward the horizon and walking toward the bodies strewn across the ground were the only thing she had seen and all that she remembered.

After assuaging her fears and holding her close until her cries had ceased, Primus spent some time telling Turia the story of how they first met and then how he planned a house for the two of them to look and how many rooms they would need to build for any children they were to have. It had taken a while, but Turia eventually came back around and began to engage in the conversation, becoming lively and more animated, extending the talk of what their life would be like and how they would sit together as an old man and an old lady, looking out over their estate as their family went from here to there, and of all the grandchildren they would have.

Although that night had appeared to make Turia better, Primus could still see the toll it was taking on her. The worry of whether he would be killed or not was eating away at her, and Primus wished that either Sodom, Gomorrah, or Angra would launch either a single city attack or that they would all declare war and march on Meftif.

The tedium of waiting was worse than Primus could have imagined, and he wished that they would attack, not so he could fight but just to give Turia some peace of mind that one way or another, the war would be over sooner rather than later.

Three months after the three cities allied against Meftif and the night after one of Turia's visits, Primus lay in bed, reading by candlelight a book he had taken from the library about the history and construction of the citadel in the center of the city, which had been constructed of relatively small bricks made of carved white limestone originally before being replaced by larger blocks of the same stone over time. Then the door to the barracks began to slowly open.

Primus noticed the slight movement and, matching the speed, closed the book while reaching beneath the bed, groping slightly for his weapon. Though he knew that it was most likely to be Thak or one of the lieutenants, there was always a chance that it was someone who meant him or his men.

His fears were once again unfounded, as once the door was open wide enough, and just as Primus was starting to rise, Thak stuck his head through the door. He spotted Primus immediately due to the candle and motioned to him to stay quiet and put out the flame. Primus did so and, following Thak's still silent motions, stood up and followed him out into the training field, closing the door slowly and gently on the way out. Once they had put some distance between themselves and the barracks, Thak finally spoke.

"I'm sorry to do this now, Primus. I know it's late, and I know you're probably tired and need some sleep, but this can't wait," Thak said, the urgency in his voice clear as he picked up speed, nearing a full sprint by the end of his short sentence.

"What is it? What happened, Thak?" Primus asked, his own voice urgent as he kept pace with the older man.

"We received a missive from one of our spies. Targrave called everyone of note to a meeting at his estate. Everyone except you, that is. But I'll sneak you in through the servants' quarters, through the back gate. You'll be able to listen to the missive. You just can't be heard," Thak said as they entered the city, running headlong between the dark alleys and side streets toward Targrave's manor.

"Are we going to be attacked? Or have they created something we don't know about? Some new engine of war?" Primus asked as he felt his gut clench within him.

If we're attacked now by something new, I don't know if we'll have the time to build something that could defend against whatever it is. And then Turia will be danger, Primus thought.

"I don't know, Primus. The summons was urgent, but the only thing I was told was that our spies have information about their activities. We'll have to see how bad it is when we get you in there," Thak said as they slowed to a walk, now at the front of Targrave's estate.

Primus and Thak said no more as they pushed the gate open and began to make their way quickly but quietly around to the back. From there, Thak pushed on the door, although it stayed locked. After a moment of shaking the doorknob first left, then right, and up and down, suddenly, an audible *click* was heard, and the door swung open.

"It's a problem with most of the doors in the city. You can force the tumblers to fall if you shake it in a certain pattern," Thak whispered as he swung the door open.

"How did you figure that out?" Primus whispered back.

"Years ago, my wife was pregnant with our first child, and she wanted something from the market. I can't remember what it was. Anyway, she locked the door after I left but fell asleep before I got back. I had to break in to my own house. It took me most of the night to figure out the pattern, and I've had to use it a few times since. Now go *on*," Thak said softly, inclining his head toward the now-open door. Primus entered the kitchen and quickly found the door to the hidden passageways within the manor.

"Once you close that door, you can listen for voices or look for light from the crack underneath the door. Stay quiet and out of sight. I'll go around the front and go in in a minute so you have some time to get there," Thak whispered as he closed the door and was gone.

Primus shuffled forward and up the hidden stairs, and before long, he was able to see the thin golden bar of light shining from beneath the door. There was muffled conversation beyond, but it was too faint to make out, so Primus grabbed the knob and twisted gently. The door began to swing outward on silent hinges, and when the gap was just wide enough to let the voices in, he stopped and waited for Thak to appear. He did not have to wait long.

"Ah, Thak, you're here. Good. Please, come in and sit down," Targrave said.

"Thank you, sir, but if you don't mind me asking, why did you summon us here at this hour? Your message only said that something important was delivered from a spy," Thak said as Primus heard a chair slide across the floor.

"Yes, I wanted to make sure that no one else knew or overheard. I won't waste any time. The cities are moving to launch an attack against us," Targrave said grimly, and the silence that followed was absolute.

Chapter 8

The silence and darkness seemed to close in around Primus, and the very walls around him seemed to shrink inward, while the only thing he could hear was the muffled sound of his heartbeat, as even his breathing had stopped. He looked around feeling dazed, as if he had suffered a blow to the head. Primus guessed that the others must have had a similar reaction, as it took over a minute for shouting to erupt, with everyone trying to make themselves heard over the din. Eventually, someone won out.

"So we know they're moving. All we have to do is mobilize our men. I mean, we've been training the newer soldiers for three months just for this, and everyone who served previously are already back with us and have been for at least a few weeks. We know that we have enough men to at least put up a decent defense. The only question that remains is, when exactly do they attack?" the man said. Primus did not recognize the man's voice.

"They'll attack soon, that much we all know. They want to try and upend the established order we have, and the best thing they can do is to attack as soon as possible before exactly this happens," Thak said.

"What do you mean by *exactly this*?" Targrave asked.

"I guess I should expand on that. Exactly this means what we're doing now. Convening to discuss how and where to place our men and defenses. How best to kill their men or how best to stop them from getting here. Tell me, General, how did the spies find out the information?" Thak asked.

"They reported that the men had abandoned their posts at Gomorrah. The training grounds were empty, and several ships had been unmoored at some point in the night. There's no other reason that our spies or I could think of. The dates on the missives are also indicative of this. The dates from the spy in Angra are from a little more than a week ago, and from a few days later, Sodom, and then this one from Gomorrah just a two days ago," Targrave said.

"So they staggered their departures to make sure they could arrive at the same time. That sounds like they're moving to attack. How long do you think we have before they get here?" A third man entered the conversation.

"Based on the speed the Alabel River flows and the fact that they're upstream, I would have expected they would be here by now. My guess is that they sailed through the night and that they're hiding a little way south of Meftif. It means that we likely have only a day. Tomorrow is the last day that we'll have to prepare. After that, they'll either attack, or they'll set up fortifications and make camp so they could attack afterward at any point. No matter what, we'll need to get the men ready for combat," Targrave said.

Primus bit his tongue as he resisted the urge to shout through the wall. He wanted to rage at Targrave for his ignorance and his unwavering faith in himself and his abilities. Primus knew that the enemy, despite having a larger force, had trained just as long and just as hard as he had, and that despite not having years to prepare, they would be well aware that they could still lose this fight.

A larger army did not necessarily mean victory, especially not if you were a poorly equipped army, although Primus did not think that the enemy would be equipped much differently from what he himself would be outfitted with in just a day. Primus was thankful, however, for the knowledge that the ships had left their home cities, as this meant that the sentries in the huts he had built, who Thak had secretly garrisoned three weeks ago, had still not spotted any enemy ships sailing down the river. If they had, Primus and Thak would have been alerted to their presence.

It had only just occurred to Primus that there may have been some way to slow down or stop the ships entirely, possibly by attaching some stout logs at an angle to a large rock and then maneuvering that rock into the river so that the logs sat just below the surface. The weight of the ships, laden with men and materials as they were, might be damaged or even sink, thus improving Primus's odds.

He cursed himself a fool for this lapse until the colder and more cunning part of him reminded himself that if the ships were allowed to pass uncontested, they would believe their victory was sure, and they would be more likely to put to shore where Primus intended them to.

"I'll draw up the marching orders in the morning, and I'll distribute them to the men. They should have the chance tomorrow to see their families before going to war," Thak said.

"Good. It doesn't matter now if you or I or anyone else for that matter believes that the men aren't ready," Targrave said.

"What do you mean *not ready*? I've been saying for a while now that they're ready. For weeks now I've been saying it. Why would you think they're not ready?" Thak asked.

"I don't think they're ready because of Primus. That boy has no idea how to actually fight and win a war. And I think you're a little too close to him as well, and that friendship is affecting your judgment. You're too close, and you're not what you used to be," Targrave said, a hint of derision coloring his voice.

"Sir, with all due respect, you don't know what you're talking about. That man is an amazing fighter and a talented tactician. He has a deep understanding of logistics and a quick mind. He's not lost a single fight in combat training, despite going up against numbers that anyone else would lose against. Primus has the potential to make a great leader here, and I have no idea why you're trying so hard to say he's not or to say that he's not ready or that he can't do what needs to be done," Thak said.

His impassioned speech warmed Primus's heart, and he felt himself becoming a little emotional. He had not expected Thak to defend him to the extent that he just had, and Primus realized in that moment how high the lofty view that Thak held of him really was.

"This is what I mean. He's reckless. He doesn't actually think things through. He just does, and that will get too many men killed. I would have removed him from our ranks myself if we didn't need every single blade," Targrave said, the contempt in his voice so strong that Primus could picture the sneer Targrave wore on his face.

"Sir, he *does* think things through, and he's not reckless. He takes risks only when he needs to and no more than is absolutely necessary. You might look down your nose at him, but he's made a habit of winning, and that habit would be incredibly useful to have on our side. If you give him the chance, he absolutely can help here. Just talk to him, if nothing else. Having someone else look over what you've done and what you've written makes a bigger difference than you think since there might be options that you didn't think of or routes you didn't consider. There could be untold possibilities that would put us at a bigger adva—" Thak said before being cut off.

"Enough!" Targrave roared, almost screeching, as he silenced Thak midsentence. "I have no need of him now, and I never did. The only thing he's done is rile the men up and show them that discipline need not apply to them. He is disrespectful, a nuisance, rash, insubordinate, and out of control. He's going to get every single man out there killed if he pulls another one of his harebrained stunts, and possibly the worst thing, he refuses to learn what he's doing wrong, and on that, you are to blame," Targrave finished, and while there had been some muffled talk between a few of the men who were in the room, they had become silent, just as they had when they received the news that they would be attacked soon.

Primus felt his blood boil and his face flush. If he had received the insults by himself and outside the army, he likely would not have been able to contain his fury and would have fought with Targrave. If a friend had received insults like that, Primus would have also fought on behalf of that friend, regardless of whether or not the friend in question would fight. However, several things rooted Primus to the spot and prevented him from moving to act on his rage.

The first was that he was not supposed to be in the estate, and if Targrave found out that he was there, Primus knew he would be thrown out of the army. The second was that if he was thrown out, Primus knew that the soldiers and the city would be overwhelmed by the onslaught of enemy soldiers. The third was that he was thrown out, Thak likely would as well, as he would claim responsibility for Primus being there in an attempt to keep him in the army.

And finally, if neither of them were with the army, Targrave would set the men in place at the southern end of the city, well away from where the enemy soldiers were most likely to attack from, and he would not move them until forced to, and by that time, it would be too late. Primus held his tongue, and whatever Thak must have been feeling, he also did not speak.

"Now does anyone *else* have anything to say about this whelp? Does anyone here want to tell me to involve a boy in the matters of war?" Targrave asked. He was silent for nearly a full minute. "No? Good. Now then, Thak, are all the defenses in place?"

"They are," Thak answered flatly.

"Excellent. All the men will fight then. And yes, Thak, before you ask, that does mean Primus too. I said earlier that we need every single blade, and I did not change my mind in the brief time that it's been since I first said it. Now, all of you, get out," Targrave said.

Primus heard the sound of chairs being pulled across the floor, their legs scraping as they went. While the men inside were standing up, Primus hurriedly and quietly closed the door, attempting to time the click of the latch with the scrap of a chair.

It was well that he did. The latch closed with an audible click loud enough to be heard over the scraping sounds. However, no one in the room said anything about any sounds. All that could be heard was murmuring and the soft pounding of many feet on thick rugs. While everyone else was leaving through the front entrance, Primus made his way through the darkened passage, back down the stairs to the kitchen, and to the back door that was thankfully still unlocked.

Primus exited and made his way around the side of the manor, the same as he did with Thak earlier in the night. He waited before leaving the grounds, however, as there were several lit windows that were visible, and in one of them, Primus thought he could see Targrave moving around.

To make it so far only to be caught sneaking out of the estate and being thrown out of the army after so long, and just before the battle to decide the fate of not just Meftif but also effectively decide the fate of Crizia, was a thought that Primus could not bear. He spied Thak across the street staring up at the stars, unmoving and unblinking.

As Primus watched, he could suddenly see Thak pointing at him with his hand, which Thak kept down by his hip. He first pointed then motioned for Primus to come forward. Primus inched forward and started to leave, keeping an eye on Thak. He suddenly made a motion to stop. Primus stopped then backed up into a bush to further conceal his form.

After a moment, Thak motioned to Primus again, and this time, Primus turned his head to look at the window, from which the light was rapidly fading. Primus opened the gate just enough to squeeze through and then closed it as quietly as he could. Primus and Thak silently turned and began to walk down the street, away from the gate and deeper into the city, just as they had done several weeks ago, although now it seemed as if that walk had taken place a lifetime ago.

"Thank you, Thak, for what you did back there. You didn't have to stand up for me, but you did, and I really appreciate it," Primus said.

"Ah, never you mind about that. I wanted one last shot at trying to get him to include you on this since we really only have tomorrow left. After that, we'll either be dead or prisoners, which is the same thing," Thak said, waving his hand in Primus's direction.

"No, really. Thank you. No one has ever really done something like that before, and it means a lot to me," Primus said, his voice thick.

"Hey now, I only did what anyone else should have done. You're valuable here, and you're my friend. But your thanks is appreciated as well, and you're welcome," Thak said with a half smile.

"So I guess that begs the question. What now?" Primus asked, his voice returning to normal.

"Now? Well, now we go back, we sleep, and we get up at dawn. And we all go to do whatever you're going to do. I mean, let's face it, Primus, in just over a day, we could both be dead. People have asked me, 'How would you go about your day if you knew it was the last one you would ever have?' So I'll ask you the same thing now," Thak said. Primus was silent for a moment, thinking about what he might do if he knew it would be his last day alive.

"Well, I think I have my answer, but before I tell you mine, I want to hear yours. You're older. You've been in the army longer. You've had longer to think about this than I have," Primus said.

"If I had my way, I would spend the entire day sitting at home with my wife and children, maybe read them a book or help my wife prepare dinner. Or maybe take them all out on one last big adventure. Or maybe even just a small adventure, just into the city and to the shops to let them pick out one thing I always said we could get next time. That's how I would spend my last day if I had my way," Thak said softly, as if from far away, slowing as he spoke until he was walking at half his normal speed. His eyes were unfocused, and Primus thought he could just detect a slight silver shine in the corners of his eyes.

"Anyway, that's only if I had my way. I promised I would send them all away to keep them out of danger, and I will tomorrow, but for tonight? Tonight, they need to rest. They'll need it since they'll have to start traveling tomorrow. I hope I can convince them to leave in the afternoon, though. That way, I have the morning with them. My wife will know tonight, though. She always waits for me to come home," Thak said.

"She waits for you even when it's a night like tonight? When you're home so late?" Primus asked.

"Yes, she does. She's not always *awake* when I get home. Sometimes she's sleeping in a chair or at the table, but she's always waiting for me," Thak said, smiling again.

"That sounds perfect, and I'm glad you two will do things like that for each other," Primus said.

"We do that and much, much more. But now it's your turn. So what will you do knowing it's your last day?" Thak asked, looking intently at Primus.

"You mean knowing that it *could be* my last day," Primus said, teasing the older man slightly.

"Oh, you know what I mean," Thak said somewhat testily to Primus's surprise.

"Well, for myself, I think I'll go to Turia, and I'll either spend the day with her down by the river. Or maybe we'll head into the city and see what we can find there. I might try to convince her father one more time to let us get married before I go off to fight the next day, but he was fairly adamant the last time I talked to him that we couldn't get married until after I had earned a commission. I don't think a little thing like death would let the man actually allow me to marry his daughter," Primus said, smiling to himself.

"I'm sorry, Primus. I know that must be hard on you. And her as well. What did you ever do to upset the man so much that that's what you have to do for him to even consider a match?" Thak asked.

"Well, the truth is I really never did anything to him. He doesn't think I'm a good match for Turia. That she can do better. But I never actually did anything to upset him. I wish I had though, because at least then I could have done something to try and make things better. I wish I had broken a pot or cracked a mug or set their rug on fire. But nothing like that happened. And I think despite that Turia and I were friends growing up, it was the fact that I actually showed interest in her right around the same time that she showed interest in me that really upset him," Primus said.

"But why would that be the case? Why would that be such a problem for him?" Thak asked.

"Because I figure if it was only me, then he could have told her something along the lines of 'He'll feel differently in six months or a year' or 'He's just after you now, and you know exactly why.' Or that she would be just someone I could keep around for a while until I found someone I actually wanted. If it was just her, then he could have told her that she would outgrow me, that there were other more eligible men with better prospects than a farmer. Or that he's dangerous and will hit you. Or that if she married me, he would bar her from is house," Primus explained.

"That still doesn't answer my question, though. Why is that a problem? I mean, he could have said any of those things. Or really all of those things, anyway," Thak asked, now confused.

"The reason it's a problem is because he caught us outside one day, talking to each other. We made a promise to each other. We promised that we wouldn't love anyone else. I know that sounds stupid now. We were just barely out of childhood years. And the reason it was a problem for him then, and still is, is that we promised it to each other then. And then we immediately promised it to him when he spoke up. It was because we both had such an interest in each other and that we made it known together that he couldn't try to talk her out of it. It had been said out loud, and that lent a lot of weight to it," Primus said ruefully, wishing to himself that he and Turia had stayed quiet that day so that they would not have alerted her father.

"And that's it? There's no other reason?" Thak pressed.

"Well, he viewed it as going behind his back as well and trying to court his daughter without permission, which is partly true, but I never really courted her. We just…we fell into it, you could say. It crept up on us. And the day that we decided to tell each other and make that promise, we had talked earlier in the day about each of us having something important to tell the other. So we went around to the back of the house and sat on a bench, and we started to talk. That was when her father came up behind us and caught us midconversation," Primus said.

"Ah, so that was it then. You said it out loud, and he heard it, and it was before you had said anything to him. Were you planning on talking to him?" Thak asked.

"I was. I actually told Turia right before her father walked up that I would talk to him the next week, and she told me I should talk to him the next day, which I had agreed to. We then repeated the promise, and there he was. So he missed the most important part of it for himself, but I'm not so sure he would have said yes in the first place. Like I said, he never really liked me much, and there was no explanation for it," Primus said.

"Well, it sounds like you tried after that to make things right. If he still can't see that after all this time, then I don't think there's much hope for fixing it. But he at least promised you that you could marry his daughter after you earn a commission," Thak said reassuringly.

"Yes, yes, he did. And if this plays out the way that we think it will, then he won't have much choice in two days," Primus said with a smile.

"No, he absolutely won't. I can just picture the look on his face now. At first, he'll be angry you're back. Then he won't believe you when you say you've done it. Then he'll see the commission, and he's going to just sink into himself. I just hope I'll be there to see it. I'm sure it'll be funny," Thak said, a broad smile now splitting his face.

"You're right. He'll really have to eat his words then," Primus said, chuckling.

"I could actually be there if you wanted. That way, he'll have someone else present who can verify that you really did get your commission. He could try to argue it, but if I'm there, I don't think he'll try," Thak said.

"Are you offering me help to get married?" Primus asked.

"I am. You don't have to say yes now, but think it over tomorrow. I'm almost home anyway. We're three houses up," Thak said.

"Thank you, Thak. Again. You're really a true friend. You know that, don't you?" Primus asked, his voice once more thickening.

"I'm just trying to do the right thing. If that makes me a true friend, then I'm glad to do so. This is me, though, so good night, Primus. I'll see you day after tomorrow," Thak said as he turned and walked to his front door.

"Good night, Thak. I'll see you day after tomorrow," Primus said, waving to him as he went.

Primus watched his friend enter his home before turning and slowly making his way back to the barracks. He knew that he would have to retrieve his gold in the morning so that he could spend some time with Turia, especially since he was planning to take her into the city.

He did have a good idea of what he wanted to do, but he was not sure exactly what order he wanted to do it in. The only thing that mattered to Primus was that he would be able to see Turia, possibly for the last time. And that was the best way he could possibly imagine to spend what might be his last day alive.

Chapter 9

When Primus awoke at dawn the next day to the sound of someone knocking at his door, he felt the heavy realization of what today was settle on his shoulders. It had been one thing to discuss how his possible last day alive would play out late at night with a friend. It was another thing entirely to wake up and know that that day was now upon him, and it settled with an almost tangible weight, pressing down on him like several thick wool blankets.

It felt more difficult to move, harder to breathe, and even his mind seemed slower than normal, as if honey had been poured over all of his thoughts. Simultaneously, Primus's vision seemed to have become even sharper, and details that he had previously not noticed or had seen but not given much thought to were suddenly vibrant. He could see a small crack on the wall opposite the doorknob, as if the door had been slammed open too many times and damaged the wall.

He noticed on the man across from him that there was a small stain at the neckline of his tunic that did not come out when the garment was washed. Primus rolled out of bed and removed the case that held his weapons and armor. Primus noticed a smudge on his sword from where he had touched it with his thumb several days ago, and he felt as if he could count the number of links in his mail shirt, as well as a little bit of tarnish that was appearing on the rimmed edge of his shield.

The knocking at the door had not stopped, and although Primus did not answer it, one of the other men in the barracks did, although what they said was too soft for Primus to properly hear. The man then informed the others that Thak was gathering everyone to the training field. He had an announcement that he said was of the utmost importance. Primus did not rise. He only continued to inspect his armor and weapons for any defects or other imperfections that could cause any kind of problem the next day.

Once he was satisfied with the state of his equipment, Primus pulled on his mail shirt and belted on his sword to stop the bottom of the shirt from swinging. He then slung his shield across his back and grabbed his helm, tucking it in the crook of his arm. He also retrieved a pouch filled with the gold that he had earned during his training and tied it to the belt on his waist. He ignored the looks that the other men shot him as he stood tall and left the barracks and headed toward the training field.

Primus took his place in the middle of the crowd, in case Targrave was present. It had only now occurred to him that if Targrave *was* here and he spotted Primus dressed for war, he might begin to suspect that Thak had spoken with him prior to calling the meeting, or perhaps that somehow, he had been listening to Targrave when he delivered the news of the impending attack.

His fears proved to be unfounded, however, as Targrave was nowhere in sight, and as the men continued to fill the field, it became increasingly apparent that it would only be Thak who would be speaking. The murmuring of the crowd seemed to be louder than usual, which made Primus wonder if the heightened senses he was experiencing were due to the knowledge that it might be the last day he would be able to use those senses.

It would make sense. I know there's a good chance I could die tomorrow, and maybe I'm just seeing and hearing more as a result. Almost like I'm trying to take in everything around me, and everything stands out more as a result, Primus thought as Thak raised his hands to silence the crowd.

As Thak spoke, Primus found he was unable to concentrate on the man's speech. What he heard, though, was much of the same he had heard the previous night. Primus heard the gasps and whispers around him, and many were asking each other if they thought it was true or if they would be facing the full might of the forces that Sodom, Gomorrah, and Angra could muster.

A few men asked if it would be wiser to flee with their families rather than stay and fight. Several of the whispers, however, were praising Primus, with many of them saying they were grateful that he had implemented the traps that he had, along with the battle formation that he and Thak had designed. And several more confidently said that they would not lose so much as a single man during the battle, while others belittled the courage of the enemy forces.

Thak let them whisper among themselves for a moment before continuing his speech, saying that the preparations had been completed, and with them in place, they were all in a strong position, and they would defend their homes and their families. Finally, Thak told them that the rest of the day was theirs to use how they pleased, and that if they had any family they wished to see, any friends they wished to speak with, or anything else they viewed as important, they should use their time wisely and make the most of it.

He ended it by warning them to be back no later than an hour after sundown, as they would all need a good night's sleep so they would be fresh and ready for the coming battle.

Thak bade the men farewell and walked off the stage to attend to his own matters, and the men began to disperse from the field. Primus stayed where he was for a moment, allowing the crowd to thin out before he attempted to make his way to Turia's home, south of the city.

He walked slowly, taking in the feeling of the warmth of the sun on his skin, the feeling of the breeze across his face, the smell of the crushed grass under his feet, and the smell of bread baking wafted out of many of the houses Primus passed on his walk.

He made his way at an unhurried pace, savoring every sight, sound, and smell. He stopped to smell a small vase of flowers that sat in a window three houses away from Turia. He closed his eyes and inhaled deeply and slowly, enjoying the moment. When Primus opened his eyes, he saw a woman standing near the oven.

He heard her approach, but she had not said a single word, only stared at him with a mild curiosity. Primus took a step backward and rose to his full height before flashing her a smile and waving at her before turning and walking away. Before he lost sight of her, Primus saw the woman wave back to him.

Primus arrived at Turia's house and knocked on the door. Before anyone answered, however, Primus took his helm from the crook of his arm, where he had carried it since this morning, and placed it on his head, adjusting it so it sat properly and did not obscure his vision even slightly. Primus only waited a moment before the door was answered by Turia's mother, who did not speak but smiled at him. She stood to the side while extending her arm and invited him into the house. Turia's father sat in a chair reading a scroll just inside.

"So you're back, are you?" he said in a disinterested tone of voice, his eyes never leaving the scroll.

"Yes, sir. I was wondering if I cou—" Primus started.

"No, I have not changed my mind now that you've joined the army. You still cannot marry my daughter until you've earned a commission and proven yourself in battle. There is no battle, and you've not proven yourself. Turia isn't home either, before you ask, and no, I will not tell her that you came by. Leave," he said as he shook the scroll slightly, straightening out the parchment.

Turia's mother had left the room as soon as Primus had entered, and she returned now with Turia following closely behind her.

"Father, no. Primus, I'm so glad to see you. Why are you here, though? I thought you were still training?" Turia asked as she crossed the remaining distance between them and hugged him tightly.

"Well, I guess you could say I'm actually done with training now. Sodom, Gomorrah, and Angra are going to attack," Primus said in a low voice. He felt Turia tense in his arms, and out of the corner of his eye, he saw the scroll in her father's hands drop slightly, as if in shock at hearing the news.

"When?" Turia asked softly.

"Most likely tomorrow. The ships carrying the men down the river have already left each city, and based on what the spies told us and when the soldiers left, they'll be here tomorrow. And although they may *not* attack right away, there would be no reason for them to wait to attack if they're in enemy territory," Primus said.

"So they told you that you could leave for the day?" Turia's father asked.

"Actually, yes. Me and everyone else, actually. They let us go for today so that we could meet with our friends and family. *Anyone* who we care about. I'm here to spend what might be my last day alive with Turia," Primus said.

"Of course, I'll be glad to. Let's go now," Turia said hurriedly, pulling away from Primus while keeping ahold of his arm as she began pulling him toward the door.

"You're not going anywhere, Turia, but he *is* leaving, and he's leaving *now*," Turia's father said from behind his scroll.

"All right, that's enough. Turia, just be back no later than an hour after sunset, and enjoy yourself. Primus, just…don't be you from before the army," Turia's mother said, stepping forward and opening the door as she did so. She ushered them out of the door and quickly closed it behind them. From inside, they could hear Turia's father start shouting, but Primus and Turia quickly left.

"I'm sorry that I caused so much trouble today. I hope your mother is going to be all right," Primus said once they were a few houses away.

"Hm? Oh, that. No, no, that's actually fairly normal every time I leave. My mother has to shoo me out of the house. My father won't even let me leave much anymore," Turia said.

"I'm sorry. Did he ever say why?" Primus asked.

"Only that he didn't want me running off to see you because he suspected that I had before. Sneaking out at night is way easier, but sometimes, I can get away with it during the day, as long as he goes off to look after the barges," Turia said.

"Ah, I see. Turia, I wanted to come see you today, and I had it in my head that I would have asked him if, because of the coming battle, he would allow us to get married," Primus said softly.

"Oh no, I'm so sorry, Primus. I'm sorry that he's the way he is," Turia said, nodding in the direction of her house.

"Honestly, by now, I'm used to it. There isn't much I can really do to change his mind. The real thing, though, now is I have to wonder if he'll actually let us get married after the battle," Primus said.

"If there's one thing I can say about him, it's that my father gave his word to you, and he's never backed out of something he's given his word on before. I don't think he's going to start now," Turia said.

"Are you sure? He didn't even look at either of us and lied about you being there," Primus said.

"It was an old standby of his, something he joked about getting made into a sign or a plaque for the house. He would always say he only has his balls and his word, and he won't break either of them for anyone," Turia said, imitating her father's voice and speech patterns.

"You've gotten really good at that," Primus said, laughing hard.

"I've had years of practice," Turia said with a fleeting smile. "So I guess it's really happening then. They're actually going to attack."

"Yeah, and Targrave still thinks they're coming from the south. I know he got to where he is in a time of peace, but this is just ridiculous," Primus said, disgusted.

"He still won't even look in your direction?" Turia said, sounding shocked.

"Not even an eye. He's tried and failed to beat me in the combat arena so many times it's actually kind of funny. But tomorrow is going to be the real test. We won't be able to hide the traps and fortifications, the scouts, or anything, really, for that matter from him anymore. Either my dream comes true and we won't have to answer any questions, or it doesn't and I'll be out of the army," Primus said.

"But do you really have to fight? You really have to go out there and fight off three separate cities all at once?" Turia asked in a small voice.

"I do. Regardless of whether or not my dream comes true, I still have to be there. They need every man who can fight, and besides that, the men all seem to like me. Almost all of them know about the traps that we built, if not all of them, but they haven't said anything about it. If they had, we would know, because Targrave would have ordered them to be taken down and destroyed, and I would have been thrown out. Thak would be too," Primus said.

"And the fact that you're still there means that no one has told Targrave," Turia concluded.

"Exactly. Thak and I haven't really said anything to the men about who came up with the plan, but because I've done so well in the combat arena, creating strategies that win consistently, I think they know it's me. They trust me, Turia, and they'll be looking to me to help lead them not just to victory but also to save their families and homes," Primus said.

"But why not Thak? Why can't he do it? He's been in the army longer, and they know that. Could you maybe try and act like you're sick or something?" Turia begged.

"I can't. If I don't fight, it would shame me. I won't earn anything, my commission, any honor, or glory from the battle, and I won't be able to show my face near any of the men again," Primus said gently.

"It just seems like too much to ask of you. You haven't fathered any children. You don't have a real home. You've lost your family, and now you're being asked to risk your life and maybe give it up to protect the people who spat on you and treated you like dirt," Turia said, now quite upset.

"Come on, Turia. It's going to be fine. I'm not going to get hurt, and this is a chance for me to make it right with everyone. I was awful to most of them as well, and this way, at least I can make amends for that. Yes, I've lost a lot, but I still have you, and the only way we can make this work is that I have to go out there tomorrow and fight like everything I hold dear depends on it," Primus said.

"It's not fair," Turia said softly.

"No, it's not, but that's how it has to be. But I don't want to sit here all day thinking about what I lost or what I could lose. Today might be the last day I'm alive. I want to spend it with you doing some things we both want. I brought the gold that I earned with me so we can go and pick out a spot to eat, r go get some new trinket or bauble or anything else, really. It's my treat," Primus said with a smile as he held up the pouch and shook it slightly. The sound of coins clinking was clearly audible.

"How much do you have?" Turia asked in amazement.

"Well, everything, really. I don't need to buy new clothes there or armor or weapons. I don't pay for meals or for beer either, and I'm not charged anything to stay in the barracks. So I've been able to save everything I've earned so far. So I've made my decision about what I want to do with what is possibly my last day alive. What do you want to do?" Primus asked with a smile, taking his helm off for the first time since leaving Turia's house.

Turia said nothing as she took Primus by the hand and led him toward Meftif. Once there, they browsed several shops in the market and bought some breakfast, as it was still early. Turia suggested a place she had had in mind for a little while now. Their breakfast consisted of several pieces of dough that had been left runny, which were poured in small amounts onto a hot pan.

They were allowed to cook for a time before flipping them and exposing the now browned side of the pastry, which had risen quite a bit. The cook then poured a thick brown liquid over the top of the pastry and sent Primus and Turia away. The pastries were light and fluffy and, where none of the liquid had touched them, tasted somewhat bland. However, where the liquid had been poured, the pastry tasted very sweet, especially once some of the liquid had been absorbed.

After eating, they bought a mug each filled with the juice of oranges and wandered around the city for a while, not looking for anything in particular but just anything that caught their attention. Primus spotted a play that was going to start soon and asked if Turia wanted to go in and see it, which she did. After renting their seats, they stopped by a fruit stand that was inside the theater, and they each bought something for themselves. Turia chose a mango, while Primus opted for an apple.

Together, they sat and watched the play, which was about three brothers who moved away from home and went their separate ways.

On each journey, after they built a house, each house was knocked down by a man who wished to take what little money and food they had.

The first two brothers each built their houses quickly and without much thought and so were knocked down easily, but the third brother built his home out of sturdier material. When the other two brothers appeared to the third and youngest, they begged for his help. After a time, he agreed and welcomed them into his home. Shortly afterward, the man who had destroyed the homes of the two older brothers appeared and tried to destroy the third brother's home. However, they stopped him, and he was given to a law setter, who sent the man to the dungeons, and the brothers lived together from then on.

After the play, which both Primus and Turia had enjoyed for the numerous verbal and visual jokes, they wandered around the city a little more, and this time, Turia made a suggestion. She wished to stop and see the birds that had been brought from all over the world. While there, they fed several of the birds and held them. They even found one that seemed to speak to them in a harsh voice, but they soon realized that the bird was simply repeating what it heard them say. They stopped to admire and pet several other animals. Then it was time to move on.

By now, it was early afternoon, and it was time for the midday meal. Primus found a stall that was selling meat, cheese, and beans wrapped in a bread so thin that it could bend and move without tearing. While neither of them knew just quite what to call it, the meal was delicious, and they made their way deeper into the city, now moving at a leisurely pace, weighed down as they were by the meal.

Around an hour later, once they no longer felt quite so full, they sneaked away to find a dark corner of an unused building somewhere so that they could do now as they had many times in the past. Once they had found a place, they did what they had come to do, steaming the glass of a nearby window as they did. But after their exertions were through, they heard someone outside the building shout for their friends to come over and investigate. Primus picked Turia up and held her in his arms as he quickly and quietly made his way out of another door in the building.

He was just in time as the others had found their way into the building and were looking for the trespassers. Primus made his way down to an alleyway then stood near the corner, listening for footsteps in case they had been spotted and pursued. Their fears were unfounded, however, as no one was following them. However, they could hear the shouts of the men, their shock and surprise as they realized what had taken place, as well as the order to find whoever had been in that building.

Primus left then, still carrying Turia, as they made their way back to a busier part of the city. He looked over his shoulder occasionally to make sure they had not been spotted and were not being followed. Once they made it back to the market, Primus set Turia down. They walked together, albeit slowly for Turia, who somewhat shakily made her way deeper into the market before stopping near a shop that only sold beer. They looked at each other then, panting, before they burst into laughter.

"Oh, that was great!" Turia said.

"Did you see their faces?" Primus said, bending over slightly from the force of his laughter.

They continued to laugh for a time, joking with each other about what they had just done and the reactions of those who they had just escaped, keeping their language vague so that they did not alert anyone nearby who might be listening.

After their mirth had subsided, they headed off to find a place for their evening meal, finding a shop that sold various fish, some of which was smoked while others had been cooked in oil and breadcrumbs. There they stayed until sundown, eating and drinking their water and beer, alternatively talking of nothing important and looking deeply and lovingly into each other's eyes.

Eventually, though, the time came where they knew that it would be foolish to continue, so Primus and Turia stood and left. Primus left the gold on the table. As they made their way back toward Turia's house, they continued to talk and laugh, making jokes that only the two of them would understand. Two houses from home,

Turia stopped Primus, who spun around slowly to face her. They stayed there, staring at each other for a while.

"Please just promise me one thing," Turia said softly as she hugged Primus tightly around his neck.

"What's that?" Primus asked as he hugged her back.

"Just promise me you'll come home to me in one piece," Turia said.

"I promise. I love you so much," Primus said, hugging her a little tighter.

"I love you too," Turia said, her voice muffled against his chest.

"You should leave, though. Either tonight or tomorrow morning," Primus said. Turia lifted her head, her eyes shining with a film of tears as she looked at him incredulously. "I know you don't want to, and you wouldn't otherwise go, but please, for me, I want you to go. You'll be safe from any danger then, and I can focus on doing what I need to do," Primus continued.

"I will not abandon you here. I will *not* leave you behind," Turia said forcefully.

"You're not going to abandon me. You're actually going to help me if you leave. If you're not here, I don't have to worry about what happens if the soldiers get past us or beat us or even if just a few of them leave the battle to come down here and start to terrorize everyone here. If a few of them get loose here, the damage they could cause by themselves would be bad enough. Knowing that you're home and that you could be hurt then…I don't know if I can handle that," Primus said.

"I don't care about that. I won't leave my future husband alone to face down one of the largest armies ever by himself. My father might want me to go, and you might want me to go, but I'm staying here whether you like it or not," Turia said, her voice becoming angrier as she spoke.

"If I go out and fight and win and I come back and find out something happened to you, I wouldn't be able to live with myself knowing that there was something I could have done to stop it or knowing that I told you to leave and you didn't listen.

"I know you're stubborn, but please, just this once, the only time it might ever really matter, I *need* you to leave, and I *need* you to be safe. And if you don't listen, I'll tell your mother and father about it tonight after you think I've gone back to the barracks," Primus said.

"My father won't listen to you, and you know that," Turia said harshly.

"No, but your mother will, and she can convince your father to leave. And if they're both going, they're going to take you with them," Primus shot back.

"Look, Primus, I don't want to fight. If they try to make me leave, I'll just leave them behind in the crowd and come right back. I won't leave, and you can't make me go, no matter how dangerous it is for me to stay. I can't leave you here by yourself. Can you please accept that?" Turia asked, her eyes shining again, leaving Primus to stand in silence for a while.

"If I really can't convince you to go, and if you'll really leave your mother and father to come back and wait this out, then I guess I really can't do anything more," Primus said, hanging his head in defeat.

At least not directly. If I have to, I'll try to get to Thak tomorrow and have him send a few soldiers over to make them leave. I won't let her get hurt, no matter what, Primus thought as he hugged her tighter. They released each other, and they embraced, whispering that which was only meant for them to hear for a moment, and then they released each other. Turia gave Primus's hand one last squeeze then turned her back and made her way home.

Primus stayed where he was for a while, desperately trying to think of any other alternative to allowing Turia to stay. However, he discarded every idea as either impractical, or it would take more time than he currently had. He had hoped that Turia would see the danger that was present and would listen to Primus's reasoning, and while she did see the danger, she had refused to concede the point that if the battle did not go according to plan, and that if Primus was unable to overcome Sodom, Gomorrah, and Angra's soldiers, there would be nothing to stop them from laying waste to anyone and everyone around them.

Though Primus knew that they would need to capture Meftif, he knew that such a large force could easily secure the city then begin moving out into the houses beyond, killing indiscriminately to instill fear into the citizens and make it so that they would not have the will to fight back. Turia could be one of them.

I'll figure something out by morning. Maybe if I sleep, I can find an answer here. Or maybe Thak will know what to do or at least have an idea that I haven't yet. I'll have to try and catch him early though. Otherwise, he'll be too busy trying to get everyone to the battlefield to help me, Primus thought as he turned on his heel and began to make his way back to the barracks.

Although he had not completely given up on the idea of finding a way to make Turia leave, he was not trying so hard as he had earlier.

The only real way to get her to leave would be if the battle spills out and enemy soldiers are chasing us, and there was already a ship or a barge on the river. I'll lead her there, watch her get on, then turn to fight the soldiers right behind us to give us time and shout at the captain to leave before Turia can get off. That might be the only way, but the chances that there's a boat waiting are next to nothing. I just hope I can find a solution to this, because if I don't, if any thoughts about Turia or what might happen to her intrude while I'm in the middle of the battle and my concentration slips, if I lose focus for even one second, I know that could be the end of me, Primus thought as he left behind the rows of homes before turning his mind to the coming battle and reviewing everything he thought might be useful in the fight to come. He slowly made his way through the darkness.

Chapter 10

Primus was staring at the same spot on the ceiling that he had noticed two hours ago. He had been lying awake for hours now, although dawn was still two hours or more away. He had gone to bed the previous evening reviewing everything he believed he would need for the expected battle, as well as anything he could do to make Turia leave.

He had been unsuccessful in trying to formulate any kind of plan that would allow him to remove her from the danger, and although there had been several promising ideas, they would require more time or resources than he currently had at his disposal. So Primus had turned his attention to the upcoming battle, working out the final details needed for his plan to succeed, such as exactly where he would move to during the battle and when. Targrave would lead from the back, so Primus knew that he would need to make his way closer to the stand that was being brought out.

Targrave believed that he was too valuable to lose in the fighting, so he had built for him a wooden platform which stood four feet high, on top of which was a smaller second platform, this only two feet high, and on which would rest a chair for him to sit in. Primus knew that this was to be either lifted and carried or dragged into place. It was built with the purpose of allowing Targrave to sit above the battle and direct it from the back, although it appeared to Primus that the platform was still vulnerable to arrows or spears or, if the enemy got close enough, thrown knives or daggers.

Although Targrave was planning to stay far away from the front line of the fight, Primus knew that that could change at a moment's notice. He knew that he was to be positioned at the front and that Targrave was hoping that Primus would be overwhelmed by the enemy soldiers, and it was possible that he would be. Therefore, Primus would withdraw from the front from time to time, seemingly to catch his breath, although what he would really be doing was moving closer to Targrave's seat.

If Targrave were to fall in the fighting, Primus was planning to use the platform for himself to stand up and call the men to him, to rally them around himself. He would have to climb up the platform and stand exposed, leaving himself vulnerable to attacks. However, if he were to win this fight, Primus knew that he would have to show himself braving the same dangers that the men were facing themselves or to even put himself in greater danger than they were in to inspire them to fight and win.

This was all the more important because if Targrave were to die, whether he was a competent commander or not, the death of their leader would still risk many of the men throwing down their weapons and fleeing the battlefield. If that were to happen, then there would be no hope of defeating the combined forces of Sodom, Gomorrah, and Angra.

This and more Primus thought of as he drifted off to sleep, which took quite a while. Eventually, sleep came, and he dreamed of Turia and their day together at first, but soon his dreams became strange and twisted, dreams that his planning shaped but that knowledge of the coming battle created. He witnessed many things, like fantastical beings who could not exist, men who held beams of light in their hands as if they were swords, while others flew through the clouds on the backs of huge winged beasts, before Primus felt things around him twist.

Primus woke up immediately on feeling the twist in his dreams as he had not been deeply asleep. Although he had spent months preparing for a fight, although he had spent the previous two days coming to peace with what was about to happen, the knowledge that he would be going to war in just a few hours had prevented him from sleeping soundly.

So Primus lay there in the darkness, not moving, only trying to breathe and think. Every few seconds, a thought of the battle would present itself, only for it to be snatched away by some inane thought. Eventually, however, the night did soothe his mind enough that he started to doze slightly. It was not real sleep, but it would suffice for the night, or at least Primus hoped that it would. If he was unable to fight because he was too tired or if he made the wrong decision because his mind was foggy and clouded, then not only would he get his men killed, but he would also get himself killed as well. Eventually, though, after dozing off and waking again for what felt like the twentieth time, although it was likely only the fifth of sixth time, Primus stood quietly and left the barracks, only stopping to grab his equipment.

Outside, Primus donned his armor and weapons and began to walk around, staying close to the barracks in case the alarm was raised. The sky had just begun to lighten far off to the east, although it would still be hours before its warm glow washed over the land. Primus noticed something up ahead, only a little distance from him. It appeared to be Thak and Targrave walking together through the barracks.

It was quiet out, but Primus could still not hear what they were saying nor guess what they were talking about. Primus started after them and, trying to be as quiet as he possibly could, tried to close the distance and eavesdrop on their conversation, hoping it would provide some more insight into Targrave's plans. He did not get close enough to hear anything before a lone figure entered the training grounds, running full tilt toward the barracks.

Primus increased his speed as well, no longer caring if he stayed quiet. He no longer wished to eavesdrop. As the runner drew nearer to the two men, Primus broke out into a run as well. Of the two, Primus was both faster and closer, and he reached the men seconds later, both of them turning their heads, looking for the source of the pounding footsteps behind them.

"Primus? What are you doing up? You should be sleeping," Thak said before Targrave could speak. Primus did not miss a beat.

"I was sleeping earlier, but I woke up and couldn't go back to sleep, so I went for a walk, saw you two walking and him running toward you, so I came over," Primus said quickly, not allowing Targrave a chance to speak first.

"You went for a walk before sunrise in your armor and with your weapons?" Targrave asked, his voice dripping.

"Considering the news that we could be attacked at any second, I'd rather wear it and be prepared. Also, our friend is almost here, and I've got a bad feeling about whatever it is he's got to say," Primus said as he moved slightly to his left, stepping out from the center of the path. The runner slowed and stopped in front of the three men, leaning over on his knees for support for a handful of seconds, breathing hard.

"Captain. General. I have urgent news," the man said.

"Out with it, man. Speak!" Targrave barked.

"Our scouts have reported ships on the river. They've stopped nearly level with the city, and the soldiers are pulling ashore as we speak," the man said, gaining his composure.

"What?" Targrave asked simply, and even by the pale light beginning to rise from the east, his skin was as pale as a sheet.

"How many have left the ships? And were you seen?" Thak asked quickly.

"No, sir. I wasn't seen. Neither were the scouts. The enemy only just started to leave the ships when the message came, and it wasn't long ago. They're still a ways away, and we have as little time to prepare, but they're already getting in formation to attack," the man said.

"Wait, you said scouts. What scouts?" Targrave asked harshly.

"Scouts stationed along the river, put there to let us know when ships had been spotted and where they were putting ashore," the man said quickly.

"I never ordered any scouts along the river," Targrave said, shaking his head slightly in disbelief.

"I took the liberty, sir. Seemed like a prudent measure to keep us apprised of the enemy intents, location, and which direction they intend to attack from," Thak said.

"You? But how did…when did…" Targrave trailed off.

"Shortly after the cities announced they had banded together to attack us. I didn't want them sneaking up on us in the middle of the night or sooner than we expected. Now, sir, if you'll excuse Primus and myself, we have to go and wake the men," Thak said as he turned to walk back through the rows of buildings, tapping Primus on the shoulder with the back of his hand.

Without a word, Primus turned, and the two broke out into a full sprint, shouting that the soldiers were here, pounding on doors to wake up the sleeping men. After around one minute, a gong began to ring out from somewhere near the entrance of the barracks. The call to arms had been raised. Primus and Thak stopped running and instead stood by the side of one of the buildings.

"That was some pretty quick thinking there. I didn't actually have an answer for him if he had asked us who ordered it," Primus said.

"I told you before, you let me worry about lying to his face. I've been rehearsing that line for a while now. I'm glad he seemed to believe it, although we didn't exactly give him much time to think it over," Thak said as he watched the men hurriedly ready themselves.

"Well, thank you. But we better get going. Send out the men you assigned to each trap. I'll take my place," Primus said.

Thak nodded and went off to find the archers that he had selected. Primus knew that the archers would get to the traps fairly soon. Thak had only selected the fastest runners for this, as time was of the essence.

Then Primus put all other thoughts out of his mind. The archers would be where they needed to be. The army would march where they were needed. The only thing that concerned Primus was the timing of the attack. He hoped that news of the attack would come later, when the sun was already rising, or even better, if the sun were already above the horizon.

The only real hope we have now is that the traps and poison will do their jobs. If the enemy soldiers leave their ships and assemble into battle formations before we're ready, they may be slowed enough by the traps that the sun has time to rise. If they deal with the traps and poison too quickly, then the sun will be rising right behind them, and we'll be stuck fighting half blind. If that happens, we'll have a harder time winning this than I thought, Primus thought as he made his way toward the first group of men as they were moving into formation.

He took his place at the front and waited for all the rest of the men to organize themselves, which did not take very long. While he waited, Primus noticed several men with bows break away from the rest of the men and start running through the training fields then out into the desert.

They were wearing tan robes that were long and flowing, colored to look exactly like the sand that they were running over. Thak had had the idea to give the men something to hide themselves weeks ago while talking with Primus about the speed with which they had completed the project, and Primus approved.

It had taken longer than anyone would have liked to get organized, but finally, the call came to leave the camp. The men set off at a run with Thak leading the way and Primus close behind. Primus thought back to one of the lectures, this one from around two months ago, where they had been instructed to not think about what the enemy would or will do but to think of what they *could* do.

Although the enemy could have sailed south, they did not, and now that they were on land, they could march or they could run. They could see the bowmen or they could not. They could fall for every trap, or they could fall for none.

They could do anything. At least so far, they've done everything we thought they might—landing spot, size of army, direction of attack. Even though I had hoped it would be during the day, I knew they would probably launch their attack in the dark. Either catch us asleep, waking up, or even outside of that to make us come to them and not be able to see because of the sunrise, Primus thought as they passed through the gates and into the desert.

They turned east and headed toward the spot that Primus and Thak had designated while maintaining their pace. Primus looked over his shoulder and noted that while everyone else was running, Targrave was riding on horseback.

This did not surprise Primus, however, as a man of his station would be expected to ride. What *did* surprise Primus was that behind Targrave, the platform that his seat rested on was being pulled on runners that Primus had not previously seen, and pulling the sled were four oxen that Primus had never seen in or around the training grounds.

Targrave must have had them standing by to pull his little platform to where he thought the attack would come from. Blasted idiot. Where are the oxen going to go after we get to the battle sight, eh? Where were you planning to stash them? Primus thought, bitterly wishing, as he had so many times before, that Targrave was *not* in any position to give orders to anyone.

They arrived at a stretch of desert that, months before, would have been no different than any other stretch of desert for hundreds of miles, and Meftif was now a blurry outline on the distant horizon. Now, however, there was a low tumbled wall that rose to around the height of Primus's hip, now much deeper than what he had originally intended.

Wind and the consistent trampling of feet from building the traps had left a deeper trench that would hem in the movements of the enemy soldiers somewhat, restricting them so that rather than allowing the entire army to form a battle line, instead, any men who wanted to climb out and face the enemy would be faced with a climb up a sand wall. This would slow them down, possibly trip them or their fellows below them, and make it easier for Primus and the others to move around the sides of the trench and pick them off as they tried to join the fight or make them easier targets for the archers.

"Thak, Primus, both of you come with me now," Targrave said.

Primus started at the sound of his voice. He had not suspected that Targrave could have sneaked up on him so easily. He led Thak and Primus over to a spot near the trench and mostly out of earshot of the rest of the men.

"And just *what* exactly is *this*?" Targrave said in an overly calm voice, his face placid. However, this very calmness was indicative of an anger that surpassed all other emotions.

"This, sir, is nothing you have to worry about. Regardless of how you feel about it, you don't need to worry about it. Everything has been taken care of. All the preparations have been made. You just need to yell out *attack* when it's time to fight," Thak said quickly and softly, like someone who was trying to calm a spooked animal.

"Oh, all righty. I see. Nothing to worry about. Except for one. Teeny. Tiny. Thing," Targrave said, smiling, his head tilting slightly to his right. "That little thing called disobeying a DIRECT ORDER FROM YOUR COMMANDING OFFICER!" His voice rose until he was shouting in Thak's face, his rage turning his face first pink, then rose, until finally, his face resembled a plum in color.

Several veins stood prominently from his forehead, and a large bundle of nerves was visible, pulling at the skin of his neck with enough force that it appeared that they might tear free of their fleshy prison and strangle both Thak and Primus.

"Actually, sir, I never disobeyed your orders. I was still able to help oversee the planning and some of the construction, as you ordered, which were completed on time. I simply realized that there was also a chance that they could attack from a different direction, and I wanted to make sure that we were well defended on all sides," Thak said in the same voice, still trying to calm Targrave down. Targrave's face maintained a purple hue as he took several deep breaths before speaking in his overly calm voice again.

"And just when did you have the time to dig a trench from here to the river?" Targrave asked.

"We actually did that over the course of a few months during the three-day runs. It's shallower down by the river and deeper here, which we didn't do intentionally, but it worked in our favor. The point was that if they landed on the river, try to get them to follow what looked like a path so we could determine where the battle will actually take place. Now I would love to sit here and keep answering questions all day, but right now, I need to go and organize the defensive line since we can't see where the enemy is, and they could be here nearly any time. So if you'll excuse us," Thak said, trying to extricate both himself and Primus from the situation before the questions were directed at Primus.

"Not so fast there. We can't hear them running. We can't feel the ground shaking, nothing. The lieutenants are currently organizing the men into a battle line that, I must note, is not one that we discussed at any time and that I've never seen before. No, I have a few more questions that need answers. First, how long has this been going on for? Second and more importantly, who's idea was this? Thak, I know you're going to say that this was yours, but the formation, the trench, and the length of time says to me that you didn't do this alone. Who helped you?" Targrave asked in a mild voice, his eyes drifting over to Primus as he finished.

"No one, sir. I did this on my own," Thak said, and Targrave made a noise in his throat.

"Very well then. Primus, Captain Thak, you will both hand in your shields, weapons, and armor when this battle is over. You will then be flogged for the insubordination and released from the army. Primus, I expected as much out of you, but I had thought better of my captain of the guard," Targrave said, and he turned and walked back toward the men.

"That went well," Thak said dryly after Targrave was out of earshot.

"So I guess that's it then," Primus said, defeated.

"No, not by a long shot. Targrave is going to try and get the men into a formation he approves of, and that'll take quite a while. But if your dream is really going to come true, then it won't matter what he said here, since if he dies and I survive, I'll inherit command, and I won't have to follow through on what he just said. Besides, he only said that to us, so we're the only two who know. As long as Targrave doesn't make it, we'll both be fine," Thak said with a soft smile.

"And you want to risk both of our careers here on the possibility that a dream I had months ago might actually come true?" Primus asked, incredulous. He had believed Thak to be more reasonable than that up until that moment.

"Well, partly your dream, but mostly owing to the size of the army we're going up against. Also the fact that a lot of things can happen between the start and end of a battle. After all, some of the men aren't exactly the best with a bow. Maybe someone trips and an arrow goes flying, or maybe his little perch is too visible and would make for an excellent target that someone forgets to shield," Thak said with a strange sideways look.

"Thak, I…I don't think I completely understand what you're getting at here," Primus said cautiously.

"Targrave could have retired before now, but he liked having this power a little too much, and everyone can see now that he's an ineffective leader. Regardless of your dream, I doubt he'll live to see the end of the day. One of them will get him, if not one of us," Thak said simply.

"Even if he's not an effective leader, we can't kill him," Primus said, looking away and shaking his head, shocked that such a thing would even be mentioned, let alone seriously considered.

"Why not? There's going to be enough confusion and chaos here that anything could happen, and who's to say what they really saw, eh?" Thak said.

"And you think we could get away with that?" Primus asked.

"I do, if only because no one will say a single word about this to anyone else. They all see what you and I see, and they won't shed any tears for him if something unfortunate happens. If it were any other commander, I would have the same response you did, and if it was anyone else, really, my response would be the same. This is wrong, and we shouldn't talk about it or do it or anything of the sort. Now then, let's take our places," Thak said.

What Primus heard troubled him. Although he knew Thak was correct in saying that there would be enough chaos to hide anything any of them did, turning on Targrave like that, despite everything else that had happened and despite everything between them, would not sit right with Primus, no matter the justifications he had heard. Although, if someone were to turn on Targrave in the middle of the battle, it could help the situation tremendously, as there now would not be a bumbling fool issuing commands that made little sense.

Primus was torn now on what the best course of action would be. Even as the light of dawn was starting to appear and the sky was beginning to turn blue, he wondered if he should try to tell Targrave about the dream he had had so long ago. He had just made up his mind to do exactly that when Thak walked up to Targrave and tried to get his attention. Targrave nearly struck Thak, raising his fist and pulling back slightly before shouting something at him, although what Targrave had said was unclear.

The men were mostly quiet, so it was not noise that obscured Targrave's shouts but rather Targrave himself, fairly spitting with rage, which meant that anything he could have said was lost in an incoherent jumble of words that sounded more like the growl of a beast than the words of a man. Thak stepped back then and simply looked toward the horizon and the direction of the rising sun, which was just starting to crest the horizon. Another man ran up at that moment and caught Targrave's attention, pointing at a rising plume of dust off in the distance.

Although it was still far off, the presence of the plume was in and of itself something that stuck fear into the hearts of everyone present. The enemy soldiers were closer now. The forces of Sodom, Gomorrah, and Angra would arrive soon, and the battle would begin. Men would die.

Up until that point, as the men were organizing themselves, there had been some laughter and some conversations, friends and strangers trying to lighten the mood and keep up their spirits. That, however, was now gone, and all was quiet as the men who were not in their positions yet rushed to get to them.

There were several tense minutes of men moving, the sound of footsteps and panting, jangling armor and swords being drawn, axes being hefted, arrows being knocked, spear hafts being ground into the sand so they would stand upright and ready for use. And then all was eerily quiet.

The sun fully crested the horizon and began its long march across the sky, and the light was blinding and caused everyone to either look away, squint hard enough that they were effectively blind, or to shield their eyes from the light. Primus was simply grateful that the enemy soldiers had not yet reached their position. Before long, the sun had crawled into the sky and hung a handsbreadth above the horizon when the sound of screaming finally became apparent.

Though Primus and the others had heard sounds in the distance, it was unclear what they were. Now, however, the screams of the wounded drifted over the dunes and set everyone on edge. Primus heard several men around him muttering under their breath, cursing the need for the traps. Primus shared their sentiment, and he wished with everything he had, and as he so often had before, with every fiber of his being that it had not been necessary to build the traps, not necessary to set archers with poison arrows in positions where they would shoot officers and commanders, along with a random assortment of men marching behind them.

Primus guessed that it was not as much the injuries that some of the men had suffered but the poison taking its toll on the men marching toward them. Those two things, however, he had guessed, must have slowed their advance to such a degree that they missed their opportune time to attack, which would have been just before the sun first peeked over the horizon.

As it was, based on their speed, Primus estimated that it would be only another quarter of an hour before the men would come in sight of the end of the trench. As they currently were, they were visible at the other end of the trench as a shifting sea of darkness, the result of the dark clothing and armor they wore, as opposed the vibrant red that Primus and the men with him wore.

Primus looked around, trying not to move his head much. Around him, he saw men preparing themselves for what was to come. Some he saw close their eyes and stay perfectly still. Some were using prayer beads. Some were smoking, while another was playing with a dagger, while yet more bit their fingernails. Each man seemed to be preparing themselves for war in their own way, gaining the strength of mind needed for what was to come.

Primus looked forward again, closed his eyes, took a deep breath, counted to five in his mind, and exhaled while also counting to five. He resumed his normal breathing after this, and while his body felt slightly calmer after this, his mind turned instead from the coming fight to his deepest desire, something he had told no one else, not even Turia.

His desire was simple yet complex. His desire was to meet the men who had killed his family and to understand why they had chosen his home, out of so many others, and why they had killed his family when other families had been allowed to live. Despite all of that, Primus still was unsure of what he would do if ever he were to meet the men responsible for this.

He did not know whether he would try to forgive them and move past the hurts they inflicted upon him, if he would try to kill them in return and visit the same hurts upon them, or if he would beat them until they were almost dead but allow them to live. Or if given the chance, would he take them into the desert, only to break their legs and let them walk back?

If I meet them, what would I do? I do want to see them pay for what they did, but how? Do I want to see them dead? If they're dead, do they have their own children who would want revenge? Would I just hurt them as badly as they hurt me? Primus thought as the drumming of the enemies' feet could just be felt through the sand.

Could I even ever find them? No one was really able to see what kind of ship or boat that they sailed away on after they destroyed my farm, and it's just as likely that they're from a city south of here. I mean, I hope that they're here in the armies of one of the cities, but the problem is that they wouldn't know me, and I wouldn't know them. What am I supposed to do then? Primus wondered as the drumming became louder and more incessant, heralding the arrival of the armies by several minutes.

Primus opened his eyes then, putting any thoughts of retribution or forgiveness out of his mind. There was a battle to be fought, and concerns of what only may be or could be were best left for later. *If* there was a later.

The sea of men in front of him had expanded, no longer just a dark shape that shifted and moved like liquid shadows as they had appeared earlier. Primus was now able to pick out individual men, although they were still too far away to make out anything in detail. Primus removed any other thoughts in his head, allowing his mind to become as a clear pool on a still day, reflecting everything yet touching nothing. The time for conscious thought had passed, and now Primus knew that he would have to rely on his instinct and his training to walk away from the battle, much less walk away unscathed.

Despite allowing his mind to calm itself and his breaths coming long and deep, it still did not stop Primus's heart from doubling its pace and becoming as loud as the pounding footsteps of the approaching army. Nor did it stop the sweat that broke out across his back and chest or his palms from becoming clammy despite the relatively cool morning air.

Any prayer or other activities that the men were using to prepare for battle began to die down as the footsteps became louder, soon no longer confined to simply being felt through the ground but now able to be heard. The army slowed and stopped then, just out of range of the archers.

Two men came forward on horseback then, and a third horse was left behind with the rest of the army. They rode forward, and by unspoken consent, Targrave then left the safety of his men, riding forward to meet the other men. They met approximately in the middle of the two armies and began to speak with each other, although Primus could not hear what was said, as they were too far away, and even the still air could not carry their words far enough.

Several tense minutes passed with no change in the standing or bearing of the men, long enough that Primus and the men around him began to fidget as they eyed the force in front of them.

From where he stood, there was no way to tell how large the army appeared to be, and aside from the cries of the wounded, which now sounded painfully loud, there was no way to determine how effective the traps had really been and whether the hidden archers had done their part and not been caught. After another three minutes, Targrave and the other men separated and rode back in the directions they came from. Targrave, however, did not head back to his platform. He instead rode over to Thak and motioned for him to follow, and he rode up to Primus before dismounting.

"The other generals there wanted to sue for peace one last time and to give us the option of surrendering. After hearing the words of the men who rule each city, as is only polite, I refused them and told them we would not surrender and would fight to the last man. They also had one other question for me. They asked me who built several rows and layers of sharpened stakes hidden beneath the sands in pits and in small dunes on the path here.

"Apparently, along the way, they lost many men to these traps. Several rows of men fell into them, and more are being pushed in by the momentum of the army behind them. A few of their officers and more of the men were also shot by unseen archers, and even some of the men who had only been grazed by the arrows have been dying since. Now would either of you like to explain this?" Targrave said quietly.

"How many casualties did they suffer?" Primus asked.

"They estimated that they lost a little less than a quarter of their forces. The men in front, even when they stopped dead, could not stop the men behind them from pushing them onto the stakes and were killed in large numbers. Of those that came ashore, they estimate that around seven thousand are left to fight. Less, if you count those who were shot and either have already died or are about to. Apparently, the arrows had some kind of poison on them," Targrave said mildly.

"How many were we able to bring to fight today? And how many do we have total?" Thak asked.

"Why do you need to know?" Targrave asked.

"Well, sir, you haven't shared the numbers with me, and honestly, even though I would estimate we have around six thousand, knowing what we're facing might help us to know how many we need to kill. Are we still outnumbered, or are we facing a more even fight?" Thak asked.

"Well, they had conscripted a number of citizens as well as their volunteers, but thanks to some being thrown out for misconduct, a few accidental deaths, and a fair number of desertions, they were down to around nine thousand when they shipped out a few days ago. Interestingly, some fights broke out on the ships, and a few men went overboard and drowned, as well as a few more when putting ashore. They didn't lose too many from accidents, though, so the numbers weren't given. So yes, Thak, this will be a more even battle," Targrave said, a hint of disgust creeping into his voice.

"Oh, well, I'm glad to hear it, if only because it means that we won't be immediately crushed. Shall you give the command, or shall I?" Thak asked.

Targrave said nothing, only spurred his horse back to his platform and dismounted, taking a moment before he sat down. Surprisingly, he stayed silent for a while.

"Primus, you're a genius. Your traps and poison worked perfectly, and there were even defections that we didn't know about. We're only slightly outnumbered now, so we have a real chance at winning this here," Thak whispered as the older man took up a position next to his young counterpart.

"No, I'm not a genius. I only did something a little clever to even the playing field. I wasn't going to let a larger army trample us and just stroll into Meftif. If that makes me a genius, then I guess I am," Primus whispered back.

"Archers! To the sides. Swords and spears, in front. Axes in the middle!" Targrave shouted, and after a minute of shuffling and more of Targrave's shouting, the formation that they had arranged themselves into resembled a half circle with the archers on either the left or right side of the trench.

At the back of the formation, spearmen and swordsmen were in front of them. However, the pikemen and those with axes and maces were in the dead center of the formation, and as there were more swordsmen and spearmen, the ranks were quite thin in the center of the formation while the sides were full to bursting with men. The worst thing about this, though, was that no one was directly in front of the mouth of the trench.

What is he doing? Don't let them out of the trench, you idiot! When they're pressed in and can't move, they make easy targets. Please, please, please at least let us pull out our bows so we can shoot them as they're coming out of the trench. Targrave, for the love of everything holy, don't let them out of the trench, Primus raged silently, further cursing Targrave for a fool.

Primus knew that if the bodies of the dead soldiers grew at the mouth of the trench, it would form a wall that would make it much harder for them to leave the trench, and it would make them easier targets as they crested the top of their grisly hill. It would give them the high ground for only a moment. However, they would be unable to capitalize on the higher position due to the rain of arrows that would pierce them as soon as they climbed atop the pile.

The way that Targrave was organizing things now, the enemy soldiers would be allowed to walk out on to open ground where they stood a fairer chance. But Primus did not want them to have a fair chance or really any chance at all. He wanted to dictate the pace of the battle, when it started and how it progressed, and most importantly, how and where it would end. Even if the number of men they were to face in combat was roughly the same as their own, the training of each army would come into play some, but the battle could be decided purely by luck rather than on the skill of the men or the planning of their commanders.

Primus could then hear, as if from a great distance, the enemy commanders giving their troops a speech. The voices were too faint to make out. However, the roar of the men was quickly followed by the rumble of stomping feet and the harsh sounds of sword pommels, axe flats, mace handles, and spear flats clashing against shields as the men beat them together, working themselves into a frenzy.

A horn blared from somewhere within the army, and the thrashing sea of bodies surged forward, pouring through the gap as a flood determined to wash away all that stood before them. They would sweep over the land and sweep away Meftif and its people as if they were no more than flotsam.

No order was given to Primus, Thak, or any other men around them to draw bows, knock arrows, or fire, even for the archers at the back of the formation. There was no order for the men to charge or even brace themselves against the charging men. There was only deafening silence from their commander.

As one, every man raised their shields and readied their weapons, overlapping their shields to form one long wall that wrapped around them, from one end of the trench to the other. There was no time left to think of new plans or try and make something new out of the formation that existed in the seconds left before the oncoming army slammed headfirst into Primus. He breathed in deeply, and out.

Turia.

The combined forces of Sodom, Gomorrah, and Angra slammed into Primus and the men around him with both the force and the sound of a waterfall, pushing them backward a step as Primus and every man around him set their shoulders against their shields. Primus tucked his head behind his shield as well to protect himself. Helm or not, a blow to the head could be devastating, especially in the middle a long and drawn-out fight, which Primus had suspected this would be.

He then felt a sword scrape along his side, but his mail protected him from the blade, just as a spear nearly pierced his left knee. Only luck had saved him from being crippled, as he had adjusted his stance to accommodate the new weight pressing him backward. The point of the weapon missed his flesh, and as the blade was turned vertically, the cold metal tugged at his skin as it slid harmlessly past his knee.

Defense alone was no way to win a fight, so Primus drew back his right arm and thrust it forward beneath the shields. The blade met with some resistance for the briefest of moments before sliding farther, although now there was a subtle vibration that ran along the blade, barely detectable in the hilt of the sword.

Primus pulled his arm back and felt more resistance on the blade, which ceased once he had brought his elbow beneath the wall of shields. The upper third of the weapon was a deep crimson. Thick rivulets of blood ran down toward the tip, flying off the end and splattering against the legs of the man to his right as someone screamed.

Again and again, Primus thrust into the men in front of him, seeking to damage the opposing force in any way that he could. Several times he had shoved against his shield, pushing men backward a step before allowing the momentum from the shield push to carry him out from behind the safety of the shields. Each time he did this, Primus was able to clear a small space in front of him and was able to kill or maim at least two of the enemy soldiers, oftentimes more, and the sand began to grow dark beneath their feet. And although Primus was usually safe behind his shield, that did not mean that he was safe from every injury.

Several times, when he had shoved the enemy away and sallied forward, he had been forced to cross blades with a soldier. Although the encounters were brief, they happened often enough for him to collect dozens of small injuries, mostly scratches and scrapes and more bruises than he could count. A sword had caught the sleeve of his mail shirt just below the armpit and torn the links, although the blade had missed his arm by a hairsbreadth.

Another time, a man wielding an axe had stepped over one of his fallen compatriots and attempted cleave him in two. Primus angled his shield slightly to deflect the oncoming blow and pushed his shield arm far to the side as soon as he felt the blow land, and the momentum carried the axe down, burying it in the back of a fallen soldier who was so covered in blood it was impossible to determine which side they had originally fought for. Primus responded with a cut of his own that split the man's skin open from his right hip to his left shoulder. The man released his grip and stumbled back as he attempted to hold his innards in their proper places while blood sheeted from the wound.

Immediately after Primus had slashed the man with the axe, a man missing two of his front teeth had rushed to him and attempted to stab him with a spear. Primus stopped the spear with his shield and stepped forward to attack in return, but the man who stabbed at him pulled back quickly and spun his spear around. The haft struck Primus on his right forearm, nearly causing him to drop his sword, leaving an angry red stripe twice as wide as his thumb. The man once again tried to skewer him, but Primus sidestepped the attack, and as the man overextended and stumbled, Primus stabbed upward, beneath the man's ribs, and he fell to the ground, twitching slightly.

Another wound came from a cut on his left arm, close to the shoulder. Primus had sallied forward again, and after killing one soldier by stabbing him in in the chest and another by braining a helmetless man with the pommel of his sword, another soldier with a sword lunged at him. Primus stopped the blow with his shield. However, he had misjudged the angle of the thrust, and the blade deflected off his shield and sailed toward his shoulder.

Primus tried to turn to avoid the blade but was unable to move enough to avoid the weapon, although he barely noticed the cut after the sword had passed him, as it was not deep and did not pain him overly much. By now, the soldier who had stabbed at him was so close that Primus would have been able to count the individual eyelashes, too close for either of their weapons to be of much use. Primus used his other shoulder to shove the soldier back a step while also taking a full step back himself, which created enough space for Primus to slash at the man's throat. The last three inches of his blade disappeared for a moment before exiting the other side of the man's neck. He fell to the ground clutching at his neck, and the spray of blood painted an area several feet wide, soaking Primus in even more blood.

Primus fell back from the front for a moment to catch his breath. It felt like he had been fighting for a full day, although in reality, it likely had only been around thirty minutes.

Primus looked around and was surprised by what he saw. The front had held somewhat in his area, likely owing to the men around him doing what he had been doing—using their shields as cover until the time to strike was right. At some point, the order to fire at the enemy soldiers had been given, but because of their placement, the archers had to fire either up into the air and hope their arrows came down on the enemy and not their own men, or they would need to find several areas with less of their own soldiers and fire in between the men, although that risked Meftif's soldiers being filled with arrows from their own.

Primus shook his head, shaking the battle rage from his vision, and started to make his way closer to the platform where Targrave sat. From what Primus could tell, despite the relative success that Primus and the group of men around him enjoyed, the battle was going badly.

The semicircle of men that Targrave had initially organized as the battle line was starting to unravel like a skein of yarn thrown into a windstorm. There were not enough men concentrated in one area to provide a unified battle line, and because they were so spread out, Meftif's soldiers would start to tire far sooner than the soldiers they fought against, who would seem fresh each time a new one stepped up and took the place of a slain soldier.

What's more, Primus could see by the way that the men were moving that many of them had been injured, although how badly they were hurt varied greatly from one man to the next, but more and more men were falling back from the front lines, some clutching the bloody stumps of their missing hands, arms, or fingers. Several men fell back and were trampled by those around them as they lost their legs, usually around the knee. While the noise of battle was deafening, the screams of the wounded unsettled Primus in a way that the harsh clashing of metal and war cries could not.

The screams of the wounded were sometimes shrill, sometimes low screams, and some rattled Primus's teeth and sent shivers down his spine. The low moans of shocked men who had lost full limbs before the full-throated screams began were especially unsettling, but the very worst that Primus heard was the screaming of those about to die of their injuries.

Some screamed for their mothers, while others screamed for their wives, and still others called out for names that could be their children. The despair and loss present in each of the overlapping voices gave Primus pause, and he wanted to do nothing more than stop and weep for the families of the men who either were dying or had already died, as well as the men themselves.

But no matter how he felt about it, the wounded and dying would have to wait. There was still a battle to win. Twice, Primus was stopped when the battle line had grown thin enough that there was a real risk that the enemy soldiers would break through, and Primus jumped into the fray each time, letting out a savage bellow as the corners of his vision darkened slightly, and he lost himself in the spray of blood.

The sensation that followed was one of numb disassociation, almost as if he stood outside his body and was looking down on it while someone else was controlling his actions. This did at least allow him to kill and maim without much need for conscious thought, for deep down, Primus knew that if he stopped and thought about his actions too hard, it would leave him in such a state that he would be unable to continue fighting.

A third time the line weakened, and a third time he dived back into combat to help the beleaguered soldiers. Primus lost his helm when a man with an iron-bound club ran toward him and struck at his head. Primus had just killed another man, this time by first slicing the arm of the man he was fighting, cutting through the muscle and down to the bone. And while the man was occupied, Primus slipped behind him and hamstrung the man before flipping the blade and driving it downward, between the man's shoulder blade and ribs.

When the man with the club charged him, Primus raised his arm as if to strike at the club. However, he was holding the sword backward, with the point facing toward his shoulder. There was not much Primus could do, and he clumsily raised his shield to try and block the attack at the last second. The club skated off the shield and struck Primus in the side of the head as he was leaning away.

His ears rang, and spots danced before his eyes as the force of the blow tore the helmet away from his head and sent it flying across the battlefield. He might have died then if not for the fact that the man with the club had lost his balance after mostly missing his attack, leaving him standing on one leg while simultaneously flailing his arms. Still dazed and feeling weak, Primus saw an opportunity and moved to take it.

As the man righted himself, Primus stepped directly in front of him and jerked his shield up. The rim of the shield caught the man under his slackened jaw, driving his teeth together and shattering several of them. Though the force of the blow was not strong enough to kill the man, the sensation of breaking enamel was more than enough to cause him to drop his weapon, and Primus was able to face his weapon forward and stab the man in the throat before he recovered.

He removed the sword from the man as he began to go slack, releasing another shower of blood, further coating Primus in the substance. He fell back behind the battle line. He made it out of the crush of men and bodies and dropped to one knee, his sides heaving and his head spinning. He stayed there for an indeterminate time, although it was likely only around a minute, until his head began to clear and his legs felt strong enough that they would support his body.

Primus rose slowly, sucking in a breath when he reached his full height as the world seemed to tilt around him, and spots once again swam before his eyes. He took another moment to survey what he could of the battle. The formation appeared ready to break, and if it did, there would no longer be a front to the battle, and it would essentially be every man fighting for themselves without direction. If that happened, the chances that Primus or any with him would live to see the end of the day would be slim indeed.

The losses they appeared to have suffered from poor troop placement, while not fully apparent, appeared to be devastating so far, and the front appeared to be thinning everywhere. Primus continued to make his way toward Targrave's platform, his stride becoming steadier with every step, and his vision was becoming clearer as well.

Primus intended to tell the older man that he was losing the battle and the war and that something would have to be done to change their fortunes soon, or they would all die. Even if they were to somehow win this battle, Primus knew that Targrave would put him to death for insubordination, to settle the grudge that Targrave held against him, but he also knew that if they lost, most of their soldiers would be executed. Meftif would be lost as well, and Primus was under no illusions as to what would happen to Turia if that came to pass.

If it's the last thing I ever do, I'll find some way to make Targrave see reason before he gets us all killed. We need a new battle plan, and I need to use those firepots, Primus thought as he drew closer to the line again. The only way to get close enough to Targrave's position, the only way to be heard over the cacophony all around them, was through the middle of the battle.

Primus looked toward the back of the platform but knew he would not be close enough to make himself heard. At some point, Targrave had apparently rallied several of the men to him, and they formed a protective semicircle around his platform that was several layers deep.

Primus dived back into the fray, fighting now not just with determination but desperation as well. It all would come down to whether or not he could survive long enough. The first man who stood before him was wielding an axe with a long beard but a short handle. On his arm was strapped a small shield roughly the same size as a platter. Primus slashed at the man's left arm, hoping that with one arm to swing instead of two, he would more easily be able to kill the man. He misjudged the distance, however, and only scraped the man's forearm. The man immediately retaliated with a crosscut that was much faster than Primus anticipated.

Primus could only raise his shield a few inches before the blow landed, and when it did, it sheared off the upper six inches of his shield, which, while dented and notched in several places, had otherwise remained intact up until now. Primus staggered for a moment, and the man closed the remaining distance between them, raising the axe over his head with his right arm only, his left arm positioned slightly in front of him and bent at the elbow for balance.

However, he maintained his position for perhaps a full second. That was too long, and Primus brought his sword up as quickly as he could and, with as much force as he could muster, sliced the man's left arm off near the shoulder before he had moved more than an inch. He dropped his axe and fell back onto the ground, clutching his bloody stump and turning pale, groaning in pain and shock.

Primus looked to his left then, toward Targrave's platform, noting that the men whom he had earlier seen clustered around the platform to protect Targrave were archers. Primus looked around at the battle before him and hesitated a moment before looking down at his sword, from which blood still dripped from the tip. At his feet lay the man who Primus had just maimed, dying as he bled from his wound, his arm inches from Primus's toes.

Allowing his eyes to drift back to his own body, he was shocked to see just how much gore covered him. Not much of his skin had been untouched by blood, and this, combined with the sweat that poured from his body, was staining the sand underneath him a dark appearance. He looked again at the ground, now looking to the wider battle, beneath the two armies, the land now bore a sanguine appearance.

Shaking himself slightly, Primus spun quickly on his toes to assess exactly where he stood. Meftif was still a distant smudge, and the tide of soldiers seemed endless around him, a sea of dark tunics. Nearer to Targrave, the archers had dropped their bows and were now using their swords, spears, axes, and daggers to try to hold back the advancing forces from their commander, and suddenly, this all seemed very familiar to Primus.

He started running, his earlier fatigue and pain vanishing. He knew what was coming, and he knew that there no way to stop it. He realized now that this would be a desirable thing. The only question that remained, however, was would he get there in time to prevent the men from breaking and running? Despite Targrave's poor leadership, and despite the fact he had gotten many of them killed, Targrave was still in command of the army, and with his death would come the risk that the rest of the men would flee rather than continue to fight.

The world seemed to slow around Primus as the moment drew nearer. A soldier stood before Primus, turning to face him as he made his mad rush to the platform. Every detail on the man's armor was clear. Primus could have counted every link in his mail shirt, every scratch on his sword, every drop of blood that stained his arm.

Out of the corner of his vision, Primus saw the spear flying through the air, coming from his right and slightly behind him, as he knew it would. This time, however, he chose to stay silent as the weapon hurtled through the air toward Targrave, who had left his chair and was now standing several feet back from the edge of the platform, holding a shield that Primus did not remember seeing but must have been on the platform somewhere. Targrave was bellowing orders at the men beneath him and gesticulating wildly, although whatever orders he was giving were inaudible to Primus.

Targrave never had the chance to even so much as look up, and the spear found its mark, burying itself just under his heart, sliding through the chain mail as if it were made of the flimsiest paper. Targrave took half a step back and threw his head toward the sky in a soundless howl as he felt the force of the impact, and the spear slid to a stop, the tip emerging from his back and tugging slightly at his armor. He stood posed like this for a moment and then fell onto his side, and he was no more.

Soldiers on both sides stopped fighting to watch as Targrave died, and a great cheer went up from the soldiers of Sodom, Gomorrah, and Angra, while almost no sound came from the soldiers of Meftif. Primus continued his run toward the platform, using the lull in the battle to cross the remaining distance mostly unobstructed, save one man who tried to bar his way. Without breaking stride, Primus leaped into the air, and while aloft, he thrust his sword downward into the man's back before pulling his sword out as he dropped back to his feet. The maneuver was so smoothly done that it almost appeared as if it had been practiced.

Primus made it to Targrave's platform and half jumped, half climbed the low walls and stood atop the platform. From his vantage point, it was clear that while both sides had suffered heavy losses, Meftif's soldiers had lost more men, although how many more was still impossible to tell, and they would not know until they had counted the dead.

Primus's original plan had been to use his firepots to scare the enemy soldiers and break their morale. His next plan, which he had tried to formulate in secret once the trench had become deep enough, was to use the pots while the soldiers were in the trench to both terrify and also to decimate their ranks. That plan was forgotten once Targrave had set the men in the formation that he had. Primus needed to think of a new plan now, and he needed to think of one within the next handful of seconds.

Think, Primus, think. Winning too obviously to destroy moral. Too spread out to work like the trenches, not spread out enough to make some kind of flame wall. Actually, maybe there's something there. Use the flames to force them back toward the trench...yes. Primus's thoughts raced until he settled on a plan that was so simple, he was surprised he had not thought of it earlier. And it appealed to his better nature as well, as it would result in fewer deaths for the men he fought with.

Jumping down from the platform without speaking to any of the men, several of whom paused when they spotted him, Primus ran toward a small three-pronged stick that was sticking out of the ground at a nearly vertical angle. He pulled the stick out and began to dig in the sand. After just a few inches, he uncovered one of the boxes he and Thak had buried several weeks ago. The boxes were full of the firepots, and there were several more scattered around the area, each marked with another three-pronged stick.

Primus removed a number of the pots, placing them on the sand next to him. He reached for a torch on which was tied two rocks to spark the flame. All of these items were in each box that had been buried so that each man could light their torch and, with it, light each firepot. Primus fumbled with the stones for a moment due to the blood that stuck to his fingers growing sticky, and the sand clung to his fingers and would not come off easily. Primus had a hard time gripping the stones hard enough to spark a flame, and precious seconds were lost.

After what seemed like an eternity, although it was really only moments, a spark shot from between the stones, and the torch burst into life, flames reaching skyward like dull orange fingers. Primus threw the stones down and gathered several of the pots under his arm before turning and running back to the platform.

Setting the pots on the top of the platform and jumping up using only his right arm while holding the torch in his left, Primus bent at the knees and grabbed a pot. Using the torch to light the strip of fabric that was wedged in place by the stopper, Primus drew back and, with his full strength, hurled the fragile orb into the mass of shifting bodies. As luck would have it, a soldier's raised weapon struck the pot while it was aloft, and the pot shattered, sending long ropes of pitch in all directions, which burst into flame an instant later.

Each flaming tendril landed on a different man, and their thrashing both disrupted the men around them and caused cries of fear and alarm to go up, as in that moment, it appeared that the soldiers simply burst into flames. Primus knew their confusion would not last long, however, and he wedged the torch between two of the small wooden logs that made up the floor, lighting two more pots and throwing them in quick succession. He was not aiming for the same place every time, as the soldiers gave a wide berth to any flaming man and refused to go near the area again for a short while after.

"You there! Go back to that hole there and bring me back more of those clay pots!" Primus shouted, pointing at one of the men standing below him. The man nodded and worked his way out of the throng and sprinted to the box, returning shortly after with his arms full.

"Sir! What else do you need?" the man asked.

"If there are any left there, I need the rest of those pots brought here. Once you've done that, and if he's still alive, find Thak and tell him to get some for himself," Primus said loudly, and the man nodded before sprinting toward to the buried box.

"The rest of you, bows out! Find your targets!" Primus shouted as he lit and threw two more pots much closer to the platform, which distracted the enemy soldiers long enough that the archers were able to kill the remaining soldiers and ready their bows.

Firing through the thick greasy black smoke that rose from the bodies proved to be incredibly effective, as it was much harder to block arrows if you could not tell when an archer might release an arrow. From his position, Primus watched as dozens of soldiers at a time were cut down by the archers while continuing to throw pots. Soon though, he began to run out, and just as he reached his last remaining pot, several more men suddenly burst into flame from every corner of the battlefield. Primus realized that Thak and the others must have started throwing their own, spreading further chaos.

"To me! To me, men! Drive them back! Drive them back toward the trench!" Primus shouted. Through the fire, smoke, and confusion, he could see Meftif's soldiers cut down the enemy soldiers, some soldiers who had stopped and were rubbing eyes that started from the smoke, and other soldiers who writhed as they burned.

"Archers! Move up! Fire to the center of their forces, drive them back, riddle them with holes!" Primus shouted as he leaped from the platform. He struck the ground in front of the archers and crouched as dozens of arrows whizzed overhead, like so many giant and angry black wasps. Standing, he jumped through the smoke and began to lead the men away from the platform. Small pockets of soldiers were clustered densely together, trying to fend off the thickets of spears that began to thrust at them, although they were met with limited success.

Primus's voice seemed to have rallied the men, and they began to fight with renewed enthusiasm as he personally led the steadily growing number of men on what was rapidly becoming a relentless forward march. Whether it was due to the unexpected charge, the fire, or possibly the scorpion venom that had been utilized so many hours ago, Primus began to drive back the tide of soldiers, falling on some of them while their backs were turned, cutting them down before they realized he was there.

After a short time, Primus ordered all the archers to go around the battlefield and to climb the sloped hills on the outside of the trenches. They were to bring with them as many arrows as they could carry and any remaining firepots that they could find.

Once above the battlefield, they rained arrows down and the occasional firepot and caused as much devastation as they were able to, as well as picking off any men who managed to escape the reach of Primus's swords and spears or who managed to avoid being forced back into the trench. Once they were out of arrows, they were to take up their other weapons and rejoin the fight.

It took several more minutes of hard fighting before Primus glimpsed the men reaching the tops of the hills, and soon after, they began to rain arrows down on the enemy soldiers. It was still minutes more before he detected a slackening in their resistance. Just as he was shouting, trying to rally the men again for another push, a soldier with a large gash on his shield arm feinted toward Primus's shield arm with his sword, which was bent and chipped and missing its upper half. Primus had raised his shield to defend himself, but fast as he was, he was unable to stop the jagged piece of metal before it struck him in the gut.

The air rushed out of his lungs as he tried to prevent himself from doubling over while unable to breathe, which would have made him an easy target, exposed as he was.

The soldier who had stabbed him twisted the blade and ripped it away, ripping several of the links and breaking rivets on his armor and tearing away a rather large piece. Primus's stomach was now exposed, free of its metal cage, vulnerable to any pokes or prods from spears, pikes, swords, and arrows. Several shallow scratches now wound their way around in a rough circle just below his ribs.

Primus was pulled back into the protective wall of his own men, and before he disappeared into them, he watched the man who had been standing to his left gut the attacker with a sword that was still very much intact. Primus was surrounded by his own men, all of whom looked at his desperately moving chest, their fear etched clearly on their faces.

After several seconds, the muscles in his abdomen unclenched, and he was able to breathe again, his first breaths coming in large ragged gasps. Ignoring the questions of concern from the men, Primus rose to his full height and moved toward the battlefront, determined to end this quickly.

I'm running out of parts of me that aren't scratched or cut yet. Any longer here and I might take a hit that'll actually be a problem, Primus thought as he dived back into the red haze that had become so familiar.

The fighting had dragged on, and Primus found that despite all the training from both before and after joining the army, his arms and legs still felt leaden, and his breathing had deteriorated from the smooth and controlled pattern it had been earlier into ragged gasps that, no matter how many he took, never seemed to fill his lungs enough.

Eventually, Primus fell back, just as he had earlier in the battle, so that he could regain his composure. Stopping for a moment to appreciate how the battle was progressing, Primus saw that he had nearly driven his enemies back into the trench, and from somewhere within the army, Primus could hear Thak shouting to keep fighting, and that they had almost made it, although where exactly his friend was, Primus could not be sure. It was difficult to tell where a single voice was coming from amid the screams of the dead and dying and among the battle cries and clashing of metal.

Primus stayed back from the front line for several minutes until his breathing had returned to something that resembled normal, and though his arms and legs still were heavy, they were not so heavy as before, and he felt he would be able to rejoin the fight. He made his way back to the front, only to be showered as the man in front of him fell to the side, headless.

Primus killed the man, and three more before the crowd of soldiers suddenly became much thinner, and he realized that they had succeeded in pushing their opponents back into the trench. Several more soldiers ran to join the archers, though no one ordered them to, and using whatever arrows they had left, they continued to pour arrows on the army, who now were nearly helpless against the onslaught.

Though they lifted their shields and crouched behind them, the soldiers could not block all arrows at once, and the archers were standing too far back to be attacked with the weapons the soldiers had. The crouching men made it more difficult for those who were trying to back away from Primus's march to do so, and they often tripped their fellow soldiers, which opened the fallen men to the archers above, and their bodies would further trip the soldiers.

Suddenly, a cry went up from the soldiers, and they all tried to take several steps back, although several more fell over. They took their weapons in both hands and raised both hands and their weapons toward the sky before turning the points toward themselves and offering the handles to Primus and the soldiers around him. Primus waved his hand, and his men shouldered their weapons as the desert fell silent for the first time in hours.

"We wish to surrender. We cannot continue to fight, and I wish to see the men under my command spared from death. Whom among you do you call leader?" said a man who was missing three of the fingers on his left hand. The bloody stumps glistened in the sun, the raw flesh still twitching from time to time from the sting of the air.

Thak then appeared next to Primus, who was relieved to see that his friend had survived the battle, though not unscathed, as several cuts were visible on his arms and legs, and his shield was missing.

"They're asking to talk to who's in charge," Primus said hoarsely, almost unable to believe what he was hearing.

"Mmm. Well, that'll be you then," Thak said in a low voice and with a slight smile and a small nod. Primus could only look at his friend, dumbstruck, his mouth slightly open like a fish who had been lifted from their watery home.

"M-me? But why me? Why not you?" Primus whispered to Thak, almost demanding an answer from the older man.

"Because you rallied us and led us to victory," Thak said simply.

Primus did not respond, only turned to face the now surrendered soldiers. He sheathed his sword, squared his shoulders, set his jaw, then stepped forward and out of the crowd.

"I speak for those with me. You asked for your men to be spared, and they will, as will you. You will surrender your weapons first, and then you will assist me in looking for any survivors here, your men or mine. Men, clear a path. Thak here will designate an area for you to pile your weapons in. You will be taken back to the city where you will be judged. Your men will be escorted back to their ships and be allowed to leave for home," Primus said, raising his voice for all to hear and attempting to speak with as much power and authority as he could, knowing what rested upon his shoulders now.

"Your terms are generous. Might we also clean ourselves and wash the stench of death from ourselves?" the man asked.

"You may, *after* we search for survivors," Primus said, and he stepped back and turned halfway, standing in profile to both armies, while the soldiers of Meftif moved to form a corridor back to the field. Thak moved to stand in a spot relatively free from blood, crossing his hands in front of his body.

Without a word, the defeated army moved forward and began to drop their weapons in front of Thak. After a while, Thak left the

WARRIOR ETERNAL

pile and strode over to where Primus stood on a flat stretch of ground separate from the two armies who were separating the dead and dying from the injured.

"Well, your dream turned out to be completely right, but you also pulled us through that. I'm not entirely sure how you did it, but you kept the men from breaking and running, and you were able to bring us to victory. I know I speak for everyone when I say I'm proud of what you've accomplished today," Thak said, his voice thick.

"Thank you. It really means a lot to me to hear that. I just wanted to make my commission, like I promised Turia and her family a long time ago," Primus said distantly.

"The death is getting to you, isn't it?" Thak said concerned.

"Hm? Oh, I'm sorry, Thak. After everything that happened today, I don't really feel like myself. I know it'll take a while for me to come to terms with everything that happened here, but I'm just glad that we're all still alive," Primus said.

"Well, if it's any consolation to you, seeing as how I've got the most authority now, since Targrave is dead, I think you've more than earned a rather large commission. I don't know if I'll be able to get you Targrave's position, but since I don't want it, I think there's a good chance you'll be put in charge of Meftif's army," Thak said with a smile as he scratched his jaw.

"Wait, are you saying what I think you're saying?" Primus said, unable to believe what he was hearing.

"Congratulations, General Primus," Thak said, holding out a hand.

"Thank you, Captain," Primus said as he grasped Thak's forearm firmly. The two men released their grip and turned to walk toward the battlefield. They walked forward, speaking of nothing important, and Primus suspected that Thak needed this almost as much as he did to begin coming to terms with the horrors of war.

While in the middle of the battlefield, however, a loud humming started, causing everyone to stop and look for the source of the noise. Primus looked around as well before a glow caught his eye. The glow was coming from around his stomach, from him.

All around the battlefield, all eyes turned toward Primus, and a small ball of white light began to form around his midsection, slowly growing until it had consumed him, growing brighter all the while and causing everyone to shield their eyes. Then just as suddenly as the humming had started, and as suddenly as the light appeared, the light vanished, and the humming stopped.

After a time, everyone lowered their hands and cast about, looking for any danger that might be present. There was no danger, but it rapidly became apparent that there was no Primus either. He had vanished without a trace. A large section of sand was all that could be found, glowing brightly, the color a light turquoise, and it appeared to be the only thing that was left of the newly minted General Primus.

Chapter 11

Heat and light. These were the only two things that Primus felt and saw. He had no sense of weight or direction, and while the light was bright, it was not blinding to him, only as bright as fresh white linen hung in the sun, and while it was warm, it was not unbearable, only a mild discomfort. He could obviously breathe, move, and speak, but there was nowhere to move to. He could speak, but every sound out of him was muffled, and he heard himself speaking as if through several layers of cloth.

Strangest of all, however, was the sensation that Primus had no weight. He felt as light as a feather, as did everything he carried, and occasionally, while moving about, his armor or weapons appeared to rise and lift off his body as if they had a mind of their own. At one point, to see whether they did or not, Primus removed his dagger from his belt and held it at arm's length with his thumb and forefinger. Primus had expected the blade to move toward his feet when he released it, or at least in some kind of downward direction. He had not expected the blade to remain motionless next to him.

He watched the blade for a moment, fascinated by the way it moved now that its own weight did not pull it in any direction. After a while of watching the dagger, Primus grabbed the hilt and spun the weapon, and it continued to spin without slowing down for over a minute. Primus reached out and took the weapon, examining it thoroughly for any signs of damage or that the weapon had been altered in some way without him knowing.

He was unable to divine anything from studying his weapon, however, and it still felt as if it were a normal dagger in his hand, and he knew that just hours before, he had studied every inch of every weapon he had about himself. And so he sheathed the dagger, seeing nothing else around him, even so much as a speck in the distance.

While he could turn around, move his arms or legs, and otherwise use his body in the same way he would normally, it seemed as though Primus could not actually *go* anywhere. There was no sensation of movement at all, regardless of whether or not Primus was trying to move or was still, and even actions that could potentially have moved him seemed to have no effect, which Primus discovered when he tried to swim in an attempt to move anywhere or make anything that could be considered progress.

After speaking first, then pleading, then raging for a while, attempting to move himself, and playing with his dagger, Primus simply leaned his head back on his arms and began to wait. He did not think that he would be stuck in this state forever, but he did not know how long it would be before he was freed from his current predicament.

Eventually, I'll get out of here. Wherever here *actually is. I wonder how long I've been in here as well. It can't have been more than half an hour. Maybe an hour at most*, Primus thought as he drifted, not bored, but no longer fascinated or intrigued by his surroundings nor the effect that they had on him.

He felt no fatigue or desire to eat or drink despite the battle having taken place before he was able to eat anything for his morning meal and having no water to drink for the day. However, he knew that that would change soon, and it would only worsen his discomfort and make his current situation more unpleasant.

Suddenly, there was a point in front of him, a dot no larger than the head of a pin. Before Primus could move to fully face this new feature, however, the point suddenly expanded rapidly, and it was now clear what the point was. It looked like a window into the world.

Primus began to tilt himself to look at it, but the window was now large enough that he could have stepped fully through it without touching the whiteness around him, and suddenly, the whiteness was gone, and Primus felt his weight for only a second before he dropped six or so inches onto the ground.

The rush of heat was intense, hotter that it had been earlier just outside Meftif and hotter than it should have been for the time in the day. Primus looked around for a moment, expecting to see his soldiers or to see Thak, as well as the prisoners he had set to looking for survivors and gathering the dead.

What he saw, however, was nothing of the sort. The dunes of sand in the desert to his left were taller and more well-defined. There was no trench. There were no soldiers or prisoners. To his right was a river, but the riverbank was lush and verdant, far more than what it should have been, and the shape of the river itself was also not as it should have been. There was a city visible upstream. However, the outline of the city did not match that of Meftif.

I'm not sure where I was earlier, so where am I? Am I near Sodom? Gomorrah? Angra? If I'm closer to those cities, then will they execute me for what I did earlier today? Have they even heard the outcome of the battle? Primus thought as he looked around, curiosity and panic aroused in equal measure.

Oh, come on, Primus, use your head. None of the other cities could have heard about their defeat yet. No message could get there that fast. I don't know if I'm close to any of those cities or if I'm just somewhere else in the middle of the desert, but staying here and thinking all day won't get me anywhere. I'll follow the river. Surely there has to be a town or a village or a city or even just a fisherman or farmer who can point me in the direction of home, Primus thought as he stood up and began to make his way toward the river.

On looking down at himself, he realized that he was still covered in blood and gore from head to toe, and he reeked of desperation and death. Realizing quickly that whatever or whoever he found first would likely take him for a threat, Primus decided quickly that he would step into the water and attempt to get as much of the drying gore from his body as he could.

He knew that he would miss some of the filth, but having a little in a hard to see or hard to reach place was significantly easier to explain away rather than his appearance now, which was more akin to having bathed in the runoff of a battlefield.

He reached the water and readied himself to step in, bracing himself for what was surely to be a cool swim. Although Primus could swim, he could not swim particularly well, so it would be better for him if he stayed in shallower water. It also meant that Primus could more easily defend himself as the water would not slow him down as much, and he could listen for anyone who might be trying to catch him unaware.

Unfortunately, Primus was entirely unsuccessful, and before he had advanced more than ten feet from his initial position, a group of what appeared to be soldiers crested the top of a nearby hill and spotted him. At least, Primus assumed them to be soldiers, owing to the spears and shields they carried and what appeared to be weapons dangling from their waists.

Over flat ground, rested, fed, watered, and with a bit of a head start, it was possible that Primus could have outrun these men or, if he was not faster, outdistanced them. Primus, however, would only have a head start of one hundred or so feet and would likely not be welcomed with open arms into any village or city he came upon if he decided to follow the flow of the river as his escape route.

I must look like I slaughtered an entire village, Primus thought as he looked down at the now-dried blood that coated most of his body, which came away in great crusted flakes when brushed. The thought of trying to pass it off simply as dirt that had been smeared over his body was almost immediately discarded as well, due in part to the stench, and because even a dullard would be able to tell the difference between dirt and dried blood.

Primus knew he could fight his way out of the situation if he needed to, but here he found himself hesitant to engage these men. The battle he had participated in only recently had left him with no desire to see more death. Though there was nothing he could do if they attacked him first, and he knew that it was a distinct possibility that he would be forced to fight once again.

The only two paths left to Primus at this point were to kneel and attempt to surrender to these soldiers and hope that he was not immediately executed, and the other was to attempt to swim across the river and try to use the river to lose his pursuers.

Each of these, however, had significant drawbacks. Swimming was hard enough for Primus, and the added weight of his weapons and armor might drag him under the water, and there was no way of telling how deep the water might be. Primus had heard rumors of rivers that were over three hundred feet deep in places, and the possibility of being dragged to a watery grave was more than enough for Primus to discard the option.

Even if he succeeded in crossing the river, he would have to run *away* from the city and into the desert, and he would still be pursued by these men and likely many more. The city was not far away, and it would be foolish of the soldiers not to send one man back to alert the city that they had an invader in their midst.

Primus could have an entire army chasing him then, and they would be able to travel faster than he could, especially if they had a ship or even just a barge, to say nothing of any men on horseback, meaning that he would be pursued over the water as well as on land on both sides of the river. All they would have to do was wait for Primus to grow tired, even if that took a week.

Kneeling and presenting his sword to these soldiers, surrendering his weapon and his freedom, also meant that he might be surrendering his life at the same moment. It was possible, however slim the chance may be, that the city upstream was friendly to Meftif, or at least did not actively seek war with the city and its people. If they were ambivalent or friendly, Primus could at least clean himself and rest a little before the return trip. If they were hostile, however, then there were two possibilities.

The first was that Primus would simply be executed as an enemy soldier, no different from any other prisoner. It was possible that this could be delayed by requesting to stand before a law setter and trying to argue his way out, but this would be unlikely to succeed given the recent battle. If word of their loss had reached this city already, Primus knew there was no hope of being released or even of being imprisoned. He would be handed over to the executioner without so much as a second thought.

The second possibility was a little better than the first, but it would at least grant Primus several extra days of life. The possibility that word had somehow reached this city, informing them of the death of Meftif's former commanding general, the minting of a new general, and that that general just so happened to be Primus, meant that there would at least be a chance that he could bargain his way out of death by offering to trade himself in exchange for something they wanted, whether it was prisoners, greater trade, a voice at a negotiating table, or any number of things.

There was the vanishingly rare chance that whichever city this was had not heard of the war or battle and was entirely unaware of the events of the past several months. For however miniscule the chance was, there was still a tiny chance. However, it was one so low that Primus discounted it entirely.

Primus finished reviewing his various options in around ten seconds, and upon realizing that there was no good way out for him in any scenario, he decided that the best and only course of action available to him would be to surrender. Fighting the soldiers when he did not have to would be a waste of time, and if the people were friendly to him, it would not be wise to make an enemy out of them without just cause.

By now, the soldiers had come closer, and Primus was more easily able to make out what they were wearing, and it gave him pause. They wore what appeared to be cloth caps over their heads and what appeared to be leather tunics with a leather pouch to cover their groin. There were no markings or insignias anywhere to identify them, and their leather was all of the same dye.

The weapons hanging from their belts were strange as well. Their handles were wrapped in a blue-dyed leather, and the blades were not straight but curved, like the crescent moon, and only one side was sharpened. What could be called the tip of the weapon appeared to be somewhat sharp as well and was ground in a triangular shape, and there was a hook that pointed backward toward the handle. The shields they carried were not wooden, as Primus's had been, and they were made from a material he could not place, although he was sure he had seen something like them before.

The men, too, Primus realized, were different. They were of a darker complexion than he was. Their hair and eyes appeared different too, although they were too far away to be sure. What Primus *was* sure of, however, was that these men were shorter than he was, and although Primus had always been taller than most of the men he knew, these men were substantially shorter than himself, so much so that Primus estimated he towered over them by more than a foot.

Primus removed his sword and his daggers, plunging them into the sand beneath his feet. He took two large steps backward, and he knelt, bowing his head as if in prayer. He simply waited out the remaining seconds until the soldiers would arrive, striving to keep himself calm. Memories of the recent battle rushed back, the memory of the cold bite of metal cutting through his flesh, the cries of the wounded, and the visceral fear for his own life was still fresh.

When the soldiers arrived moments later, they shouted in alarm at the sight of Primus, and after leveling their weapons at him, several of them began talking over one another and talking to Primus. However, for all their tongue that Primus understood, they may as well have been speaking to the sea or to the wind, and when he tried to respond to them, looking up slightly as he did so, it appeared that the same was true for them.

All right, so we don't speak the same language. That's more than a little bit of a problem. As far as I remember from the training, over a thousand years ago, everyone in the world agreed to speak and write the same language since it made trade and sharing knowledge so much easier. Did some people never adopt that? But if that's the case, where am I? Primus wondered as they gripped his arms and hauled him to his feet. Several of them shouted with further alarm as the upper layer of dried blood cracked and fell to the ground, exposing the sticky fluid that was left clinging to Primus's flesh.

Primus mimicked trying to wash himself in an attempt to communicate with these men, but his attempt did not appear to be successful, and a man grabbed an arm each and began to march him toward the city farther upstream. All the while, Primus wondered where in the world he could have ended up to have encountered these men who did not speak like him.

He knew that if they did not speak like him, they would not write like him, and that would make any attempt to get himself back home to Turia and Meftif immeasurably more difficult, never mind making the actual journey back, which could take weeks, or longer, if he truly was in some forgotten corner of the world.

They made their way to the city, and Primus was shocked by the outer walls, specifically the lack of outer walls. The city was more or less open in all directions, and one could enter or leave from any side. Most of the buildings were rather low-ceilinged and made out of the same type of mud bricks that Primus had used previously. There were no large structures, or at least none that Primus would have considered large, the fortress at the center of Meftif being the first thing that came to mind.

The buildings that lay closer to the edge of the city were much smaller than even Primus's home was before it was destroyed, and the same could be said about Niran's home, where he had stayed for so long. What little Primus could see through their windows, the interiors were shabby and not well maintained. The people Primus passed as he was led into the city proper cowered at the sight of him, and it was not hard to guess why. Something that did leave Primus guessing was why there were not more people around.

The city appeared to be much more sparsely populated than it should have been, even for a city that was so much smaller in scale than Meftif. Although it could be considered crowded by other standards, Primus realized that these people must not have the wealth or respect that Meftif had commanded. And without those two things, their access to resources must have been lacking.

Primus also noticed that the people themselves appeared to be frailer than he was used to seeing, with some appearing to be so gaunt he was surprised those people were able to remain upright. Farther into the city, the shops were simple stalls, selling none of the animals, foods, or goods that Primus was used to seeing, and what little trade he witnessed as he was led past was done with copper-colored disks, not coins.

Primus was then led inside a larger building and taken to the back, and he was placed into a cell, still wearing his blood-soaked clothes. The door was closed and locked, leaving Primus alone with his thoughts. Outside the cell, several soldiers were arguing loudly with one another, about what, though, Primus could not tell. He simply sat on a small cot that had been pushed into a corner of the room before lying on his back and propping his head up using one arm and crossing his legs. He was now at the mercy of his captors, so now it was time for Primus to plan.

Planning an escape from his cell would not be difficult, nor would planning his exit from the town. Planning to navigate back to Meftif, planning to steal some of the food in the market if needed for his trip, planning to fight if need be. There was much to plan, and at the moment, he had all the time in the world to do it in.

Chapter 12

As night began to fall outside, Primus could still hear the shouting, although it was now much less frantic than what it had been earlier in the day. Since he had been imprisoned, his cell had not been opened by anyone, although several people who seemed important were brought before the cell door to stand and observe for a moment. Each time, several panicked voices were audible, each trying to speak over one another and gain the attention of the observer.

Although none of them deigned to speak with him or even to shout at him, the word had been spreading that this mysterious blood-soaked invader was incapable of speaking their language. Or at least Primus assumed this is what was his captors had been telling each other, as he had no way to be sure of anything they said.

It became apparent after several hours that Primus would be staying in the cell for the foreseeable future, so he did his best to make himself comfortable on the straw mattress he lay on, and after removing his tunic and standing only in his short pants, he removed his mail shirt as well, folding and layering the metal on the floor in a corner of the room that was relatively clear of filth. He then rolled up his tunic and set it against the wall to form a soft, if somewhat crusted, pillow.

The blood that coated his body felt as if it had fully dried now and came away in great chunks when he moved, breaking into pieces as it hit the ground. Once night had fully fallen. Most of the activity outside ceased, although not all.

There were still people running back and forth, occasional shouts and cries of alarm that went up, and every once in a while, there would be the sound of someone or something striking the ground with force, which was inevitably followed by several angry shouts. Primus suspected that several of those running pell-mell had run into each other in the darkness and were being berated for it afterward.

At long last, two men stood in front of the door to the cell. One of them carried a torch and ring of keys, and one of them carried a tray and a pitcher. Primus could not tell what was in the pitcher, but he noticed that the tray contained half a loaf of bread and a small wedge of cheese. The man carrying the food was let inside the cell, and the door was quickly locked behind him.

He approached Primus slowly, fearfully, and the closer he got to the cot, he began to shake more and more, hard enough to almost knock the bread, cheese, and wooden plate they rested on off the tray. Primus also noticed the pitcher, which must have been full of water, was sloshing around as well, spilling some of it on to the sand-covered floor.

The man set the tray of food at the foot of the cot, and the pitcher he lowered gently on to the floor, his eyes never leaving Primus. He then backed away quickly, nearly tripping over his own feet as he tried to get back to what he most likely viewed as safety from this strange and evidently dangerous man.

Before the door could be unlocked and opened, Primus stood and, rising to his full height, turned to face the man who had brought him his food. The man yelped and tried to press himself into the door in an attempt to get away from Primus. Primus faced the man then bowed his head in thanks before flashing a warm smile to the man.

"Thank you. I'm so hungry and thirsty," Primus said to the man, smiling again.

The man appeared to go pale as Primus spoke, and the other man with the keys stood in place, key next to the lock. They both stared wide-eyed at him as he sat on the edge of his cot and proceeded to eat the bread and cheese, all the while making satisfied noises while consuming the meager meal.

This seemed to make the two men realize that he was appreciative of the food and drink and did not intend to do them any harm. Slowly, the door was opened, and the man who still stood in Primus's cell backed away through the door, which was subsequently locked, after which, the two men vanished.

Primus was left alone to continue to eat in darkness and silence. He did not even hear so much as a rat squeaking in the gloom. After savoring the last morsel of food and nursing his last few sips of water, Primus lay himself down to sleep. Despite the events of the day and the exhaustion that dragged on his limbs and slowed his mind, Primus was unwilling to fall asleep, even though the meal, slight though it was, caused him to feel ever more tired.

If I go to sleep here, there's a possibility that I never wake up. One of my jailors could open the door in the middle of the night and slit my throat. Then again, if they were going to kill me, they had more than enough time to do that earlier today. Not to mention I ate that food without even considering that they might have poisoned it. Now that I thought about it, though, I do have to wonder what, if anything, they did to it. I've survived a lot recently, but I don't know if I'll actually make it out of here. I wonder what they think I've done?

I showed up out of nowhere, no tracks in the sand for them to follow, no disturbances for them to try to track down. They must think I murdered a village, but they're not going to find anything close to here. And to top it off, I'm dressed like a soldier, not a common criminal. I don't know what I can do or say either to help myself, because they don't understand anything I say, and I can't make sense of anything that comes out of their mouths.

I'll have to try and communicate with them somehow. If they don't speak my language, it's unlikely they can read it. And it's just as likely I can't read their language either. I have to work something out though. Otherwise, I'll rot in here.

I could try to break out, but I don't know how strong those bars are, how deeply they're embedded in the walls, even what they're really made of. They could be stronger than the metal I've dealt with up until now, or maybe they're different blends of metals. It brings a smile to my face, thinking back to my time working with the smiths. I never thought I would need to give too much attention to the metallurgy of anything other than mine and my enemies' weapons and armor, Primus thought.

It had been a long time since he fully had an internal discussion with himself like this. There was a time when he would occasionally find a quiet place and speak out loud to no one. Those words eventually became thoughts, and the desire to have a discussion with himself waned over the years, although it did not abate entirely.

These inner discussions often allowed him to work through problems and find solutions that would otherwise have eluded him or sometimes would open doors to other avenues of thinking regarding certain parts of some problems that he had not considered.

In some instances in the past, they had allowed him to create structured arguments that would give him the best chance of winning. Or in other instances where victory was not something that was desirable, arguments with Turia being one example, these internal conversations would allow him to structure things in such a way that while he would lose or end in a stalemate, Primus would at least be able to get his point across clearly and concisely.

The only problem is that even though I've started this again, at least for now, I know that it won't help me much at the moment. I don't have a way to get out of here. I have no friends here. I don't even know where I am. It's not like I need to do this right now to plan an escape. I'm just doing this for comfort because I can. Although... Primus allowed his thoughts to drift away slowly as he stood and walked over to the bars in the small window that was nearly level with the ceiling in the corner to his right.

The bars themselves were too high and the window too small to climb out of, but the wall itself was made of mud bricks, and while they were undoubtedly several layers thick, digging through them would not require much more than a simple stick. The trouble that immediately presented itself was that there were no such sticks anywhere inside the cell. Only a straw bed, some sand and loose straw on the floor, his wooden plate, clay pitcher, and his mail shirt.

While a circular wooden plate would not be of too much help initially, Primus knew that he would be able to use it to help dig through the wall after a time, and the pitcher would be useful for dumping the sand and mud out of the window. The only other thing of note was the mail shirt, whose broken links were sharp.

Knowing that an escape attempt might be needed, Primus gathered up his mail shirt quietly and began by pressing it into the wall with the plate with as much of the damaged section facing the wall as possible. He then began to twist it back and forth, and soon there was a growing mound at his feet as the sharp metal dug into the hardened mud.

Primus stopped then because he realized that if he managed to dig a hole in one night through the wall, it would do nothing but attract the wrong kind of attention. If this was going to succeed, Primus would need to be slower and take his time, gently removing a little of the wall at a time, until the moment was right to escape. Primus then gently laid his shirt back on the ground and walked over the area where the mound was, flattening it and spreading it out, such that it appeared that he had only been pacing in his cell.

Primus then lay down on the cot, still using his tunic as a pillow, and did his best to fall asleep. It took longer than he expected, for despite his exhaustion, his mind continued to hum with questions to which he had no answers. After controlling his breathing and focusing on counting his breaths in and out, counting in batches of ten, he was eventually able to slow his mind enough that he began to drift off to sleep.

* * * * *

Primus sat bolt upright in bed, heart pounding, covered in sweat, breathing hard. He looked around, head whipping wildly from side to side as he attempted to get his bearings. He was still on his cot and in his cell, and the light of dawn was starting to creep into the sky, which had assumed a pale blue color. The visions that haunted his dreams seemed to dance before his eyes for another second or two. The images were superimposed, like two faces stamped on the same side of a coin, and then they faded.

He stood on the sands before Meftif, the battle raging around him. The smell of burning flesh and blood filled his nostrils, and dark smoke blotted out the sun. A sea of thrashing limbs and bloody body parts swirled in front of him, a sea of faces, battered and bruised. Some were missing parts of their faces, but of the faces that Primus could make out, they all had dull and lifeless eyes, like those of a dead fish.

They screamed and lashed out, blaming Primus for their deaths, shouting at him how he had killed them and how much it hurt. Primus had snapped awake shortly after his nightmare began, and while he knew that what he had done was right, he took no pleasure in it.

Will I see them every night? Primus wondered as he looked out of his small window, trying to get his breathing under control. Every face he had seen with those lifeless eyes were soldiers he had killed or wounded so badly that they would not have survived. Each man's lifeless and accusatory stare had bored into his very essence, and it felt as if they were seeking to rip him apart from the inside.

I know they can't hurt me. I know they're only dreams, and I know I did the right thing in the end. I just need to keep telling myself that they're not real and that everything is fine. I do need to calm down, though. I feel like my head is in the clouds. Still, no one told me that this would be the price of being a warrior, Primus thought as he strove to calm his racing heart.

He began to do as he had done the previous night, focusing on counting his breathing, but rather than in batches of ten slow breaths, now it was a count of five as he inhaled and a count of five as he exhaled. He also imagined his fear and strain flowing into the bed and then the floor with each breath, just a little at a time. After what felt like an hour, although in reality, it had only been around five minutes, Primus's heart slowed to a rate where each beat could be distinguished from the one before and the one after, and he no longer felt as if his dreams were tearing into the fabric of his being.

After a little more time had passed, he was able to fully relax his clenched jaw and other muscles, and he swung his legs over the edge of the bed to await another day of sitting in the cell alone, save the occasional visits from guards and the like. He hoped that his jailors would see fit to give him another meal soon, as now that his panic had subsided, he found that he was ravenous. While this was most likely from his previous meal, Primus was also sure that his early morning fear had led to at least a small part of his current hunger.

He did not have to wait as long as he first thought. He heard the sound of people making their way to the markets and the braying of a nearby ass being particularly loud. A man was led to Primus's cell, which was subsequently locked by the jailors. Primus was unsure what to make of his latest visitor.

He was a short man, even by the standards of those he had already met, and had a rather rotund belly, which protruded quite a bit. He was bald, although whether his head was simply shaved or if he actually had no hair, Primus could not be sure. His eyes were quite dark in color, appearing almost as if his iris was black and not some dark shade of brown.

His other features were not particularly noteworthy, his jaw not particularly square, his lips not overly large, mouth not overly wide. The only other defining feature of his face was his nose, which was somewhat longer than normal and slightly hooked.

He wore only what appeared to be a white linen cloth that was wrapped around his waist and attached with a small hook, and a single strip of gold-colored fabric was attached to the front, in line with his naval. On his feet were leather sandals of a similar design to Primus's own. This did not give him any hope of familiarity or understanding, however, as there were only so many ways that one could make a leather sandal.

The man had brought with him a small three-legged stool, which he set on the floor before seating himself facing Primus. He said nothing for a moment, only staring at him with an all too familiar intensity. But Primus could not feel any malice in his gaze. If anything, it felt more akin to curiosity, as if this man was just as unsure of who Primus was as Primus was about the man himself.

The man began to speak then, telling Primus something which held no meaning for him but which he knew was not meaningless. Primus could understand nothing more of the man's speech than he could the previous day. However, he did begin to notice certain sounds repeating themselves several times, and he began to imagine just what this man could be saying to him, although Primus did not speak out in return at any point.

Despite the fact that this man appeared to be friendly, it did not mean that whatever he was saying to Primus was anything good. For all he knew, this man was telling him how he would be executed in the afternoon.

The man spoke for several minutes without interruption, either by Primus or the guards outside the door. Finally, he finished and gestured to Primus, as if expecting him to speak. Primus looked around for a moment then down at his own bloody hands before looking back at the man.

Primus opened his mouth then and began to speak. He told the man of the battle he had participated in and of what happened after the battle, which had led him to sitting in the cell. The man seemingly did not understand anything Primus said, but he did not interrupt at any point. When Primus finished, they both sat in silence for around two minutes.

The man then drew into himself, crossing his arms and tucking his chin. He stared into one corner of the room and began muttering to himself, as if he was beginning to understand whatever was going on, and that it would take much more effort than simply sitting down and talking. After a moment, he raised his head and looked Primus squarely in the eye.

"Wjat," the man said slowly, pointing to himself. Primus looked at him askance for a moment. "Wjat," the man said, faster this time and with more confidence while still pointing to himself. Comprehension suddenly dawned on Primus then, and he realized what the man was trying to do.

"Primus," Primus said while pointing to himself. He did not slow down his speaking. However, this did not seem to be a barrier for Wjat. Primus then looked down at himself and patted himself in several spots, showing how simultaneously sticky and crusty his skin still was before mimicking washing himself. Wjat quickly saw what Primus meant and said something to the guards at the door, who promptly left.

When the guard returned, he was carrying another plate of bread and cheese, although now there was what appeared to be some dried meat strips as well. The guard set the items on the floor near the door before producing a set of manacles. The guard opened the door, and Primus allowed himself to be shackled before being led out of the building and through the streets to the nearby river.

Once at the river, Primus was led into the knee-deep water, and Wjat motioned for him to remove his clothing. Primus stripped and, standing naked in the water, was unshackled and given a potful of what appeared to be an oily paste, the color of pale ash. Primus dipped his hand into the pot and pinched some of the material between his fingers, bringing them to his nose. The material had no odor, but that was not necessarily indicative of safety or danger.

Wjat again motioned. This time, he appeared to be dipping his hand into the pot then scraping the contents against his arm before appearing to scrub vigorously. Primus dipped his arm into the waters of the river and did as Wjat had shown him, and to his delight, he discovered that the material was gritty enough that it could scrub the dried blood from his limbs.

While this was happening, a group of women carrying tied bundles of clothing also approached the river, evidently to wash the garments. They stopped to stare at the strange sight before them, speaking in low whispers to one another as they observed this tall stranger bathing. Primus motioned that he was going to go out slightly deeper, using his hand to signal how deep he was going to go, which was only to around his waist. Wjat looked at the women then back at Primus. He made a sideways motion with his head then shrugged.

Primus made his way into the waist-deep water and began to scrub himself vigorously, welcoming the feeling of whatever strange scouring his body was receiving. After a while, he was clean from the waist up, and the women were engrossed in their washing.

Primus walked out of the deeper water, standing with just his calves in the water, and proceeded to scrub his legs as well. When he was finally clean, he walked back out of the water, where he was given a skirt almost identical to the one that Wjat was wearing, although Primus did not remember seeing an extra garment on either of the guards or on Wjat.

Primus donned the skirt and held out his hands, allowing himself to be shackled once more and led back to his cell. There, Primus was surprised to see that the straw mattress had been replaced, and the filth that he had left on the bed due to not washing before sleeping on it was gone. Somewhat more worryingly, however, his mail shirt was missing, along with his bloodstained tunic. Primus was led back into the room by Wjat, who also unshackled him, rather than the guard.

Wjat sat, and so did Primus. Wjat then retrieved Primus's morning meal, although before passing it to Primus so he could eat, he first pointed to each of the items on the platter and spoke the words for them in his native tongue. Primus repeated the words until Wjat was satisfied with his pronunciation.

After Primus was finished eating, Wjat continued to point to different objects around the room and repeated his earlier process. Primus had realized earlier that Wjat was teaching him the language, and Primus began to hope that once he knew how to speak this strange new language, even if he was not necessarily fluent in it, he would at least be able to explain his situation and get home sooner. And with the spark of hope rekindled in his heart, he strove to learn how to speak like Wjat, promising himself he would throw himself into this with the same zeal as he had when he decided to become a warrior. His life and freedom hung in the balance, as well as his future with Turia. And with this in mind, Primus began to learn.

Chapter 13

After around two weeks, Primus felt he was really beginning to get ahold of the strange language. He seemed to have a gift for it, much like when he was learning to read, and he found that he was enjoying the experience more and more. It had taken a while, but eventually, he had learned that he was in a place that Wjat called Kemet, and the river was called Aur. The names, Primus was told, would translate in his own native tongue as simply *Black Land* and *Black*.

The reason for these simple names, which did not seem to fit with what Primus had seen of the lands, was because the Aur River flooded every year. The river would swell and swallow the land on either side of the river, and the entire river would stay flooded for between three and four months at a time. Wjat called this time *akhet*, which Primus would know as inundation. When the flood waters receded, the riverbanks would be coated in a thick layer of black silt.

This layer of silt was what allowed the farmers farther downstream, where the silt would be at its deepest, to grow a gargantuan amount of crops, and the grain and other crops would be harvested once grown, and the grounds would be left alone until the floods came again the following year.

Primus also learned that the river flowed from the south and ran toward the north, emptying into a shallow sea. This had intrigued him greatly, for if one followed the coast to its easternmost point then rode or walked into the desert in that region, they would surely find Meftif there. Primus, however, was shocked when he was told it would be at least one week in the fastest ship until they would be able to even see the sea. He did not realize how far inland he currently was.

After four days, when it became apparent that Primus was not an immediate threat and was responsible for no crimes, he had asked if he may stay somewhere other than his cell. Wjat had left shortly after, and Primus had not seen him for nearly the rest of the day. Shortly before nightfall, Wjat returned and informed Primus that he would be allowed to leave his cell, but Primus would have to stay with him, and he was not to leave Wjat's home unaccompanied under any circumstances, to which Primus agreed.

The next day, Primus had requested a map of Kemet and the surrounding lands. However, no map of the surrounding lands was close enough to be retrieved. Most of the other maps in the area were in the possession of the leader of this part of Kemet, which they simply referred to as Upper and Lower Kemet. Lower Kemet may have been responsible for more of the food production, but Upper Kemet was responsible for most of the gold mined.

However, despite their many similarities and the beneficial nature of their relationship, the northern and southern kingdoms were at war with each other and had been for some time. This was part of the reason Primus had been imprisoned, as the king, a man named Narmer, was wary of spies.

Narmer and his chief adviser, Imhotep, had been in another city not far from where Primus was staying. Tin was the city where Narmer was currently ruling from, and Nekhen was the name of the city that had housed Primus's cell. The stern man that Primus had seen his first night in Nekhen had in fact been Imhotep. He had been in the city on Narmer's orders to requisition more weapons, namely the khopesh, the curved sword that Primus had seen on his first day.

The weapon was itself brand-new, having only been developed around two years earlier. They were currently only in use in small amounts. However, when Narmer requested that he be shown how effective the weapon could be, he was so impressed with its performance that he requisitioned as many to be made as the smiths could produce. When asked, Wjat said that he had heard that the weapon had lopped off a man's arm as easily as someone might flick the grain from a head of wheat or barley.

Some of the soldiers were not impressed with the weapon, however. Not because they doubted its effectiveness, for they had heard much the same as Wjat and Primus. They laughed because of the shape of the weapon, which resembled the hind legs of several animals, cattle being among them.

"The problem, though, is that Narmer wants enough to outfit his entire army, but these take time to make. They are, how you would say?" Wjat asked.

"A burden to make?" Primus offered.

"Correct. They take too much time," Wjat said.

"Is it their shape that makes it take so long?" Primus asked.

"Yes, it is. They have to be thick on the backside and sharp on one. You saw the hook on the tip, yes?" Wjat asked, and Primus nodded. "That can spin away shields or grab other weapons. That also has to be a special size, and fixing one too small or too big takes time too."

Wjat went on to say later in the conversation that he did not believe they would have anywhere near enough of the weapons to outfit the entire army. They likely would only have three or four dozen, as despite the weapon only being two years old, they had gone unnoticed until just weeks ago, and it would be unlikely that there would be enough made before Narmer was to march on his enemies in the north.

That time was fast approaching, and within another week, two at the most, Narmer intended to begin his own march, because as Wjat accidentally revealed, Lower Kemet had already begun to march south from a city called Abydos, toward Tin and Narmer. On hearing this, however, Primus pricked his ears back.

"Wjat, you said that Narmer needed every warrior to try and fight, correct?" Primus asked.

"He needs everyone who can swing a blade and heft a shield to fight. While we do outnumber them, victory is no sure thing, and they are better supplied with food than we are. They could just surround the city and wait until we began to starve," Wjat said.

"I asked because I think in this matter, I could be of some help. When I first began to speak your language, you asked me if I had killed anyone and how many, if I had, because of all the blood on me. I had told you no at the time, that I couldn't explain at the time because I didn't understand enough. Well, I think it's time I tell you what happened just before I was found, but I only ask that you believe me when I tell you this. I haven't lied to you yet, and I don't intend to from here either, but you may not believe me when I explain it to you," Primus said.

"You have been honest, and you have given me no reason to distrust you so far. What is it that you wish to tell me?" Wjat asked after a moment of hesitation.

And so Primus began to recount his story. He began with where he had been born and then spoke of his childhood, although he quickly moved on, as there was not much here that was relevant to his current circumstances, save only that it was during this time he had met Turia.

From there, he described how his home had been destroyed, his failed apprenticeship with several metal smiths, then of how he trained so that one day, he would be able to join the ranks of the soldiers.

Wjat stopped him several times to ask questions, such as why being allowed into the army meant waiting for so long. Primus explained that it would allow most men to father children and begin families before going to war so that their line would survive, along with keeping the population stable. Wjat told Primus that there was not really a standing army, and that most of the soldiers were farmers or miners or craftsmen. They would put down their plows and pick up their swords when their king called for them, however.

Primus continued his tale then, explaining how he was nearly imprisoned and how he was shown mercy. How he trained alongside the soldiers and even how they had given him a room to stay in. He then spoke of his actual training, the interest that his general had taken in him, and the friendship he had developed with Thak.

Next, Primus explained how Targrave had been threatened by Primus and how he and his friend had secretly orchestrated the defenses of the city as far away from the city walls as possible so as to minimize the possible deaths of citizens, although Primus kept secret his firepots, fearing the damage that might occur if they became generally known and the loss of life that would come with that knowledge.

At long last, Primus arrived at the information that their spies had relayed and the subsequent battle. This subject, in particular, seemed to be of great interest to Wjat, and he asked questions at every opportunity. Wjat also backtracked here, asking further questions about the mock battles that Primus had spoken of earlier, now asking Primus to tell the stories of his victories there in greater detail, and Primus acquiesced.

Finally, Primus told of the death of his commander and his victory that followed shortly after and of the strange ball of light that seemed to have brought him to Kemet. After he finished his story, Wjat stayed silent, appearing to ponder what Primus had said. The silence stretched so long that Primus began to measure the time by the passage of the sun as it moved across the sky.

"And you were minted a general before you appeared here?" Wjat asked.

"Not formally, but with the position vacant and the man with the next highest authority saying he did not want the position for himself, he could block anyone else below him from taking the position, and as captain of the guard, he also had access to the leaders of Meftif and could speak to them on my behalf. He more or less guaranteed that the position would be mine. At least until I appeared here," Primus finished sadly as he looked off toward the horizon.

"And that's why you wanted a map of the surrounding lands, especially the lands to the north. You wanted to see how long it would take for you to get home," Wjat concluded.

"Exactly. I just want to go back and hold my beloved again, more than the position I was awarded, more than the riches promised. I just want to see Turia again," Primus said as he looked out the window again.

"Well, I think I can help with that. I don't know whether to believe your story about being brought here in a ball of light or not, but everything else you've said sounds mostly accurate, other than your description of Meftif and the lands across the sea," Wjat said.

"Wait, what do you mean?" Primus asked.

"Well, no one has been across the sea. It stretches on forever, and some sailors have come back, half mad, claiming to have found the edge of the world, and by going too much farther, they would have fallen off," Wjat said matter-of-factly. Primus simply looked at the man, dumbstruck.

How does he not know about these places? I don't get it. They say they aren't too far away from Meftif's location, but they claim to have never heard of the city. They don't speak the same language, they don't have a written language, and now he tells me there are no lands across the sea and that there's an edge to the world that you could fall off. Nothing about this makes any sense, Primus thought, and he made a promise to himself to keep looking for any more information as to why there was such a lack of knowledge.

"Well, I had been told that there *were* lands, but I don't know if that is actually true or not. They might have been talking about lands to the north, not to the west," Primus said as he attempted to recover. His turnabout was not out of some realization of being wrong but out of fear. Risking being called mad and imprisoned again, for his safety and the safety of those around him, of course, did not seem wise to him, and telling Wjat honestly what had happened to him felt to Primus as if he were pushing on that boundary already.

"Well, you are from farther north, and there may very well be land there yet unclaimed, or perhaps there are people who inhabit those strange lands. Maybe you even met one or two of them before," Wjat said slowly, cautiously conceding that the world might be larger than he had previously thought it was.

"But does this mean that I'll be able to speak with Narmer? If he needs every sword he can find, and I need to get home, we could make some kind of pact," Primus asked.

"What kind of pact?" Wjat asked cautiously.

"If I fight for him or can help him plan his attack or his defenses, once he wins, I'll be provided some supplies and allowed to leave for my homeland," Primus said.

"I don't know if he'll accept that or not. Narmer is not like other men. He does not think or even feel like we do. He stands above it all, and in his inscrutable gaze, we should pray for his mercy," Wjat said reverently, and Primus suddenly realized that Wjat worshiped him not as a man but something closer to the divine.

"True though that may be, I still wish to try. If I don't, it's possible that I'll never make it home, and I'm sure that I would need Narmer's permission to leave Kemet, so this will serve both of our purposes. Narmer gets an extra sword and mind to assist with planning, and I can go home, provided I survive the battle," Primus said earnestly. Wjat was silent for a time, staring out of his window and into the sky beyond. Eventually, he stirred.

"I will send word to Tin, and I will pray for both Narmer's mercy and for your success," Wjat said, and before Primus had a chance to say anything, Wjat had leaped from the table and rushed out the door. Primus knew that his instructor would not be going to Tin himself, for he was guarding a prisoner who was potentially either very dangerous or very valuable, but that did not answer the question of where he had gone.

There were no books or scrolls to read, as there was no system of writing that existed in Kemet. And Primus was prevented from leaving Wjat's home as he was still a prisoner. He tried to entertain himself at first by imagining conversations between Turia's parents and himself. He eventually moved on to other people whom he intended to speak with when he returned.

Eventually, however, he fully exhausted his imaginary friend and family group and began to wander the small home in search of something else to occupy his time until Wjat returned. After eating the heel of a loaf of bread, which tasted rather bland compared to the various breads that he was used to, Primus put the bread away, knowing that eating to satiate his boredom would mean coming home fat, and while no one would have called him vain, Primus did take pride in how his body looked.

Realizing that staying inside alone all day with nothing else to do would drive him mad, Primus walked out of the front door and stood with his face turned to the sun. After a simple moment of enjoying the warmth against all his exposed skin, he walked back inside while leaving the door open. He then began to glide through the motions he had become so familiar with in training, using a rounded piece of wood and a pillow as a sword and shield replacement.

Primus continued to move his body through the flowing motions of each form of combat he knew, paying extra attention to his stance, not focusing on power or speed but on his precision. He kept up with this even as several women of the town gathered around the door and window to watch him. He simply chose to ignore his onlookers.

After he was pleasantly warm from his practice, he began to move his body, lifting heavy objects he could find inside Wjat's home, some he lifted over his head, some he laid on the ground and raised them away from his body, while others he tried to lift using only his legs. Primus continued to lift the various objects around him until he was in need of a bath, but nothing he was moving was large enough or heavy enough to strain his body, so while his limbs were slightly tired, he was nowhere near as tired as he had been on some of the days during his training.

The thing that Primus really wanted to do, however, and the thing that he was missing that surprised him the most was that he wanted to run. He wanted to go and run up the river for a day and a half then immediately run back for a day and a half. Using the time to fully stretch and relax his mind would help tremendously, and it would hopefully allow him to come to terms with what he had done during the battle for Meftif, as he called it in his thoughts.

Though Primus was not a coward, he was waking every night in a sweat after seemingly being transported back to the battle and seeing the faces of the men he had wounded and killed. The procession of the dead never seemed to end, and their hauntingly blank stares bore into Primus's mind, enthralling him, making it so he could never look away. And then, as always, he would wake up.

He never seemed to wake Wjat up, however, and several days ago, Primus had asked him if he ever woke up in the night due to strange noises. Wjat had told him that occasionally, a jackal or some other such animal might be nearby, or they might knock something over in the darkness, but that was the extent of him waking up. Primus then asked if he had awoken recently, but Wjat told him that nothing had awoken him in months now and followed up by asking Primus the reason for bringing it up.

Primus told him that because he was a stranger in this land, he had not been sleeping well, and he thought he heard something outside, but after a while, he heard nothing more, so he went back to sleep. Wjat, it seemed, had believed him, and the matter was not discussed again.

Although the nightmares bothered Primus, he understood that at least for now, he would have to keep them to himself. It would not help his situation if he started to talk to others about these nightmares. His chief reason being that if word of those nightmares somehow made it to Narmer or someone close to him, such as Imhotep, it could cause them to not to see him as the great warrior that he was trying to present himself as. If that came to pass, Primus truly believed that he would never see his home again.

After several more hours and more time spent trying to maintain his body, followed by eating small amounts afterward, Wjat finally arrived back to his home. It was late enough in the day that the sun hung low on the horizon, like the yolk of an enormous egg, which would soon touch the horizon, breaking open and bleeding its colors into the surrounding sky. Wjat looked tired, and he was covered in dust and dried sweat, as if he had been running nonstop since Primus had last seen him.

"You look terrible," Primus said as the man seated himself at the small table in his kitchen.

"I feel terrible. It took me a long time to find someone who could deliver your request and longer still to convince them to take it to Narmer," Wjat said.

"But you were still able to find someone, yes?" Primus asked, trying not to sound urgent or too eager as he retrieved an untouched loaf of bread and started a fire to cook dinner. Primus had previously discovered that Wjat was older than him only by four years and that he had been married before a crocodile had killed his wife while she was washing their clothes one afternoon. As a result, Wjat's, and now Primus's, duties included cooking, and as Primus had discovered, he himself was a terrible cook.

"I did, and they've already left for Tin. It's a few days away on horseback, but hopefully, we will have word from Narmer within two weeks, although we may wait a month," Wjat said as Primus laid a medallion of cut beef on a hot stone and attempted to cook it.

Wjat did not have very much to season the food with, and it generally tasted quite bland. Primus had asked Wjat about the lack of spice, and Wjat replied that no one had access to very much. Primus was shocked to his core when he learned that salt was worth its weight in gold and sometimes more than its weight in gold.

"Well, hopefully, we will hear back sooner than later. I would love to see home again," Primus said as he continued to cook, this time keeping his stone farther away from the center of the fire so that it would cook slower.

"I hope so too, Primus. And I hope you find what you are looking for," Wjat said as he took a long drink from a waterskin. The two men sat in silence until the meat was done, and they ate in silence as well.

After they finished their evening meal, Primus asked if they might walk to the river so that they may clean themselves. Wjat eventually agreed to go, not for the first time questioning why Primus insisted on washing himself daily, as Wjat washed himself once a month at most. At the river, Primus washed and was accompanied, as always, by the same group of women who seemed to follow him any time he went outside or attempted to maintain his body.

After he was clean, they returned to Wjat's home and spent some of the evening going over areas of the language that Primus already knew, this keeping them both occupied. Then they retired to bed, Wjat being particularly exhausted after a long day and retiring early.

The following four days passed without incident. However, on the fifth morning, a man rode into Nekhan at breakneck pace, and he stopped before Wjat's home. Wjat went out to greet the man, and the two began discussing something in a low voice. Primus was unable to make out what they were saying, both because Wjat had asked him to stay inside and to stay away from the door. After several minutes, the rider left, and Wjat returned to Primus.

"Before you ask, yes, that was a message from Tin. No, not just from Tin but from Narmer himself," Wjat said, sounding awed by the revelation.

"And? What did he say? I need to know what the message is. What are the details?" Primus asked, once again trying to hide the urgency in his voice, although he was far less successful than he had been several days earlier.

"He requested that we depart for Tin as soon as we are able to, for he wishes to speak with this great warrior from an unknown land. That he believes that you could aid him in his conquest. He also said that horses would be provided to us at the stables so that we may leave without further delay. The rider said that he had been given something from Narmer that would prove what he said was true, but it was for the stables," Wjat said.

"Good. When do we leave?" Primus asked as he stepped forward and squared his shoulders.

"As soon as you help me pack some food and some blankets and anything else that we might need, but only what is absolutely necessary. We travel light," Wjat said as he turned to the cupboards and began to gather supplies in his arms.

Primus said nothing, but he ducked into the room he shared with Wjat and began to gather the items they would need for their travels.

Chapter 14

The road to Tin, if it was deserving of such a grand title as road, was uneventful for Primus and Wjat, and they encountered no others as they rode north along the narrow trail that served as their road. The trail would nearly disappear at times and was at most no wider than an animal path. The sun was far hotter than what Primus was used to as well, and being out in it all day was much more difficult than it had been in Meftif. He also found that he was stopping to refill his waterskin more often than Wjat did, although neither mentioned anything about it.

Neither of them spoke much after the first day, apart from the occasional request from Primus to revisit some of the harder-to-pronounce words and phrases that he had struggled with in the past. Primus's silence stemmed from his desire to perfect his arguments to Narmer. No matter what would happen, Primus was sure that he would have to fight both before and during the coming battle. For his part, Wjat also preferred to travel in silence.

While Primus knew that he would have to fight in the battle if he were to win his freedom, he was also sure that he would have to win in some kind of test of arms to even be allowed to fight. According to Wjat, Narmer had a bit of a penchant for single combat, and he enjoyed watching his warriors battle each other, sometimes to the death. Primus was not as concerned about this now as he was when he first heard it.

While he knew that it would be possible that he would have to fight to the death, Primus was not as concerned because he viewed it as not being particularly likely to happen with war this close on the horizon. The king needed every man who could swing a sword to fight, and possibly losing one or more of his men to Primus's sword, while not unacceptable losses, would still likely be viewed as losses that Narmer would not want to incur with a battle so close at hand.

Of course, it could very well be the case that Narmer simply would not care about the lives of some of his men when he knew that he outnumbered the forces of Lower Kemet. The idea that a man could be so callous to those who served under him filled Primus with a level of disgust that he had not realized he was capable of feeling.

A ruler, king or otherwise, only rules because others allow him to. If the king lost the support of his people and they turned against him, he would have no other choices. He either gives in to their demands and gives the people what they want, or they overthrow him and rule goes to someone else. But a king also needs to have the support of the army behind him, maybe even more than the people.

If he lost the support of the army and they turn on him, even if the people don't rise up, no king couldn't hold on to power. There would be no one to really enforce any laws or edicts that the king passed down, and with the weapons they would have, there would be no real way to stop the army either. All it would take is for a weak king or a powerful but mad king who humiliates the wrong commander, and that person could lead their forces right up to the king and take the crown by force.

It would be one thing, too, if there was only one commander who rose up and dethroned the king, but if there are two or three, or even more, then that could tear a land apart, brother fighting brother, for control of the throne and whatever is left afterward. Now that I really do think about it, one king who is a poor enough leader could cripple an entire empire, Primus thought.

He had had more than enough time to have these types of long and uninterrupted thoughts on his trip so far, but Primus found that if his thought went on too long, it would become tangled in the web of his other various thoughts and opinions.

When this happened, he would spend hours mulling over various aspects of any subject that happened to catch his fancy, be it something as small as the motion of a bird's wing or the turning of the stars. Eventually, he would rouse himself and go back to sitting in the saddle, focusing on his upcoming audience with Narmer again, until his thoughts were lost again.

Riding would often help rouse Primus from these thoughts, as it was something that, until now, he had never done. When Primus had told Wjat at the stables that he did not know how to ride and that he was never taught how to do so before, Wjat had been incredulous.

"How can you claim to be a soldier but not know how to ride?" Wjat asked.

"Because it was never a part of my training since we didn't use mounted soldiers. Some of the other cities were making small groups of mounted soldiers, but no one had done it on a large scale," Primus explained.

"Yes, but how, though? Have you ever even sat on horseback, whether they were moving or not?" Wjat asked.

"Well, if you mean to ask if I had ridden a horse at any time in my life before this exact moment, the answer is no, no, I did not," Primus said. He managed to keep an even tone despite the mild anger that he felt at being the subject of another man's scorn.

"Well, you do at least seem to be a fast learner, and learning to keep your balance is one of the harder things to do, but that is something you can learn on the way to Tin. You take the reins of the horse, and you hold them in your hands. To turn the horse left, pull left, and to turn right, you pull right. To make the horse walk forward, tap your heels against the horse's flanks, and to make the horse stop, you pull backward on the reins with both hands. Now do you think you can remember all of that?" Wjat asked.

As he had described every motion of the reins, he demonstrated their movement while holding on to his own reins, and he also raised his left leg off the ground and mimicked the kicking motion that Primus was supposed to use.

It took Primus two tries to mount the horse, as it was much farther off the ground than Primus took it to be, and there was nothing he could use to give himself a leg up besides grabbing a large fistful of the horse's mane, which he tried to avoid doing, both for fear of injuring the animal and also for fear of what the animal might do if he were to injure it.

It could throw me off or take off running and drag me behind it, or it could mule kick and injure someone else or any other number of things that could go wrong. It's still an animal, even if it's been brought to heel, Primus thought as he settled into the saddle, the molded leather of which felt cool against the insides of high legs, which rested bare against the saddle.

Primus realized soon after they set off on their journey that he would need to protect his legs from this direct contact as the leather would soon begin to scrape away the skin on his thighs, and if it continued for too long, the insides of his legs would be raw, and the bloody sores could easily get something in them that caused his legs to swell like dead bloated pigs and leave him bedridden for weeks while he healed, if he ever could heal properly.

To avoid this, Primus found two small squares of fabric in his pack, something that he had seen Wjat use before to wipe sweat off his forehead, and stuck one under each leg. While this did not entirely fix the rubbing issue, it did alleviate most of it, and the small patches of skin that still touched the leather soon slid against it, as each became wet with perspiration.

The motion of the horse as it walked was of gentle swaying, and from time to time, it would lull Primus into an almost trancelike state, leading him to daydream. During one of these times, Primus had a sudden realization that the swaying reminded him of Turia, and he nearly made a comment to Wjat about having a living thing between his legs that was moving as a joke, but he thought better of it before he opened his mouth. He did not want to upset his guide with any reminders about his deceased wife, intentionally or not, and a comment of that nature, even if in jest, could still hurt him deeply.

During the day, while hot, things were relatively calm, and there was not much to speak of. But nightfall, on the other hand, brought with it a much clearer and more present danger. After the sun set and darkness swallowed the land, Primus and Wjat would sit by their fire and sleep in shifts.

The jackals and other small desert animals would come out and lurk at the edges of the light, their eyes glowing a soft pale green color. Closer to the water, enormous crocodiles would make their way into and out of the water, often without either Wjat or Primus hearing them.

For such a large beast, they were incredibly quiet, unless they began to hum. When they did, a note of pure bass would resonate throughout the reeds and rushes that lined Aur's riverbanks, and the water would twist and move in unnatural ways around them. The largest of these that Primus had seen so far appeared to be eighteen feet in length, a great lump of rough skin with a mouth as wide as both of his outstretched hands put together and a jaw as long as his entire outstretched arm. Occasionally, the two men would hear the animals hunting in the night.

A great splash of water, the squeal of a surprised animal, followed by their desperate bleating would pierce the air for a brief time, which then would be followed by profound silence after the crocodiles were done rolling through the water. Even the frogs and insects that lived at the water's edge would go silent when the crocodiles took an animal, and it set Wjat more on edge than it did to Primus, although the younger man understood perfectly why it seemed to affect Wjat and the severity of it.

Although they encountered no humans during the night or the day and the only animals they encountered were those found by night, Primus could not help but feel like he was being watched at all times. It was an uncomfortable feeling, as if he had an army of ants marching over his skin, and the urge to look behind him was ever present, although when Primus looked back, there was never anyone there.

Once, Primus even turned his horse around and rode back for a short while at a full gallop. He found nothing, however. No one hiding in the reeds, no one visible on the other side of a dune, not even any tracks besides their own. When Wjat caught up to him and asked him just what had put the idea in his head that he should go running off like that, Primus told him exactly what he had been feeling and how he had been unable to rid himself of that feeling.

"Ah, that. Most feel it through here since it's so empty, apart from the animals. The idea that there must be at least one other person here and that they're watching you stems from the fact that out here, alone, you're more likely to die to something, be it the thirst or the animals or something else. That no one is watching you means that you feel like someone is watching you. Don't worry, the feeling will pass once we reach Tin," Wjat said soothingly.

"And when will we reach Tin?" Primus asked, unsure if he should feel relieved or not.

"We should see it by sundown, but whether we make it to Tin or not before dark, however, is another matter entirely. We might be spending another night here by Aur, and I can only pray that we do not encounter anyone so close to Tin," Wjat said.

"Why should we be worried about encountering anyone outside of the city?" Primus asked.

"Because of the bandits. They prey on travelers, and rather than spend all their time in the middle of the desert in a small camp with only themselves, they often make camp near a city. They're closer to their prey and also closer to where they can spend the gold that they've stolen, with very little fear of retribution," Wjat said.

"No one will stop them?" Primus asked, shocked that such a problem had not already been solved.

"No, no one will stop them. If we imprison or execute a few of the ones we could catch, more will simply take their place, and we cannot imprison everyone who would do this. Usually, in a city, if you're caught stealing, you lose the hand that you stole with. This far away from a city, though, there is no one who can help you. The bandits rob you, and then they leave," Wjat said nonchalantly.

Primus was shocked that despite all the gold and power Narmer seemed to have, he was not interested in trying to stamp out the bandit threat. Regardless of a war, maintaining peace among the people was paramount, and allowing for this to continue appeared to be nothing more than negligence.

I have more than enough experience with that. Sure, they never found the people who burned my home, but they found many others and even tried, for a while, to increase patrols south of Meftif so that no one sailing from there would be able to just appear, pillage, and leave without meeting at least some resistance. But now that I think about it a little more, they definitely would have a harder time with that than we did.

The river seems to stretch farther than anything we know, and if the bandits live close to a city like Wjat said, a few may even have homes inside a city. Stolen money to pay for it, but it's still theirs. Then what? Who's to say what really happened? I guess I can see the problem they're facing. Maybe if they had a group of men dedicated to hunting down bandits? Maybe something like that would help them? Questions for later, and I need to think this through a little better, Primus thought as he watched the river flowing to his left.

Before too long, he gave himself over to the sounds of the water and allowed himself to daydream once more. Late in the day, when the sun was just a fingerbreadth above the horizon, a hazy outline appeared on the river ahead of them.

It was low, and the heat of the day caused a rising effect to ripple off the ground, making the air shimmer, although the outline of the city of Tin was unmistakable. Or at least that was what Wjat told Primus. Without the large central citadels of the cities he was familiar with, Primus had no way to identify what was a city and what was just an illusion caused by heat.

They turned around then and rode back the way they came until the city was no longer in sight. There, they built their fire and made their camp. They built their camp not where Wjat had suggested but instead about fifty yards farther upstream and within an embankment that had been worn into the surrounding desert.

Wjat had resisted being made to camp more along the open road, reasoning that they would make easier prey for any bandits. Primus argued that if they made their camp against the embankment, it would trap them there, and if bandits were to appear and try to slit Primus's and Wjat's purses, their throats, or both, it would be easier to fight off the bandits without a wall behind them. Wjat then tried to challenge Primus's honor and courage by claiming he was too scared and was not really a warrior, that he was only a coward.

Primus heard this while his back was turned as he was unloading his horse. He stopped moving then, and seemingly everything around him went silent as well, as if even the frogs and insects had taken notice of what had been said, and they eagerly awaited a response. Primus closed his eyes slowly and inhaled once through his nose before he opened his eyes and slowly exhaled through his nose as he attempted to keep his temper in check.

"You know something, Wjat? I know you never did believe my story, and you don't have to. Stand in front of me now, and we'll settle this," Primus said, his voice low and hard.

"I've had enough of hearing about this imaginary battle, these imaginary lands, and most of all, your imagined *fighting abilities*!" Wjat said, growing louder with each statement until he was screaming at the end of his sentence, which was when Primus turned to face him.

"I'm not running," Primus said as he advanced, holding his arms wide as if for an embrace. Wjat ran forward and balled his fists up, swinging wildly at the direction of Primus's head. He easily sidestepped and stuck his foot out. Wjat quickly fell onto the sand, scrambling to get back up. Primus simply stood in place, facing away from his guide.

Wjat charged again, and without looking, Primus ducked the wide blow, leaning his head and upper body far to the left before jumping and twisting. Despite his massive size, Primus was still faster than Wjat could follow, and the side of Primus's foot connected with Wjat's right eye and cheekbone. The force of the blow was strong enough that Wjat's head snapped backward, all his forward momentum stopping with the impact, which threw the man to the ground.

Primus continued to unload his horse after this, leaving Wjat on the ground groaning, rolling slightly, and drooling over himself as he attempted to regain the conscious use of his body. Primus finished unloading his horse then moved onto Wjat's, which was had not been touched since Primus had stopped his horse just before their argument.

Primus had just finished unloading Wjat's horse before the man began to stir, attempting to sit up by using his elbows as leverage. His strength had not returned, however, and his arms soon gave out, leaving him once again lying on the ground, unable to anything other than groan.

Primus retrieved his waterskin, which was close to empty, although it did still hold a fair amount of water, and after Primus unstopped the waterskin, which was held close by a strange sort of wood that appeared to have been pressed together and not the smooth and fibrous wood he was used to, Primus poured the remaining water over Wjat's face, which caused him to sit upright and sputter.

While crouching at the edge of Aur, Primus remembered that Wjat had once told him the wood was something called cork, and it came from trees that were even farther south than Upper Kemet, and Nubians traded with the peoples there and also with the Kemet's. While not strong wood, it was malleable enough to be squeezed into the necks of bottles of all shapes and sizes and was useful to prevent losing or spilling any liquid one might want to keep, be it water, wine, or anything else.

Primus filled his waterskin and walked back to what was supposed to be the fire, which he had started to build before waking Wjat. Wordlessly, he began to gather some more driftwood that lay scattered along the riverbank as well as running his hands through the dead grasses that ran along the river as well, pulling out much-needed kindling.

Returning to the pile of smoldering kindling with the needed materials, Primus set about building a proper fire rather than a few dead grasses that a single spark had ignited earlier and then been allowed to die out. It only took Primus five minutes or so, but a towering fire soon blazed, and lit the land for dozens of feet in every direction, bringing a soft glow with it.

At night, Primus felt Kemet was surprisingly cold, and the sandy landscape felt somehow more inhospitable and rather barren. As such, the fire was most welcome.

Primus stood and retrieved Wjat's waterskin from his horse, along with a small amount of their remaining provisions, including some dried meat that Primus began to chew on after he sat back down, gazing at the fire without really looking. Across the fire, Wjat sat against his blanket, which was rolled in a tight bundle, also staring into the fire without seeming to see it. The silence was all-consuming, only broken by the occasional crack or spark from the fire and the ever-present droning of the frogs and insects. After a while, Wjat finally stirred.

"So that's the warrior spirit, is it?" Wjat said slowly and thickly, almost as if his tongue was so swollen he had trouble speaking past it.

"It is, and I'm sorry, Wjat. I just didn't see another way to end that once you started trying to hit me. But that's what separates a warrior from a butcher. I went only as far as I needed to and no further. I didn't want to hurt you. Well, more than I already did, I mean," Primus said softly.

"Oh, is that what happened? I just remember arguing with you. Then I tried to hit you twice. Then the next thing I remember clearly was water being poured all over my face. You kicked me? Where?" Wjat asked, sounding confused.

"I kicked you in your face. Looks like it was across your right eye, cheek, and a little of your forehead. It's already bruising," Primus said, and he was right. A large bruise was starting to spread from around the middle of Wjat's cheek to the middle of his forehead in the size and approximate shape of Primus's right foot. His eye was nearly swollen shut. His brow ridge appeared almost deformed due to the swelling. And despite the darker complexion, the large bruise that Primus noticed had already acquired a hue so purple it verged on black.

"Is it?" Wjat asked thickly.

"Yes, and you shouldn't touch it. If anything is broken, I don't want you to make it worse," Primus said suddenly, and the slight harshness in his voice caused Wjat to flinch badly.

"All right, I won't touch it," Wjat said.

"I'm sorry, Wjat. I didn't want to do it, and I didn't mean to kick you so hard either. Do you remember why we were fighting?" Primus asked.

"It's fine. I'm sure you didn't mean it as hard as you did, and I don't remember why. Actually, a lot of things aren't clear right now. Why were we even fighting?" Wjat said, sounding troubled now in a befuddled sort of way.

Primus then explained to Wjat why there were fighting and the initial reasons each of them had disagreed on. Wjat then asked Primus to explain one more time why he was there, so Primus told Wjat his story again, trying to keep his words small as he realized that Wjat truly had been hurt quite badly. After he listened to Primus's story, he showed the appropriate awe and sadness where needed. It felt much more genuine compared to the last time Primus had told the story.

At the end of his story, Primus offered to stay awake with Wjat for a while so that he did not feel lonely in the night. Wjat thanked him then proceeded to tell his own story. Primus sat and listened politely to his guide's story, doing much the same as Wjat had done previously, and they spoke of things that Wjat wanted to, topics he was curious about, or Primus answered questions. It was late in the night before Wjat's mind started to return to what it had been earlier in the day, and the man began to get his wits about him.

Primus once again apologized to his guide, and Wjat apologized as well, having not expected things to have escalated as quickly as they had. Soon after the apologies were exchanged, Wjat felt that he had recovered enough from the blow to his head that he was willing to try to sleep, and he simply rolled over and promptly began to snore.

Primus stayed awake a while longer, knowing that he would need the rest before his audience with Narmer the next day. However, knowing that Wjat was injured and needed the rest more, Primus was more than happy to stay awake to ward off any bandits that might appear in the night or any animals that encroached on their camp.

Despite the made and accepted apologies, the earlier violence still did not sit well with Primus. He realized that he could have killed Wjat with that kick if it had connected somewhere sensitive, such as his temple. Primus was also glad to have controlled his actions afterward. In the moment after the kick had landed, he had *wanted* to continue to hurt Wjat in a similar way to the enemy soldiers during the battle of Meftif. For a moment, Primus had almost envisioned himself back there, and it took a greater effort of will than he would have liked to admit to stop himself from continuing.

Knowing that he had resisted this made it no easier to bare, however, and the memory of the law setter sprang forth, as if of its own accord. Primus closed his eyes for a moment and breathed deeply, and when he opened them again, it was as if he stood before the law setter again, but this time, it was as if he were watching from the perspective of one of the men or women who watched it happen rather than being the person the law setter spoke with.

After a moment, Primus allowed the memory to fade, and night once again washed over him. He thought back to that day and how so much had been hanging in the balance. He thought of how things might have been different if he had been barred from joining the army or how things might have changed if he had been forced to wait a year.

Primus rose from his spot near the dying fire to collect more wood and kindling, stoking the fire until a pillar of flame reached into the sky, thinking all the while. Primus continued to think until the sun began to rise in the east.

Once morning arrived, Primus woke Wjat, although it took him several attempts to do so. Once he was awake, Wjat appeared to move with more care than normal. His face and eye were still swollen, even more so than the previous night, and the bruising looked far worse in the naked light of day than under the cover of darkness. Wjat helped Primus catch some fish by the river and helped cook it as well before helping him load their horses and ready them for the journey.

On the remaining road to Tin, Wjat was talkative, far more than he had been previously, and even offered to teach Primus some of the more difficult aspects of his language. Strangely, though, Primus noticed Wjat kept farther away from him than he had the previous day or any day since the start of the trip, and Wjat praised Primus for even the smallest of things that he seemed to do right. This confounded Primus for quite some time until the answer became painfully obvious.

He's afraid of me. He's afraid of what I can do or what I could do, so he's trying to keep me happy and placated, Primus realized, and that knowledge pained him more than he first thought it would. He was about to say something to Wjat, but as soon as he opened his mouth, Wjat exclaimed and pointed forward.

"Ah, look, my friend! The city of Tin! We're close now, so look sharp!" Wjat said happily.

"Look sharp?" Primus queried.

"Yes, my friend! It's an expression that means keep your eyes opened or stay alert or something of that nature," Wjat explained.

"What do I have to stay alert for?" Primus asked warily.

"For thieves on the city streets, for urchins and beggars who will trick you. But most of all, stay alert for those in Narmer's court, for they will try to use you. They will try to bend you to their will and use you to gain his favor. That is, if they take a liking to you. If they do not, then prepare for them to try and maneuver you into a spot that will make you look weak or that will put you in greater danger," Wjat said as they rode past the pillars that formed the entrance and into Tin.

Primus looked around as Wjat guided him and his horse through the city. It was much the same here as it was in Nekhen, with low buildings built of mud bricks and wider streets, lacking the large structures that Primus was familiar with. The people looked much the same as well, although there were more of them in Tin than there were in Nekhen.

Wjat led the way through the city and toward the only building that Primus would have considered to be of a normal size. It was a square building, constructed no differently than most of the others, the main feature of the building being its size. The building could easily fit three of the smaller homes side by side and was twice as tall as the other buildings, but other than its size, there was not much else that was notable about the building.

At least, Primus thought that there was nothing special. Once he and Wjat had stopped by a horizontal pole and tied their horses to it, which Wjat said was its purpose, they stepped around the corner, and Primus beheld something he had not thought he would see. In a large area above the door, the brick had been carved away slightly, leaving a large image standing in relief from the rest of the building. It was a stylized scorpion with claws opened and tail pulled back, as if to strike.

While there may have been no writing in the land, the message that this image sent was immediate and unmistakable. Just like the animal that had been carved into this building, the man inside was dangerous and could strike at any moment, and above all else, he would survive and thrive in even the harshest of conditions. It caused Primus to pause for the briefest of moments and made him question the wisdom of coming here.

Do I really want to or even need to reason and bargain with a man who uses the scorpion as his emblem? I used scorpion poison to help win my war, and I heard the screams and moans all throughout the battle. Now I have to trust that this man will help me despite the imagery he's using? Sure, maybe that'll work, but it might just as well get me killed. This worries me, Primus thought as he stepped forward and through the entrance.

Inside, there were many windows that allowed the air to move freely and which kept the building from feeling so hot, and in fact, it actually was somewhat cool inside. Several tapestries and pennants were hung along the wall, bracketed by the windows, which themselves were also bracketed by torches. The room was otherwise bare of all ornamentation, save another scorpion, smaller than the first, which was carved the same way as the first and which rested above a carved wooden chair that appeared to serve as a throne.

Despite the lack of decoration, the building and the king who inhabited it seemed to radiate a sense of purpose unburdened by the frivolities of peace or pleasure. This was the lair of a military man, and lair seemed to be the best way that Primus could describe it. It was darker, breezy, and the sand-covered floor was barren of any rugs or other tables, and the only chair in the room to speak of was the throne itself.

Austere would have been a compliment. And despite that, the coiled power that seemed to radiate from the throne filled every available inch of the building and made Primus want to rush back to

Meftif even faster so that he could march on Sodom and Gomorrah, so that he could fight his enemies and win.

Primus and Wjat walked the length of the building, stopping before the empty throne, and waited. Primus took the time to examine his surroundings with greater care, for now that the initial excitement was over, the hall itself seemed rather gloomy. And despite the wealth that Narmer had, it appeared none of it had been used to build or maintain the hall to make it appear more welcoming to guests, nobles, or commoners.

This struck Primus as strange, for surely meeting other nobles would best be done in comfort and luxury, not in what could pass for a storeroom. Before Primus could think too much on the subject, however, a man wearing a large gold rectangle on his chest appeared. The emblem, whether it was chased to raise the material underneath or the gold around it had simply been chiseled away, was another scorpion, this one with claws and tail faced toward the ground, the tail arching up and around it's body, as if viewed from above. In both hands, he held a pennant that displayed the same symbol, painted in gold.

"His Most Exalted Royal Excellency, King Narmer, son of Menes, Scorpion I," the man said in a loud voice, announcing the imminent arrival of the man whom Primus had heard so much about.

Narmer walked in from the left, the same as the man who announced him. His step was measured but not overly slow. In profile, his chest was deep and his back broad. His arms and legs were muscled, though not to the extent of Primus. His nose was not hooked, and his cheekbones were prominent.

When he turned forward and seated himself, it became apparent that he was short, much like the rest of his people, with a long thin goatee that stretched down from his chin to his chest and was around four inches long, curling slightly at the end. He was the image of a warrior king.

He was wearing a white linen shirt that was unadorned and left his arms bare. His sandals were of a fine make and appeared to be painstakingly stitched together with very fine thread. In his left hand, he held a wooden flail of the type that Primus had seen many times, meant to be swung at the flanks of various animals such as cattle to help move the animals from one field to another to graze.

In his right hand, he held a crook exactly like the type used by shepherds, and it seemed as though Narmer was trying to give the impression that similar to a shepherd, he was here to guide and protect his flock.

On his head was a white crown that took the same shape as a vase, with a slightly narrow bottom which had cutouts around the ears so it would sit properly on his head. The narrow bottom widened then bulged slightly, perhaps half an inch in total, around the middle of the shape, followed by a severe narrowing that flared once again near the top. Overall, the crown gave the impression of a vase fitted with a stopper before being worn.

As Primus noted the shape and design of the crown, it also became apparent that Narmer was wearing some kind of paste on his face, dark blue in color, all around both of his eyes, and Primus wondered what purpose it could serve.

Perhaps it helps to keep the glare from the sun out of his eyes? I can't think of any other reason for a man to wear something like that, unless it's part of their way of life that I don't know about. Either way, I shouldn't say anything until after Wjat and I leave and maybe not until we're far away, Primus thought as he eyed the man in front of him. Overall, Narmer radiated power and command in the same way the hall had when Primus first entered, although this time, he suspected that the feeling would not wane.

"So this is the man I've heard much about in the past days. A man who appeared from nowhere, who emerged from an orb of light whilst dripping blood. Some say you're a murderer. That you killed an entire village to become so drenched in blood and that I should have your head mounted on a spike. Others say that you've come from a distant land to aid us in our hour of need. That you will help me to stamp out my enemies in the north and unite Kemet. You arrived in damaged armor and with a notched sword dripping in still wet blood, though no battle could be found, and no slaughtered village could be found.

"You are something of a mystery to us, and the land that you claim you hail from is far to the north yet looks much like Kemet does. I inquired as to your supposed homeland, and no one could tell me if this place exists or not. Since I do not know if what you say is true and correct, I cannot accept you into my army to assist me with this fight, and I cannot risk allowing you to roam free within our borders," Narmer said. His voice was deep and commanding and seemed to reverberate throughout the hall, as if the hall itself was designed to channel his voice and amplify the sound.

"Sir, uh, Your Excellency, if I may speak?" Primus said, his own voice sounding meek and quiet by comparison.

"You may. Regardless of the truth of your story, a man who does not speak our language and must learn it even as our children do, who no one has ever seen before in any city in Upper Kemet, nor town nor village, yet also does not seem to have been a part of any city in Lower Kemet from what my spies have told me, deserves a chance to be heard," Narmer said, his voice booming forth once again.

His message, on the other hand, was very clear, even if Primus thought he had not explained himself particularly well. Primus was an unknown in this situation. He could be a spy from one of the other cities or even from an outside force that was hostile to Kemet. He did not look like them, he did not sound like them, and he did not speak their language.

All these things made Primus a threat to Narmer, and the only reason Primus still seemed to be alive was because the king wanted to hear what had happened from Primus himself, and then Narmer would act as a law setter would and judge him.

Primus also realized that there must have been voices on either side of Narmer's ear, one telling him to kill the bloody stranger to avoid the possibility of a spy no matter how much help they could potentially be, and another who voiced that the stranger should live because he could be the deciding factor in whether Narmer won the upcoming war or not.

The fact that Narmer had given both of these sides a voice when speaking earlier was the thing that gave Primus hope that he could somehow get out of this, whether it was by using his mind to think his way out of the situation or his body to fight his way out. Knowing that what he said next could be the difference between living and dying, Primus chose his next words carefully.

"Sir, I would like to give you the account of how I came to be here, from the beginning until now. I believe I can fill in any gaps or holes in my story where information currently does not seem to exist, and once I am done with my story, I intend to ask for your permission to fight with you, and if you win your upcoming battle, I would like to be given the supplies needed to return home," Primus said, matching the more formal speech of the king.

"I will hear your account and judge for myself the merits of what you say. If what you say merits me keeping you alive, then you will also be required to fight before the war, that I may judge how you will best serve me in this venture," Narmer said.

Well, no turning back now, Primus. Either you tell your story and he believes you and you fight for his amusement after, or he doesn't believe you and he orders your execution. I could probably make it to my horse, but I won't make it far outside of the city, and staying on the road between the cities would only get me discovered and brought back. And the desert is too empty to try and cross it or even just hide there until it's safe, Primus thought. He closed his eyes, taking two deep breaths. Then he began to tell his story.

Chapter 15

"And you say that all of this truly happened to you, and you truly only wish to go home?" Narmer said, and he straightened up in his chair. The king had slumped against one arm and rested his head upon his fist, where he had sat unmoving since around the time Primus had described his encounter with the law setter.

"It did. Whether it sounds true or not, everything I described happened," Primus said, nodding slightly. He had been speaking for quite a while now, but the king had listened with rapt attention and only interrupted on the very rarest of occasions. This only happened when Narmer felt Primus did a poor job of explaining something important.

One such instance had been when Primus explained the idea to keep the enemy soldiers farther away from Meftif. Primus had laid out his plan for the king in much the same way that he had when creating it. The king had then asked him why he hadn't used the walls that already surrounded the city for defense rather than going into the desert and building defenses so far away.

Primus had answered that it seemed a prudent measure to keep the enemy soldiers farther away from the city so they could not set fire to any of the buildings within and to avoid fighting in the narrow confines of Meftif's streets. Large as the city was and large though the buildings were, fighting in the streets would not offer much benefit to Primus, as even though he knew the layout, he and his men could have been ambushed at any time.

Additionally, fighting a force that was numerically larger in front of someone's home meant possibly putting the residents in danger and furthermore opened the entire city to being searched building by building. From top to bottom, the city would have been searched to ferret out any soldiers who might have hidden themselves if Primus were still victorious, a process that likely would have taken weeks to complete.

Narmer also questioned the use of poison from a scorpion and, further, why only have some small groups of archers hide with a limited number of arrows. Primus responded that they would not have had enough time to outfit the entire army with poisoned arrows, and keeping such arrows in the armory where any could be injured or killed due to carelessness did not seem wise. Keeping them hidden in the desert, only to be used when needed, seemed a more prudent measure. On the whole, however, Narmer had elected to listen rather than to speak.

"And if not for the impending war here and the distrust that it brings, you would have made for your home already," Narmer said.

"If I believed that my best chance to return home lay with simply leaving and riding as hard and fast as I could with as many supplies as I could carry was my best option, I would have already tried to do that. For example, I could have done it last night after Wjat and I fought a little. I could have taken any gold he had on himself or on his horse, most everything else he had, and tried to bring it here to sell or trade for what I would need before riding north. Yet here I stand," Primus said.

"I see. So even though you had the chance to escape, you felt it better to plead your case and be given leave of the land after performing a service to me so that I would be more likely to release you," Narmer said.

If I end up having to do the same thing again before I get home, I need to make it a little less obvious that I'm trying to present my fighting ability as a service that someone can use as long as I get to go home after.

Sooner or later, I'll end up fighting for someone who won't let me go, which is what Narmer sounds like he's suggesting he could do or might do even if I fight for him, Primus thought, and he began to make a mental list of things to avoid for the remainder of his trip home should he run into another king who was going to war and called for every man who could swing a sword or hold a spear.

Making things more difficult, however, was Primus's preparations and victory. Downplaying these would mean he would be more likely to simply be executed as an enemy spy with an interesting story, whereas speaking too highly of these could save him from that fate, only to become the foremost military adviser and not be released from the service of whomever he was forced to swear loyalty to.

That would leave Primus no other choice than to beg, borrow, barter, or steal supplies to make the return journey home, only now with an angry kingdom following him.

"Well, that's not to say...what I mean is, um. It's not, uh, it's not exactly ho—" Primus stammered.

"While that may not be how you interpreted your request, that was how I have interpreted it, and with sovereign authority over these lands, my interpretation is the one that truly matters," Narmer said, and Primus felt his stomach lurch.

No, please no. Not like this. Almost anything else would have been better than what he just said, Primus thought, his mind beginning to race, trying desperately to think up a plan of escape that did not involve what he had been thinking about just moments earlier.

"That does not mean I am blind to your plight, Primus. The war for who will rule all of Kemet will soon be over, and the final battle will be waged not far from here. If you wish to fight, you may. If you survive the battle, you will be permitted to ride for home after a rest period of several days, the exact number of which you will decide. For if what you have told me is true, your home lies far to the north of our borders, and you will need your full strength to return," Narmer said, and Primus tried to hide his excitement.

"Thank you, my king," Primus said as he bowed his head, not quite willing to believe that he would be allowed to leave after the battle.

"Do not show your appreciation yet, for you have not yet fulfilled your duty to me to fight. Something you have spoken of today at length is your ability to quickly and efficiently win a fight, whether it be single combat, a group of men, or an entire battle. Let us put that to the test," Narmer said. He paused then, one which started short but quickly grew into a long drawn-out silence. Primus considered his options and whether there would be a way out of this at all. Inevitably, Primus sighed and looked to his left, away from Wjat and Narmer, lowering his head and then swiveling to look Narmer in the eye once more.

"How do you wish to test me?" Primus asked bluntly.

"You will come back when the sun reaches peak of its arc, as it is pushed across the sky by our sun god, and you will fight three men of my choosing. Two of them you will fight at once, and one of them you will fight by themselves. You may use any weapons or armor you wish, or none at all. If you are defeated, I will decide whether to spare your life based on how well you fought. If you are victorious and you prove that your story is true, then you will spend the rest of your time before the battle as you deem fit.

"Should you wish to train, our armories are open, and our soldiers willing. Should you wish to rest, we have fine wines and many women to satisfy you. And should you require anything, simply make one of my servants aware. Tonight, you will eat and sleep in the servants' quarters. Simply come back at sundown, and you will be shown the way. Now go, both of you," Narmer said, and he rose from his chair without another word and made for the hall through the same hidden hallway he had entered through.

Wjat bowed deeply as Narmer rose. Primus bowed his head in the same manner as he had earlier. The two men turned and began their long walk out of the hall.

After so long in the shade, the sunlit expanse was blindingly bright, and the two shaded their eyes with their hands for a moment while they adjusted to the increased brightness. Wjat started toward the Aur River, generally in the same direction as they had entered from.

Primus followed closely, staying nearly level with him. Once they had left the city, Wjat walked a little farther before turning to his right and walking to a section of the river where the reeds and grasses were absent.

There, on the banks of the river, mere feet from the water, Wjat stopped and stared out at the water without seeing. The occasional boat passed, and the fish occasionally jumped. The man was not looking at the sky either, through which several birds flew and a distant whiff of cloud could be seen, soft and wispy.

Primus stood next to Wjat and gazed in the same direction, allowing the river's current to sweep away some of the thoughts that troubled his mind and carry him to a fleeting peace. Primus quickly lost track of time, although he retained a general feeling of its passage. He could have been standing by the river for several hours, or it may only have been minutes. Wjat muttered something under his breath then, and it sounded like a question.

"What was that?" Primus asked.

"Do you really intend to fight Narmer's soldiers?" Wjat asked again softly.

"I do. It's the only hope I have of returning home," Primus said just as softly.

"You do remember, though, that those are not really soldiers you're fighting. They're farmers or fishermen or craftsmen. They might have been taught to fight, but they aren't really soldiers," Wjat said without looking at Primus.

"I remember, Wjat, and I know that that means many of them have families of their own. I know that if I kill them, I take away someone's husband or father and leave their home weakened," Primus said.

"Yes, but Narmer enjoys watching a fight to the death," Wjat said, finally turning to look at Primus. Primus simply continued to stare at the river.

"I remember. I'll try to win without killing them, but if I spare them and Narmer says that the only way I leave is if they die, then I won't hesitate," Primus said, his voice hard.

"You'll be killing for someone's amusement, not because you truly need to," Wjat said, his tone accusatory.

"You were the one who told me about that before, and you didn't seem to have much of a problem with it at the time. But ignore that. You just said that I would be killing for someone's amusement, and you sounded upset when you said it. Before, when you described Narmer and anything to do with him, you seem to revere him. You view him with a sense of awe. Now you sound like you never want to see or hear anything from him again," Primus said, finally looking his friend in the eye.

"He views the death of his people as a cause for celebration and enjoyment. Does that not seem wrong to you?" Wjat asked, incredulous.

"It doesn't matter much now whether it's good. It simply is. Whether it should or should not be. He rules these lands, and I am an outsider. It's not my place to disagree with his methods, especially not when my own freedom hangs in the balance," Primus said as he looked away, his tone of voice leaving no room for discussion. Silence once again reigned over the two men, broken only by the sounds of the water.

"What happens if Narmer decides he likes you better serving him and fighting for him? Do you have a plan then?" Wjat asked.

"Then I fight my way past anyone who stands in my way. Anyone," Primus said, looking Wjat in the eye as he did.

"Do you understand what you're saying?" Wjat asked, astonished that anyone would have the temerity to insinuate what Primus stated he would do.

"I do. And I also know that I cannot, and will not, be held here by Narmer to fight for his amusement. I don't know exactly what it was about the man, but something about him does not sit well in my mind, and the less time I spend around him, the better," Primus said.

"Yes, but…" Wjat trailed off. Primus looked at the man and sighed.

"I'm not going to kill him or anything like that. I'm just going to hit him really, really hard. And hopefully, that would make him reconsider keeping me around, along with anyone else who wants the same. It might even give me enough time to get away before anyone decides to send soldiers after me," Primus said with a slight smile, reassuring Wjat that no permanent harm would come to the king.

They continued to talk for a while longer, with Primus using Wjat to try and plan out what weapons and armor he would need, if any at all. Eventually, Primus decided that he would use the armor. He initially had not been in favor of it, but in the end, he conceded that if he was not able to block or avoid an attack, it would be better that the armor was on him to absorb some of the impact from the blow. The armor might even save him from a more devastating injury.

The benefit of the leather armor was that it was more flexible and a lighter weight than his old chain mail armor, although the obvious tradeoff was that it would provide less protection than his old armor would have.

Primus then asked after his weapon and his armor, and Wjat told him that his armor had been damaged. That it had already been melted down. Primus's sword, on the other hand, had been lost, apparently having fallen off of the camel that was transporting it, and those whom had been tasked with transporting the weapon had ridden back over their tracks and looked all throughout the desert. They had been unable to locate the weapon, and in the end, they had no choice but to return empty-handed.

After finishing their discussion, they went back into Tin, and Wjat showed Primus some of the more important buildings, as well as pointing out nobles and generals from around Kemet. Wjat said that they had all been summoned here for the impending war. If they possessed their own forces, they had been instructed to bring those forces with them. Otherwise, they were instructed to bring with them any man who would be able to fight, and they would be outfitted once they arrived.

"You mentioned something back in Nekhen about having a shortage of stones for the war, and even though that struck me as a little strange, I didn't say anything about it at the time. What did you mean by not having enough stones?" Primus asked.

"Oh, well, we discovered a way to create a stone mace that is incredibly effective. The process to make them, however, is both time-consuming and not always guaranteed to work," Wjat said.

"Oh? Well, why is the stone so effective for a mace? Why is it time-consuming? And why won't it always work?" Primus asked.

"The stones have to be of a specific size, or it would be too heavy to swing properly, which is why it's so hard to find stones that are the right size. They're so effective because they don't weigh much, but they can break bones easily, and the leather armor is of little protection. The reason that it's time-consuming, and also the reason that it doesn't always work, is because of the method that's used to actually create them.

"We take the stone, and we make it hot, as hot as we possibly can. Great fires are needed to create these maces, and men working pumps to blow air across the fires are also needed. Once we make the stone hot, we take the stone from the flames and drip water from the Aur onto the top. Just a single drop, perhaps two, at a time. If the stone cools too much, we must put them back in the fire until they are hot again, and water will be dripped over them again.

"Sometimes it's the very first drop, sometimes the stone must be heated several times, but in the end, the rock will crack in the middle, and this allows a hole to form from the top of the stone to the bottom. The rest of the stone is strong, but the middle is hollow, and a split stick is inserted and wedged in place, the same way you would fit an ax-head," Wjat explained.

"Well, I can see why that would be time-consuming, and although you didn't tell me why it doesn't always work, I think I know. If the crack splits the stone entirely, or the crack forms in the wrong place, you can't use the stone, and you have to start again, right?" Primus asked, and Wjat nodded.

"You have only seen the scorpion carvings so far, but many cities have carvings of a similar nature, and paintings as well. We can carve on the stone heads anything we wanted to. We don't do this because that would make them less effective as weapons, but I heard a rumor that Narmer has decreed, if he wins the war, he will have an image of it carved onto a mace that will be used in ceremony. More than that, I can't say," Wjat said.

As there was not much else to do in Tin at the moment, Primus and Wjat bought a little bit of food and simply wandered around the city aimlessly, but as it was already late in the day, they did not have much time to wander before the sun began to set, and they headed for Narmer's hall. There, they were greeted and subsequently led through the city by a wordless servant.

The servant led them to a large stone manor, from which several servants could be seen going back and forth. The building was not large enough to really be considered palatial, but neither could it be mistaken for anyone else's home. Only Narmer could have lived here, and Primus guessed that of everyone he could see, roughly two dozen people lived here, most of them servants, although some children could be seen running and shrieking in delight as they played.

Primus and Wjat were led into a long low-ceilinged building that rested next to the manor. Once inside, the servant briefly announced that the two men he had brought with him were honored guests of the king and were to be treated with respect. They were given food and wine, and although Primus ate his fill, he did not drink much of the wine that he was given, as he did not want to feel fuzzy-headed going into the fight the next day.

The evening was uneventful, and after listening to some of the servants speaking with one another about certain things they found interesting during the day, such as one of the nobles bringing with them not just their wife but their mistress as well, Primus asked where he would be sleeping and was led to a small bed near the corner of the building. Wjat already occupied his own bed, having been led there earlier in the night after imbibing two cups of wine too much.

As Primus lay down to sleep, he allowed his mind to wander and drift through all the events he had experienced recently. Fantastic visions, akin to a waking dream, filled his mind. At some point, Primus fell completely asleep, and his story and memories provided the backdrop, but the visions shaped and molded how they appeared, and things were no longer what they once were.

Part of a dream involved Primus standing on Targrave's platform just before the battle, and Primus spoke to the crowd of soldiers, but all the soldiers were Wjat and Narmer, though Primus could not hear the words that came out of his mouth. He was only aware of their blank eyes, like small white stones, staring back at him. Then things shifted, and Primus was desperately running after Turia as she ran away, both on foot and later on a cart.

Morning arrived all too soon, and Primus was awoken by the servants, who showed him to a small armory nearby. Primus cast about for the weapons that he would use in the coming fight. Though it was still early, with the sun resting just above the horizon, Primus knew that he would need to pick and familiarize himself with whichever weapon he chose for himself, and he would need to try to find armor that fit him as well.

While Primus could fight with a spear, he detested the way it felt in his hand and the way it made him change his fighting style. Despite the added danger, Primus believed that the best way to fight was close to his opponent. Being so close came with the risk that he would be hit by someone or something from the side or from behind, or he could be caught off guard by reading his opponent's movements the wrong way.

But being so close meant that Primus was aware of many small details, such as how his opponent was standing or how they planted their feet, and details such as that could tell him where they planned to move next, how they were going to strike, and sometimes even how much force was behind the blow. However, for Primus, the reasons ran deeper than just the practicalities of fighting in closer proximity.

It's easy to hide behind a shield and duck my head behind it and thrust my arm forward. Just like that, I can kill someone I haven't even seen and can, with almost total safety, kill anyone who gets within ten feet of me. That never seemed right to me. That so much death can be caused from a distance.

The same goes for archers. They can kill dozens or even hundreds without ever actually stepping on a battlefield. Yes, I know they're necessary and without them, a war can't be won, but so much easy death is more like slaughter than it is an actual fight. At least up close, I can say I stood before an enemy and lived while they didn't.

There's no question of who a better warrior is then. I'm surprised I'm having this conversation with myself, but now I'm more surprised that I can't even explain it very well to myself. If Turia or Thak or even Niran asks why I preferred this, I'll have to come up with a better answer before I see them again. If *I see them again. At this rate, I'm not sure that I will,* Primus thought as he scanned the short rows of various weaponry.

The swords had a differently shaped hilt and pommel, and they were also several inches shorter than his old sword at the blade, and the pommels were also smaller than what Primus was used to. Primus picked one up and balanced it in his hand for a moment before swinging it slowly at first, then quickly.

He did this to determine how the blade would feel in his hand later and was disappointed by how lightweight the end of the blade felt, realizing quickly that there might be too little weight at the tip, and there was no way to compensate by placing his other hand on the too small handle.

Primus put the sword down in disgust, picking up each and every one he could find in the armory, even the broken blades. All of them had the same problem, too little weight and too small pommels. He briefly considered using some of the other weapons in the armory but just as quickly discounted the idea. While he was proficient with most of the other weapons here, Primus felt that he fought his best with a sword. He considered asking one of the servants if they knew if a khopesh was in the armory or if one would be available to use in the fight.

After briefly considering this, he rejected the idea. It was not out of concern or fear for the other men he was going to fight, even though there was a good chance they were simple farmers. It was because Primus remembered Wjat telling him that the idea and design of the weapon were new and that few had yet been crafted. Additionally, it would be a new weapon entirely with a different weight and balance, and it would require Primus to spend more than he had this morning to learn the small intricacies of the weapon.

For example, even though the length was something Primus was used to and expected, the curvature of the blade would put the balance of the weapon out of what he was familiar with and comfortable with. That could result in him not taking the opportunity to strike when it appeared. Or believing there was an opportunity to strike and taking it, only to be injured or killed by one of the other soldiers.

Primus knew he could overcome the weight and balance issues, but he also knew that it would take at least a day to go through every movement he was familiar with and at least two more to become proficient. This way, he could learn the weapon thoroughly and not be caught off guard by some facet of the khopesh he was unaware of. Perhaps it was easy to catch his own shoulder or shield with the backward-facing hook, or perhaps it was harder to recover from a missed attack.

These were all uncertainties that, if Primus had been forced to contend with them on the battlefield, could have spelled the end of him and still could. If one of the oddities of the weapon that he viewed as a problem or a weakness showed itself to be a strength, Primus would have immediately found a method to integrate it into his fighting style.

Primus also knew that there was a chance that something he viewed as a weakness *was* a strength, and it could very well be used against him. If that were to happen, Primus knew he would be at a severe disadvantage, owing to his unfamiliarity with the weapon. Ignoring the maces other than to test their weight, Primus also proceeded to ignore most of the other weapons as well, settling on a sword that, while shorter than his original weapon, was the closest in length and width.

The shield was another matter entirely, as they were wooden frames covered with rawhide made from the skin of cattle. There were no other options for shields. This was due to the fact that no one in Kemet built shields like Primus was used to, heavy wooden planks nailed together and secured with a band of soft metal to aid in catching a blade.

The armor was also made of leather, and while Primus had hoped that his new armor would both be lighter and more flexible, the leather was only lighter and not much more flexible than his old armor.

Primus took his weapons and armor and walked out into the sun. For the next several hours, he practiced with the new weapons.

He was attempting to fit a week's worth of practice into a space of just three hours or so. Fortunately for him, his new sword was close enough to his old sword that Primus felt he would be able to adequately wield it once he was done practicing. The shield was another matter, however.

In the past, Primus's shield would be attached to his arm at two separate points. One was a leather strap that secured the shield to his forearm, and the other was a small leather strap that he could hold in his left hand. The shield he held in his hand now was very different, being both substantially taller and wider than he was used to, and only one wooden bar was fastened to the back using wooden nails.

The shield was designed to be held vertically and roughly as tall as the midpoint of Primus's chest. The shield was also possibly even designed for the bottom to be placed on the ground, anchoring it in place and providing the user extra stability and support. Primus could see that after anchoring the shield in this fashion, it would be quite difficult to move anyone in that position. Primus even conceded to himself that using a spear whilst anchored could prove to be quite a problem for anyone attacking or defending, especially if the technique was used by a group of soldiers, not just individuals.

Now if only that group could move, then that would really be a force to be reckoned with. Otherwise, they would be vulnerable to arrows or anything else that could be thrown or shot from a distance, or they would be vulnerable from the side, unless they set shields along their flanks, Primus thought as he set about trying to work out how he could use the shield to try and bash away his opponents.

This had been easy when his old wooden shield was strapped to his arm, as all Primus had had to do was to draw his arm back and swing, but with only one point to secure his grip this time, it was proving to be more difficult than he expected.

Eventually, Primus realized that the best option for him to achieve the same type of effect would be to simply turn his palm skyward and grip the bar that way. Then he simply stepped forward and shoved his arm forward and was able to use the new shield in a similar manner to what he was used to, although things like jumping and spinning into his opponents and using the spinning motion and his forward momentum to knock his opponents off-balance and dash their shields out of the way were now completely out of the question.

While this was impractical to do in many situations, it was incredibly helpful as an opening attack, at least to Primus. No one would really expect someone to attack with their shield as the first thing they did in a fight or battle. It was also useful because as Primus had discovered when he first tried it in a fight, his forward momentum would carry him behind the defensive lines of most of his opponents.

Although Primus had appreciated this in Meftif, making use of it often, he knew that it wouldn't make much of a difference in Kemet. Partly due to the difference in weapon design and balance, as well as is armor and shield, but also because Primus suspected that warriors and soldiers would have reacted very differently to it, and the same tactics that he had relied on in the past likely would not serve him well here.

Once he was done familiarizing himself with his new equipment, Primus broke to drink, although not to eat. A full stomach now would only make the battle to come harder due to slower thinking and a slower body. Otherwise, Primus left his shield and weapon with the servants before proceeding to do nothing and speaking with no one, choosing only to watch the river and the many boats that now rested on the water, which gently lapped against the banks of the river as those on the boats went about their business.

There were a number of boats that appeared to be loaded with grains while others seemed as if they were loaded with stone, and more carried other goods that Primus could not tell from a distance. For a time, Primus was at peace.

Inevitably, however, Primus knew that this would have to end, and as he was thinking this very thing, a man who Primus remembered seeing sitting at the end of the table the previous evening while he dined with the servants approached and delivered a simple message. The time had come, and the fight was at hand.

Primus walked back to Narmer's hall, stopping only to retrieve his weapon and shield. Primus entered the hall and approached the throne, raising his weapon aloft, as if he was raising a mug of ale or beer. Narmer inclined his head and snapped his fingers, which called in three men in from the right-side hallway, the one Narmer had not entered or left from the previous day.

Narmer then began to speak with the three men who were standing behind him and staying where they were. Primus could not hear what Narmer was saying. Everything seemed extremely quiet. While Primus could tell that Narmer's booming voice should be heard resonating all throughout the hall, Narmer might as well have not been speaking.

After a minute, perhaps two, Narmer suddenly clapped his hands, and the fight began. The two men who stood behind Narmer rushed him then, each of them wielding a shield of the same design as Primus had. One used a short spear, and the other used a short sword identical to the one that Primus used.

Primus reacted by stepping to the right, out of the range of the man with the sword, and he caught the spear on his shield, the wielder thinking he would be able to skewer Primus for an easy victory. Primus retaliated by swinging hard at the spear haft that was tantalizingly close.

Primus was rewarded with a hit, although it was not strong enough to cut through the haft in its entirety. It did damage the haft. But the tip of the spear was stuck in the shield, and this provided an anchor point closer to Primus and was what had allowed him to damage the spear at all. This second point, the first being the spear wielder's hand, made the spear haft much sturdier, and the wood had not flexed in the slightest.

When the spear was fully removed from the shield, the spearhead was still intact, but Primus knew that he would be able to cut through it again or break it if he just hit it hard enough. As the spear user retreated to give himself more room to swing his weapon, the swordsman rushed him in an attempt to kill him before he had recovered. The swordsman underestimated Primus, however, and Primus caught the weapon on his shield after raising his arm just a little.

Primus stabbed below the shield then, catching the man on his hip. The wound was not deep. Only a small bit of the blade itself appeared to have actually made contact with the swordsman's skin as evidenced by the thin red line that traced along the edge of the blade.

The man hopped backward, favoring his left leg, and the spearman was nearly at Primus's throat. Primus hopped backward several inches and retaliated by stepping forward and lunging back at the spearman with his own thrust before twisting his hand and leading with his knuckles instead of the blade.

Punching the spearman squarely in the chest hurt Primus, however. Since the leather armor was a little pliable, it did not hurt as badly as it could have. It threw the man back several feet and caused him to drop his spear. He used his free hand to clutch his chest as he began to gasp for breath. Primus let the man stumble backward, and he pivoted hard on his right foot, pushing hard as if to jump, trusting that the swordsman would be there.

Primus's blind swing connected with the shield of the man who had been trailing him, splitting the wooden border of the shield and collapsing it somewhat. Primus pushed his attack, ramming the man with his shield in the manner that he had practiced earlier. Primus whirled around and viciously kicked the man behind him as he was reaching for the dropped spear, breaking his arm.

Primus returned to the man in front of him and charged toward him while the man was trying to close the remaining distance. Primus then tucked his shoulder behind his shield and sprinted forward two strides, the impact jarring Primus as he reached around the shield and blindly cut downward.

There was a howl of pain, and Primus stopped dead. The swordsman fell backward and clutched at a cut on his arm that appeared to have gone about one quarter of the way through the muscle. Primus stopped and turned to Narmer then and stared at the king for the moment.

"Spare them, my king, for they have fought bravely!" Primus said loudly.

"They will be spared, Primus, but your fight is not over. The fight will continue," Narmer said loudly.

Primus turned toward the final man, who charged toward him while swinging a mace, which Primus deflected with a small movement of his shield. The man had too much momentum to slow down, and Primus tripped him as he went past. The man fell to the ground hard and scrambled to get back up, but Primus was on top of him and plunged the sword into the sand next to the man's chest.

The man froze in place then, and it was clear that Primus was the winner. Primus waited for a moment, holding the position until long after it was clear that he had won. Primus then slowly stood and turned to face Narmer, his face set like stone. Narmer began to smile and slowly clap his hands.

Chapter 16

It had taken Primus some time to convince Narmer not to have the last man killed, although it had not taken nearly as long as Primus had feared it would. After only perhaps a minute or two of discussion with Narmer in his private chambers, at Primus's request to speak alone, Primus was able to change Narmer's mind and convince the king to allow his last warrior to live. Primus had then asked Narmer why he would order the death of a warrior or warriors that he might need for the upcoming battle fight and die before the battle.

Narmer had told him then that as most of his soldiers were not professional soldiers, but rather ordinary men who had been somewhat trained to fight, requiring them to only very occasionally fight to the death was a loss that Narmer deemed acceptable. He then added that what men he lost, he gained more from the stories that came after.

Narmer would allow rumors to spread that he was a king who would not just allow for such things but also encourage these things, oftentimes watching. These rumors would terrify enemy soldiers and eventually find their way to the ears of rulers of lands beyond Kemet. This would, Narmer hoped, dissuade anyone from trying to invade Kemet. The frequency of battles to the death was rare as well, with only five of them ever having taken place. That was all that it had taken for the rumor to begin to spread.

Due to the infrequency of the battles, there had never truly been any need to fear for most of the soldiers, and the rumors spread far enough and wide enough that they would do much of the work to spread fear by themselves. In addition to this, the people of Kemet were almost totally loyal and devoted to their king, to a degree that Primus was not familiar with, and that loyalty meant they were willing to overlook certain things. If their king requested it, the people would provide it.

After this, Narmer declared that Primus would stay with him until the end of the battle, which was going to be in around a week if the reports from the north were true. Narmer also told Primus that Imhotep would be there as well. Finally, Narmer told Primus that he would be allowed to know at least some of the planning and the work involved in the final stages of planning.

This greatly surprised Primus, who had only hoped to be fed and clothed until the battle. However, after having proven himself in combat, and more importantly, proving that at least some of his story was true, this meant that even though Narmer had the utmost confidence in both himself and in Imhotep to prepare and plan for a battle, Narmer had decided he trusted Primus enough to let him see the plans that had been drawn up. He also showed himself to be open enough that he could allow alterations to his plan if he viewed those alterations to be valuable.

Due to the size of the battle to come, and despite the risks that it entailed, Narmer deemed it to be important that someone other than himself check over the plans that had been made. Narmer later expanded on this view. He believed this because no matter how carefully one man could plan, another man could spot a weakness that was hidden to all except themselves. Primus was surprised by this greatly, as he had not expected the king to be as aware of the need to consult as he was, although secretly, he welcomed it.

His experience with Targrave showed Primus what happened when someone had too much confidence in themselves and dismissed anyone and everyone who offered any amount of criticism, whether positive or negative. Primus knew that he could make mistakes, and oftentimes, he would make small mistakes, and many of them.

They usually involved small movement mistakes, taking a half step forward to close some distance for one. He would be too close to an opponent, which meant that sometimes Primus had to shift his weight or balance more than he wanted to, potentially leaving himself open to a counterattack or putting himself in greater danger than what was necessary.

After the audience with Primus, Narmer had reentered his hall, only to bid everyone within farewell soon after. He personally led Primus back to his home, talking all the while. Once inside Narmer's home, Primus was given a midday meal, and he talked of many things with Narmer during the meal, such as Narmer's upbringing and Primus's plans once he returned home. Primus was also able to speak more freely than he had before once he noticed that Narmer had relaxed somewhat. When asked why that was, Narmer began by explaining what his daily life was like, something that Primus would never have thought to ask.

Primus found it interesting to learn what went into running a kingdom successfully and the various ins and outs of life as the ruler of a kingdom, and the topic consumed most of the next two hours. Narmer became increasingly lively during their conversation, talking louder and less formally than he had previously, first merely speaking then speaking while moving his hands and even his feet. Primus suspected that despite all the power and command Narmer had, he had no one to call a friend, and Primus was quickly learning how distant it could make one appear.

They talked so long that night was falling, and it was now time for the evening meal, and even though the meal was apparently ready, Narmer instructed Primus to wait to eat. They did not have to wait long, however. A man who was announced as Imhotep walked in and sat down, and the meal was promptly served. With a start, Primus realized that he had seen this man before.

He was one of the more serious-looking men who visited Primus's cell the night he arrived in Kemet, distinguishable by his rather prominent hooked nose. Primus nearly opened his mouth then and mentioned this, but something about the man gave him pause. Somehow, he did not think Imhotep would appreciate it being said that he had been in Nekhen at a time to size up Primus before Imhotep could say something for himself.

Beyond that, Primus held his tongue for another reason. He was unable to pin down exactly what it was about the man, but something about his mannerisms or speech patterns gave Primus the impression that he was not to be trusted, and the less time Primus spent around him, the better.

The meal proceeded without incident, and Primus only spoke when spoken to, and never for very long. The following week was spent with Primus training in the mornings and into the early afternoon with a khopesh, and his late afternoons and evenings were spent with Narmer and Imhotep as they laid out their final plans and made any adjustments.

Primus was of some help here, and he was able to recommend several small improvements to the battle plans. For example, the battle was to be fought near a large rock formation, one wherein archers could be placed not just on top and on the face of the rock formation. Several blocks of archers could be hidden behind the formation and would emerge to shoot the enemy soldiers from slightly behind them on command.

Narmer had praised the move for the surprise and confusion it would cause while Imhotep railed against the idea, calling it a cowardly way to fight. Primus and Narmer argued with him until he agreed to take their side. However, Primus was not convinced that Imhotep would actually go along with the plan when the time came.

Imhotep was the type who, in an argument, would eventually be won over with long and well-reasoned arguments, only to immediately revert back to his original point of view or close to his original view if he could no longer defend it.

The first time Primus had entered the room with Narmer to go over the plans, Imhotep had objected, and it took Narmer and Primus the better part of an hour to convince Imhotep to allow Primus to be in the room while they were discussing their plans and a further half hour to convince him to hear anything Primus had to say about the plans.

In the end, the only thing Primus could do to convince the man was to walk over to the table with a map of the battle area and make an immediate suggestion that could help. Primus walked over and studied the map for several minutes then suggested the archer placement.

This led into the argument about the right way to fight a war, and it was at that time that Imhotep called Primus a coward. Narmer's fury seemed as if it would bring the roof down, crushing anyone caught save for the king himself. Imhotep quailed and reversed course immediately.

He accepted the addition to the plans and Primus being allowed to stay without question. However, it was apparent he did not trust Primus and seemingly never acknowledged anything that the younger man said. At least, not until Narmer acknowledged what had been said, at which point Imhotep would offer a response, be it a question or a comment. Occasionally, he would raise a concern to Primus, but for the most part, Imhotep tried to act as if Primus did not exist.

Mutual distrust aside, the week proceeded without further incident, and Primus was now fully proficient with his new weapon of choice. The day before the battle was uneventful as well, and Primus preferred it that way.

Without Thak and Turia or anyone he knew around him, Primus had little desire to leave Narmer's home. Toward the end of the day, Primus ate a large meal early, begging the kitchen to allow him to eat earlier so that he would not be slowed down by it at any point prior to the battle.

After a while, the kitchen gave him some food, and Primus ate and drank his fill, opting once again not to have any wine before a battle. He then opted to simply lie on the riverbank and watch the boats go by for a while. As the sun set behind him, Primus then stood and removed his clothing. He collected a jar of the same mixture he had used the day after he arrived in Kemet and scrubbed his body from head to toe.

Once he was clean, Primus sat back down on his folded clothing and allowed the slight breeze and the cooling night air to dry him, and he resumed his silent vigil. Once he was completely dry, Primus made his way back to Narmer's home, where he quickly and quietly found his way to his room. Once he was back in his room, Primus sat down on the bed and looked out of his window, thinking of all that had been and all that would be.

He was interrupted by a knock at the doorframe, and the curtains that separated the room from the rest of the hall parted as Narmer walked in. He silently walked to the window and stood there, placing his hands a little wider than shoulder width and leaning heavily on his arms, allowing them to hold his upper body as his chest fell and shoulders rose. He maintained this pose for nearly a minute before speaking.

"So tomorrow is it then. The last day either of us may have as free men or among the living. How did you spend your day, Primus?" Narmer said, his voice surprisingly quiet.

"Well, I practiced some with my weapon and shield, inspected every tiny detail, and then laid by the Aur and just watched the river for a while. I bathed, ate, and came back here just now," Primus answered honestly.

"What were you thinking about while you were laying by the water?" Narmer asked.

"I wasn't really thinking about much. I was more content just to sit and observe for the day, not to wrest meaning from meaninglessness," Primus said.

"Is this what you did before your previous battle?" Narmer asked.

"No. When I was in the same position last month, I spent the day with Turia. We wandered the city for a while and got into a little trouble. We watched men on a stage pretend they were characters from an old story, and then I took her home before I went back to the bed I was given," Primus explained.

"Ah, I see. So tell me, why do you not do something similar this time?" Narmer asked.

"I don't see much reason to. Most everything that I want to do, I want to do with Turia. I know you could order someone to be with me for the day and to do the same things we did, but it wouldn't be right. It wouldn't feel the same, and besides that, she's my betrothed. I refuse to pretend as if we are not," Primus said.

"Yes, but you could be killed tomorrow. Surely you want to experience all the pleasures this world has to offer at least once more?" Narmer queried.

"I could, but I think that if I did, I would regret it once I made it home. I couldn't hurt Turia like that. It might hurt her enough that she no longer wants me. I won't willingly let that happen," Primus said.

"Well, on that matter, I perfectly understand. I myself, however, will be spending the night with a woman." Primus raised an eyebrow at Narmer. "I can't fool you, can I? Oh, all right, with several," Narmer said with a shrug and a slight smile.

"Well, it sounds like you're going to have a good night. For my part, I think I'll sleep soon. I want to be well rested before the battle, which is also part of the reason I've eaten earlier in the night and did not plan on anything for my morning meal," Primus said.

"You're not eating in the morning? The battle likely won't be until closer to midday, maybe later than that. You can stay awake tonight, drinking and making merry for hours to come still. I can arrange for nearly anything your heart desires," Narmer said.

"Thank you, but I would prefer to remain here for the night," Primus said.

"Well, I did try at least to make the night a little more enjoyable for you. Still, if there is anything you need, please come and find me," Narmer said as he made to depart the room.

Primus watched him as he was leaving, only to be surprised when the king stopped at the doorway, the curtains parted and with a hand on the doorframe. After a moment, he turned to look over his shoulder at Primus.

"You should know something though, Primus. Your stories of words written down and immortalized in your homeland stirred something here. Such a thing has never existed in Kemet, but if I should win tomorrow's battle and unite my people, I have ordered that a system of writing will be created. Over the last week. I have spent some time with those who will become my scribes. I hope you don't mind, but I've decided to call them as you called them in your homeland," Narmer said.

"You have? And what will your letters look like?" Primus asked.

"They'll look like things we know. Storks, crocodiles, waves on the river. We're making this because of you," Narmer said, turning his head and staring straight ahead.

"I, um…wha…be-because of…me?" Primus managed to stammer out.

"Yes. We realized that even though we have always gotten by without having it, if we wish to tell a story one hundred years later, we now can. It'll mostly be used to keep track of the gold and grain we have, who bought what and when. And of course, they will write of my victory if I should win. But I've also provided instructions to them that even if I do not survive tomorrow, your story will still be written down and preserved. You will not be forgotten here, Primus. That much I can promise you," Narmer said.

"Thank you" was all that Primus could get out after half a minute of silence. Narmer nodded in an almost imperceptible movement and departed. Primus sat down on the bed, feeling dumbstruck.

He had not expected that his time here would be remembered and had failed to consider the fact that writings about himself could be passed down through the years, to be read by anyone who could read years afterward, and likely well beyond his own death.

The knowledge was strangely moving, even though Primus could not say why it was affecting him so. He also took comfort in the knowledge that the people of Kemet would one day learn how he had helped them, even if it was an indirect way of helping.

It did not matter to him that most written things would be concerning trade. What mattered to him was that was the same way that writing had started in Meftif. A simple way to keep track of what one owned and was owed, but by Primus's time, books and scrolls too numerous to mention on every topic or subject he could imagine were there to be read by anyone. Primus felt a strong sensation arise in his chest, and he realized that it was pride. Pride at having helped lay the foundations for what he was sure would be a similar future for Kemet.

With thoughts of the kinds of stories and epics that could be written, Primus lay himself down and fell asleep, where fantastical visions danced in his head. Primus had no nightmares that night nor any strange dreams to speak of. He slept easy for the first time in more than a month and awoke more rested than he thought possible.

Primus then went to the kitchens and retrieved a light meal that consisted mostly of some small strips of dried meat and two small purple fruits with pink insides that Primus had once known the name of but had now forgotten. After his small meal, Primus left the hall and found Narmer outside. He was already mounted upon his horse and dressed for battle.

Primus went back inside and retrieved his armor and weapons. Once he, too, was clad in the garments of war, he returned to Narmer and mounted his own horse, which a servant had brought out from the stable.

"So where are we going?" Primus asked.

"We are only going a few miles north of here. There wasn't much on the road between Tin and Nekhen, but farther north, there are actually quite a number of cities you haven't visited. I hope I can convince you to stay for a time, that I may show you the wonders of Kemet," Narmer said.

"I'm sorely tempted. In a way, I will be able to see many of the wonders since I have a long journey north ahead of me. I'll have to stop for supplies and to sleep at least sometimes," Primus said, and they set off.

Narmer led Primus to the northern edge of the town, where around two thousand had gathered, all dressed for war. Narmer took his place at the head of the column of men and signaled Primus to follow closely behind him. Primus rode next to Imhotep, where they sat in silence until they heard a shout from Narmer, signaling the advance.

They rode north along the road for around ten miles or so, Imhotep and Primus each as silent as the grave and studiously trying not to look at each other. The column eventually reached a certain rock formation, and in the distance, they could see a dark blot advancing toward them over the golden sand, like a stain of pitch. As they drew level with the rocks, Primus saw Narmer twist in his saddle and motioned for some of the group to begin to move behind the formation according to the plan.

Primus sat with Narmer and Imhotep as they came to a stop, with Narmer in the middle and Primus on his left, while Imhotep sat on the right. They waited for half an hour before the opposing force came fully into view. They were garbed in much the same manner as all the men who stood behind Primus, leather armor and rawhide shields. Most carried spears, and some carried swords, while others carried maces. How many archers there were, Primus could not tell, and that worried him greatly.

Narmer gestured with his hand for Primus and Imhotep to stay where they were and proceeded to ride off toward the enemy forces. A singular figure on a horse detached itself from the army and rode toward Narmer.

Once they were in the approximate center of the empty space between the two armies, they stopped and remained motionless for a while before some small movements could be seen. Primus suspected that the two were gesturing quite a bit. Whether it was in anger or not, though, he could not tell. After around fifteen minutes, the two separated, and Narmer rode back.

"What did they have to say for themselves?" Imhotep asked once Narmer had rejoined his warriors.

"They will not cede to my claim, for they wish the unified crown for themselves," Narmer said, practically spitting the words out.

"It seemed he had a fair bit more than that to say," Primus said, trying to imagine what a conversation like that would entail.

"The meaning was the same. Ready the men. They will charge at us soon, and I do not wish to stray too far from our archers," Narmer said as he turned his gaze back to the army they faced.

Primus and Imhotep turned their steeds around and rode back along each side of the column of men, each shouting to prepare to charge that they were about to fight for the future of their families.

Once they arrived at the end of the column, they turned and rode back to the head of the column at full gallop. As they arrived, they watched Narmer dismount, and both Imhotep and Primus followed the king's lead.

A great shout went up from the opposing army, and Primus felt the ground below his feet begin to tremble ever so slightly as the army began to rush headlong toward Primus and the army behind him.

So once again, I find myself staring down a charging army whose stated intent is to kill me and everyone with me. Once I get back, I need to make sure that there is no way we'll be attacked like this again. Anything else is madness, Primus thought as he stood idly, waiting for the order from Narmer to ready his weapons and charge.

When the enemy force had nearly halved the distance, Narmer turned and said something to Imhotep that Primus could not hear. Imhotep turned and signaled to an archer that had been behind him since they left Tin, and the man raised a bow he carried.

The man turned to the rock formation and drew the bow quickly before loosing an arrow at the formation, which clattered loudly off the rocks. The sound echoed loudly, and the men who were stationed on top of the formation stood and drew their bows briefly before raining arrows down on the charging army, felling many of them.

As arrows continued to rain down, the army drew closer, and Primus continued to grow tense as he waited for the signal to charge. He could hear the men behind him whispering and talking in low voices, and he heard several of them shift in place as they began to fidget.

Primus could feel his own emotions rising, although he felt more anger than fear. It frustrated him that Narmer was waiting so long to order the charge, because Primus knew that it would take the men distance to get up to speed so they could hit the enemy soldiers with their full force. It was a relief to him then that mere seconds after thinking this, Narmer bellowed his order.

"CHARGE!" Narmer's voice echoed off the stone formation to their right, bouncing off and reverberating. How long the voice continued to echo was lost to Primus, as were most other sounds as he charged forward.

Running full speed next to the king, they and several other warriors left Imhotep behind as they charged toward the line of soldiers in front of them, who themselves had not slowed their headlong rush despite the arrows that continued to rain down upon their men.

The two groups met with a ferocious and deafening crash that rang forth across the desert. Rich with the ring of metal and the dull thuds of arrows and spears striking shields, and rising above it all, as if in discordant song, were the cries of the wounded. Primus had tucked his head and braced his whole body as he reached the line of rushing warriors, and he slammed his shield into another as he entered the oncoming horde.

Primus's arm buckled under the impact of another man hitting him in the same fashion. Due to the way he was holding his shield, when Primus's arm collapsed inward, his arm closed, but the shield was kept close to his body, and the momentum Primus carried was not lost, allowing him to knock the other man to the ground. This came at the cost of his own balance, however, and Primus struggled to slow himself down without tripping or falling over and being trampled.

As he steadied himself, Primus looked around and saw that he was now behind the enemy front line. He realized that not only was he surrounded by soldiers, but those soldiers also did not seem to realize that Primus was not one of their own men. Immediately, Primus realized his advantage and began to hack and cut at the men all around him, killing many before they realized what had happened.

A few soldiers realized the severity of the problem they found themselves facing, and some turned to try and fight Primus. Most did not make it very far, only partly turning around, and most of the men Primus was fighting held spears, which were useless in such close quarters.

One man with a short sword was able to turn around and lift his shield, and rather than try to hack through the shield or batter it to pieces, as he had done when fighting Narmer's soldiers, Primus simply thrust his weapon past the man's shield and used the backward facing hook to catch the edge of the shield and rip it from the grasp of the wielder.

The man stumbled forward, his grip starting to fail, and as he straightened, Primus slashed upward and cut the man diagonally from his right hip to his left arm. Primus allowed the swing to continue, and the blade of his khopesh buried itself in the left temple of another soldier, who dropped to the ground like so much empty sackcloth.

By this time, soldiers were beginning to notice in greater numbers that Primus was not an ally, and they were beginning to turn on him faster and with increased ferocity to their strikes, a far cry from the unsuspecting men Primus had cut down earlier. Primus knew that he had to make it back to his own men soon, or he would die to the men around him.

Primus had the advantage here again as he simply turned and cut his way through the few men that separated him from the front line. Once there, he kicked the man in front of him in the back, sending him flying into a crush of warriors, who promptly skewered the unfortunate man.

Primus naturally wanted to avoid the same fate as the man he had just kicked, and he jumped back toward the safety of his own men before they had time to react and whirled around to continue fighting the soldiers he had just emerged from. This made it appear as if Primus had always been there with them and made it less likely that one of them would turn on him and stab him in the back without realizing Primus was fighting for them and not against them.

Shortly after this, Primus dropped back from the front to rest for a moment. He had not been fighting for long, but already, he felt as if he had run at a full sprint for hours without stopping. His heart pounded, sweat coursed down his body, and everything was once again visible in stunning detail. Primus could have counted each individual hair in Narmer's beard were the king in front of him.

Once he had recovered somewhat, Primus decided that it would be best for him if he found the king and fought next to him. His reasoning was simply that once the battle was over, it would be better to be closer to the man who ruled, and he would be protected from anything Imhotep might have planned. Primus had the distinct feeling that even after the battle was over, he would still be in danger due to his actions and status as an outsider.

Whether this was actually true or not, Primus was unsure, but a nagging itch in the back of his mind would not stop telling him that he would be in danger in the same way that the hairs on the back of Primus's neck would stand up when he was alone and felt as if he were being watched.

Primus began to look around for the king and spotted him at a distance. Apparently, he had been resting the same as Primus had but was closer to the front, and he had already gathered several warriors around him. He appeared to be getting ready to make a push forward and through the enemy line.

As Primus made his way over, he watched Narmer raise his hand as if he were signaling, and shortly after, there was a great cry that went up from the back of the enemy soldiers. Primus was surprised to hear it over the din of the battle, and it confused him as well.

Why would they be screaming toward what sounds like the back of the army? All the fighting is at the front, Primus thought. After a few more steps, Primus belatedly realized Narmer's signal was for the hidden blocks of archers who had just been ordered into action. Primus increased his pace and attempted to close the remaining distance before the king went back into combat. But just after Primus realized what was going on, the king turned on his heel and charged back into the fray with several of his warriors clustered around him.

Primus arrived at the front several seconds later, arriving at a scene of swirling confusion and thrashing bodies. In the scant few minutes that he had rested within the safety of his own men, the front had dissolved into pockets of fighting, sometimes one man against several, or small pockets of two and three at a time, all struggling to stay alive in the midst of spraying blood and severed limbs.

Narmer had disappeared into one of these pockets, although Primus had no idea which one. Choosing the one closest to him, with a group of two of his own men fighting against three others, Primus entered the fray. He caught a spear on his shield and hacked at the splintering haft. As the spear was pulled back, the blade detached from the haft, leaving its owner with a useless blunted stick.

Primus turned his attention to one of the other men and tried to press his newfound advantage when he felt the shattered haft impact his right thigh, poking several small holes in him. The spear haft pulled back, and Primus could feel the shards of wood pull free, groaning as they did.

Primus immediately returned his attention to the man, now more wary and with a very slight limp, blocking two more quick thrusts from the man before deflecting a third. The man stumbled forward, and Primus brought his khopesh down on the man's collarbone, just where it met his neck. The man collapsed, clutching at his wound with his good arm.

The man beside him shuffled forward and overreached with his own lunge and was stabbed in the gut. He pulled himself off the spear and fell onto his back, cupping and recupping his wound, trying to hold back the flow of blood and organs that spilled forth. Primus and the remaining soldier were joined by three others then while two more joined the enemy.

Slowly, they began to push back the men in front of them. Primus killed one, while the other three fell to the blades of those around him. Primus motioned with his shield to move forward while another two men joined. With seven strong, they moved to help two others who were outnumbered, and slowly, they grew their numbers as they assisted more of their own.

Eventually, Primus spotted Narmer's group, now down to just the king and two men, and he shouted at those with him to follow as he made his way to the beleaguered king. Three soldiers stepped in front of him, but by now, Primus's group was over twenty strong, and they made short work of the soldiers. Primus looked up from his latest kill and looked about for the king again. The king was not where he had been, and Primus spotted him again shortly thereafter, now down to just himself and his last warrior.

Primus ran forward and closed the remaining distance, careful not to get in the way of any other soldiers. He made it to the king and surprised all of them by jumping and, with both legs, kicking the man who had been harassing the king. Primus's momentum carried his kick far beyond the man Primus had hit, and he landed amid a group of four soldiers.

Primus scrambled to his feet quickly, hacking at the legs of everyone close by while he attempted to stand, causing three of the men to hop away, while Primus struck a fourth in the thigh, nearly severing the limb. This bought him enough time to get to his feet and get back to the safety of the king and the men with him.

They now turned their attention to the remaining three soldiers and made short work of them. Primus and Narmer looked at each other and nodded, and by unspoken consent, they retreated to the center of their group for a moment to rest, chests heaving as they gasped for breath. They spoke not a word, and each man used the opportunity to evaluate how the battle was proceeding.

Primus guessed that a little less than half of the original force he had faced was left, and what was left was rapidly shrinking. It seemed as though no one had seen where the additional archers had been, and they had proven to be far more effective than Primus first realized. As he inspected the field, Primus saw several clusters of soldiers nearly as large as his own forming, but many more were far larger than his own. These groups had mostly succeeded in reforming an unbroken advancing line.

Suddenly, Primus could hear Narmer laughing, and Primus turned to look at the man. The king stopped laughing, and a wide smile took over his face as he surveyed the battlefield. He had reached the same conclusion Primus had.

A horn sounded just as Primus was about to say something to the king, and the battle around them slowly came to a stop. The horn sounded a second time, and a great groan went up from the enemy soldiers, while those around Primus began to cheer.

"So does that mean what I think it means?" Primus shouted over the cheering.

"Yes, my friend, that it does! We've won!" Narmer shouted back.

"What about their leader?" Primus shouted back.

"I killed him earlier in the battle. With this victory, I now rule all of Kemet!" Narmer shouted, and he jumped in the air at the statement, crowing like a rooster from the thrill of victory.

"And you will make a fine ruler indeed, Scorpion King Narmer!" Primus shouted.

All of a sudden, a low hum could be heard filling the air, quickly increasing in volume until it had drowned out all other noise on the field. Everyone stopped and looked for its origin, both curious and fearful of the noise.

Suddenly, a ball of white light no larger than his fist appeared on Primus's stomach, and it began to grow larger, quickly enveloping him. The humming increased suddenly in pitch, and the ball vanished. Narmer began to call out for Primus, but no response was received, for when the ball of light disappeared, so, too, had Primus.

Narmer quickly realized this and ordered several soldiers to search the battlefield while he went to speak with the adviser of the former ruler of Lower Kemet. The man still held some authority and would treat with him while the soldiers would search for the missing Primus.

Chapter 17

Primus blinked twice as his eyes adjusted to the bright white nothingness that surrounded him. He looked around and realized that he had been returned to whatever strange plain he had been to a month ago. Whatever his situation had been when he had been taken from Kemet no longer mattered, and wherever the place that he would be taken to now was the only thing that held any sway or meaning for Primus. He rested a little more, his breathing returning to normal, and he began to look around his environment, hoping for some answers.

It was the same blank white expanse that he had been stuck in right after the battle of Meftif. And now after another battle, Primus found himself stuck again. He could still speak and move about as he had the last time, and the feeling of being weightless had returned, although the onset of the ball of light appearing and the humming sound that preceded it had both come about much faster than they had previously.

Last time I was brought here, after my first battle, it was nearly an hour before the light appeared, but this battle was only just finished. And it hummed for longer last time as well, not to mention the ball of light took time to grow before. Now that happened almost immediately. I didn't have any time after the battle to talk with Narmer or anyone else. I hope I figure out what's happening, and soon.

Maybe it's taking me home, though. It brought me to Kemet before, so maybe this is the return journey. Maybe I was supposed to accomplish a task, and the light is here to bring me home. I'm covered in blood again, and I stink like death, so if the light isn't taking me home, hopefully, it'll drop me next to a river. That way, I can at least clean myself up before I have to deal with another city or land where I don't speak the language.

I mean, come on, Primus, you were transported from your home to a land a thousand miles away. No one ever heard of your home, your language, you, your battle, and none of it appeared on any map they had. They couldn't even find anyone who had heard of people who lived in the area, much less a city. Something strange is going on, and hopefully, I can find out what it is, either here or when I get home. If I get home, that is. Maybe even if I'm in a place like Kemet, maybe this time, I'll be closer to home. Either I can try and escape or I can try to convince someone to go with me on a journey.

Primus's internal discussion might have gone on longer, but just then, the whiteness around him faded back to reality. The light by his feet began to disappear, and it was shortly after this that Primus dropped onto the sand once again, falling only around one or two inches. Primus looked around, trying to gather his bearings.

He was still in the desert, but now he was next to a riverbank that held many trees of different varieties, and the sheer number of animals that Primus could hear from the thick grasses and reeds surprised him. He did not know if he was still in Kemet, but it was obvious to him that he was not in Crizia, nor was he close to Meftif. None of the trees here grew in the density that Primus saw, and some of the trees he saw he knew grew elsewhere. Primus also spotted several birds of a species he did not know.

Rather than dwelling on any of this, however, there were several things all vying for Primus's attention. The biggest of these was the fact that downstream, almost out of sight but not quite, Primus spotted what looked like a farm. But it couldn't be a farm, for the field seemed to have been plowed next to, and possibly inside, the river.

Even from a distance, Primus could see the shimmering water that filled the grooves that had been painstakingly carved into the ground, and the water appeared to flow directly from the river into the field. To Primus, this made no sense, as flooding a field like that would cause the crops to become too waterlogged and die. In Primus's experience, the smiths had heated metal until it melted, and then, using a stone core, the smiths would pour the metal into a mold and allow it to cool around the core.

Once the metal was cool enough, it would be removed from the stone and would take the shape of a tube. From there, the single tube would be joined with others and secured in place with molten pitch poured on the places where the tubes joined.

The resulting length of tube could be placed anywhere on a farm, while the other end was placed in the Alabel River. And as long as the farm itself was plowed deep enough into the ground, the end of the tube could be capped or uncapped, and the crops could be watered whenever the farmer deemed it necessary.

Primus decided to wash himself of the blood and dust that coated his body, this time walking to the top of a low nearby hill to look for anyone who could sneak up on him, the same way the soldiers of Kemet had a month prior. Seeing no one, Primus went back to the river, removing his weapon and shield and hiding them beneath a nearby bush. Next, he removed his armor and placed it close to the river's edge before finally removing his clothing, right down to the sandals he wore.

Though there was nothing and no one around, Primus slowly and carefully entered the water. He did not know what, if any, animals lived in this part of the river that might try to make a meal of him. Before he got deeper than his knees, Primus had an idea that he hoped would tell him where he was, or at least if he was no longer in Kemet.

Primus immediately turned around and rushed back to the shore, where he retrieved his weapon from beneath the bush. He then went into the sun and tried to stay as far away from the trees as was prudent so that Primus could at least make an attempt to retrieve the khopesh if anyone should appear.

After debating with himself for a moment, Primus decided to simply plunge the weapon into the sand as deep as he could force it. Afterward, Primus returned to the river and began to look for two stones of differing sizes. Retrieving his stones, Primus then went and put both of them next to the khopesh, one of them he placed at the end of the shadow that the pommel cast, and the other was placed to the side and away from the first stone.

Satisfied for now, Primus went back to the river and began to wash himself, taking special care to pull any wood shards or splinters he found out of his thigh. Once he had cleaned himself, using handfuls of sand from the riverbed near the shore to scour himself, Primus retrieved his leather armor and proceeded to scrub it the same as he had himself. He repeated the process with his clothes, although they were still stained by blood.

After removing as much gore and filth from his clothing and equipment as possible, Primus left the water. It had been nearly an hour since he first entered the water, and he was eager to see if his idea had worked. Before checking on his weapon, however, Primus laid his clothes and armor out to dry, choosing to drape them over a low tree branch.

Primus walked to his khopesh and checked the position of the shadow of the pommel. The shadow no longer sat on the rock, instead having traveled to his right, moving closer to the river. Primus then placed the other rock on the pommel's shadow and removed the weapon from the sand. Below him, the two rocks sat apart, and Primus used the tip of the khopesh to draw a straight line between the two stones.

I'm a little surprised that that worked. All right, so now I have my east-west line, and since the sun moves from the east to the west, that means I'm facing north right now. S, the river flows from north to south, the same as every other river I know of, except the Aur, and since the Aur flows from south to north, I know for sure that I'm not in Kemet, Primus thought, feeling pleased with himself.

Retreating to the shade of the nearby trees, Primus collected two sticks and placed them so that he would easily be able to find his direction, placing them on the ground just outside the shade. He then went back into the sun fully and retrieved his blade.

Returning to the water one final time, Primus took the khopesh with him and scoured it under the water until he had removed all the blood that was visible on the blade, hilt, and pommel. He stood and placed his weapon atop his shield under the bush and entered the water to submerge himself one final time.

After holding his breath for a while and enjoying the feeling of the water flowing over his body and the peace it brought, Primus surfaced and made his way back to shore. There, he found a spot to sit against the base of the tree from which hung his clothing and armor. Seating himself on a large flat-topped rock, Primus leaned his head back against the tree and began to watch the river and the riverbank.

Fish jumped, turtles lounged on rocks, and birds flitted about between the trees, which themselves moved under a slight breeze. The gentle susurrations provided a backdrop of the soundscape of nature that Primus found himself listening to as his body dried. Primus sighed, content for the first time since the battle of Meftif. Here, there was no war to fight, no battle to be had, no one to kill. Primus knew that this would not last long, but he cherished the tranquility of the moment.

Since the moment he joined the army months ago, he had spent nearly every day fighting or training, and twice now, he had participated in large battles that had nearly ended his own life. Over the course of six months, Primus had spent all but a few days either fighting or preparing to fight, and the constant threat had begun to wear on him.

After an hour, perhaps an hour and a half, Primus roused himself and stood, brushing off the small amount of sand that had accumulated on his legs. After checking his clothes and armor to see if they were dry and finding that little moisture remained, Primus donned his clothing and armor before realizing the trouble he found himself in.

So now what? I can go north, well, generally northward, with the curve of the river. Going upstream, I could find a town or city and start to make my way home then, but going downstream could be the same thing. Not only that, even though I've never been to the coast, I know that there will be towns and villages, probably a city as well. I don't know which way will actually help me at this point, though.

Upstream and northward, I can start making my way home. Downstream and southward, I might find a more populated area with more resources to start making my way home. But I could be a thousand miles away from the coast for all I know, and maybe the mouth of the river isn't actually near a city. But then again, I might be near the source of the river, and there might not be any cities or towns farther north. Upstream or downstream? Either way, I think my first stop will be that farm downstream a little way. Maybe they have some food or can at least point me in the right direction. That is, as long as I can understand what they're saying, Primus thought as he made up his mind.

He would make his way to the farm, and afterward, if all went well, he would head upstream. Primus also decided to ignore some of the lessons from the time he had spent in Tin and Nekhen. Going downstream would mean more people, but more people could mean a greater chance that Primus would be dragged into a conflict he had nothing to do with and no real desire to be included in.

Primus did realize, however, that this could cause a problem for himself if he had nothing of value to present to anyone who could provide him safe passage. The only thing Primus could truly offer would be his skill as a warrior and as an adviser, as had been the case with Narmer.

It had been too long since Primus was a farmer, and despite the waterlogged farm in the distance, Primus knew that whoever it was would have developed their own methods for farming and watering their crops. As such, Primus knew that there was not much he could accomplish by sharing his farming knowledge.

Primus also spent time as a smith, but he had not been a smith for long enough to have accrued a store of knowledge that could be shared with any other smiths. Aside from very specific things, such as the metal tubing that Primus knew of to move water, there was little of value in this area for Primus as well.

Even if he were to share the knowledge of the tubing, Primus did not know how to build the stone molds that were used to pour the molten metal, nor could he accurately describe how one of the molds looked to someone who had never seen one before, and his almost total lack of artistic ability meant that he could not even draw a portrait of one to show what it would look like.

Primus could read and write, but only in the language of his home, which was something he had not been asked to share with Narmer. The king had elected to make his own system of writing, and Primus had not had a chance to see what the writing would look like.

If this new land also had no system of writing in place, Primus could try to share his own. However, this would only work if there was no written language. If writing already existed here, then Primus would once again have nothing of value to offer short of his skill with a blade.

And just to rub salt in that wound, I'll probably have to learn another language, and this time not just how to speak it. The way things have been going for me, I'll probably be stuck learning how to read and write as well. I still don't understand it, though, how any society could not have writing when they've built cities. I really hope I can get some answers to these questions here, Primus thought as he collected his weapon and started toward the farm.

Chapter 18

Primus lay on his bed staring at the ceiling, marveling at the turn of events as well as just how much his fortunes had shifted in the past weeks. His visit to the farmers had gone better than expected, although he realized that neither of the languages he spoke could be used to communicate with them. Their home appeared to have been made of bundles of reeds that had been woven and tied together so closely that they functioned more as sturdy beams of wood, and clay appeared to have been smoothed into shape and allowed to dry in the sun.

The farmers themselves had medium brown skin and black hair, which was curled on top of their heads while straight on the sides and bottom. They were clad in sheepskin skirts that were cut off perhaps two or three inches above the knee, and they had initially reacted with some shock, fear, and distrust at the sight of Primus when he first appeared to them. However, Primus was able to point to numerous small cuts and scrapes as well as the holes in his leg to show that the bloodstains on his clothes seemed to have come from mostly himself. His stomach had rumbled loudly shortly after this, and the farmer took a measure of pity on him and gave him some food.

After some time, Primus was able to make his position somewhat understandable to the farmers. He was not quite sure how it had happened, but it seemed as though the farmers realized that Primus was a lost stranger and needed more assistance in getting to wherever he was going than they could provide. Toward the end of the day, they had prepared a place for Primus to stay for the night. When morning came, the farmers wrapped some food in a blanket and pointed south.

Primus followed the river until he found a large well-worn path that cut through the surrounding area. Following the road, Primus passed numerous farms farther away from the river yet still covered in water. However, from a distance, all Primus had been able to see was the flooded field, and he had missed the smaller details.

The farm he had first encountered was one of many, and they were connected by an intricate design of channels and canals that crisscrossed the land. The result was that there were many farms, most larger than Primus was used to seeing. Although it was obviously not planting season, Primus was amazed by the amount of food that these people would be able to grow. Growing curious, Primus stopped by the corner of one field and dipped his hand into the water, which was surprisingly deep.

The handful of dirt that Primus brought back up was silt, but of a different variety than that of Kemet. Instead of the black silt that filled the Aur, the silt here was gray and claylike. The color caused Primus to cast his mind back to his encounter with the farmers, and he suddenly remembered that there had been an abundance of clay pots. He chastised himself for forgetting the farmer's home so quickly. They were the same pale gray as what he held in his hand now, and Primus realized that the silt could be pulled from the water and dried to form a clay, which these people evidently made a great many objects from.

Primus had been alone on the road at first, but soon the roads swelled with people from all stations in life. Some appeared to be dressed like the farmers in their sheepskin skirts, and a few wore a shirt of similar material. Others were clad in skirts of uncolored wool that went as far as their knees, while still more wore skirts that went nearly to their ankles. And finally, a scant few were dressed in thin wool clothing that had been dyed in vibrant colors, the skirts of which nearly always fell to the ankle.

Most everyone who was not dressed as the farmers were wore gold, silver, and copper rings and bangles on their fingers and wrists, while some were more akin to bands of metal that wrapped around their upper arms. Precious and semiprecious gemstones were visible in some of these ornaments as well, leaving Primus to wonder exactly what these people created that allowed them to display their wealth so lavishly.

Some of the wealthier people were also reading off clay tablets, and Primus was able to catch a glimpse of what was written on them at one point. What he saw was a series of vertical and horizontal lines, along with triangular and circular holes, all of which were spaced quite closely together, forming a tangled web of writing that Primus could not make sense of, no matter how hard he tried. Primus had been hoping to catch a glimpse of writing that would be familiar to him, or at least something he could try to pry meaning from if he stared at it long enough.

After two more days, the road had swelled even more, and Primus now spotted mostly men, along with a few women, who looked very different to the group with which he found himself traveling. Several appeared to have a lighter skin tone, more akin to an olive in color, and they wore garments similar to those of the majority of people Primus traveled with. Others were of a darker complexion, and all had hair the same shade of black as those Primus traveled with. The difference was in their clothing and speech.

These people were garbed in vibrant clothing of nearly every color, with long veils laying over the top of the hair of many of the women. The veils were stitched with golden thread to form intricate patterns, and they spoke an entirely different language from anything else Primus had heard in Meftif or in Kemet, and different still from the language of those whom he traveled with. Primus once again was in awe at the sheer number of languages that existed outside Meftlf, although it troubled him as well.

Nothing that had been spoken sounded even remotely like the language he and everyone he knew had grown up with. He had not even heard so much as a single familiar word, and even when people were speaking in their native languages, the way they structured their sentences sounded nothing like the way Primus knew a sentence to be structured. This would make it more difficult to learn, as Primus knew he would have to do if he wanted to make it home.

As night began to fall, Primus spotted a city on the horizon, although he knew that he would not make it inside before sunset. What surprised Primus was the size and scale of the city. It was around one-fourth the size of Meftif, and from a distance, Primus could see several prominent buildings within the city proper. This included a large structure that could have been some kind of large hall for a ruler to receive guests. Upon reflection, Primus conceded to himself that the building could be used for other purposes, including for religious reasons.

The time Primus had spent in Kemet had given him a brief understanding of the many gods and goddesses the people had worshiped, along with the shrines that had been erected to provide a holy place for each to be offered prayers.

Primus had not paid much attention to these stories and tales when he had stayed in Kemet, believing that he would not need to remember the details of such stories once he made his way home. Primus could only hope that these people did not worship the same deities or at least would not expect him to offer prayers of his own.

Primus nearly tripped then, and he returned his attention and thoughts to the road he walked. However, his attention was inexorably drawn to the distant city, and while Primus believed that there was something vaguely familiar about the shape of the city, he also believed that if someone were to press a dagger to his throat at that exact moment, he could not name what seemed to be so familiar even if his life depended on it.

As the sun touched the horizon, those on the road made camp, sharing their food with Primus as they cooked. As he sat down to eat, Primus realized exactly why the city's design seemed at once so familiar yet so different. The city was surrounded by walls that appeared to be both high and wide and which encircled the city in its entirety, although after a moment, Primus believed *encircled* might not be the correct term.

Even at his current distance, Primus could see that he was not facing the city directly but rather slightly from the side. As a result, Primus noted that the city appeared to have been constructed like an enormous square rather than the circular shape of Meftif and its walls. When Primus got closer to the city the next day, he finally saw the true size and shape of the walls. The walls were still shorter in height than what Primus was used to, these only being around two hundred feet or so in height, and the central building appeared less imposing the closer that Primus got to it as well.

Passing the walls, Primus noted that rather than simple clay that had been dried in the sun, as the farmers' homes were, these walls had been built from bricks that appeared almost like the bricks that Primus had seen used so often in Kemet. Primus stopped, however, and he looked more closely at the brickwork in the walls, surprised by what he found. The bricks were similar to those from Kemet, yes, but there were some differences that were just as striking, such as the faint sheen on the bricks, almost as if they had been cooked rather than simply being allowed to dry.

Primus left the walls of the city behind and made his way into the heart of the city. After peering into every building that had doors or windows that were not barred, Primus found what he was looking for—a large building whose interior was decorated with inlaid gold and silver. Carvings adorned the walls, and pillars carved in the strange shapes and strange human-animal creatures dotted the building. Rows and rows of shelfs stood, and on them each sat stack upon stack of clay tablets of all shapes and sizes. Nearly every single tablet showed the same markings that Primus had seen previously and were equally as inscrutable. There were some tablets that Primus thought he might be able to make out what was inscribed on them. They had several holes next to several objects that appeared to be grain, although he could not be sure.

After wandering around the library for a while, Primus eventually stumbled upon a group of four men sitting on benches that faced each other and seemed to be energetically discussing something. They all wore the same plain white clothing, and each of their skirts were so long they nearly touched the ground. Unlike those whom Primus had seen traveling, each man had had his head cleanly shaved.

They wore no jewelry or other ornamentation, but their hands appeared to be softer than most others, and Primus guessed them to be scribes. They all froze when they spotted Primus, their eyes not leaving the khopesh that was hanging from his belt. Primus attempted to ask them a question in his native tongue, only receiving confused stares back.

He tried twice more, first faster and then slower, but still received no response from the men. Primus tried several more phrases in an attempt to communicate with them, but each time, the response was the same. The men appeared to grow less worried as Primus continued speaking, appearing more intrigued than scared now. Primus stopped talking and looked first down then to his right, shaking his head in each direction. He was silent for a beat before his eyes lit up.

"I'm sorry, but I'm not sure where I am. Could one of you help me?" Primus asked, but not in his own language. The question was asked in the language of Kemet.

The eyes of one of the scribes lit up as well, and he spoke quickly and excitedly to the others around him for over a minute until one of the other scribes said something. The scribe who spoke first leaped from his seat and began to quickly make his way toward one end of the building.

The man stopped before he had gone more than three steps and turned back to Primus. The man pointed at Primus twice quickly then pointed at the ground twice and just as quickly before raising both of his hands with his palms toward Primus, using both hands in a pushing motion before turning and rushing out of sight. Primus took the man's motions to clearly mean *stay right where you are and don't move.*

Primus occupied his time by looking at several statues that he had earlier failed to notice, which dotted several alcoves. Many figures were carved. Some appeared to have been created with the intent to show a deity, while others showed animals, and still more seemed to show ordinary men.

What set these statues apart from many others that Primus had seen was the color. Each statue was beautifully painted, each detail exquisitely presented, and although Primus could not have possibly known who each statue was meant to represent, he knew that he was in the presence of great men.

Sometime later, the scribe who had left earlier returned with another scribe in tow. Just as with the previous four, this scribe was shaved and wore the white clothing of his fellows, and his hands appeared as soft as those of the others. Where this man was different, however, was in his eyes, which shone with an intensity that Primus, until now, had associated only with those who could sense a victory for themselves was close at hand. The man approached Primus, stopping several feet short and looking him over.

"So this is the stranger from Kemet that I was told about," the man said.

"Could you tell from my speech or from my equipment?" Primus asked in disbelief. He had not expected it to be so easy to communicate with someone from this city.

"Your speech, friend. My fellow scribes have heard the language of Kemet spoken before and recognized it. However, you must excuse them, for they do not speak it themselves," the man said.

"Well, I'm just glad to be able to talk to someone since no one else here seems to speak my language," Primus said, a palpable sense of relief washing over him as he spoke.

"I am sorry, friend, but we're speaking your language now," the man said with a smile.

"Oh, forgive me, I meant *my* native tongue. I speak the language of Kemet because I stayed there for a time," Primus explained.

"Ah, I see. Well, perhaps one of us here speaks your language. Please forgive me, but I do not know your name. My name, as you would pronounce it, is Gilgamesh. I was named for the ruler of Uruk, a city not far from here, which was the first to become as heavily fortified as it currently is," Gilgamesh said, evidently quite proud of his name and the history it carried.

"Well Gilgamesh, my name is Primus, and I was born in a place that no one seems to have heard of, and I'm trying to get home. I'm a professional soldier, and I just recently helped to finish a war in Kemet," Primus said.

"Welcome then, Primus, to what we call Kengir, what those in Kemet would call Sngr. The Akkadians to the north also call it Kengir," Gilgamesh said.

"Thank you for your welcome, Gilgamesh. I wish I had received such welcome in Kemet, but they were fearful and distrusting of me at the time. Fortunately for me, though, Narmer was able to grant me passage home as long as I fought for him in his attempt to unite Upper and Lower Kemet," Primus explained, and when he was finished, Gilgamesh turned and said something to the other scribes, which caused them to burst out laughing.

"You did not tell us that you also have such great wit. That is a fine jest, Primus, but you could not have possibly fought alongside Narmer," Gilgamesh said as he wiped at his eyes.

"I'm afraid I don't understand what there is to laugh about," Primus said as he looked about confused.

"You couldn't have possibly fought with Narmer, King Scorpion II, which was his official title. Among the people, he was simply known as the Scorpion King. He warred and ruled nearly a thousand floods ago," Gilgamesh said.

"Ah, you're correct. I'm sorry. I'm afraid that so long on the road might have muddled my thoughts. I am still looking to go back to my home, however, and I'm in need of supplies and a route. I also need a map to find my way. Is there a chance I could speak with the ruler of this city that I may beg for safe passage home?" Primus said smoothly, trying desperately to maintain an air of unshakable confidence, mixed with road weariness. Behind the confidence, Primus was confused and now fearful.

What does he mean a thousand floods? If the floods here are anything like what they were in Kemet, they come once a year and last for several weeks. But how? How in the name of anything sacred could that have been a thousand years ago? I fought with him days ago, Primus thought as the urge to panic grew stronger.

"Yes, I do forget myself. Please, come with me and we will get you something to eat and drink. I believe that the brewers have just introduced a new beer. Just the thing for the weary traveler. Our ruler is currently not within the city, which you would know by the name of Kish, but you may speak with him when he returns, as long as he grants you an audience. However, I think you'll have a very good chance of meeting with him as you are a professional soldier," Gilgamesh said.

"Why would he want to meet with a soldier so badly?" Primus asked.

"Because several other cities have declared war on Kish. You may not know it, spending time in Kemet, but here, each city is ruled by a different lugal, as we call them, but you would know them better by the title of king. Currently, our lugal is engaged in a war with several kings," Gilgamesh said.

"And because he's going to war, he needs every soldier he can find, correct?" Primus asked flatly, his spirits falling.

"Exactly. Sargon will be pleased, however, as anyone who has seen war will be greatly appreciated, as he will need their experience," Gilgamesh said.

"So when can we expect him back from, what was the name of the city you mentioned earlier?" Primus asked.

"Uruk is where Sargon is now. However, that is because he is currently tearing their walls apart. He will be back soon, but the fury of the other cities will follow him. Ur is the city he is the most concerned about, as they are the wealthiest in Kengir," Gilgamesh said.

"Ur? Where is it that makes it so wealthy? Is the city built on top of a gold mine, or is the lugal out raiding other cities or countries? Is he waging war with every other nation he can find on a map?" Primus asked, trying to determine the best course of action as well as whom he could or should side with if he must offer his services once more.

"No, there is no mine with gold in most all of our homeland. No, we trade with Kemet, with Elam, and many others. You've seen some of these people on the road here, I'm sure," Gilgamesh said.

"I did, but what could you offer to trade if not gold? I did not see any mines for anything else on the way here. It didn't appear to be the case in the city that much was made here either, aside from many shops selling pottery and some fabrics. How then did Ur grow to be so powerful and wealthy?" Primus asked.

"Ur is situated more or less at the mouth of the Buranuna River, which empties into the southern sea, and most of the goods from the sea trade pass through the city, which is why they have grown so wealthy. I doubt if there is another city in the world that could match the wealth on display, even in Kemet. As for what we trade, it's food. If you have not seen a map of Kengir, many of our cities are located between the Buranuna and the Idigna Rivers, although if you came directly south, you likely heard the name Idiqlat," Gilgamesh said.

"I did not hear the name while traveling. Why, should I have?" Primus asked.

"No, not necessarily. Idiqlat is the name that the Akkadians, who live in the north, call it. Coming from the north, I'm surprised that you did not hear it. In any event, I did not finish with your questions. Where we are, it is very easy to farm. So easy, in fact, that we have massive amounts more food than we could ever possibly eat, and in a greater variety as well.

"We simply sell the extra that we don't eat. The copper we use for many things, including our weapons, we get from an island in the northern sea, silver from the mountains in the north, gold from Kemet and Elam, and tin from across the southern sea," Gilgamesh explained.

"So all the gold and jewels I saw on the road were all brought here to trade for your food? Can you really grow enough for the other nations and yourselves?" Primus asked, awed by the sheer amount of food that would have to be produced to satisfy that many people.

"More nations and people could be fed by what we grow without straining anything here. Take Kish, for example. As a city of around forty thousand people, we would have enough grain and beer to drink for years if we stored all the grains and barley, although we would have to plant new fruits some years. However, I believe that the harvest of apples and dates would be enough by themselves," Gilgamesh said.

"I suppose I should ask, although I do feel rude to do so, could we continue this conversation while we eat? I've traveled far, and

I'm famished," Primus explained, hoping to see more of the city and gather more information about the people and the conflict while also secretly hoping that he would spot a way out of the situation.

"Of course, we can! Please forgive me. I did not realize how long we have been here for. Follow me, and you may feast until your belly is full to bursting, and then we will drink until you see two of everything," Gilgamesh said with a wide grin as he turned and began to lead Primus out of the library.

On his way out of the library and all the way out into Kish proper, Primus tried to be as vague as possible about the location of his home. Despite how he tried to avoid the questions around his home, he was forced to answer some of the questions directed at him.

Primus was able to somewhat turn this to his advantage after describing the physical location of Meftif, which Gilgamesh said sounded as if the city was located in a stretch of land considered empty and just north of some verdant plains that Primus vaguely remembered being south of his home.

Primus was unable to pinpoint the exact area, however, as there was no map readily available for him to begin to plan his journey home. Despite the lack of a map, Primus learned that the trip would only last around two weeks on horseback, although the trip could be made in one week provided that Primus and anyone with him traveled by boat instead by horse.

Primus was able to learn some more about Kengir as well, such as how goods could be moved more quickly from the northernmost cities to the southernmost before those goods could spoil. The goods were loaded onto flat-bottomed boats and barges, which would then be attached to two oxen.

The oxen would then tow the boats down one of the countless canals that had been dug. The oxen were able to lead the boat and set the speed by walking next to or in front of the boat thanks to towpaths that had been cleared next to the river, which made for a much easier journey and a quicker delivery of goods.

Primus also learned more about Kish and some of the surrounding cities. In addition to each city being ruled by its own lugal, each city also had a patron deity who would watch over the city and provide good fortune and good health to those who lived within. The deity of Kish was called Zababa, and it was partly at the urging of the high priest that the previous lugal stepped down from the throne, leaving the open seat to Sargon.

From everything that Gilgamesh was able to tell him, Sargon was cut from the same cloth as Primus himself was. He was a military man, highly intelligent, capable of making the correct decisions in times of stress and without all the details, and had garnered a reputation for confounding his enemies. He was viewed as an outsider, however, as he had been born in the northern reaches, which were controlled by the Akkadians.

Gilgamesh went on then to explain that the Akkadians and the *black-haired people* lived alongside one another since the founding of the first cities, *black-haired people* apparently being the literal translation of what these people called themselves. After pressing Gilgamesh a little more than he would have otherwise thanks to the beer, Primus learned that they would accept being called by a different name as long as it was the Akkadians doing the calling.

The name was the *Sumerians*. Gilgamesh made it clear that he was no fan of the name, going on to tell Primus that using that name was somewhat of a mild insult to them. The Akkadians looked down slightly on Gilgamesh and those like him, believing them to have grown soft in the years they lived in cities. Primus promised never to call Gilgamesh or any of the black-haired people by that name whilst in any city.

Eventually, night descended on Kish, and Primus needed somewhere to sleep. Gilgamesh offered him a room for the night, promising to help Primus find accommodations where he could stay with little money until Sargon returned to Kish. Primus thanked him, and together, they stumbled out into the streets and eventually to Gilgamesh's home.

The home itself appeared to be made from baked bricks, the same as the outer wall. When Primus mentioned it to Gilgamesh, he burst out laughing. Primus waited for his mirth to subside before asking again why the bricks would be so similar. Primus had been laughed at too many times in Kemet for this to upset him, as he was ignorant of these people's lives, customs, and habits.

"The reason this is so funny t-to me, P-Primus, is because baking the brick, the bricks, is what makes them special. Makes them strong, and makes th...makes them last. It's as the gods commanded. Our finest bricks and our pottery, those are...th-those...those are the things we may bake that aren't bread," Gilgamesh slurred out eventually, hiccupping several times.

Primus was pleasantly surprised when he entered the home as the floor was covered in reeds and was far softer and springier than what it should have been, and Primus spied a light gray substance underneath some of the reeds as they flexed under his feet.

Primus turned around and looked for Gilgamesh, only to see him disappear up a ladder at the front of the house. Primus walked back outside and turned toward the ladder, looking up and expecting to see Gilgamesh making some kind of hasty repair, only to be utterly confused when Gilgamesh reappeared and beckoned him up the ladder, a bedroll over one shoulder.

Primus climbed the ladder and was astounded to see Gilgamesh's family lying on the roof, wrapped up and sleeping. He looked back and forth at Gilgamesh and his family, mouth agape, as he tried to understand what he was seeing, all while Gilgamesh giggled uncontrollably. After nearly five minutes, Gilgamesh calmed himself down enough to speak.

"It's too hot inside at night to sleep comfortably, so we all just sleep on the roof since it's cooler. The clay keeps too much heat. I've got a bedroll here for you. Now lay down. We have a lot to do tomorrow," Gilgamesh said.

"What's tomorrow again?" Primus asked, his tongue feeling thick.

"Tomorrow, I need to teach you to speak my language and also find you a map," Gilgamesh said as he turned over and made himself more comfortable. Primus simply walked over and unrolled his blankets and went to bed.

The following two weeks proceeded much as the first day had, with Primus learning to speak the language of Kengir and also some

Akkadian. Not much, but some words and phrases, enough to get by if he needed to, along with something of the history of Kengir. The only other thing to do was await the return of Sargon.

Primus was surprised to learn that scribes had as much political persuasion as they did, and when it was reported that Sargon was getting close to Kish, Gilgamesh arranged it so that Primus would be staying in the palace so that he could be received by as early as possible. It seemed that Sargon had heard something about a man from beyond the northern reaches, north of the edge of the Akkadian lands.

So Primus now lay in a soft bed, thinking over everything he had learned these last weeks, and he thought over how he could make his case to the lugal. He was initially planning on making his case that he could introduce Sargon to the rulers of Meftif and promise aid in his battles, but he eventually discarded the idea as he had no idea if it was actually one thousand years since he last saw his home.

Eventually, Primus gave it up and resolved to attempt to build a speech in the morning, just after he had awoken and eaten, for soon after, he would have to find a way to get himself out of Kengir and on the route back to his home.

Chapter 19

Primus stood before the age-stained doors to Sargon's chamber. The doors themselves were intricately carved with scenes of farmers harvesting their crops, of workers building walls and temples, of women weaving clothes and spinning clay into vases and urns, while still others showed soldiers marching along a road.

Under other circumstances, Primus might have requested to move his meeting with the lugal to a later time, feigning illness or perhaps debilitating hunger that would force him to meet later in the day while actually studying and gazing at the doors. As it was currently, Primus stood in quiet fear before these carved doors.

He was not fearful of speaking with a king, a lugal, or someone of importance, as he had done several times before now. The reason for his fear was twofold, with the most pressing reason was that Primus was unsure what he was going to say or do or what he could offer the lugal. When Primus had gone to bed the previous night, he promised himself that he would be get up in the morning and write his speech down on the clay he had been provided, or he would at least go over a some of the things he wanted to bring up to Sargon.

However, when Primus awoke the next morning, the sun had not quite yet crested the horizon. One of the palace slaves had been sent to wake him, and it was their duty, so he was told, to inform the honored guest that Lugal Sargon would receive him shortly. Primus had quickly dressed himself, finding it slightly harder to fit into his shirt after so long without training his body.

After Primus had dressed, he was led through the palace until he stood before the door to Sargon's chambers. At this time, the slave left Primus, informing him that he would be shown in shortly. Primus had been trying to collect himself since, attempting to make something of a coherent statement and plea for help.

Thus far, he had met with limited success. Sargon was from the northern area of Kengir and was an Akkadian by birth, and it had been a substantial amount of time since he had seen his home. However, Sargon had been on the throne in Kish for less than a year and was apparently only around five years older than Primus, although he had heard conflicting numbers whenever anyone spoke of his age.

Much like Primus, however, Sargon was a strategist and a warrior. Unfortunately for Primus, the lugal had already seen several more successful battles than Primus had, and he was just now returning from Uruk, the best-fortified city in all of Kengir and with the highest walls. Sargon had apparently gone to the city with a small force of men, and with only those men and his will, Sargon had conquered the city and destroyed sections of its walls.

He had enjoyed much of his success during the light fighting that followed because Uruk itself was only lightly garrisoned at the time. The majority of the soldiers had gone with Uruk's lugal on a campaign farther to the south, apparently to put down a rebellion in a city whose name might have been Umma, if Primus decided to trust a hazy memory, half submerged in beer.

The name of the lugal who ruled Uruk was lost on Primus, but he knew that invading someone's city and destroying their prized walls was sure to anger a proud lugal, and as a result, an attack was sure to come to Kish before long. Primus racked his thoughts, trying to remember something else about the lugal with a missing name, and gradually, he started to remember.

The lugal of Uruk was the latest in a line of lugals who attempted to claim the entirety of Kengir for themselves and had faced tough fighting to conquer the cities when he had taken them, and several cities had been in open rebellion, including Lagash and Umma. As a result, he spent most of his time away from the city that he called his home, and that was when Sargon knew that it was time to strike.

How exactly Sargon had conquered the city, no one could say for sure, as no reports had come in from those who were there. Conversation focused more on the destruction of what Primus had later learned were the sacred walls of the city and the wrath of the god of the city for the desecration of what was rightfully theirs. That, and the swift revenge of the lugal who claimed himself king of Kengir.

How Primus was supposed to treat with a man who had done all of this and had been fearless enough to challenge the conqueror of Kengir, he was not sure, but he hoped to appeal to Sargon's warrior spirit, as well as a desire to be back in his homeland. Primus decided then that that was the best approach, and that further thinking on this matter would only harm his chances of an easy journey home.

Once again, Primus's eyes were drawn to the doors before him and the delicately carved images. He inhaled deeply and was met with the faint aroma of cedarwood, and he suddenly remembered something Gilgamesh had taught him not long after his arrival. Cedar was not just a prized wood because of its naturally pleasant scent and resistance to being eaten by termites, but it was a holy wood used only in the construction of palace and temple doors, as well as the support beams for the same. That, and that it came from cedar forests that grew in the far northern reaches of the lands, along the old shallow sea that Primus had once wished to visit, made the wood incredibly valuable to the lugals and high priests.

Primus's thoughts were interrupted when the doors began to swing inward, and a richly painted room with vibrant colors met his eyes. Gold, silver, and copper had been used here in an even greater abundance than the rest of the palace. Sumptuous tapestries rich in color and design had been hung all over the room, and Primus even spied several gemstones dotting the walls, although what type of stones had been added to the walls and even some statues Primus could not be sure, as his attention was drawn elsewhere.

Specifically, his eyes quickly found and rested on the partially turned figure of Sargon. He was clad in an ankle-length skirt that had been dyed in a rich purple color, while an ornamental dagger hung from a belt studded with gold rivets. His arms and chest were bare of clothing, although he wore several armbands, rings, and bracelets on each arm, and around his neck hung a golden pendant bearing a design that, from a distance, Primus could not make out. Sargon's hair was not entirely visible, as the top of his head was covered by an ornate cap, which itself appeared to be held in place by a golden band. What was left of Sargon's hair fell from under the cap and was curled, while his beard had been immaculately and painstakingly curled into incredibly small curls that, at a distance, appeared to give the beard a wavy appearance akin to distant ripples. On his feet, rather than the leather sandals that most of the other people in Kengir wore, leather boots were visibly sticking out from the bottom of his skirt.

As Primus entered the room and started toward the lugal, Sargon's gaze turned toward him. His dark eyes sported heavy bags, and despite the confident manner in which he presented himself, Primus noted great strain in him. The hard line of his throat, just visible past his beard, in addition to the bags under his eyes. As Primus got closer, the fine web of delicate lines that stretched from the corners of Sargon's eyes to his hairline appeared. His shoulders were rigid, as if he had been carved from stone, and his mouth, which appeared finely carved and expressive, also sported a matching pair of lines around the corners.

"So this is the stranger from the north," Sargon said as he turned to face Primus.

"I am," Primus replied simply.

"I'm told you found your way to my city without food, water, and looking as if you had just arrived from a battle. Then you say that your home cannot be found on a map, yet you insist that it is there. Yet now you stand before me in a time of war, when my enemies surround my city, and you would ask me to let you go? To give you safe passage?" Sargon finished, skipping most of the introduction and pleasantries that Primus had expected, and as he now realized, would have counted on to help in his appeal to Sargon.

"I would ask that. My only desire is to return home, and safe passage through these lands would be appreciated greatly," Primus said.

"In a time of war, you wish for me to allow a possible spy to simply walk away from Kish? Do you think I am a fool?" Sargon asked dryly.

"Of course not, and I meant no such disrespect, my king. I only wished to ask that I be allowed to return to my home in the north. I understood you to have hailed from that land as well. Surely you would not deny someone their desire to return to their homeland?" Primus asked, fighting the urge to smile as he saw a potential route to gaining his passage home.

"Yet you intend to take me for a fool. You do not speak the language of Kengir well enough, and I will not ask you in Akkadian either, for I have no desire to hear the language of my home defiled by one such as yourself. Be truthful now, an speak the language of your homeland. Be you Elamite, Guti, or some other abomination that seeks to weaken us from within? Speak!" Sargon barked, his anger rising fast enough that Primus feared he would lose his chance.

"I, of the city of Meftif of the land Crizia, wish to return home to my betrothed, my home, and my station as a likely general within their armies," Primus said in his native tongue.

Sargon took a half step backward, placing his right leg back somewhat and turning his shoulders so that his left pointed more toward Primus in an unmistakably defensive stance. Sargon scowled then, dipping his head slightly and glaring at Primus, though whether in anger, fear, curiosity, or some combination of the three, Primus could not tell.

"What manner of trick is this?" Sargon said softly in Akkadian.

"It is no trick," Primus said, also in Akkadian. However, his speech was slow and halting.

"Then explain yourself. Start by telling me your name and how exactly you came to be within my city. You may ignore what you have done in Kish since you arrived, as I know you spent time with the scribe Gilgamesh to learn the language we speak," Sargon said, switching away from Akkadian.

Primus proceeded to tell the story of how he came to stand before Sargon, starting at first with a brief description of his childhood, followed by the death of his family, some of the time he spent as a smith, his self-imposed training, his run-in with the law setter, his time training with Meftif's army, formulating his battle plan, the battle itself as well as the trouble with his first general, his victory over the three armies he had faced, the strange events afterward, his time in Kemet, his meeting with Narmer, his contributions to the planned battle, the battle itself, the strange events that repeated themselves after the battle, and what Primus had done once he arrived in Kengir and until he reached Kish.

Despite being told earlier that he could skip the telling of what happened after arriving in Kish, Primus decided to finish his story entirely, although the only things of note that he could add was the learning of the history of Kengir and scouring everything he could find for any mention of his home. When he finished, Primus's throat felt raw from talking for so long, and he looked about for something to soothe his parched tongue. He was shocked at how much time had gone by, as it was now late morning with perhaps an hour remaining until noon. Primus walked to the other side of the table and unstopped a jar of watered-down morning beer, which he poured into a nearby cup and sipped lightly while he waited for Sargon to speak.

"And you could find no mention of your home anywhere? Even with several of the scribes searching for the records?" Sargon asked after a long silence.

"I found absolutely nothing, and the same is true of the scribes. Nowhere is my homeland mentioned, even in legend. But why do you ask, my king?" Primus queried.

"You may simply call me Sargon, Primus, and there's no need to be so formal with me now. I've heard the languages of everyone, every land, and every people who trade with us, and even the nomads who live along the fringes of Kengir. Tribes like the Guti sound more like dogs barking than anything human. Elamites and the mountain valley people all sound a very specific way, and even Kemites have brought some Nubian slaves.

"I say this because out of every language I've heard and out of every people that I've dealt with, your language is completely unique. Akkadian and Sumerian languages may be very different in how they sound, but at least there are a few similarities, and there's a common tongue from even further back, although that's now so long ago that no one knows quite what that sounded like, but we think we can guess it. Your language is even further removed, and nothing like it exists in the world now. Primus, I think I believe your story," Sargon said softly, the wonder plain in his voice.

"You honor me with your belief in my story. Will you allow me safe passage then to attempt to return home?" Primus asked.

"I will. You will have no trouble in Kish, and rather than just allowing you safe passage, I will come with you," Sargon said.

"Forgive me, Sargon, but why do you wish to come with me? I'm afraid I don't understand," Primus said.

"I *will* be coming with you for several reasons. First, even though I believe your story, that doesn't mean I trust you. You could just be a scout who is going to inform Meftif of the current weakness of Kengir so that you may attack and conquer us while we are otherwise engaged. The second reason is that for too long, I have not visited my home, and I wish to do so before the coming war. And third, I promised my warriors that they would wash their weapons in the northern and southern seas. When I told them this, I meant that I would lead them to victory, and we would control all of Kengir, but now I think I may be able to allow them to actually wash their weapons in the northern sea," Sargon said.

"And doing that will allow you to keep your promise in the truest sense. Thank you, Sargon," Primus finished.

"We will make ready to depart at once. I don't know if anyone has told you the truth of what is going on here, but if they have not, I will do so briefly," Sargon said.

Sargon spent the next half hour or so informing Primus of the goings-on, how several lugals had attempted to rule over all Kengir, but no one had done so successfully for a particularly long time. Rebellions and other lugals with ambitions to rule often destroyed the fledgling empires. Against this, Sargon had already declared war on the current ruler, making Kish the sole city to stand against the might of all Kengir.

He then briefly described how the current ruler, a priest-king originally from Umma named Lugalzaggesi, had come to power and chosen Uruk as the city he wished to call the center of his power, rather than Kish, which had been the previous seat of power. Sargon then described how, even at that moment, Lugalzaggesi was visiting several cities and commanding the ensi, or governors of the cities, to stand with him and fight against Sargon.

"If he succeeds in rallying every governor to his cause, it will be myself and Kish as the only city to stand against the might of a nation. I tell you all of this so you understand something of my position. I wish to go with you and even stated I would travel with you, but I will not truly be able to do so. I am needed here to oversee the defenses of the city and make sure that I would not come back to a smoking ruin," Sargon finished.

Primus was silent for a time as he pondered Sargon's predicament, wondering how he could turn the situation to his own advantage. He was silent for a few moments until a wide smile broke out on his face.

"Sargon, I think I have a solution to both of our problems," Primus said, and he quickly explained his plan to the lugal. Once Primus finished, it was Sargon's turn to ponder in silence, contemplating the feasibility of the plan.

"And you're sure that this will work? You're sure that we could do this?" Sargon asked.

"No, not really," Primus admitted.

"Then how do you expect me to stake my empire, my future, my life, and the lives of my children on this?" Sargon demanded.

"Because it's the best chance you have. Recruiting as many of your fellow Akkadians as you possibly can gives you the best chance to win because your forces will match those of Lugalzaggesi. You can promise them greater wealth and more power once you take the throne, as I suggested, or you can offer them anything else they need or want. They would only have to march for you," Primus said.

"Even after so long, though, do you really think they would march to war with those they've long considered friends and neighbors?" Sargon asked.

"They will if they march behind one of their own. Without you to lead them, the Akkadians will stay where they are. But with you to lead them, you could usher in an Akkadian age. All the stories that I've heard about you before now made it clear where you came from, and the other Akkadians will see you as their path to rule as well," Primus said.

"That will put me at the mercy of the Akkadian cities," Sargon said pointedly.

"What difference would there be then between calling on them to help? If you don't and somehow win this war, you'll be at the mercy of Umma, Uruk, Ur, Lagash, and every other city. Yes, you may not have much to fear from anyone you place in command of those cities, but the people could rise up and rebel against you and put you to their mercy. You said it yourself. Lugalzaggesi was not at Uruk because he was putting down a rebellion. If you call on the entire other half of your nation to help, the people who make up large numbers of people in the cities you wish to control, then you will need their help," Primus explained.

"I still don't like this. It feels as if I'm shackling my fate to the other Akkadians. As proud as I am of my bloodline, relying on anyone else to help me win this war makes me feel as if I've not proven myself. It's as if I did not have the strength to defeat Lugalzaggesi myself," Sargon said bitterly.

"You said it yourself earlier today. You *don't* have the strength needed to stand against him, not when he has the potential to have fifty governors and their forces marching with him. You need the help of the Akkadians, whether you like it or not," Primus said.

"But what about the walls of Kish? Are you sure that this is the best way?" Sargon asked, the pain in his voice almost imperceptible.

"It is. Unless we have a way to further shield your warriors from arrows and stones cast at them, then we may as well surrender now and beg for Lugalzaggesi's forgiveness," Primus said.

"I still do not like this. But I will go to the Akkadians, and I will plead for their help. Along the way, I'll escort you to your home so that you may once again look upon the high walls of your city," Sargon said.

"Thank you, Sargon. I can't tell you how much this means to me," Primus said, relief washing over him. "So when do we leave?"

"Within the hour," Sargon said, and he leaned over a table and began to move grains around that rested on a map, which Primus guessed represented the placements and garrisons of soldiers, and the two men fell to discussing their journey.

Chapter 20

Primus looked into the depths of the campfire, unsure of what he should think or how he should feel. It had been nearly two weeks since he and Sargon had left Kish with ten warriors, and Primus was so close to his home that he could almost taste it. They were all camped around a large fire that burned inside the circle of four-wheeled wagons that had been outfitted with light armor and in which rode the soldiers.

Primus had asked after the wagons, discovering that the wagons were the original form of another type of four-wheeled wagon that had been outfitted for war. They had apparently been used for the last nine hundred years or so, and chariots, which were built for warfare, were constructed differently from the wagons they had all traveled in so far. The soldiers would enter the chariots from the rear, one archer and a chariot driver. Both men would be armored, and javelins were mounted on exterior quivers to be hurled at enemy soldiers.

True chariots were constructed using lightweight materials and were lightly armored, with modified wooden shields that were slanted forward slightly. While light, the chariots were powerful and much faster than any man could run. As such, they were the terror of the battlefield, and few could hope to slow even one of the horse-drawn monstrosities, much less stop it.

The horses, however, were not horses but were apparently more closely related to a donkey, although they were taller and much faster than an ass. Primus had been surprised to learn that horses had not yet been domesticated in Kengir, but Sargon had planned to change that. Prior to their leaving, Primus had learned that Sargon had made some changes to the usual type of battle formation as well as helping to make a new type of bow made from several layers of different types of wood and held together with a sticky substance made from rendered animal fat that Sargon had called glue. The battle formation and the plan that Sargon and Primus had put together to use it, once Sargon returned home, was already in place and being taught to the soldiers that remained in Kish.

The plan consisted of removing some of the bricks that made up the walls of Kish, creating extra windows that an archer might fire an arrow through, or that those who used slings could use to fire rocks out. Heavy pots were also being brought in from every town and village friendly to Sargon so some could be filled with water and others with oils. Once in place on the wall, these pots would be heated then poured over the walls to scald those below. For the outer defenses of the city, a second plan had been created and put in place. As tall and strong as the walls of Kish were, Sargon was only too aware of how easily the walls that protected them could become a prison from which there was no escape.

Primus had initially suggested that they seal the gates to the city and pack the inside with a mound of loose clay so that breaking the doors down would be impossible. If the gates were sealed this way, even setting them ablaze would do little to help Lugalzaggesi. Sargon, however, declined to implement this and reasoned that it would only make escape impossible if defeat became inevitable. Sargon went further, telling Primus that during the battle, the scribes that traveled with Lugalzaggesi would be working out how much dirt to pack against the side of the walls to create a ramp that would allow soldiers to walk up to the top of the wall and engage the soldiers atop the ramparts.

To slow the advance of the soldiers, the doors would be left unblocked so that groups of soldiers could leave the city and harass the soldiers building the ramp. The soldiers' formation consisted of a phalanx in the center, slowly advancing, flanked by bowmen and slingers, as Sargon called them. Behind them would be some of the more heavily built wagons pulled by oxen and piled high with replacement weapons, essentially turning them into mobile armories.

Some of the chariots would then ride out, passing in between the two armies and around the phalanx, shooting arrows and throwing javelins into the opposing army. Once past, they would continue to ride until they were behind their own men again before turning around and making another pass.

Sargon's plan involved fewer men inside the phalanx, now only being six rows deep, holding large bronze rectangular shields horizontally in front and above the heads of the others to protect from arrows and stones, thrown bricks, or even smaller clay rounds that could be launched quickly and accurately from slings. Though they were not as lethal as an arrow, they still hurt and could injure a man quite severely. Primus, too, had begun to work on a plan, but it was a plan that could only come to fruition if Sargon succeeded in rallying the Akkadians to his cause.

Since they had left Kish, Sargon had gone to every town and village, as well as some of the larger cities located farther to the north. At every stop, he had attempted to recruit soldiers to join his army and assist in his fight with Lugalzaggesi. He had met with some success, although few of the towns and villages pledged their full support. Many of the Akkadians promised to aid Sargon, though the numbers of men they could pledge were low. Many of the individuals left for Kish shortly after a visit from the lugal, and Sargon's forces were beginning to grow. However, it was fewer than either Primus or Sargon would have liked to see.

Still, there was some hope, as neither of them were sure as to the size of the army they would be facing down, and Sargon's victory at Uruk had roused many in Kish to fight, as well as many from outside the city. Some of those who were close to fighting age were conscripted, along with those who were otherwise considered too old. Together with the volunteer Akkadians, the two men hoped to be able to match the forces of Lugalzaggesi, if not amass a larger force than he had at his disposal.

After nearly a week of traveling and after many new volunteers, Primus revisited his addition to Sargon's plan. Primus had initially thought to place several archers using the new, and by all accounts, far more powerful bow made from materials composited on the backs of chariots and to use them to keep any other soldiers busy with more consistent passes.

From what he had been led to believe, Sargon's bow was roughly the same weight and length as the previous bows but was three times more powerful and more accurate at a longer range. Putting these on some of the chariots would mean that some could harass soldiers at close range, while others could do so from long range. Combined with sending the long-range chariots to ride alongside the forces they were attacking, the result was that attacks could now come from all directions, and this would sow confusion in the enemy soldiers' ranks.

He broached the topic while riding in Sargon's covered wagon, and after some time had passed, Primus succeeded in convincing Sargon that this very tactic would be necessary, and much later into the conversation, Sargon admitted to Primus that he had thought it over and realized how much the idea could shift the balance of power on the battlefield. Sargon had a scribe take down the instructions and give them to some of the conscripts at the next town they entered to take back to Kish.

The day after this, their party stopped by the shore of the northern sea, and everyone, including Primus, washed their weapons in the water and fulfilled half of Sargon's promise to his men. There was much celebration afterward, and Sargon spoke of it in every speech or meeting he had with potential soldiers thereafter.

Primus remembered all of this and more as he sat next to the fire, now so near to his own home, and he began to think of what he might say to Sargon and his men when the time came for them to part ways, or what Sargon might wish to say to Primus. For that matter, Primus was not sure what he would say to Turia or Thak when he arrived home. However, the closer to home he got, the more uneasy Primus began to feel.

He thought back to how Gilgamesh had described hearing that Narmer had unified Kemet so long ago. He thought back to how Sargon had reacted to hearing him speak in his native language and how no one alive today spoke anything that was even remotely similar, and Primus was forced to tear his mind away from the growing feeling of disquiet.

My home is close by. I know it is. It has to be. It's the largest city in one of the most well-traveled areas in the world. It stood for hundreds of years and will continue to stand for hundreds more. Thousands of years, in fact. It's right there, and I'm almost home. Hold on, Turia, Primus thought. He retrieved his bedroll and laid it out, simply turning over and going to sleep without speaking a word to anyone.

When they broke camp in the gray light of predawn the next morning, Primus and Sargon rode wordlessly through the desert. It was perhaps an hour until noon when a shout went out from the wagon driver. Primus did not bother to wait for the covered wagon he and Sargon traveled in to stop, instead opening the door and stepping outside, matching the speed of the wagon before rapidly slowing from a run to a stop.

There was nothing. There was no city, no river, no verdant farms leading up to Primus's home. Off to his right, he could see where the dried riverbed of what used to be the Alabel River, but ahead of him, there was nothing that even resembled ruins, much less a functioning city. Only a barren waste as far as Primus's eye could see.

No one spoke to Primus as he slowly walked away from the soldiers who had traveled with him and into the wastes before them. Eventually, after what felt like an eternity, Primus stopped and simply looked from his left to his right. Slowly, he reversed course and started to look from his right to his left, as if he could remake the world if only he believed hard enough and looked again.

Primus's breath caught in his throat and became ragged. His shoulders fell forward and slumped in despair, while his eyes acquired a glazed look as they slid across the vacant landscape. He jumped a little when a heavy hand suddenly and very lightly appeared on his shoulder, and Sargon stood even with Primus as his mind reeled from the implications of what he saw.

"I'm sorry, Primus, but it looks like there is nothing here and no one around for miles," Sargon said softly.

"I won't accept this. I *can't* accept this. I refuse. There has to be something here, even if it's buried in the sand. I'll lead the way. Come with me," Primus said quickly, shaking himself into awareness and ignoring the calls of Sargon and several of the other soldiers as he sprinted forward.

Toward the place where Turia's home should have been, Primus continued to run at a dead sprint, leaving the other soldiers far behind. He only hoped that he would be able to find something, *anything*, to show him that someone lived here, that there had once been some*thing* here.

Before long, Primus stood before the place where Turia's home should have been, and in a place where Primus had stood so many times in years past, there was only more desert that stretched as far as Primus could see. He dropped to his knees then and began scrabbling in the sand as he started to dig. After several inches of sand had been cleared away from a spot in front of him, Primus reached into his belt and removed his dagger, which he used to help clear away some more sand.

It took nearly another minute after this before Sargon and the other soldiers were able to catch up to Primus. They stopped and looked at him, as if no one present was capable of helping the man before them to dig. After he had cleared away nearly two feet of sand in front of him, Primus suddenly felt resistance on the very tip of his dagger. Primus redoubled his efforts and hacked at the grains before him as he fought to free whatever the object was from its earthy tomb.

It was a book. A leatherbound book with what once could have been an intricately carved cover, the pages faded and yellowed severely. Primus gingerly ran his fingers over the cover, the bottom corner of which broke off when touched, and slowly, Primus opened the cover along with several pages. The words printed on the page were almost illegible due to age, the ink having faded until it nearly blended with the page itself. Slowly, Primus deciphered some of the words that had been written so long ago, reading them to the assembled warriors.

"Today marks the anniversary of our victory over the forces of Sodom and Gomorrah. I will be going to the festival today to celebrate," Primus read out slowly. He tried for several minutes to make out anything else, but in the end, he gave it up as hopeless.

"I'm sorry, Primus. It seems as if you really have been telling the truth. But there's nothing here anymore. No one has lived here for thousands and thousands of years. If you truly did call this place home, then you are ancient indeed," Sargon said softly and solemnly.

Sargon motioned to his men, and they wordlessly turned and left Primus to mourn the loss of his home and everything he had worked so hard to get back to. Primus stayed as he was for a long while before he wordlessly returned to Sargon's wagon, which the lugal stood next to. He waved his guards away as Primus drew closer. The younger man said nothing when he reached the wagon, merely turning his back to it and resting against it as he gazed out into the endless expanse that had swallowed his home.

"What would you do if it were you, Sargon? If everything you ever knew vanished in the blink of an eye? How would you handle that?" Primus asked.

"I'm not sure, Primus. I really couldn't say how I would feel if everything I thought I knew turned to dust in front of me," Sargon said slowly, appearing shaken by the thought.

"Sargon, all I've been trying to do for months now is to get home. And now I make it all the way here, only to find out that everything I was trying to get back to was ground into sand before Narmer was even born. What did I do all of that for?" Primus asked.

"You did all of that because you believed it would lead you home, and it has. It's just that now your home is gone, and you must make a new one for yourself," Sargon said.

"And just what exactly is that supposed to mean? Make a new home for myself?" Primus said sarcastically.

"I mean exactly that. You can make a home for yourself anywhere you wish to, and you may begin to rebuild your life. If you assist me in my war when we get back to Kish, you will have your original position. I will make you a general and put you in command of many men, and you will have your choice of women from my court to bed, either for a night or for your life if you wish to take a wife," Sargon said.

Primus did not respond for a long time as he considered Sargon's offer. He did not want another woman, but it pained him to realize that after enough time, Turia would have taken another man as a husband at her father's insistence. Primus also knew now that there was no way to return home, and for him, that wound was still too raw to consider anyone else sharing his bed yet. All the rest, while not being home, eventually could be similar enough that Primus could at least try to fool himself into believing he was home.

"All right, Sargon. If you agree to make me a general, I will fight for you, but for women, I think I will wait before I take you up on your offer," Primus said.

"I'm glad to hear it, Primus. Now then, shall we ride for Kish?" Sargon asked as he opened the door to the wagon.

Chapter 21

Primus exited the wagon that he and Sargon had shared, stepping out onto the waste-strewn streets of Kish for the first time in three weeks. After finding nothing left of his home, Primus had initially said nothing to Sargon, only stepping into the wagon and listening vaguely as Sargon went on to describe the history of his home as honestly as he could. While Primus did not pay much attention to the man, choosing to ignore him in favor of his own thoughts as he stared out the window, he did hear everything Sargon said. Due to this, he occasionally heard Sargon deviating quite a bit from some of the things Primus had learned during his time with Gilgamesh.

Primus believed that the differences he heard were due in part to the differences between his education and Sargon's education. Sargon had lived in the palace since he was made cupbearer for the lugal at the time and learned the history as it was passed down directly rather than some kind of historical facsimile that was distributed to any who could read or to foreigners who learned to read the densely packed symbols.

Whether this was actually true or just what Primus had come to believe due to his incomplete knowledge and his obstinate refusal to properly listen for the first days of the journey back, Primus certainly could not say. For his part, Sargon had talked the entire rest of the day, filling any moment of possible silence with the sound of his voice.

Though Primus had initially been annoyed at the constant chattering of the man across from him and almost asked him to stop on several occasions, he never said anything to Sargon. When they stopped for the night, Sargon and his warriors set up several games for themselves. Games of strength, speed, agility, and much more. They all invited Primus to compete with them, but Primus declined, opting instead to sit in silence and watch them without truly seeing what they were doing.

The next day had proceeded much the same as the first. However, Sargon continued to talk, almost as if he couldn't stand the idea of riding in silence after spending the previous two weeks traveling with and talking to Primus. During that time, in addition to conscripting some soldiers and taking volunteers for others, the two men had spoken at length about many topics.

Everything from hunting and fishing to which wines and beers paired best with which foods, and their interests in certain attributes that women possessed, as well as their childhoods and upbringing. Primus, at first, believed that after two weeks of traveling together, learning all that they had from each other, Sargon was simply not used to the silence that would have reigned supreme over the remainder of their journey. But by the end of the second day, and after hearing Sargon ramble on for nearly an hour about the proper alignment of weapons on a rack in the armory, Primus quietly revisited his assumptions.

If he actually just wanted to hear the sound of his own voice, he would just look out the window and keep talking to himself. If he was trying to get my attention, he would have done more than just talking, and he hasn't discussed anything that's actually important to him, like the coming war. Unless that isn't the point. Unless...unless that was never the point, Primus thought. He seized the opportunity at the first chance he got.

"Sargon?" Primus queried.

"Yes, Primus?" Sargon answered back quickly.

"Yesterday and today, all the talking yesterday, the games last night, and all the talking from today. Did you do all of that for me? For my benefit?" Primus asked slowly, his speech halting and unsure.

"It was, it is, and it's going to be for tonight and the rest of the nights until we get back to Kish," Sargon said.

"Why, though?" Primus asked.

"Because you just had your entire view of the world and everyone in it shattered. You feel as if you've just lost absolutely everything that's important to you, and to a large degree, you have. I've watched others go mad from similar losses, and some have lost their minds from losses that don't come close to comparing to yours," Sargon said softly.

"But why would you try to lift my spirits and save my mind? Or anything that could pass for my mind after learning something like what I did," Primus said, curious as to why the man would try so hard for him.

"Because I like you, Primus, and I would be a liar if I said that I wouldn't consider you to be my friend. I can't just leave you to sit and suffer alone like you would have otherwise. What kind of a man would I be if I left you like that? And what would happen to you if I did? If you lost your mind, how badly could you hurt the people around you? If you lashed out, you would be hard to stop," Sargon said.

"You say that like you think I would hurt those who I consider my friends," Primus said, suddenly wary of the man across from him.

If he thinks that, then he views me as either a threat or a possible threat to his rule, his safety, and his budding empire. Even if he says he's my friend, he probably views me as a threat to him, Primus thought.

"I say that because I've watched it happen before. Sometimes some of my generals have a little too much beer or wine and hurt someone when they don't have their wits about them. A state of grief like yours is similar to having too much wine or beer to drink, and you could hurt someone without meaning to, whether with strength of arms or with a carelessly said word or phrase," Sargon said, and Primus suddenly understood.

He doesn't really view me as a threat then. He just wants to make sure that I don't hurt anyone if I let my emotions run away with me. He actually is a friend to me, and he's trying to ease my loss, Primus concluded, and his expression softened.

"Well, I thank you for your concern, Sargon, but I don't think I've lost my mind quite yet. I've lost everything I worked to get back to and everything I was trying to protect, and I understand how that looks to you. I appreciate your concern, and I thank you deeply for it, but for now, I think I won't need it," Primus said with a small quiet smile.

"Hm, well," Sargon said, looking briefly at the floor and shrugging before continuing. "Only if you're sure of yourself."

"So tell me. When we stop for tonight to make camp and sleep, are the games still going to be played tonight?" Primus asked, his smile widening.

That night, Primus played the games that he had somewhat watched the previous night, finding that he was both faster and stronger than most of the other soldiers, with Sargon being the only man present who could match him in terms of speed, strength, and agility. While Sargon was more accurate with thrown spears and javelins, Primus won many of the contests. In his endurance, however, Primus had no equal, and he received much praise from the warriors with him. Many asked how he had achieved it. However, it was now very late, and Primus promised that he would tell them the following night, as long as they all promised him that they would hold nothing back in return for the games the following night.

In this manner, they made it back to Kish six days after they had left what used to be Primus's home, arriving back to find the roads and city in turmoil. Once within the city, it became apparent to Primus why it had appeared so chaotic from outside the walls and why the roads had been choked with people. The city was packed with people, far beyond the forty or fifty thousand that Gilgamesh had originally stated could live comfortably.

Easily double that number crowded the streets. Filth and waste lay strewn about, and next to the walls, many people sat in their own refuse, the slightly wider streets near the gate allowing for slightly more open air so that the stench was more tolerable. Everywhere he looked, Primus saw people carrying small bags and huddling together, looking suspiciously at anyone who was too close. Given such confined conditions, however, this could only truly be done when someone stood directly in front of another person. It did not take Primus long to realize why Kish seemed to be overpacked with hordes of men, women, and children.

"They must have fled from Lugalzaggesi's army, thinking that they would find safety here," Primus said as he looked out of one of the windows.

"They'll be disappointed then. If this many people are here, Lugalzaggesi can't be more than a day from Kish, two at most. Oh, and before I forget, you'll want this," Sargon said, and he reached below the bench that he sat upon. Under the bench, he moved a curtain aside that had been dyed to look exactly like the floor and walls around it. From behind the curtain, Sargon pulled a small clay bottle out and uncorked the bottle before pouring a small amount of liquid onto his chest and neck directly under his nose.

"And just what, pray tell, is *that?*" Primus asked, although he noted the sweet scent that filled the air.

"Someone created this recipe a long time ago. So long that we don't remember who had done it first, I'm afraid. But do what I did. Pour a little on yourself and try to get it under your nose," Sargon said as he offered the bottle.

"I will, but what *is* it?" Primus asked as he took the bottle and sniffed at it, filling his nostrils with a pleasant aroma.

"We've taken to calling it perfume. I can't tell you what goes into it or how it's made beyond that you can buy it in several different scents. It's expensive, though, I will say. Really, only the nobles here can afford it, myself included, and certain well-off merchants. We can use it to block the smell of waste when we're in the streets," Sargon said.

Primus poured several drops of the liquid onto his chest, and a soft scent of flowers began to fill the air he breathed. The smell of human filth became less severe in his nose, although it did not abate entirely. They were close to the palace when the streets became too overfilled with people, and the warriors who had come along with

Sargon and Primus left their wagons as they began to push the people back, clearing a path to the palace steps.

Once inside, Sargon was accosted by seemingly every adviser in his retinue, all shouting over one another as they vied for his attention. Sargon shouted, bellowing at them all for quiet, and the room became deathly still. Sargon then gave instructions that in an hour, all present were to return, and Sargon would receive them in his chambers. Until then, he wished to bathe and wash the grime of the road from his body.

He took Primus by the arm n and led him into a room with a large stone tub decorated with symbols carved into the alabaster stone that he did not recognize. Pointing them out to Sargon, Primus asked him what they were and what the purpose of the tub was, to which Sargon burst out in laughter.

"This is a stone bathing tub that was brought here by one of the rulers of Kemet. *Pharaoh*, as they have taken to calling their kings, much like we call the rulers of cities lugals, although the pharaoh rules Kemet in its entirety. I even heard the people treat him as a living god who rules using the body of a man. The symbols are the writing system that is used in Kemet," Sargon said.

He then called in several servants and palace slaves, and he instructed them to fill his tub and the one that Primus was to use, as the pharaoh had apparently brought two of the heavy stone basins with him when he visited sometime in the past. Primus thought to ask when this might have been, but no one knew the answer at the time, and Primus convinced the servants not to take the time out to find it, as he did not really need to know, and it was only idle curiosity.

After this, water that had already been warmed was brought in by the jar, and the stone basin was soon full of lightly steaming water. Without waiting for the servants to leave the room, Primus shed all his clothes before stepping into the tub, gasping slightly at the temperature of the water, which was hotter than it looked. Several servants attempted to help him by reaching for his arms, intending to help him slide into the water, but Primus waved them away while trying, only too late, to hide his nudity.

Not long after settling in, the servants left after Primus convinced them that he needed nothing besides a scrap of rough cloth and some of the slurry mixture of ash and water that Primus had used to clean himself the previous times he had bathed. Shortly after the servants left, two palace slaves came into the room and deposited the requested items before wordlessly leaving the room.

Primus allowed his muscles to relax slightly, and he slid deeper into the tub as he allowed the hot water to begin easing his mood and his mind. After enough time had passed, and after the water began to cool a little, Primus cleaned himself and exited the tub. He was supposed to call for the servants so that he did not accidentally slip and fall on the slick stone, but he was unwilling to request help where none was needed.

Once Primus had dried himself with a square of linen, he dressed in the fresh clothing that had been provided to him, a light blue ankle-length skirt and some sandals. Reflecting on his sandals, Primus decided that before the battle that was to come, he would find himself some boots to wear, much like the ones t Sargon had been wearing the day Primus first met him.

Leaving the bathing room, Primus met with Sargon in his chambers just as he appeared to finish dressing. Before they had a chance to say much of anything to each other, Sargon's generals and several scribes entered the room and immediately began shouting over one another. As each man attempted to make himself heard and to have his issue addressed, the overlapping voices quickly grew out of control until it seemed the walls themselves rang from the clamor.

Sargon opened his mouth and bellowed at the men assembled before him. His cry was loud enough to drown out all of those around him, and it went on long enough that even the two most insistent men could not make themselves heard above the noise and eventually quieted down.

Sargon then pointed to each man in turn and requested to hear from them one by one so that he would not miss any information. He also told them all to continue with the most pressing matters, issues that would require his immediate attention only, as there was much he still needed to do before the coming battle.

Each man spoke in turn, just as ordered, and it became clear to both Sargon and Primus why the generals all seemed so agitated. Lugalzaggesi *was* just a day away and would be camped before the city gates by evening the next day, and with him, he brought soldiers and ensi from no less than fifty cities and towns.

The reason Kish was so crowded was due to all the farmers and villagers who had come when Lugalzaggesi began his march, for they knew their fields would be burned and their crops trampled. Additionally, the city was overcrowded due to a number of boys and men who had come seeking to be a part of Sargon's army.

Due to the crowding, and despite the excess food that was grown, the city would soon begin to starve and would not be able to withstand a siege for long under these conditions. Furthermore, if they were to arm every man of fighting age, they would now be short of weapons that would be critical to replace the copper weapons once they became too damaged or lost their original shape. Each man would be allowed one weapon and one shield, and no more.

Sargon met with each challenge as it was given, and the scribes recorded his instructions dutifully. In just under two hours, Sargon had given instructions for how to fortify the city further against attack, learning in the process that the small windows that had been created to fire arrows through had been completed, and that one soldier had decided to see just how protected one would be by going down to the road and shooting at the hole. The arrow had struck the brick around the hole but had not damaged it in the slightest, and it showed no indication of weakening the wall.

Sargon also solved his weapons problem by ordering the soldiers to go from one door to the next and confiscate anything within the city that was made of copper so that it could be quickly melted down to make weapons. The issue of food, however, was one that could not be solved at present. The only solution would be to defeat Lugalzaggesi so that the farmers could return to their homes and to draw on reserves of grain in other cities that would find themselves under Sargon's control.

The issue of protecting the prospective soldiers from quickly being killed was another matter. The same general who had informed

Sargon of the shortage of weapons also informed him that there was not enough material left over to make anything that could be considered armor, and the same man rightfully pointed out that even if enough copper were to be found to arm them all, they would still be unable to protect their men. This issue had taken the most amount of time as there was no easy solution to the problem. In the end, they simply decided there would be no way to provide enough armor, and Sargon gave the order that unarmored men were to be in the centers of phalanx formations.

All this was to be done as quickly as possible, and the smiths were to work their forges day and night until the battle began. The women and children who were to remain in Kish during the battle would still be assisting by helping to work the ovens that baked the pottery and hardened the clay. They would not be making jars, however, but rather creating orbs of clay of varying sizes, but they were to be baked in the same way as the bricks that built the walls and palace. This hardened them far more than simply leaving them to dry in the sun, and when cast from a sling, the baked clay projectiles could kill.

The sun was beginning to set, and Sargon ended his counsel. His final instructions were to find a meal and return to their families for the night. Sargon had bid Primus stay and eat, and the lugal called for a meal to be brought to them. Together, Sargon and Primus ate their fill. Neither man said much during the meal, for they were both famished after traveling for so long, and the planning had taken much of their remaining energy.

They said their goodbyes shortly after, and Primus found his way back to his room to sleep. Primus disrobed and lay himself down, taking only the time to snuff a tallow candle next to his bed. His eyes heavy, Primus blinked once long and slow, sighing as he did. When he opened his eyes, however, Primus was perplexed to see the sun hanging just above the walls of Kish before quickly cursing himself.

I only just closed my eyes, and it's already midmorning. I didn't even dream. I guess traveling consistently for three weeks eventually took its toll. Well, I guess it's time to find myself a meal and figure out what I can do before I walk straight into another war, Primus thought as he got up.

Asking several servants around the palace where he might find Sargon, Primus eventually discovered that his friend was no longer in the palace, instead having gone to visit several forges and ovens, as well as to oversee the final placements of men and materials before the battle, leaving Primus alone to use the day how he pleased.

Rather than spend the day training his body or going to assist Sargon or the ovens or the smiths, Primus decided he would spend the day reading some of the many tablets of baked clay that resided within the palace library. While there, Primus remembered the tub he had bathed in, and he realized that he had heard the previous night that the stone basin had been carved in Kemet. He realized now that he might be able to translate the language or find someone who could translate it. Perhaps something on the tub was relevant in some way to him.

Primus jumped up from his seat, taking care not to scatter the various tablets that he had collected and had been in the middle of deciphering. He asked after every scribe in the palace before finding one who could read and speak the language of Kemet, and once he found the scribe, Primus set about convincing him to read the writing to him.

Eventually, the scribe relented, but Primus was disappointed on learning what the tub said, as it was simply a message of friendship between the two nations. Primus asked when the language was first written down, but the scribe could not answer him, as the scribe did not know when it was first written, saying only that the written language appeared to have been introduced by a king who ruled long ago. Primus hoped that it had actually been Narmer who had commissioned the language, keeping his promise to Primus.

Around an hour before sunset, Primus realized that the city had become still for the first time since he had arrived. Worried, Primus began to scour the palace, asking everyone he met along the way what the cause for the silence was, only to receive the same response from each servant. None of them could tell him why the city had suddenly become still.

As the sun was setting, Sargon sent a message to Primus, requesting to meet him in his chambers. Primus made his way through the palace, and with the vanishing of the light, what little sound there was emanating from the streets of Kish had vanished as well, save only for the glow of several ovens and forges visible in the distance. Primus nodded at the guards standing at the entrance to Sargon's chambers and walked past them, finding Sargon standing on the balcony and looking over the darkened city.

"I sincerely hope your day was fruitful, Primus, because I personally feel as if I accomplished absolutely nothing today," Sargon said without looking at Primus.

"If you feel like you've done nothing, then I know I've done nothing with my day. I read some of the history and stories that you keep in your library, and I chased down a scribe who could read and speak Kemet. Otherwise, I've done nothing worth noting," Primus said.

"At least you got to *enjoy* what might be your last day alive. But the real reason I called you here is because I have some questions I was hoping you could answer for me," Sargon said.

"I'll try to give you what you're looking for," Primus responded.

"What did you do when you faced down the battle for your home? I don't mean the battle itself. I remember what you told me of that. No, I mean what did you do the day before?" Sargon asked.

"If you mean what I did with what could have been my last day alive, then I spent it with my betrothed, the same as my friend Thak did, along with many others," Primus answered.

"I had hoped to hear that. I would have spent the day with my wife and my children, but I couldn't. I sent them north to one of the smaller villages to hide until the battle is over. Even if we lose this tomorrow, they will still live," Sargon said.

"I'm glad you succeeded in convincing your wife to leave. I tried but failed, and she insisted that she would stay with me," Primus said ruefully.

"Hm. Well, from what you told me, she did seem strong-willed. But now to another question. What would you do in my place right now, Primus? The men are as ready as what they can be. We have as many orbs and weapons made as what we're likely to by morning, and I have a gargantuan army camped before the gates of my city.

Would you attack first, or would you wait to be attacked, and when?" Sargon asked.

"If I was in your place right now, if I stood in your boots, well, I think the first thing I would do is to have an extra cup of wine, just a small one. Second, I would have the guards wake me before dawn, and I would attack Lugalzaggesi while he sleeps," Primus said.

"You would cut him down while he still lays safe in bed?" Sargon asked, shocked.

"I would. It would depend on the size of the army you face, but if they outnumber you severely, then you need to take advantage of every trick you can find," Primus said.

"Every dirty trick, more like. Still, the element of surprise would be very strong indeed and could give us the needed push to win this. How would you attack?" Sargon asked.

"I would ride out in a chariot, followed by every chariot I could find, shooting flaming arrows and throwing javelins into their camp, setting their tents alight and causing as much chaos as possible. While I was busy doing that, I would have several phalanx formations close in from the back and sides, trapping Lugalzaggesi in place. With luck, he would be so shocked and unsure that he would surrender on the spot, and if not, just shoot at him from the walls and chariots. I would ride into Kish as much as I could to replenish my supplies then ride back out," Primus said.

"And of the men who aren't in a phalanx?" Sargon asked.

"For any who aren't already in their positions, I would create a larger group that would begin fighting with Lugalzaggesi's men, and they would exit the city and stand before the army so that they would be hemmed in on all sides," Primus said.

"And in the dark, they couldn't be sure of the size of my forces, and the added confusion would aid in forcing him to surrender," Sargon said, following the same line of reason that Primus had.

Sargon continued to talk with Primus for a short time as they worked out the timing. Then he bade Primus good night, informing him that a guard would wake him when the time for battle was near. Primus slowly walked back through the palace, heading generally for his room but not paying much attention to where he was going.

His mind was no longer working, however, and his thoughts were as still as an untouched lake. Eventually, Primus gave up on trying to make his mind behave and create new comprehensible thoughts, simply allowing the stillness to wash over him as he made his way back to his room and into his bed.

It was still dark when the soldier who had been sent to wake Primus nudged his arm, whispering that it was time to get up. Primus groaned and rolled out of bed, his eyes heavy lidded and bleary. He ran a hand down each cheek and stood, walking to where he had laid out his garments earlier in the night.

His weapon and shield would be provided when he met with Sargon and the rest of the soldiers, but he had worn the blue skirt worn and a pair of boots he had spotted outside one of the closed doors in the palace, along with a decoratively dyed cloak and gold clasp that Primus did not remember being in the room when he retired for the night. He guessed that the soldier who roused him had brought it, as Primus had seen similar garb on most of the other soldiers throughout his stay.

Primus donned his clothing and made his way through the darkened palace, directed where to go by guards and soldiers stationed every so often. In the same manner, Primus made his way into the streets and before the main gate of Kish. The gate already stood slightly ajar, the heavy doors having been pulled slowly and quietly aside. Outside the gate, separated by perhaps a quarter of a mile, was the army of Lugalzaggesi, with only a few sentries patrolling the low earthen walls that the army had erected as a defensive measure. The hills were only waist-high to Primus, but he knew that they would still cause a problem for anyone who got close enough to scale the small embankment.

Primus spotted Sargon and made his way over, stopping only to grab one of the large shields made of interwoven reeds, a spear, and a small hand scythe in place of a short sword. Primus was surprised to see that among the spears and maces and other instruments of war that he expected to see, he saw many objects he would not have thought to bring to a battle.

Wooden hammers and mallets of all sizes and shapes were on display, as well as plow blades, large and small, that had been hurriedly attached to various poles. Pitchforks and long scythes were also among the makeshift weapons he spied, and behind them were rows of copper-headed spears and javelins, arrows bundled together thickly, and behind those sat a small mountain of variously sized and shaped orbs of baked clay.

"So are you ready, Primus?" Sargon half whispered as the younger man approached.

"I've been asked that in some capacity before each fight I've had, and my answer hasn't changed much since the beginning. I'm nervous before the battle because I would rather just be in the middle of it instead of waiting and worrying about what *could* happen," Primus said.

"I'll take that as a yes then," Sargon said, and he turned to say something over his shoulder to one of his generals, but Primus could not hear what it was.

"Follow me, Primus. You and I will take the lead in the two chariots. Together, we'll each lead a line of them around the camp, circling around behind them and following each other's lines back toward Kish. Right now, a phalanx is around each of the three sides of the camp far enough away that the darkness will hide them. Once we make our first pass, they move in, and the doors will open. The majority of my men will rush the front in their own phalanx. And above it all, arrows and stones will rain down from the ramparts, causing even more confusion in their ranks. So what do you think, Primus? Is this the attack we planned, or is *this* the attack we planned?" Sargon finished with a wide smile and a hint of relief in his voice, almost as if he did not believe his own eyes.

"This is it, all right. I hope to see you after for a morning feast of champions," Primus said with a smile and a nod as he made his way to the front of one of the two columns of chariots.

"And feast we shall, for we will be victorious! Oh, and before you go off on your own, I have something for you," Sargon said, leaving a puzzled Primus standing behind his chariot. He did not have to wait long, however, for in less than a minute, Sargon had returned, resplendent in a helm of gold, engraved such that it matched the look of the hair under the helm.

"This is for you, my friend. My generals all have one, and seeing as how I promised you that you would be a general after this, I thought, why wait?" Sargon said, and from behind his back, he produced a carved and engraved helm closely resembling the one he himself wore. Sargon offered the helm to Primus, who haltingly took it.

"Are you sure that you want to give me something so valuable before the battle?" Primus asked.

"I am. It denotes not only your station but also your proximity to me. As long as we win this battle and defeat Lugalzaggesi, I will take his place and rule all of Kengir, and I will also claim all the lands to the north as well, where my fellow Akkadians live. I will rule both the northern and southern kingdoms, something that has never been before. Stick close by my side, and you'll live in comfort after the battles for the other cities. That gold helm names you not just as an adviser and general but also as my friend," Sargon finished softly.

"Then I would be honored to have it," Primus said just as softly, and he donned the helm, which was even heavier than it appeared.

"Then luck be with you, and may Enlil smile upon you, Primus," Sargon said as he extended an arm, which Primus grasped. They stood there for a moment in silence before parting ways, each knowing that they might never see each other again.

Primus mounted his chariot and stood behind the driver, hefting the new bow that Sargon had commissioned. He pointed it toward the gap in the door and drew his arm back, testing the strength of the bow's limbs. The draw was heavier than Primus expected, surprisingly so, and he knew that this would cast an arrow with far more force than anything he had previously used in Kemet or in Kengir and was closer in strength to the bow he trained with in Meftif.

Satisfied with the weapon, Primus settled in to wait for the order to attack. Around half an hour later, the sky had changed colors ever so slightly from dark black to a slightly lighter shade of black, and the order for the attack was whispered through the line of chariots and to the men behind.

Ever so quietly, the door was opened to the night and the enemy camp beyond. To his right, Sargon raised an arm and held it aloft for a moment before bringing it down in silence. The chariots began to move, but only at a trot, and the two lines widened once away from the walls of Kish. The sentries did not notice until the chariots were halfway to the camp, and they fervently began blowing horns and shouting, frantically trying to raise the alarm.

Sargon bellowed into the night sky, joined by Primus and warriors both within and out the city as the countryside echoed with war cries. The noise was deafening, and the chariots increased their speed until the pair of asses that pulled the chariot were at a full sprint.

Primus grabbed an arrow and swung it through a torch that burned on the front corner of the chariot, lighting a strip of cloth. Drawing his arm back with sudden ease, Primus released his flaming arrow and cast it deep into the camp. Where exactly his arrow landed, he was not sure, as dozens of flaming arrows arched their way to the camp from the chariots, and the cloth tents burst into flame as quickly as tinder held before a smith's forge.

As Primus rounded the side of the camp, firing arrows all the while, he suddenly spied black blurs within the flame, as if giant angry wasps were darting about in the conflagration, and it took him a moment to realize that they were the silhouettes of arrows from the now advancing men behind him, Sargon, and the camp. The soldiers must have been shooting over the tops of the chariots and into the camp, and with each wave of arrows, the cries of the dead and dying grew louder.

Primus rounded the back of the camp and passed by Sargon. Each man flashed the other a vicious battle grin as they passed by, continuing to shoot into the camp. Nearing the front of the camp, Primus reached down for an arrow, only to grasp at air twice before finding a shaft. Upon loosing the arrow, Primus looked down and realized that he had shot so many arrows that his quiver was nearly empty. Looking back up to the gates of Kish, Primus could see several wagons full of weapons being rolled out by the corners of the doors while soldiers poured through the gate like so much blood from a wound.

Primus's chariot pulled up alongside one of the wagons, and his arrows were partly replenished, though not fully replenished, or the men at the end of the line may not have enough for themselves. Then the chariot was off again, following a similarly wide loop around the camp, which was now under attack from all directions.

The three groups of men who attacked from the sides and rear were already almost upon the short wall that had been hastily put in place, having run to their current places before arranging themselves in formation and beginning to slowly advance. Behind the rows of shielded men, archers fired arrows into the camp and at enemy soldiers who stood silhouetted against the light of the flame. Primus passed by these men, firing at anything that moved.

Every fourth arrow or so, Primus stopped and reached for a short javelin and attempted to hurl it into the camp, hoping to skewer a soldier. Primus could not tell whether he actually hit anyone with a javelin at a distance, but he thought that he had not, as the weapons were much like spears, and they proved difficult, if not impossible, to aim properly with the amount of practice that Primus currently had.

Three more times, Primus circled the camp, each circle growing wider and taking more time to complete, depleting his weaponry more and more each time, and each time he replenished his arrows, Primus was given fewer. The wider circles were owed to the growing size of the armies, as Lugalzaggesi, in his camp, attempted to fight a multifront battle, but the dwindling supplies were cause for concern for Primus.

I can probably get one more pass out of the arrows I'll have left, but then I'll have to put the bow down and join one of the phalanx formations. Hopefully, they have more arrows or even a sling over there for me to use. I really would prefer not to be overcrowded in the middle of the formation, constantly at risk of being trampled by my own men or trampling them myself, Primus thought as he accepted his meager supply of arrows and rode once more around the camp, now picking his targets carefully in an attempt to make each shot matter.

Primus counted another four men that he was sure he hit with his shot and back around to the gate. Primus looked up and realized that the archers and slingers who had previously manned the ramparts were no longer above him. Realizing that something was amiss, Primus whipped his head around, looking about the battlefield for Sargon, intending to warn him that something was wrong.

Primus quickly realized that his alarm was unneeded when he saw several archers and slingers exit the city and sprint to the battle, their weapons gleaming in the torchlight. By now, the chariot had slowed to walking speed, and Primus simply stepped off the back, flexing his knees slightly from the impact. He turned and made his way toward the battle, looking about for Sargon.

Primus spotted his friend making his way back from the edge of the battlefield. Even at a distance, Primus could see the blood that coated the mangled remains of his spear, and arrows stuck out of seemingly every available inch of his shield at every conceivable angle, though his helm appeared intact at a distance, and he walked without a limp or any other noticeable injury. Primus began to run, closing the distance between them in short order.

"How goes the battle, General Primus?" Sargon said as his friend and newest general approached.

"Every available man has come down off the walls and joined the fighting here. The camp is in ashes, though I can't say how many are dead yet," Primus said.

"Excellent. They're surrounded entirely, and we caught them completely by surprise. It hasn't been long, but I think we might have won the battle already, and all that's left now is to wait for Lugalzaggesi to realize it," Sargon said.

"Speaking of Lugalzaggesi, where is he?" Primus asked.

"He's somewhere over there," Sargon said, pointing to an area that was close to where he himself had been previously.

"You've fought him?" Primus asked.

"No, but I spied him among his men, moving around and bellowing orders, trying to make his men fight harder. But I think his men know, and I think even more importantly than that, *he* knows that the battle is lost," Sargon said.

"So what's next from here, then?" Primus asked.

"I think we'll keep fighting for now, but really, we only have to wait for him to give it up as hopeless, however long that takes. If we have to stay here until noon, then we stay here until noon," Sargon said.

"I have to say, I'm glad we could pull off the surprise attack. You really must have inspired some kind of loyalty from the men, and I believe they would follow you anywhere," Primus said.

"Well, now all that's left is to start preparing for Lugalzaggesi's surrender. We'll need to enlist some from Kish, but we'll need to bury the dead, collect the arrows and javelins, take stock of how many prisoners we have, and I'll need to think of something to do with Lugalzaggesi," Sargon said.

"Wouldn't it be easier if you executed him?" Primus asked.

"It would, but his reign has been cruel, and while it would make many feel better to kill him, I won't kill him. He will be a prisoner in the palace afterward, but he will be allowed to live," Sargon said.

"Afterward?" Primus queried.

"After the conquest of his other cities. I've already thought up a way to prove to any naysayers, any detractor in any city, who is in command. And without shedding a single drop of his blood. Oh, and I'll need to think of a title for myself, maybe just *king of Kish and Akkad*," Sargon said.

"You'll have to forgive me, Sargon, but how exactly do you intend to do that?" Primus asked, his incredulity growing like the soft light now emanating from the east.

"I'll put him in a yoke, like the ones we put on oxen who plow our fields and pull our barges down the canals. He will be tied naked to it then be led into each city after it has been defeated, if they even fight once they see Lugalzaggesi imprisoned like that. It will be humiliating to lead him through the streets of Umma, Lagash, Nippur, and so many others. Ur will be especially sweet, although I will have a problem there when I leave," Sargon said, turning inward slightly and becoming pensive as he spoke of the seaside city.

"Why? What's in Ur?" Primus asked.

"Hm? Oh, nothing too important. It's just that I've heard some stories about a man there. He's been speaking of only one god instead of the many that exist. He calls himself Abraham," Sargon said.

"Do you think he could pose a significant problem?" Primus asked.

"No, he's just one man. Rather than execute him for blasphemy, I'll cast him out of the city," Sargon said.

"How is that any different than just killing him though? He and any family he has will die in the wastes," Primus argued.

"It's possible, but he will only be barred from the cities as long as he continues to waste his breath. When he stops, he will be allowed back in. And before you ask, he may choose if he wants to live with some of the farmers outside of a city. If any are willing to take him in, that is," Sargon said, to which Primus had no reply.

They continued to speak of other matters for several more minutes before a horn sounded. The long and slow note blared for half a minute, during which time the fighting stopped as everyone looked for the source of the noise. Then another horn sounded, and another, and before long, the very walls of Kish seemed ready to shake themselves apart under the noise from the horns, which now sounded unnaturally loud.

The horns stopped, and silence fell on the battlefield for a moment before Sargon's soldiers began to cheer, jumping up and down, hugging one another and waving their weapons in the air. They had won, and as the sky began to turn pink in the light of the rising sun, Primus and Sargon looked at each other, dazed by their sudden victory. Sargon began to laugh then, his mirth seemingly building from deep in his belly before bursting forth and rolling over the land. Primus soon joined him. Eventually, their laughter subsided enough that they were able to breathe properly again.

"Well then, Sargon of Akkad, or should I say *Sargon, king of Kish and Akkad*, I believe you are now in control the empire of Kengir," Primus said.

"Please, Primus, I'm Akkadian. I've called it Kengir most of my life, but I think I'll call my new empire by the name I heard as a boy," Sargon said.

"What name is that?" Primus asked.

"The Sumerian empire has fallen, but now a new Sumerian empire is born," Sargon said, his mouth stretched in a half smile.

"Then I will call it the Sumerian empire, the same way you do," Primus said, and he extended his arm just as Sargon had done earlier.

"Thank you for your help, Primus. I would have had a much harder time in this war without having you around to talk to, to trade ideas and create new strategies. You've more than earned your station," Sargon said as he took his friend's arm.

A low hum began to fill the air, barely audible over the celebrations of the men but growing louder, until all could hear it. The blood drained from Primus's face, and his eyes became as large and round as chariot wheels. He released his grip on Sargon's arm as he began to stagger backward, bowing his head and grasping it in his hands, hunching his shoulders.

"No, no, no, no, *no, no, no*! Not again!" Primus shrieked, his terror bursting forth as the humming reached a fever pitch, and a ball of white light appeared in front of his stomach, quickly expanding to envelope him completely.

Suddenly, the ball disappeared, the humming stopped, and the world grew dark and silent again. Sargon looked for his friend, ordering every man who would not be busy burying the dead after the battle or watching prisoners to search Kish and the surrounding farmhouses, leaving no room unsearched. Sargon further surprised his men when he informed them that he would be joining them in their search for his missing friend.

* * * * *

Primus's breath came quickly and in short gasps. His mind raced, and tremors wrecked his limbs while he fought the urge to release tears that he had not realized he was holding back. As fast as one thought could form, another snatched it away. Much sooner than he expected, the bottom began to open underneath Primus, and he fell slightly to the ground, but because of his panic, Primus was unable to stay standing, and he fell hard on his side.

Scrambling to his feet, Primus wheeled around, trying to take in everything all at once. He was in the middle of a field. Stalks of wheat and barley grew tall, and the heavy heads hung low, burdened as they were in what some part of Primus knew to be nearly harvest time. To the right of where he fell ran a river whose name he did not know, and to his left was a vast plain that stretched on to the horizon.

Primus threw his head back and screamed an aching lament to the heavens above and all who may be close enough to hear, tears spilling from his eyes, caring not for who may be close by as the true hopelessness of what had been happening to him started to become apparent. Primus knew that he was in another land, and he feared how many years had passed in the minutes it had been since the light had taken him, fearing whatever war or battle he would be drawn into next.

End of Book 1

BOOK 2

Chapter 1

Warrior Eternal

Ancient

Primus dropped the two or so inches to the ground as the ball of white light opened up around him, depositing him onto the hot sand near a fast-flowing river, over which now familiar ships prowled the waters. The design of the ships told him that he was back in Kemet.

Ah, good. Well, at least I have more of an understanding here than I did with the Trtsu-Bharata. That battle against the Vedic tribes took quite a while, and with nine tribes and the Bharata together, someone's probably going to try and be clever. Call it the battle of ten kings or something.

I wonder who's pharaoh now? Last time I was here, it was Thutmose III, and we had more than enough battles against the Syrians. With any luck, whoever rules Kemet now won't be quite so bloodthirsty. Still, I'd rather be fighting the Syrians than the Hittites or the Babylonians, although I do miss Kish. The Akkadians as well. They were a little less refined than the Sumerians, but I still miss them. I can't help but wonder, though, what exactly they would all think if they could see everything else that's happened since I fought with them.

Shaking himself slightly, Primus inhaled deeply and looked down at his armor, which was ruined in several places, before sighing deeply in disappointment. The design of the armor itself was not to his liking. However, it had proved to be extremely sturdy, withstanding far more punishment than he had expected.

Primus threw down his weapon and shield before removing his armor and what little clothing he wore beneath it before walking forward and into the Aur River. The warm water was soothing against his flesh, which burned as if with fever from the battle he had just participated in.

While the battle itself had not been a particularly hard fight compared to some of the other battles he had participated in, it had been an exceptionally long fight, and it had taken much from him. The Babylonians, in particular, stood out in Primus's memory, both for their bloodlust when he fought for them and their stubborn refusal to surrender when they obviously lost when Primus fought against them in the end.

While Primus scraped the drying gore from his body, he strove to not think about the Babylonians too much, as their seat of power was too close to the last true friend he had, that being Sargon. The king had once ruled from the city of Akkad, which Primus had never seen nor visited before it had been ground back into clay by the Gutians.

It had taken Primus quite a while to piece together the events that occurred after his stays in various lands. While he had been back to Kemet several times, he unfortunately had not been able to spend much time in Sumeria after his time with Sargon. Or rather, as he would be known now, Sargon I.

Sargon ruled for many years after, and he built his legend up somewhat with the people, attaining an almost godlike status and having apparently served for forty years as the gardener of the gods. Despite the stories, Primus had known the truth and the man behind the truth. He also learned that several hundred years after he fought for Sargon and helped him create an empire, that empire had been torn apart by men from the hills and mountains. They called themselves the *Guti*.

They were an illiterate people and were much like the early people of Kemet in that way, even uniting under one banner. However, they rode for the cities of Kengir, namely the city of Akkad. They overthrew the king and attempted to govern the empire that Primus had helped create, and although they may have destroyed the city Sargon had ruled from, they themselves had not ruled for very long. From everything Primus had learned in Babylon, which was built shortly after he disappeared, the Guti could not govern effectively as they could not read or write, and they refused to adopt any form of written word.

The result was they could not keep everything running smoothly, as the nation had relied so heavily on the written word that it nearly collapsed without it. Incursions by Elamites from the west, as well as other nomads or mountain people, and a famine devastated the Sumerians and wiped many of them out. Eventually, the Guti were overthrown, and the Sumerians once again ruled, but they were unable to stop the decline of their nation and their people.

The only thing Primus had absolutely been able to attribute to the decline was an increasingly low yield of crops. Primus had asked to see the records of yields, and thanks to the friends he had made in years past, he had been allowed into the archives to have a look around. It was thanks to an increase of barley production and the almost complete non-planting of wheat that Primus was finally able to parse out what had happened.

In the several thousand years that the people had been farming the land, the land itself had absorbed some of the water, and with it, small amounts of salt. While it was not much each individual season, over the generations, salt built up both in and below the soil, and since barley was more resistant to salted soil than wheat was, it made sense to plant more of a crop that would actually grow.

Whether due to incomplete records in Babylon or possibly something else entirely, Primus could find no more information on the downfall of the Sumerians. The Elamites also disappeared as a people, becoming several different groups, some nomads, others forming more permanent settlements.

Out of all the lands that Primus had so far visited, Kemet had so far stood the test of time. It was not without its changes, however, as their religion, which had been a small part of their daily lives when Primus had first visited, had grown dramatically. Gods and goddesses for every conceivable event or disaster existed. Most had animal heads, and the legends about the founding of the nation had grown immensely in the nearly two thousand years that had passed since Primus first set foot in Nekhen.

They also avoided the same trouble with their crops, which Primus guessed was accomplished by allowing the river to flood and recede naturally rather than attempting to irrigate a field, and the salts would return to the water and be washed out to the sea.

Their diet had improved much over the years as well, partly due to the trade network that had been established, bringing with it seeds and grains of every variety. The people themselves were not much changed from the very first time Primus visited the land, still shorter than he was and of darker complexion, although their attitudes had changed much.

But then again, it's been two thousand years. If they were exactly the same now as they had been then, I think I would be more *concerned. Still, they're at least more consistent of a people than everyone else. At least every time I get dragged back here, I can slide right in and almost pick up where I left off. Almost,* Primus thought as he finished scrubbing the last of the gore from his body.

Leaving the river, Primus collected his weapon and armor then returned to the river to wash his weapons and armor. Though he did not intend to wear it for much longer, it would not be proper if he were stroll into the nearest town naked, and it would be just as off-putting were Primus to arrive reeking of death and desperation.

While in Meftif, Primus had fought with an unrivaled savagery, almost animalistic in nature, and it was that very drive to fight and win by any means necessary that had helped Primus achieve his first victory. While Primus had not spent a large amount of time in each land he had visited, he had not seemed to age much, something pointed out by numerous people over the years. This mattered to Primus, for even though his body was not much older, his journey through the years and the near-constant war he now found himself in had worn his mind down and dulled the savage edge that he once had.

I don't know exactly when it happened, but at some point, I started not wanting to fight as much. Looking back at the first few battles I had, at first, I fought for my home and my prospective family, and after that, I fought to get home or to try and find a way home. Then Sargon destroyed that hope when I realized that Meftif was so old that not even its dust was left for me.

I mean, I still fought for him, but it was in the hope that I was building a new home for myself. After that, it's just been more of the same. At least when I show up in some town or city, they know me or at least the stories that have been passed around. The infallible warrior, the eternal warrior, the deathless one, the herald of victory. At least people are somewhat creative with the names, Primus thought as he attempted to scrub his armor and weapon.

Though the armor would not come completely clean, as that would take most of the day to clean and oil the armor with linseed oil, and if left alone for too long, the unrestrained water would begin to rust his armor horribly. Despite this, Primus scrubbed in the water to remove most of the drying blood so that he did not cause undue fright to anyone who might have been unfortunate enough to chance across him before he could find someone of importance, and being in Kemet, a captain or lieutenant in the army would be ideal.

The sight of a man covered in blood and wearing damaged armor was enough to scare most people away and had caused Primus to be imprisoned by the palace or the city guard on a number of occasions, and each time, Primus had to learn the language and convince them that he was merely a soldier who had been in the wrong place at the wrong time.

Usually, Primus met with success, although before his most recent battle, he had not been released from his imprisonment. Due to this, Primus had not learned where he was, how long it had passed since his last battle, or whom was fighting with whom. Despite this, the ball of light once again appeared and swallowed Primus, disgorging him in the vicinity of the Bharata, where Primus spent some time recovering from his long imprisonment and once again making friends with the soldiers and the ruler of the Bharata.

This had puzzled Primus, who until then had believed that it was the act of making war itself that caused the ball of light to appear to him. However, he could not say that this was necessarily true now, given that Primus had been in shackles when the battle began, as well as when it ended. He also could not explain his situation very well to peoples who he only met once, but for the Kemetese?

If anyone might have a new idea of what's going on, these people might be it. Maybe there's a god of time or something of that nature. I haven't prayed to anything in a very long time, but I'll pray to a slice of meat if it gets me out of this, Primus thought as he finished.

Making his way back to dry land, Primus draped his armor over a dense clump of reeds that grew next to him. He placed his weapon next to it before choosing several reeds and bending them flat, creating a springy seat for himself while he waited for his armor and clothes to dry.

After enough time had passed, Primus donned his mostly dry clothing and armor, retrieved his shield from where he had left it, and hailed one of the smaller fishing boats, calling them over to shore while planning his next moves.

All right, first order of business is to find out whether it's time for the evening or morning meal. I'm famished. Second, I'll see what anyone is willing to trade for a meal since I've only got a few pieces of gold and silver at the moment. Third, who's the pharaoh, and where does he hold court? Primus thought as the small boat closed in on him.

Though Primus had spent much of his time here, he still looked forward to meeting with the pharaoh every time. While it was for war, Primus appreciated the large buildings and cities that each pharaoh built to leave his own mark on history. These palaces and cities were often lavishly decorated with finely carved stone and intricately painted scenery lining the walls, as well as for their vast libraries. Primus would often spend time here between the wars he fought in to find out what had happened during his time away.

The pharaoh himself was also much kinder to Primus than the rulers of most other lands. Once, he had asked Thutmose why he and nearly every other pharaoh that Primus had interacted with were so kind. Thutmose had then told Primus that it was due to stories that were passed down from pharaoh to pharaoh, describing how an unknown warrior had appeared to them out of the desert, like a gift from Osiris.

This warrior had helped in the formation of Kemet as they all knew it, at peace with itself and prosperous. It had come as a great shock when this unknown warrior vanished just after the conclusion of the battle that unified Kemet. It was an even greater shock still when this mysterious warrior had appeared again, coming to their aid in an hour of need before disappearing again wrapped in the light of the heavens. After this, all pharaohs yet to be were told the story as babes in their mothers' arms and raised to know of this warrior.

They were to treat him with the kindness and respect worthy of someone who helped form the very nation that they found themselves at the head of, for he was ancient and wise. If kindness was shown to this warrior, the pharaoh and people of Kemet would have nothing to fear. Treat him badly, however, and the warrior would vanish again and return to destroy them with a force of soldiers not of this earth, and they would wipe the land of Kemet from the desert sands as easily as one might brush away an insect.

In this way, Primus's story and exploits had lived on through the year, and was the reason that nearly every pharaoh had been so kind to him. It was also the beginning of the tradition of hospitality, which the people of Kemet nearly always observed for fear of divine retribution, or so Primus had been told. Primus thought of all of this and more as the fishing boat made contact with the sand and silt along the riverbank, coming to a halt not far from where the now fabled warrior stood.

About the Author

Sam Hain is a first-time author and husband to Elaine. He is an engineer by day. When not solving technical problems or weaving tales, Sam enjoys long rides on his motorcycle and sampling a new scotch or whiskey.

www.ingramcontent.com/pod-product-compliance
Lightning Source LLC
LaVergne TN
LVHW041610131224
799068LV00001B/29